The streets of Manass remained empty as the priest and his barbarian bodyguards marched through the town. The procession saw few men until it rounded a corner and entered a large plaza. There, armored soldiers carrying wicked-looking swords formed a wall.

The priest bowed to the governor, who stood foremost in the ranks. "I am a Koja of Khazari," he began, a little nervous. "I bear you greetings from Hoekun Yamun, khahan of the Tuigan, who styles himself Illustrious Emperor of All Peoples. He has sent me to deliver a message. The words of the khahan are these: 'Submit to me and recognize my authority over your people or I shall raze your city and destroy all those who refuse me.' "

As Koja finished the demands, there was a murmur of shock and surprise from the soldiers in the plaza. Many eyes turned to the governor, whose face was purple with rage. "Is that all your barbarian friend has to say?" he shouted.

The priest wiped his sweaty palms on his robe. "No, Lord Commander. He also bids you to look over your walls from your highest tower."

"I've seen the reports from the sentries. Your khahan has gathered himself a sizable force of bandits. And now he wants to style himself 'Illustrious Emperor of All Peoples?' He's got a lot to do before he can claim that title," the governor said with a sneer. "Does he really think he can capture Manass with that puny force?"

Koja smiled slightly. "Yes, Lord Commander, he does."

THE EMPIRES TRILOGY

HORSELORDS
David Cook

DRAGONWALL
Troy Denning

CRUSADE
James Lowder

FANTASY ADVENTURE

Horselords

The Empires Trilogy: Book One

David Cook

Cover Art
LARRY ELMORE

HORSELORDS

©Copyright 1990 TSR, Inc.
All Rights Reserved.

Distributed to the book trade in the United States by Random House, Inc., and in Canada by Random House of Canada, Ltd.

Distributed in the United Kingdom by TSR Ltd.

Distributed to the toy and hobby trade by regional distributors.

FORGOTTEN REALMS, PRODUCTS OF YOUR IMAGINATION, AD&D, and the TSR logo are trademarks owned by TSR, Inc.

BULLWINKLE AND ROCKY ™ and © 1988 P.A.T.-WARD. All Rights Reserved.

First Printing: April, 1990
Printed in the United States of America.
Library of Congress Catalog Card Number: 89-51888

9 8 7 6 5 4 3 2 1

ISBN: 0-88038-904-4
All characters in this book are fictitious. Any resemblance to actual persons, living or dead, is purely coincidental.

TSR, Inc.
P.O. Box 756
Lake Geneva,
WI 53147 U.S.A.

TSR Ltd.
120 Church End, Cherry Hinton
Cambridge CB1 3LB
United Kingdom

To Sarah Elizabeth, who will be with us in our memories, and to Helen.

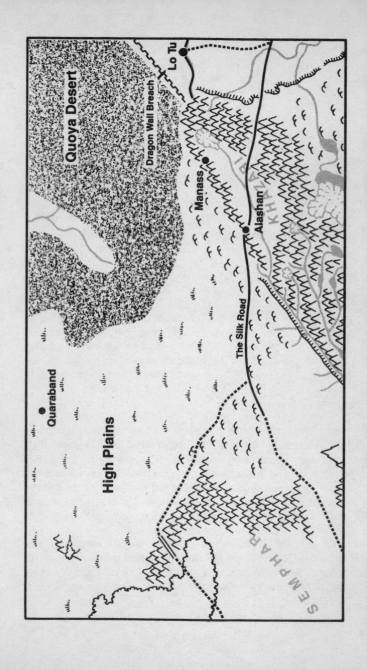

- 1 -

Quaraband

Quaraband was a city of tents. There were no permanent buildings, only domelike yurts of white and black spread out in the shallow bowl of a valley. The little round shelters were scattered in dense clumps, large and small, radiating out from the river that meandered across the valley from the south. The space between each yurt was cluttered with heavy, wooden-wheeled carts, ox yokes, racks of drying meat, hobbled horses, and camels. Here and there were wicker corrals for horses and sheep. Thin trails of smoke drifted from the cooking fires between the yurts. Farther out were herds of horses, cattle, and sheep grazing on the greening grass of the spring steppe.

The stubby grass broke through the pitted crust of old snow that still dotted the plain. White snow, green grass, and brown dirt covered the flat ground in broken patches, stretching as far as one could see. There were no trees, only gently rolling hillocks that rippled to the horizon. Dark scars from old gullies made jagged cuts across the barren land. Small clumps of bright blue and pink, the blooms of early crocus and dwarf lily, struggled against the cold to bring the first signs of spring to the land.

Chanar Ong Kho, a general of the Tuigan, seemed to glisten as sunlight played off the burnished metal scales of his armor. The light emphasized the luster of Chanar's thick braids and the thin sheen of sweat on the shaven patch at

DAVID COOK

the top of his head. The sword at his side, its scabbard set with sapphires and garnets, swung in rhythm to his mare's swaying steps, scratching out a beat as it scraped against the general's metal leggings.

Saddle leather creaked as Chanar looked back to see if his companion was impressed. The man, a gaunt rider on a black mare, lurched along, parallel to a long, winding file of mounted soldiers—a small part of the ten thousand men under General Chanar's command. The companion wore what were once bright orange robes, though they were now travel-stained and worn. His head was shaven, and around his neck hung several strings of beads, each ending in a small prayer case of silver filigree. The priest rode stiffly, bouncing with every jolt, not with the natural grace of his fellow horseman. Chanar waited with bemused distaste as the priest pulled alongside.

"Tonight, Koja of the Khazari, you'll sleep in the tents of the Tuigan," Chanar announced, as he leaned forward to stroke his mare's neck. "Even though it's only been a few nights under the sky."

"Three weeks is more than a few nights," Koja observed. The priest spoke haltingly, with a musical inflection, ill-suited to the guttural twists of the Tuigan tongue. It was a language clearly different from his own. "Even you, honorable general, must welcome a night in warmer surroundings."

"Warm or cold, Khazari, it makes no difference to me. The Blue Wolf gave birth to our ancestors in the bitter cold of winter. My home is where I stand. Learn that if you mean to stay with us," General Chanar answered. Snapping the flank of the dapple mare with his knout, the general urged his horse into a gallop toward Quaraband, leaving the foreign priest behind.

Koja let out an exasperated sigh as he watched the horse-warrior gallop ahead. Once again Koja had to put up with the arrogance of the Tuigan general. The priest was saddle-stiff, dust-caked, and sun-scorched after three weeks of constant riding. The Khazari had traveled with the general and ten thousand Tuigan warriors through forests, over mountains, and finally across the dry and empty steppe to reach the great capital of the Tuigan people. He had left the comforts of civilization far behind.

Now, the capital of these mysterious warriors, men who bedeviled the valuable caravan trade, lay ahead. This khahan, emperor of the Tuigan, could wait a few more minutes while he looked their city over.

It was primitive, rustic—and it took Koja's breath away. There wasn't a single stone building in Quaraband. The little tents—yurts—were dirty felt mounds, but the sheer number of them was awe-inspiring. There were thousands of the yurts set up upon the plain. Quaraband covered the valley floor, a mile or more in each direction. A gray smudge of smoke hung over the tents, the residue from hundreds of fires. It had an acrid tang that came from burning dung. This unpleasant fuel was a necessity, since there was precious little else to burn on the treeless steppe.

A cloud of dust swirled up in front of Koja, partially obscuring his view of the city. The line of troopers snaked past; the sound of snorting horses, grumbled curses, and creaking leather suddenly reminded the priest of where he was. General Chanar was well ahead, trotting toward Quaraband. Koja awkwardly spurred his own horse forward, hurrying to catch up.

Just at the outskirts of the tent city, the priest rejoined General Chanar. The warlord barely noticed as the dallying priest came apace. Instead, the general turned back to survey the dispositions of his men. The ten thousand riders were already breaking into smaller groups, directed by the *yurtchis*, the officers responsible for laying out the camp. Satisfied that his men were being taken care of, Chanar turned back to where Koja sat on his horse.

"Come with me. I must present you to Yamun Khahan," Chanar ordered. He spit on the ground, clearing the dust from his throat, then tapped his horse forward. Koja followed.

DAVID COOK

As they passed through the yurts, Koja studied them
closely. The round tents were made from thick felt pounded
into rugs and stretched over a wooden frame. Each doorway was covered with a loose rug that could be pulled aside
to let in fresh air and light. The roofs bulged at the very top,
where a smoke hole provided a little ventilation. Judging by
the dirty exteriors, Koja doubted the yurts were bright and
cheery inside. As they passed one yurt whose door was
open, Koja caught the thick odors of sweat, grease, and
smoke issuing from the inside.

A small troop of riders, rough-looking men with butter-
colored skin, approached the priest and the general. The
riders wore identical black robes and pointed, fur-trimmed
caps topped with long red tassels. Each man carried a
curved saber at his side. "Yamun Khahan sends these men to
escort the valiant Chanar Ong Kho to the khahan's home. He
asks Chanar to share drinks with him," hailed the lead rider
as the men approached. As he spoke, the man eyed Koja
curiously.

Chanar nodded in acceptance, then motioned toward
the priest. "Tell the khahan that I've brought an ambassador of the Khazari along from Semphar." At the command
of the lead rider, one of the escort galloped away with the
message.

The group continued in silence. As they rode, women
peered shyly from behind tent flaps and dirty, bare-legged
children ventured out to see the stranger riding by. The
riders skirted the cooking fires, where pots bubbled, filling
the air with the strong odor of boiled mutton.

Soon they reached a palisade of simple wooden stakes.
The fence was five feet high, and ringed the base of a low
hill that stood alongside the river. Beyond the fence Koja
saw five large yurts, bigger than any he had passed. The
largest yurt, dark black, occupied the top of the hill. The
others, clustered around it, were smaller and powdered
white with chalk. Primitive figures formed a printed band
around the top of each yurt.

"I've come to see Yamun Khahan, my *anda*," General Chanar announced formally to the black-robed guard at the entrance. Koja noted the curious phrase Chanar used, which apparently denoted some close bond between the general and the khahan.

The guard hurriedly pulled aside the simple gate and allowed the riders to pass through. Gray-robed servants ran forward and held the horses while Chanar and Koja dismounted. The general carefully straightened his armor, tugging at the hems of his grease-and-sweat-soaked silk undershirt. Satisfied, Chanar turned to the priest and declared flatly, "You'll stay here until I send for you." Sharply he turned and strode up the small hill toward the large central yurt.

Suddenly stranded by his host, Koja stood awkwardly still. The men of the armed escort were nearby, in small knots, talking among themselves. At intervals, perhaps prompted by a word or a thought, one of the guards would suddenly look Koja's way, stare through narrowed eyelids for a little while, and then, just as abruptly, return to the conversation.

The priest stood, then squatted, then stood again. No one made any attempt to speak to him or show him the hospitality an ambassador was properly due. Koja was hardly surprised, given what he saw was the barbarism of the Tuigan. Still, he had hoped for better.

For a time Koja was content to study the men in his escort. They might have been young men, but their faces were so heavily weather-beaten that their actual ages were impossible to determine. Long, thin mustaches were the favored style among these warriors. They had no beards and a few of the older-looking men had long ago taken knives to their cheeks, scarring them so badly that their beards could not grow. Most wore their hair in long braids that hung down in front of their ears. This was not unusual, but the way they shaved the crowns of their heads was quite distinctive.

After the priest waited for an hour or more, dusk fell.

Koja roamed a little, slowly at first to see if the guards would notice. He walked a short way up the slope, toward the banner that stood halfway between the gate and the largest yurt. It was a pole, fifteen feet tall with a crossbrace at the top. From the arms hung nine long black horsetail plumes. Affixed on the very top was a human skull. Below the skull was a golden plaque, while small dolls made of red cloth stood at the pole's base. Bits of hair and leather were stuck to these. Koja studied the standard, guessing at its significance.

A man came down from the large yurt, dressed in a black robe with silk trim, clearly an officer. He stopped directly in front of Koja. "Koja of Khazari—come. But first, you must kneel to the khahan's standard."

Koja looked at the dolls. They were idols, he realized—some shaman's spirit guardians, probably the powers of earth and sky. However, they were certainly not any of the gods he knew from his training at the Red Mountain Temple.

"I cannot," Koja said softly. "I am a priest of Furo. These are not my gods."

The officer looked at him darkly, his hand sliding toward the sword at his side. "You must. It is the khahan's standard."

"I mean no disrespect to your khahan, but I cannot kneel to these gods," Koja said flatly. He crossed his arms and stood firm, gambling that the guard would not strike him.

"I cannot take you to the khahan's yurt until you kneel," protested the officer. "You must kneel."

"Then I shall not see the khahan," answered Koja. A strained look crossed the officer's face.

The black-garbed officer stood in indecision. The other guards came up to see what was happening. The men and the officer fell into a heated, whispered conversation. Koja discreetly pretended not to notice, returning to his examination of the idols.

Finally, the officer gave in. Turning to Koja, he said, "You will come, but the khahan will be told."

"Your courage is great," Koja praised, allowing the officer to save face. The priest pointed to the skull at the top of the pole. "What does that represent?"

"That is the khan of the Oigurs," the officer said with relish. "He attempted to slay the khahan by luring him into a trap. The Oigurs were the first people Yamun Khahan conquered, so he honored them by placing their khan there."

"Does he treat everyone in this way?" Koja asked as he eyed the dubious honor.

"No, only a fortunate few," said the officer. The other guards broke into laughter as they led the priest up the hill.

When he reached the khahan's yurt, Koja looked down to the plain below. From the doorway the priest had a clear view of the entire Tuigan encampment. It was clear why the khahan had chosen this hill as the site for his yurt. The squat yurts of Quaraband stretched out below in a rough oval, following the course of river.

The tent flap was pulled open as the officer beckoned Koja to enter. Ducking his head through the opening, the priest carefully stepped inside. The khahan's chamberlain tugged at Koja, carefully making sure the priest did not accidentally step on the jamb, a sure sign of evil luck. Inside, it was dark. Koja willingly allowed himself to be led to a seat. As he padded across the heavily carpeted floor, the priest tried to focus his eyes in the gloom.

The Illustrious Emperor to the Tuigan, Yamun Khahan, leaned forward on his seat of cushions at the back of the yurt. His face was lit by the flickering flames of oil lamps hung from the roof poles of the Great Yurt. The light barely revealed his reddish hair, bound into long braids. Occasionally light glinted off the pale, jagged scar that ran across the bridge of his nose and over his cheek. A second old scar gave the khahan's upper lip a slight curl.

Not far from the khahan, General Chanar sat on the rugs, only a single cushion beneath him. The warrior sipped at the hot cup of tea he cradled in his hands. As Koja settled into his seat, Chanar leaned over to the khahan and spoke softly. The khahan listened, then shook his head gently, apparently vetoing the general's suggestion.

"So, envoy of the Khazari, what did you think of the grand council of Semphar?" boomed out Yamun Khahan from the far side of the yurt. Koja was surprised by the khahan's directness, but quickly regained his composure.

"Surely, Khahan of the Tuigan, General Chanar has told you about the conference. I am only an ambassador of the Khazari," Koja protested.

"You're going to tell me about this great conference at Semphar," the khahan ordered bluntly, scratching at his cheek. "I have already heard the general speak. What did the Sempharans have to say?"

"Well, Lord Yamun, the caliph of Semphar was, uh, surprised." Koja shifted his legs, trying to find a comfortable position.

Yamun Khahan snorted with laughter and drained his silver goblet, setting it down on the thick woolen rugs with a muffled thump. "Surprised? I send my best general with ten thousand men, a complete *tumen*, and the caliph is only 'surprised.' Do you hear this?" He leaned toward Chanar, who was sitting stone-faced while Koja talked. A servant came out of the shadows to pour the khahan another goblet of heated wine and dropped a pierced silver ball filled with herbs into it. Yamun, his face stern and unsmiling, turned back to the envoy. "This caliph didn't tremble in fear at the sight of General Chanar?"

"Perhaps he did, Khahan of the Tuigan, but never that I saw." Koja found his gaze locked with the khahan's. In the dim light, the ruler's eyes were black and riveting. Flustered, Koja could feel his blood reddening his face, even making his bald scalp tingle. The priest suddenly wondered if the khahan was some type of sorcerer. Unconsciously, his fingers fumbled with one of the small scripture lockets that hung around his neck.

Chanar cocked an eyebrow, noticing what the envoy was doing. "Your charms and spells won't help you here,

Khazari. No magic functions within this valley."

Koja stopped in surprise, slightly embarrassed when he realized what he was doing. "No magic? How is that possible?" He looked to Chanar for an answer, but it was Yamun who replied.

"Teylas, the Sky God, banished the magic—or that's what the Second Empress Bayalun Khadun tells me. I don't care how it happened. No magic makes this a good place for my capital, a safe place," answered Yamun Khahan between swallows of wine.

"Isn't life difficult without magic?" Koja asked softly.

"If Teylas wanted life to be easy he wouldn't have given us the steppe for a home. And he would have given me an easier people to rule," commented Yamun as he finished off another goblet of wine. "Enough of this. Was the council impressed when General Chanar told them my demands? Will they pay a tax for the caravans? Do they recognize me as ruler of the whole world?"

Koja thought carefully about the answer. "They were outraged by your . . . boldness, Lord Khahan. Many of them took exception to your claims. As the king of Cormyr pointed out, 'You do not rule the entire world.' " Koja heard a soft, irritated snort from Chanar.

The khahan slowly stood, stretching his legs. He was not a tall man, but was still imposing. His chest was broad and his neck was thick with corded muscles. He slowly walked with a bowlegged swagger toward the door of the tent. All the while he kept his eyes on the seated priest, the same way a desert cat watches its prey. "*Cor-meer?* I've never heard of such a place."

Koja, still seated on the woolen rugs that covered the floor, scuttled around to keep facing the khahan. Although the evening was chill, the lama was sweating in the stuffy tent. His orange robes were damp and clammy. Slightly frosty breezes slipped in through the minute gaps in the felt walls of the yurt.

"Is it far?" quizzed Yamun, tugging at his mustache.

"Great Lord?" asked Koja, confused by the sudden shift of the conversation.

"This place, *Cor-meer*—is it far away?"

"I don't know. It is a land far to the west, even far from Semphar. I have never been there."

"But this king, he talks bravely. What is he like?"

"The king is named Azoun. He is a strange-looking man, with pale skin and thick hair on his face—"

"Pah! I asked what he is like, not what he looks like," the khahan snapped.

"He was a . . . king, Khahan," Koja said, unable to think of a better word. "He was bold and seemed brave. The others listened to him and seemed to respect his words."

"He sounds like a man to meet. I will go to Cor-meer someday, and then we will see how brave Azoun is," Yamun decided, slapping his thigh. "So this king was not impressed. My words were not enough."

Koja tried to slowly and calmly explain what had happened at the council, at least the way he saw it. "The leaders came to the council to talk. They did not bring armies, only their wizards, priests, and guards. They were . . . not pleased, upset. After all, there was a huge army of Tuigan soldiers camped outside the city. Soldiers make very poor diplomats."

"Diplomats! Old men from tents that have no warriors—those are diplomats. Your diplomats meet because they are worried about their caravans." Yamun tapped one of the center posts of the yurt. "You think I didn't hear these things, envoy. Your khans and emperors thought they could fix everything without me, but I rule this land. I rule all the tribes of the land, and nothing is decided without my word," declared Yamun. "So I sent my own envoys—warriors with fat horses and bundles of arrows."

"With all due respect, Khahan, all the ambassadors saw was a great army of men and a brazen general," Koja replied, respectfully bowing his head to the floor. There was a sharp hissing of breath and a muttered curse from General

Chanar. Koja bit his lip as he realized he'd just slighted the warlord.

"A brazen general?" Yamun said softly as he turned away from Koja, twisting his mustache between his fingers. "What do you mean 'brazen?' "

"General Chanar is a warrior," Koja answered carefully, hoping that would be sufficient. The khahan tilted his head and waited for more. Nervous, Koja rubbed his neck. "Well, those at the council expected soft words. General Chanar was . . . insulting."

"These are lies, my khahan," Prince Chanar asserted as he shifted in his seat. "This *foreigner* has insulted me."

Chanar's hand slid to the hilt of his saber. Glowering, he stood and stepped toward Koja. "I say you're a liar and you will pay." There was a scraping sound as he started to draw his sword from its scabbard.

"Chanar Ong Kho, sit down," rumbled Yamun, his calm voice carrying easily over the general's mumbled threats. There was a quality of iron in the deeply resonant words. "Will you dishonor my tent with bloodshed? Stay your sword. This priest is my guest."

"He has insulted me!" Chanar insisted. "Didn't I say the council trembled in fear? That they were awed by our might? Is a foreigner allowed to mock me in your yurt?" Sword half-drawn, he turned to face Yamun. Chanar's body was tense, his back arched, his arms stiff.

Yamun strode directly up to Chanar, unflinching in the steady gaze of the general. Looking up into Chanar's eyes, he spoke slowly and softly, but with a hard edge. "Chanar, you are my *anda*, my blood-friend. We've fought together. There is no one I trust more than you. I have never doubted your word, but this is my tent and he is my guest. Now, sit and think no more of this." Yamun closed his hand over Chanar's on the sword hilt.

"Yamun, I petition you. He's lied about me. I will not let him stain my honor. I will not have this." Chanar tried to pull his hand free, but Yamun's grip kept it in place.

"General Chanar, you will sit down!" the khahan replied. His voice thundered as he spit out the words in tightly clipped fury. "I listen to this man," he said, flinging his finger toward Koja, "but do I believe? Perhaps I should if he angers you so."

Chanar trembled, caught between rage and loyalty. Finally, he slid the blade back into its scabbard and silently strode back to his seat. There he sat, staring darkly at the priest. All through the exchange, Koja stayed quiet, a slight shiver of nervousness and fear running through him. He marveled at the liberties the general had taken in the presence of his lord.

Yamun casually returned to his cushions and waved for another cup of wine. "Chanar is my *anda*. It is a special friendship, like brothers to each other. Because he is my *anda*, Chanar Ong Kho has the right to speak freely before me." Yamun paused to look closely at Koja. "You, however, are not my *anda*. It would be wise for you to remember this when you speak. The Tuigan do not take insults lightly. I should have you whipped for your words, but you are my guest so this time I only warn you," the khahan calmly informed the surprised lama. Chanar's black looks softened.

"I plead for forgiveness for offending the valiant Chanar Ong Kho. I can see that he is a brave warrior," Koja said, bowing to the general. Chanar coolly acknowledged the apology.

Yamun drew a small knife from a scabbard that hung at his belt and held it between himself and Chanar. "Brother Chanar, this priest does not understand our bond. This, Koja of Khazari, is what it means to be *anda*." Yamun drew the knife across his hand, making a small gash in the palm. As the blood started to well out of the cut, he handed the knife over to Chanar.

Chanar took the knife, turning it back and forth so the light sparked off the blade. Without saying a thing, the general pulled the tip of the blade across his hand. He bit down on his lip at the sudden pain.

As the first drops trickled out of the wound, Yamun pressed his bleeding hand to Chanar's, clasping it tight. Blood seeped from between their fingers, splattering in droplets on the rugs. The two men locked eyes: the khahan confident, the general smiling through the sting.

"See, priest, we are *anda,*" Yamun said. The khahan still showed no sign of pain. He squeezed Chanar's hand even harder, drawing a faint wince from the general. They gripped hands for a few minutes more, then released each other, the bond broken by unspoken communication.

"I am your *anda,* Yamun," Chanar announced loudly, if somewhat breathless for pain, so Koja could hear. The warrior held his hand in a fist. Yamun settled back into the cushions, paying little attention to his own wound. A servant came forward with thick strips of felt and a bowl of hot water and set these between the two men. Chanar began binding his own hand while the servant tried to fuss over the khahan

"Bring drinks—black kumiss—for my *anda* and this visitor," Yamun ordered. "I'll tend to myself."

The man disappeared for a moment, then reappeared with a leather bag. Setting out silver cups, the servant ladled the drinks and placed them before the men. Koja looked at the kumiss, a curdled white color, and sniffed at it gingerly. The priest recognized it as fermented mare's milk, a drink popular among the Tuigan. This was "black" kumiss, drawn from the khahan's own mares and considered the finest of all. Koja took a sip of the bitter drink and then discreetly set the cup aside while the other men gulped the contents of their chalices.

"My lord—," the lama eventually began, but the khahan waved him off.

"This audience is over," Yamun announced. "Tomorrow we'll hold council to hear the message of this envoy." He picked up his cup of kumiss and turned partially away from Chanar and the priest, the signal for them to leave. Reluctantly, Chanar stood, bowed to Yamun, and strode out the door. A blast of cold spring air blew through the doorway, making the lamps flicker. Koja took care not to turn his back on the khahan, which would be considered an insult in the priest's own country.

Yamun raised his hand to recognize the envoy's leaving. The hastily wrapped bandage across his palm slipped loose, letting blood flow once again from the wound. Seeing this, Koja took the opportunity to be of aid.

"Great Lord, I have a little skill in healing wounds. If I could be of some small service to my illustrious host it would bring great honor to my temple." Koja knelt down, touching his head to the floor.

Yamun turned back toward Koja, one eyebrow arched as he studied the kowtowing priest. "If you have some skill with spells, it will do you little good here. Remember, the power of magic is gone from this area."

"I know, Khahan of the Tuigan, but at our temple we are taught the secrets of herbs. It is something all of the chosen must learn," Koja explained, still kneeling.

"What if you plan to poison me?"

"I would not do this, great khahan. I have come a long way to speak for my prince," Koja explained, looking up from the floor. "You have not even heard his words."

Yamun tilted his head and studied the priest. Finally, his lips twisted into a wry grin. "I think your words have merit. Well then, envoy of the Khazari, let's see what your skills can do for my hand."

Koja sat himself at the feet of the khahan. Reaching into his robes, the priest brought out a small pouch he always carried. From it he took a small strip of yellow paper covered in script, a lump of incense, and three dried leaves. Taking Yamun's wounded hand, Koja carefully began unwrapping the loose bandages.

"The herbs are very cleansing but cause some pain, Lord Yamun," Koja warned, crumbling the leaves into the Yamun's kumiss.

"What of it? Tell me about Semphar."

"I only saw a little of it, Khahan," Koja began as he soaked a strip of cloth in the kumiss. "But it seemed like a powerful land." The lama handed the wine-soaked cloth to the khahan. "Squeeze on this, Khahan."

"If they are so powerful, then why did the Sempharans call this council?" Yamun queried, ignoring any pain as Koja washed out the wound.

Koja finished dabbing at the cut. "Caravans from east and west begin and end in Semphar, so they become worried when the merchants are attacked and no longer travel the routes to Shou Lung. Hold your hand flat, please." Koja pressed the yellow paper into the wound and carefully placed the incense on it. The yellow was immediately tinged with red. Standing, Koja reached up and unhooked one of the lamps.

"Still, if they are mighty warriors, why don't they send soldiers to protect their caravans?" Yamun asked as he poked at the paper on his hand.

"Semphar is powerful, but they are not horsemen. The steppe is far from their homeland. They did not know who ruled the lands of the steppe. There have been many tribes here and many chieftains, khans as you call them." Koja fumbled in his pouch.

"I am the khahan, the khan of khans. I rule the steppe," Yamun declared.

Koja only nodded and lit another scrap of paper from his pouch off the lamp beside him. Twice he passed the burning paper over the khahan's hand, muttering prayers. Then he touched the flame to the incense. Yamun twitched his hand to pull it away from the fire, more in surprise than pain. "Keep your hand still, Khahan. The ash must be rubbed into the wound."

Yamun grunted in understanding. For a time he watched the little ropes of sweet smoke coil upward from his hand. Finally, he spoke. "Since they do not attack me, perhaps I must go to them."

Koja started at the suggestion. "Khahan, Semphar is a

mighty nation with great cities of stone with walls around them. You could not capture these with horsemen. They have many soldiers." The khahan didn't seem to understand the greatness of the caliph. "Semphar does not want war, but they will fight."

"But they refused my demands, didn't they?"

"Only because they seek more time to consider them," Koja explained as he blew on the smoldering incense.

"They're stalling. They have no intention of obeying me and you know that, priest," Yamun pointed out. The last wisps of smoke from the incense wafted over his palm.

"Noble khahan, it takes men time to decide. My own prince, Ogandi, must hear what has happened at Semphar and then discuss it with the elders of Khazari." Koja gently rubbed the warm ashes into the blood-soaked paper. That finished, he began rewrapping the bandage around the khahan's hand.

"Then, your people should know that I will destroy them if they refuse me," the khahan promised in grim tones. His face was emotionless, and he watched Koja in silence, letting his words sink in. Koja shifted uneasily, uncertain how to react to such a threat. Then, breaking the tension, Yamun leaned forward and slapped the priest on the knee. "Now, envoy, tell me of the people and places you have seen."

It was almost dawn before the khahan permitted Koja to leave. Exhausted from the strain of the meeting and thick-headed from the wine, the priest stumbled out of the tent. The icy wind snatched at his robes, whipping and cracking them about his legs. Shivering, Koja wrapped a heavy sheepskin coat, taken from the belongings still packed on his horse, tightly about him, but it did little good for his slipper-shod feet. Stamping, he worked to get the blood circulating through cold toes once again.

The khahan's bodyguards watched the priest from where they huddled by a small fire. In the three weeks that Koja had been traveling with the Tuigan, men like these had watched over him. For the most part they had eyed him silently, but a few had been talkative. It was from these men that Koja had learned the most about the Tuigan.

Not that it was much. The Tuigan were nomads, raising sheep, cattle, and camels. But horses were their lives. They ate horsemeat and brewed kumiss from the curdled mare's milk. They tanned horsehides and made plumes from horsetails. They rode horses better than anyone Koja had ever seen. It seemed as if every man was a warrior, trained to use bow, sword, and lance.

The finest of these warriors were handpicked for the khahan's bodyguard, the Kashik. These were the men who were now watching him from around their fire. Each man was a proven warrior and killer. One of them stood and announced himself as the priest's escort.

"The khahan invites you to stay at one of his yurts," the squat guard said. It wasn't phrased like an invitation, but Koja didn't care. The command would mean a tent, and a tent would be warm.

Willingly following the guard, Koja walked slowly, sometimes stumbling over clumps of grass that broke the thin crust of snow. His tired body barely noticed. A servant followed, leading the priest's horse. Finally, the guard stopped and pulled aside a felt rug door. Koja entered and the servant unloaded his belongings. Fatigue settling on him, the priest tottered over to the pile of rugs and gently collapsed on top of them, dropping away into blissful slumber.

The sun was high over the eastern horizon when Koja awoke to someone shouting outside his tent. "Koja the Lama, envoy of the Khazari, come out."

Koja straightened his sleep-rumpled robes and stepped through the tent door. Four guardsmen stood outside, dressed in the black robes of the khahan's bodyguard. They wore tall caps of sable, the pelts turned inside-out so the hide was on the outside. The men's braids were bound with silver disks and tassels of blue yarn. Long straight swords hung from their belts, the silver fittings gleaming in the sunlight. Koja squinted and shielded his eyes from the bright glare.

"Yamun Khahan, Illustrious Emperor of the Tuigan, orders you to appear before him," said one, stepping forward from the rest.

Koja sighed and held up his hand for the man to wait, then ducked back into the tent. Inside, he hastily pulled off his dirty robes and rummaged through the wooden chests of clothes, flinging shirts and sashes over his shoulder. Finally, Koja pulled out an orange-red silk robe. It was the color worn by lamas of his temple, the Red Mountain sect. He had bought the silk from a Shou trader and had the robe specially made after learning he was going to the council at Semphar.

In a few moments Koja left his tent and set out for the khahan's yurt. As he walked along, Koja noticed the tents were arranged in rough rows, each positioned the same way. "Why do all the doors face the southeast?" he asked his escort.

One of the guards grunted, "That is the direction where Teylas lives."

"Teylas is your god?" Koja asked, stepping around a patch of mud. The guard nodded. "You have no other gods?"

"Teylas is the god of everything. There are *cham* to help him." The fellow was far more talkative than others Koja had met.

"*Cham*?"

"Guardians, like our mother, the Blue Wolf. They keep the evil spirits away from a man's yurt. See—there they are." The guard pointed to the band of stick-like figures that circled the top of each yurt.

After that the guard fell silent. There was nothing left for Koja to do but trudge along, watching in silence. They passed through the gate and marched up the hill to the khahan's yurt. This time no one challenged the priest when he reached the horsetail banner, although his escort bowed. At the khahan's yurt, Koja waited outside.

It did not take long for the priest to be announced. A servant pulled up the tent flap and tied the door open, letting a little light into the dim interior. At the far end of the tent was a raised platform, covered with rugs. Sitting there, on a small stool, was Yamun Khahan. Below the platform, sitting to the side, was an older man, his mustache wispy with graying hairs.

The khahan was dressed in formal clothing—leather boots dyed red and black, a pair of yellow woolen trousers, a blue silk jacket embroidered with dragons, and a leather coat-robe with broad cuffs and collar of white ermine. His cap was low and only slightly pointed, the brow a thick band of sable fur. From under it hung his braids, bound in coils of silver wire. Glass beads dangled from the long ends of his mustache.

For all the grandeur and might Yamun Khahan claimed, his yurt was furnished simply. The felt rugs that formed the walls were brightly dyed in geometric patterns, as was the custom, but aside from the dias there was little else in the tent. A stack of cushions rested along one wall, and an incense burner sat in the middle of the room. Oil lamps hung by chains from the ceiling braces, which were themselves carved and embellished with silver plaques of scrollwork. Behind the khahan was a stand, which held his bow and several quivers of arrows.

The old man in front of Yamun sat at a low table. Neatly arranged on it were several pieces of paper, an inking stone, and a heavy, square silver seal. Koja guessed the fellow was a scribe.

"Welcome, Lama Koja of the Khazari, to the tents of Yamun Khahan. The khan of the Hoekun and emperor of all the Tuigan people asks you to sit," said the khahan in the weary tones of a man bored with protocol.

A servant scampered from out of the darkness, bringing a cushion for Koja. A place was set for him in the center of the floor, just behind the incense burner. Kneeling on the cushion, Koja bowed his head to the floor.

"If the yurt you slept in was comfortable, I give it to you,"

Yamun offered, suppressing a yawn.

Koja bowed again to Yamun and carefully began the speech he had rehearsed for this formal reception. "The khahan does me great honors. I am only a simple envoy of my prince. Knowing that you would attend the council of Semphar, he ordered me to carry messages to you from his hand. I have brought these with me," Koja said, pulling two packets from the sleeves of his robe. They were large blue envelopes, bound with red silk string and closed with the wax seal of Prince Ogandi. Koja set the letters on the rugs before the khahan.

The khahan waved his finger, and the scribe picked up the letters. Taking these, he presented them with two hands, his head bowed, to the khahan. Yamun took the envelopes and studied the seals while the scribe returned to his seat. Apparently satisfied that they had not been tampered with, Yamun broke the first open and carefully unfolded the sheet. Uncertain what languages the Tuigan might understand, the letter had been written in both the flowing script of Semphar and the hachured ideograms of Shou Lung. Yamun scanned the page and passed it back to the scribe.

"My scribe will read these. I have no use for reading," the khahan bluntly explained. The scribe carefully placed the paper on the writing desk.

"Koja the Lama," continued Yamun, arching his back to stretch, "you are the envoy of the Khazari. Therefore, I've ordered proper documents prepared for you, stating your position and the honors you must be shown. These will keep you from being mistaken for a bandit or a spy." Yamun's eyes flicked up and down over the priest. "Show these signs and you will be allowed to pass unmolested—except where my word says you will not go. No one will refuse you because defying my word is death."

Yamun waved to the scribe once more, who scurried from his table to present Koja with a golden *paitza*—a heavy, engraved plate, almost a foot long, strung on a red silken cord.

Taking the *paitza*, Koja studied it closely. At the top was the fanciful face of a tiger, the seal of the khahan. Below it was writing, carved in Shou characters. Koja read it softly aloud. " 'By the power of eternal heaven and by the patronage of great grandeur and magnificence, who does not submit to the command of Yamun Khahan, that person is guilty and will die.' "

"Wear it about your neck and do not lose it or you may find yourself in trouble." Koja gently hefted the *paitza* and decided to wear it somewhere else.

"Now, priest, I must dismiss you. There are other things I must do. I will consider the words of your prince. When the time is ready, I will prepare a reply." Yamun abruptly ended the meeting, turning to the scribe while ignoring the presence of the priest.

Bowing one last time, Koja took his leave. After the previous night, the formality and shortness of this meeting was jarring. Perhaps, he thought, there was something he didn't understand about Tuigan hospitality.

Koja returned to his yurt to work on his reports. Since leaving Khazari, the priest had tried to maintain a careful account of his mission by writing his observations in letters to Prince Ogandi. Although Koja had sent a few missives from Semphar, he had not had the chance since. Pulling out a bundle of sheets, the priest began to carefully add the recollections of last night and today to the papers. He quickly became engrossed in the work.

It was dark when Yamun summoned Koja back to his yurt. The khahan sat alone on the dais. The scribe was seated at his little table. A wick floating in a bowl of oil provided the man with light. Other lamps were lit, casting a dim illumination against the dark. Koja was ushered in with little ceremony.

"Sit, priest," Yamun said, dispensing with formalities. Koja took his seat on the cushions in the center of the floor. "No, here." Yamun pointed at his feet. "You will look at my hand."

"As you wish, Khahan." Koja reached into the front of his

robe, getting his charm pouch.

"Priest, will you join me in drink?" Yamun asked while he watched the Koja rummage through the bag.

"You are most gracious, Khahan. I will take wine."

Yamun clapped his hands, taking care not to strike his bandage. "Bring hot wine and kumiss for me. It's a better drink than wine," he said, pointing a finger at Koja. "Kumiss reminds us of who we are. It is our blood. But," he concluded with a grin, "it is an acquired taste."

The servants appeared and poured the drink into silver goblets. As they did so, Koja carefully unwrapped the bandage on Yamun's hand. The skin around the edge of the wound was black and crusty, but there was no sign of swelling. Already it had started to knit properly. "Let the wound air," Koja advised the khahan.

"Very well. Now, for the sake of formality, read me your prince's words," Yamun requested. Reaching into his robe, the khahan produced the letters and tossed them to Koja. He leaned forward, intent on Koja's words.

The priest unfolded the sheet and squinted, trying to make out the words in the dim light.

" 'To the gracious lord of the steppe from Prince Ogandi, ruler of Khazari, son of Tulwakan the Mighty:

" 'Long have we heard of your people, and great are they in their lands! Mighty is your valor. Greatly it pleases us to have so stalwart a neighbor—' "

"What does it say?" Yamun interrupted impatiently, tapping his fingertips together.

"Great Lord?"

"What does your prince say? Tell me. Don't read anymore. Just tell me."

"Well . . ." Koja paused as he scanned the rest of the letter. "Prince Ogandi offers his hand in friendship, hoping that you will enter into peaceful trade with him. And then, later on, he proposes a treaty of friendship and defense."

"And the other letter, what does it say?"

Koja unfolded it and scanned through the lines. "My

prince has outlined this proposed treaty for you to consider. It calls for recognizing the borders of the Khazari and Tuigan lands. He says that, 'Your enemies shall be our enemies.'" Koja stopped to see if the khahan had understood. "It's a promise to assist each other against attackers."

"He does not threaten war?" Yamun asked sternly.

Koja looked at the letter again. "No, Great Lord!"

"Does he state that assassins will be sent to slay me?" Yamun fingered at the baubles in his mustache.

Koja wonder just what Yamun was getting at. "Not at all."

"Hmmm . . ." Yamun stroked his mustache. "Then why would someone tell me these things?" he wondered out loud as his gaze settled on the old scribe. The man went pale, sweat beading out on his forehead. "Why would someone tell me lies?"

"I did not lie, Lord! I only read what was there!" the scribe babbled as he frantically pressed his face into the carpets. His voice muffled, he continued to plead. "I swear by the lightning, by the might of Teylas, I only read what was written! I am your faithful scribe!"

"One of you has lied and will forfeit his life for it," Yamun rumbled, looking from the priest to the scribe. The prostrate servant began heaving with muffled sobs. Koja looked at the letters again, baffled by this strange accusation. Yamun looked at the two men over his folded hands, his mind deep in thought.

Suddenly the khahan stood, knocking the stool over, and strode to the doorway of the tent. "Captain!" he shouted into the darkness. The officer appeared within a second. "Take this dog out and execute him. Now!" Yamun thrust his finger at the scribe. With a shrieking wail the man clutched at the carpets for safety.

The scribe's pathetic screams grew louder as the black-robed guards approached. Koja slid back, out of the way of the grim-faced warriors. Yamun's visage was fixed with anger and hatred.

"Shut up, dog!" the khahan shouted. "Guards, take him!"

Three soldiers picked up the scribe and carried him from the tent. His muffled cries could be heard through the tent walls. Yamun waited expectantly. The screaming grew frantic and hoarse, then there was a dull thud and the screaming stopped. Yamun nodded in satisfaction and took his seat.

Koja realized that he was trembling. Lowering his eyes, the priest practiced his meditation to regain his composure.

The captain of the guard pulled the tent flap aside. In his hands was a bloodstained bundle—a simple leather bag. Wordlessly he entered and knelt before the khahan. "As you ordered, so is it done," the captain said as he unwrapped the package. There, in the middle of the cloth, was the head of the scribe.

"Well done, Captain. Take his body and feed it to the dogs. Set that," he sneered, pointing to the head, "on a lance where everyone can see it."

"It will be done." The captain looked at Koja in curiosity, then took the head and left.

Yamun let out a great sigh and looked at the floor. Finally, he turned to Koja. "Now, priest, bandage my hand."

Still trembling slightly, Koja took out his herbs and began to work.

- 2 -
Mother Bayalun

Yamun trotted his horse, a sturdy little piebald mare, through the camps of his soldiers. Alongside him rode Chanar on a pure white stallion. From behind came the jingling clatter of reins and hooves as five bodyguards, black-robed men of the elite Kashik, followed closely behind.

It had been days since the audience with the priest from Khazari, and Yamun was still reflecting on the events. He scowled as he pondered the contents of the envoy's letters. The prince of the Khazari wanted a treaty botween their two nations. Yamun didn't know if that was desirable, and, before deciding, he needed to know more about the Khazari—their numbers, strengths, and weaknesses. "The sleeping rabbit is caught by the fox," or so went the old saying. Yamun had no intention of being lulled to sleep by mere paper.

Dismissing the topic in his mind, Yamun slowed his horse and looked with pride on the endless sea of soldiers' tents and campfires. This was his army. He had organized the tribesmen into *arbans* of ten men, then *jaguns* of one hundred, further still to *minghans* of one thousand, ending finally in the *tumen*, the great divisions of ten thousand men. Every soldier had a rank and a place in the army, just as Yamun planned. Under his command the men of the steppe were transformed from raiding bands into a tightly disciplined army.

The khahan reined in his horse, bringing it to a stop just in front of a small group of soldiers gathered around their fire. The entourage with him clattered to a stop, too. The squad of ten men who sat around the fire leaped to their feet.

"Who is the leader of this *arban*?" Yamun demanded, tapping his horsewhip on his thigh. The khahan's horse pranced uneasily, agitated by Yamun's energy.

One man hurriedly ran forward and flung himself to the ground at the mare's hooves. In the warm spring day, the man wore only his woolen trousers and *kalat*, a stained blue tunic trimmed with red. A conical bearskin cap, decorated with goat-hide tassels, identified the man as a common trooper of Chanar's *tumen*.

Satisfied with the trooper's response, the khahan waited for his horse to quiet down. "Rise, brother soldier," he said, trying to put the nervous trooper at ease.

"Yes, Great Lord," mumbled the man, pushing himself up from the dirt. Even sitting upright, the man kept his eyes downcast. Yamun could tell the man was a tough and seasoned soldier by the large scars on his cheeks.

"Fear not, warrior," Yamun spoke soothingly. "You're not to be punished. I've some questions, that's all. The commander of your *jagun* recommended your bravery and skill. What's your father's *ordu*?" Yamun whisked away the flies from his mare's mane.

"Illustrious Emperor of the Tuigan, my father was born into the Jebe clan." The trooper bowed again on completing his words.

"Jebe's *ordu* has many tents, and he's served me well in the past. What's your name?"

"Hulagu, Khahan," the trooper answered, bowing again.

"Very well, Hulagu. Stop bobbing up and down and be a soldier." The man sat up straighter, obedient to the words of his khahan. "Jebe Khan keeps his *ordu* to the east, near the Katakoro Mountains, doesn't he?"

"Yes, Great Lord, in the summertime when the pastures are rich there."

"Have you heard of the Khazari? I'm told they live in those mountains." He stroked the neck of his horse, keeping it calm.

"This is true, khahan. We sometimes take their sheep and cattle," the trooper answered with pride.

Yamun smiled. Raiding and rustling were old and honorable traditions among the Tuigan. As khahan, he could barely keep the different *ordus* of the Tuigan from stealing each other's horses. Any Tuigan caught stealing from another was executed on the spot, but the law did not apply to non-Tuigan. Yamun tucked his horsewhip into his boot-top. "Are they easy to raid?"

"My father says it was not as hard as raiding the *ordus* of Arik-Boke and Berku—or so he was told; my father never did this," Trooper Hulagu added hastily, remembering the penalties Yamun had set. "The Khazari aren't horsemen and don't chase us very well, so it is easy to get away. But they live in tents of stone and keep their sheep in pens at night, so we could only raid them when they took their flocks out to pasture."

"Are they a brave people?" Yamun asked, dropping his horse's reins to let it graze.

"Not as brave as the Jebe," the man answered with a trace of boastfulness. "They would fight, but were easy to trick. Many times they did not send out scouts, and we could fool them by driving horses ahead of us to make our numbers seem much larger." The trooper wriggled a little, trying to keep his toes warm in the cold mud.

Yamun stroked the fine beard on his chin. "Are there many of them?"

The man thought for a bit. His eyes glazed as he started imagining numbers larger than twenty.

Finally, the trooper spoke. "They are not so numerous as the *tumens* of the khahan nor do they fight as well," he said, breaking into a big smile at what he thought was his own cleverness.

Yamun laughed at the man's answer. What he really

needed, as he had known from the start, was solid information on who and what the Khazari were like. Trooper Hulagu's memory was certainly not going to be enough. "What's the distance to Khazari?" he asked. Again the man thought, although this time Yamun suspected he knew the answer.

"Illustrious Emperor of the Tuigan, when I left my *ordu* to join the magnificent Son of Teylas's armies, I rode for three weeks, but I did not hurry and stopped many days in the yurts of my cousins along the way. The trip could be made faster."

"Undoubtedly," Yamun said, half to himself. The squat warlord paused, although he already knew what needed to be done. Leaning on the pommel of his saddle, Yamun turned to General Chanar beside him. "Chanar Ong Kho, this man and his *arban* are to ride with all haste to the Katakoro Mountains with as many men as you think wise to send. I want to know the numbers, strengths, and weaknesses of the Khazari. See that the scouts have fresh horses and passes. They must return in five weeks, no later." Chanar nodded in understanding.

Just as he was about to go, Yamun turned back. "And send someone from my Kashik who can count. Make him their commander. Let all who disobey you know this is by the word of the khahan." Yamun added the last automatically, a formula that signified his orders.

"By your word, it shall be done," responded Chanar mechanically, according to the formula of etiquette. "Is that all my men are to do?" the general asked.

Yamun stopped his horse and stared back at Chanar. "You, General Chanar, will ride to the *ordu* of my son, Tomke, and observe his camp. I want to know if his men are ready. Take the men you need and go immediately. Teylas will protect you."

"By your word, it shall be done," Chanar responded. The discussion finished, Yamun tugged his mount's reins and galloped off.

The trooper still cowered at the feet of Chanar's horse.

"Get going!" the general bellowed. The terrified Hulagu leaped to his feet and scrambled back toward his camp. With his boot, the trooper roused the men of his *arban*, sending them tumbling after their gear.

"See to the details," Chanar ordered an aide nearby. With his own preparations to make, General Chanar wheeled his horse around and galloped away, headed toward his own yurt.

* * * * *

In his tent, Koja brought out his papers and began to make notes of the day's events and sights. He had only added a few pages since his arrival in Quaraband. Looking at the meager letters only reminded him of how little he knew of the khahan. Undiscouraged, he took up the writing brush and with quick practiced strokes started another letter.

My lord, Prince Ogandi of the Khazari. Greetings from your most humble servant, Koja, envoy to the Tuigan court.

For two days I have awaited the word of the khahan of the Tuigan. There has been no communication from him. He has received your offers, but gives no sign of his opinion toward a treaty. I can do little but wait.

During this time, I have ridden about Quaraband, as the Tuigan call this city of tents, attempting to learn more about their numbers and their way of life. Using the paitza given me by the khahan, I have been able to go where I wish, with one exception—the royal yurt.

Koja stopped to ink his brush and lay out another sheet of paper. He paused before touching the brush to paper again. That morning he had gone to Yamun's tent. There he was stopped by the Kashik dayguard stationed by the gates. Showing his *paitza* had had no effect on the man and all his protests had been in vain. The guard, in his black *kalat*, made it clear that Koja was not to be admitted, since the priest's pass bore only the tiger seal. This was apparently the pass used by low-ranking officials. Koja thought about penning the story down, then decided against it.

Perhaps no one was allowed within the royal palace except by invitation.

Traveling elsewhere in the camp, I had no such difficulty, though I have been in the constant company of an armed escort, a precaution of the khahan. I carefully counted tents, making a knot in a string for every ten. By now the cord is short, twisted with little knots. There are more than one hundred knots on the cord, and I still have not ridden the extent of the camp. The Tuigan are a numerous people, O Prince.

In crafts and arts, the people are more than mere barbaric savages. They have men skilled in working gold and silver, and from the wool of sheep make a wondrously warm and soft fabric called felt. At the same time, they are among the smelliest and most abhorrent people for their personal habits.

Koja set aside his brush and pondered what he knew of the Tuigan so far. What seemed like ages ago, when he had first learned he was to visit the Tuigan, Koja had assumed that they were all uncultured savages. Chanar's appearance at the Council of Semphar—dirty, foul-smelling, rude, and arrogant—certainly confirmed that impression.

The ride to Quaraband had been no better. The entire force had traveled at a killing pace, sometimes covering sixty to eighty miles in a single day. He had joined this rank, unwashed group at their meals of near-indigestible dried meat and powdered milk curds mixed with water. For three weeks the men never changed their clothes. It was not a pleasant journey.

The Tuigan, Lord, will eat anything, nor does this give them indigestion. They are great eaters of mutton and horsemeat. They eat much game, for they are most excellent shots with the bow. Mare's milk is used at every meal, made plain, curdled, fermented, and dried. A powder made from the curds is mixed with water or, I am told, mare's blood, to make a drink the soldiers use while they travel.

Koja stopped writing when he realized that his description was incomplete. In Quaraband, he had finally been exposed to another facet of his hosts. To be sure, they still seemed to be barbarians—cruel, dangerous, and impulsive—but Koja could no longer say they were simply uneducated and unskilled. There was a surprising variety to Tuigan life.

The first thing he noticed was that not everyone traveled by horseback and lived in yurts. Mixed among the tents were households who used great, heavy carts to haul their belongings. Some families owned carts but still used yurts; others had abandoned the dome-shaped tents and lived in houses built on their wagons. Other carts carried portable forges for the blacksmiths who set up shop along the water's edge.

These smiths were skilled craftsmen. Working with silver, they made decorated cups, bowls, saddle arches, buckles, pins, and an amazing assortment of other ornaments. Others worked leather, tanning and dying horsehide for all uses. The women wove bright-colored cloth of wool and camel hair. Armorers were especially prized, and the priest had seen many fine examples of their art since he arrived.

Koja was just about to set these thoughts down when the guard outside summoned him to the door. Hurriedly putting the writing instruments away, Koja folded the slim sheets and put them in a letter pouch. Pouring water from a leather bag, the priest rinsed his inking stone and fingers, leaving a blue stain on his fingertips. At last, with what seemed proper dignity and decorum, he threw aside the tent flap to see who was there.

Outside were five soldiers wearing white *kalats* trimmed with blue, the personal guard of the empress of the Tuigan, Eke Bayalun. Koja noted their presence with a slight nod.

"Empress Eke Bayalun of the royal household requests you come to an audience with her," stated the officer of the group, identified by the red silk tassels that hung from his cap.

"I am honored by the empress's invitation," Koja answered with a bow. Judging from the man's tone, Koja decided the request was actually an order, so there was little to do but accept graciously. Gathering his things, the priest mounted the horse the guards had brought for him.

Koja was curious to meet the empress of the Tuigan. Eke Bayalun was, from what he had learned, the only surviving wife of Yamun Khahan. She was also his stepmother. Apparently, Tuigan custom required a son to marry his father's widow—or widows—mostly to ensure the women would be cared for. Her full title was Second Empress Eke Bayalun Khadun, denoting her status as Yamun's second wife. It seemed she took an active interest in the khahan's affairs.

Koja studied the guards she had sent. As empress, she was allowed her own bodyguards, much like Yamun's Kashik troopers. Koja noted, too, that Bayalun's troops must not like the khahan's bodyguard; they were widely skirting the tents of the Kashik. Finally, they came to a gate in the stockade, one Koja had not seen before. They rode through without stopping, waved on by the white-robed guards that stood to either side.

Inside the palace grounds, the escort dismounted and helped Koja from his horse. Leaving the horses behind with the soldiers, the officer in charge led him through the grounds to a large, white yurt. Before it stood a banner of white yak tails. The officer knelt quickly before this and then led Koja to the door.

The man pulled the door flap aside and informed the chamberlain that they had arrived. There was a delay, then the chamberlain returned to usher Koja into the empress's yurt. As he entered, the priest noticed two rag idols hung over the doorway. Near the one on the left was a leather drinking bag; by the one on the right, a bundle of grain. Offerings to protective spirits, he guessed.

This yurt was far more lavish than the khahan's spartan tent. The chalk-white walls were hung with patterned silks of red, blue, yellow, and white. One section of the yurt was blocked off by a carved wooden screen. The rugs on the floor were bright red, embroidered in gold and silver with leaflike curls. The two tent posts that supported the central frame were carved and painted to resemble what Koja thought were twining dragons and horses.

At the yurt's far side was a square platform, no more than a few inches high, covered with rugs. On the platform was a couchlike bed of carved wood inlaid with seashells. Blankets were draped over the curved ends. Perched on its edge was a woman, Eke Bayalun.

The second empress was a striking woman, far more graceful and attractive than Koja had imagined. Knowing her to be Yamun's stepmother, Koja thought she would be an old crone, her face bound up in wrinkles with blotchy age spots. Instead, Eke Bayalun was remarkably poised and youthful. Her face was only lightly wrinkled at the corners of the eyes and mouth, the skin stretched tight over her high cheekbones. There it was smooth and glowed with a rich buttery color. Unlike the other Tuigan women Koja had seen, with their soft, round cheeks and broad noses, Bayalun had a sharp, angular nose and chin, both straight and narrow. Her eyes, too, were different, more like those of the westerners he had seen at Semphar—lacking the fold of eyelid at the outer corner. The woman's eyes were sharp, bright, and clear. Her lips were thin and tinted with natural color.

Bayalun's hair was covered with a cowl of white silk, gathered high in the back and fanned out to drape behind her shoulders. The front of the silk wrapped loosely around the neck, and wisps of black and silver hair peeked out from under the cloth. Silver earrings, set with blue and red stones, barely showed behind the fabric. Her dress, in the style of the Tuigan, was high-necked with broad lapels and collar. The dress was black silk, while the collar was a bright red velvet. Over the dress Bayalun wore a long, sleeveless felt jacket, a *jupon*, decorated with silver coins and silken tassels. Rough woolen trousers and hard leather boots peeked out from underneath the layers of clothing. A wooden staff, topped with a golden, fanged face, lay across her lap. At Bayalun's feet were several neat stacks of paper scrolls, each carefully tied with a cord of red or gold.

Koja, startled as he realized that he was rudely staring at the second empress, turned his gaze to the other people in the yurt. The men sat to the left and the women to the right. There were three men on the left side. The first, sitting slightly out of the way, was clearly Bayalun's scribe: an old man, perhaps ancient, who hunched over his little writing table. To the scribe's left was another old man, dressed in robes of faded yellow silk. The robes were completely covered with Shou characters. This man looked quickly and sharply at Koja as the priest advanced to take his seat.

Taking his place between the two rows, Koja walked past the third man. His hair hung in loose, greasy hanks, and his teeth were crooked and rotten. The man was garbed in ratty-looking pelts, thickly layered over each other. Iron hooks, bars, plates, chain-links, and figurines were stitched all across the breast of his robes. In his lap he held a large skin drum and a curved drumstick. Koja was fairly certain the man was some type of shaman, calling on primitive spirits for his powers.

On the right side of the yurt were ten women. Two sat in the front row, facing the men, and seemed important. At the head of the row was an old crone, dressed in a warm *del*, the leather garment that served as both coat and robe to the Tuigan. Beside and slightly behind the crone was a younger woman dressed in similar clothing. She wore the headdress of an unmarried woman, a towering cone of wrapped red cloth held in place with tortoiseshell combs and silver pins. Long dangling strings of silver coins draped down over her shoulders.

Koja bowed low as he stood between the two rows of attendants. Head lowered, he waited for some word from the second empress. "Welcome, Koja of the Khazari," she said in a warm and friendly tone. "You may sit." Koja sat, making himself as comfortable as possible.

"The second empress does me great honor, more than I deserve," he said.

Bayalun smiled in recognition. " 'Second empress' is not a title I am accustomed to. Among my people I am better known as Mother Bayalun or," she informed him with a wry smile, "Widow Bayalun, even Bayalun the Hard. I prefer Mother Bayalun, if only because through me the House of Hoekun is traced."

"Please pardon my ignorance, but I have only been here a short time. What is the House of Hoekun? Is it the same as the Tuigan, or is it something different?" queried Koja. He waited attentively for her answer.

"A quick mind. You ask questions," commented Mother Bayalun as she leaned forward, setting the point of her staff on the rugs. She studied the priest's face intently with her dark, deep eyes. Raising the tip of her staff, she drew a large circle in the thick nap of the felt. "This is the Tuigan empire." Her staff tapped at the circle.

"Are the Hoekun part of the Tuigan?" Koja asked.

Mother Bayalun ignored the question. Instead she drew several smaller circles inside the first. The circles more or less filled the space. "These are the people of the Tuigan empire. These," she said, stabbing at one of the circles with her staff, "are the Naican, conquered by Burekai, my husband before the khahan." Bayalun went on to tap four other circles. "These are the Dalats, Quirish, Gur, and the Commani. They were all defeated by the current khahan. And this circle," she pointed at the last, in the center of all, "is the Tuigan. There are many families among the Tuigan." Using her staff, the empress poked the rug, leaving little dents. "These are the people of the Tuigan. There are the Hoekun, the Basymats, the Jamaqua, and many more. Each house is named for its founder. Ours was Hoekun the Clever, son of his mother, the Blue Wolf."

Koja nodded politely, though he wasn't sure he understood completely. "The Blue Wolf?"

"A wise spirit. She whelped our ancestor in the middle of winter and caused our people to be born." Bayalun leaned back and shrugged her shoulders. "The children of the House of Hoekun are all the sons and daughters of the Blue Wolf. This makes the Hoekun the royal family of all the Tuigan. I am the oldest of the house, so I am called Eke—or Mother—Bayalun."

"Then your husband before Yamun Khahan was also the khahan?" Koja noted, trying to make sure he grasped everything clearly.

A scowl knitted Bayalun's brow, but she quickly assumed a blank look. "Burekei was khan of the Hoekun *ordu*, no more. It was his son, Yamun, who was chosen to be the khahan."

"Yamun Khahan was elected? He wasn't born to become the khahan?" Koja asked in surprise. He had assumed the khahan was a hereditary rank, like that of king or prince.

"All men are born to become what they will. Such is the will of Teylas, Lord of the Sky," she explained, playing her fingers up and down the staff. "When Burekei died, Yamun became khan of the Hoekun. It was only later, after he conquered the Dalats, that the families named him great prince of all the Tuigan." Bayalun crossed her feet and adjusted her seat.

"But, I did not invite you here to answer all your questions, envoy, although they have been amusing." She gave him a slight mocking smile and watched to see what kind of reaction her gentle barb would bring.

Koja became red-faced. "Accept my apologies, Second Empress," he meekly responded, bowing his head slightly.

"Please, call me Mother Bayalun," the empress chided. Sitting back in her seat, Bayalun carefully set the staff down by her feet. "You say you are a lama of the Red Mountain," she began casually. "What teachings do you follow?"

"The lamas of the Red Mountain live by the words of the Enlightened One, who taught us how to reach peace and perfect oblivion. We seek to banish our passions, so we can understand the teachings of the Enlightened One." He paused, waiting for some sign of understanding. Bayalun watched him closely but gave no indication that she understood.

Koja continued. "If I drink tea and I like tea, my life will be ruled every day by the desire for tea and I will not know anything else. Every day I will think about my cup of tea and will miss what is happening around me." The priest's hands mimed holding a cup of tea. "Only after we no longer savor life can we truly feel everything life has to offer." Koja tried to keep his explanation simple, not wanting to confuse his hostess with the complexities of Red Mountain theology. Judging from the shaman beside him, the Tuigan were not all that familiar with sophisticated philosophical teachings.

Mother Bayalun squinted at him. "I heard it said you followed Furo the Mighty. Isn't he the god of the Red Mountain Temple? But today you talk of the Enlightened One. Do you follow the teachings of one and worship the other?"

Koja scratched at the stubble on his skull. His simple explanation was getting more complex. "We know it is a truth that Furo the Mighty is a divine agent of the Enlightened One."

"So, you practice the teachings of the Enlightened One, but pray to Furo to intercede on your behalf?"

"Yes, Mother Bayalun." Koja marveled at the astuteness of her questions.

" 'He is like the wind all about us. Felt but not touched, heard but not spoken, moving but unmovable, always present, but always unseen,' " quoted Bayalun, her eyes closed in concentration.

Koja stared at her in amazement, too dumbfounded for words. "That is from the *Yanitsava*, the Book of Teachings," he whispered.

"And you're surprised that I know it," she chuckled. "I, too, have spent my life learning the teachings of wise men.

These worthies have been my instructors." She waved a hand toward the men who sat down the row from Koja. "This is Aghul Balai of the Tsu-Tsu, a people close to the border of Shou Lung," she said, introducing the thin man in the mystical robes. "For many years he studied in Shou Lung, learning the secrets of Chung Tao, the Way." The wizened man pressed his palms together and bowed slightly to Koja.

While at the temple, Koja had heard a little about Chung Tao. It was powerful within the Shou empire, far to the east. It was said that the emperor of the Jade Throne himself followed its teachings. Koja had been taught its teachings were wrong and had heard many evil stories about its practices. To Koja, the mystic suddenly looked sinister and dangerous.

"This other," continued Bayalun, pointing to the fur-clad man, "is Fiyango. Through him, we are able to speak with the spirits of the land and our ancestors, and learn much good advice." The shaman, whose age Koja found impossible to place, smiled a toothless smile at him.

"And she," concluded the second empress, tapping her staff in front of the old crone, "is Boryquil, and this is her daughter Cimca. Boryquil has the gift to see things as they are and things as they should be. She knows the ways of the *kaman kulda,* the dark spirits that come from the north."

"With my eyes I can see them; with my nose I can smell them," cackled the hag, reciting an old, ritualistic formula. Her lungs labored from the exertion. With each gasping breath, her necklace clacked and rattled. Peering at it from across the aisle, Koja saw that it was a leather cord strung with broad, flat bones. Each bone was covered in red-inked script.

"So you can see, Koja of the Red Mountain, I have surrounded myself with people of useful skills. They advise me and they teach me." Bayalun stopped and quickly wet her lips. "Aghul hopes to convert me to Chung Tao. Fiyango worries that I will forget the spirits of earth, sky, and water, while Boryquil protects my tent from evil spirits. Of course," she added softly, "not that any spirit could enter this area." She touched the finial on her staff.

"Tell me, Koja of the Khazari, are you here to teach me the secrets of the Red Mountain?"

Koja paused for a bit, trying to think of an appropriate response. Finally, he answered, "I was never the best student of my masters, and so I only learned a little from them. These were only small things in the teachings of Furo. I have traveled instead, hoping to aid others through the services of the Enlightened One." Koja didn't lie; he wasn't the best disciple, but his skills were more than he allowed.

"I thought all of you sat in your temple and meditated," Bayalun commented, brushing a wisp of hair from her eyes. The shaman to Koja's right broke into a fit of coughing. Bayalun pursed her lips and waited until he was done. "If you are a teacher, you must stay and instruct me in the ways of your temple."

Koja swallowed uncomfortably, unwilling to offend the second empress with a direct refusal. He was not here, however, to teach, even if it might spread the belief of Furo to these nonbelievers. "I will certainly be happy to teach you of our ways while I am here, illustrious empress, but I must carry messages back to my prince in Khazari." He bowed slightly as he spoke.

"I understand," Bayalun said, relenting. She leaned back with a sigh, stroking her eyebrows carefully. Koja detected a note of disappointment in her voice. "So when you summon him, does Furo lay waste to your enemies?"

Koja started at the boldness of the question. "It is said, Mother Bayalun, that he is both wondrous and terrible, but we do not *summon* him. We live to serve our god, not to have him come at our beck and call." A tone of chastisement unavoidably crept into the lama's voice.

"I see," said Mother Bayalun, turning away from Koja. "At this time the interview is over. It is our misfortune that you are unable to stay and instruct us. But I am sure your pressing duties need your attention. You may leave." Koja bit at the inside of his lip, frustrated by his own indiscretion.

The chamberlain came forward and touched Koja on the shoulder, motioning the priest to rise. Koja hoisted himself to his feet and backed out of the tent, bowing as he went. The priest, bewildered by the strange meeting, was led back to his waiting horse. Only one man from his original escort remained. The two of them rode back toward his tent, once again following the roundabout way they had taken earlier.

"Why do we go this way? It is shorter that way," Koja said, pointing along a route that would lead them past the front of the royal enclosure and Yamun's bodyguard.

"Orders."

"Oh," the lama answered. The white-*kalated* guard trotted his shaggy-maned horse forward, expecting the priest to follow along.

Koja, inattentive to his riding, urged his horse forward, giving it what he thought was a gentle kick. The mare set off at a full gallop. Koja was slammed forward into his saddle and then toppled backward, barely keeping his hold, as the horse leaped over a cooking fire. The lama only had time to glimpse a flash of startled faces. Panicked, he dropped the reins and used both hands to cling to the saddle arch. There was another hard jolt, and his feet flew from the stirrups.

"Haii!" shouted the guard, wheeling his horse around to pursue. The man leaned forward onto the neck of his pony, slashing its haunches with his three-thonged knout. "Haii! Haii!" he cried, trying to warn everyone out of his path. The guard could see Koja bouncing and tumbling about on his saddle, feet flying in the air.

"Stop! Stop!" Koja screamed to his horse as it took a tight turn past an oxcart. He managed to knot one hand into the pony's mane while his other arm flailed about. The horse's hooves clattered and thundered, pounding over the icy ground and meager grass. Koja tossed to the right, lurched forward, cracked his spine in a hard jolt against the saddle, then felt his legs fly backward, almost up over his head. The wind whipped at his robes as the pony galloped onward.

From behind Koja there was a chorus of shouts, cries, and yells. Suddenly, a man's scream came from in front of him. The horse answered the scream and reared, almost throwing Koja off its back. The mare's breath was labored, coming in snorting pants. There was a sharp crack as its hooves hit the ground.

The jolt snapped the priest forward, flipping his body over the front of the saddle, one hand still tangled in the mare's mane. In an instant, Koja slammed to the ground, thrown completely over the head of the panting steed, a hank of mane in his hand. As he hit, Koja's head struck a stone.

"Haii-haii-hai," the breathless guard hoarsely shouted as he leaped from the saddle of his still-moving steed. He sprinted over to where the runaway horse pranced. Under its hooves was the priest, a huddled form of tangled robes. From the nearby tents ran the black-garbed men of the khahan's guard.

*　*　*　*　*

Yamun paced back and forth along the dusty streambed; it was the only action that could contain his frustration and anger. Several times he stopped to slash an offending tuft of grass with his bloodstained knout. At one end of his pace was the guardsman of the second empress, Koja's escort, spread-eagled on the ground. The man lay staked out on his back, his head pressed into the dirt by a *cangue*, a heavy, Y-shaped yoke that was lashed to his neck by twisted thongs. The guardsman had been stripped naked and was bleeding from several lash marks.

At the other end of Yamun's stride was a pallet bearing the unconscious priest. Huddled around him were three shamans, wearing their ritual masks. A piece of white cloth, set with a silver bowl of milk and bloody sheep bones, was spread at the head of the pallet. Encircling everyone was a wall of Kashik dayguards, their backs turned so that they faced away from Yamun and the shamans, forming a living wall. A strong wind whipped their *kalats* about their legs. In the distance, the smoke of Quaraband curled over the dim shapes of the tents.

Yamun stopped at the prisoner. "Why did old Bayalun summon the Khazari?" he demanded, towering over the bound man.

The prisoner, choking from a parched throat, barely gurgled a reply. Infuriated, Yamun whipped him with the knout, leaving more bloody wounds.

"Why did she summon him?"

"I—I—don't know," the guardsman rasped out.

"What did they talk about?"

The guard gasped as Yamun struck him again. "I did not hear!"

Disgusted, Yamun strode to the other end of the little compound, where the shamans worked. "Will he live?"

"It is very difficult, Great Prince," spoke one of the three. He wore a crow mask, and his thin, creaky voice echoed hollowly from it. Horse-mask and Bear-mask kept to their work.

"I don't care. Give me an answer," Yamun snapped.

"His gods are different from ours, Khahan. It is hard to know if our healing spells will have power over him. We can only try."

Yamun grunted. "Then you'd better try very hard." He turned to resume his pacing.

The wall of Kashik parted to allow a mounted rider to enter. The man, a commander of a *minghan* in the Kashik, slid quickly off his horse, ran to Yamun, and knelt before the khahan.

"Get up and report," Yamun ordered.

"I come from the tents of the Mother Bayalun, as you ordered, Great Lord."

"And what did she have to say?"

"Mother Bayalun says she only wanted to learn more of

the world," the officer quickly answered as he looked toward the prisoner on the ground.

Yamun gripped his knout with both hands. "And what's her excuse for the guards?"

"According to her, the orders she gave were not followed. She commanded the guards to escort the priest to and from his tent, and to make sure that he was not hurt," the commander explained. "She ordered an *arban* of men to go as escort, but they did not obey her orders."

"Then you must ride back and tell her to choose a punishment for the nine that deserted their posts," Yamun ordered. He impatiently scuffed at the ground with his toe.

"She has anticipated your desire and has already given her judgment. They are to be sewn into the skins of oxen and sunk into the river, as is by custom."

"She's clever and quick. She hopes this will appease me." Yamun pulled at his mustache as he thought it over. "Her judgment will do. Still, I want you to go back and tell her I'm not satisfied. For letting this happen, she must reduce the size of her bodyguard. I'll set the numbers when I return."

"Yes, Khahan. Surely the second empress will be angry, Lord. Might she do something dangerous?" The officer had heard much of Bayalun's powers.

"I don't need to please her. She'll accept it because I'm the khahan," Yamun said confidently. He turned and walked over to his captive. "And did she say anything about him?" Yamun asked, pointing at the man on the ground.

"Seeing as he is within your grip, she allows you to deal with him as you want."

Yamun looked down on the man. The fellow's eyes were wide, waiting for word from the khahan.

"He did not desert, Khahan," the officer noted.

"True. He can live, but . . ." The khahan paused, thinking. "He failed in his duties. Fetch men and stones. Crush one ankle so he cannot ride again. Let all who disobey you know that this is by the word of the khahan."

"By your word, it shall be done," answered the commander. Taking his horse, he left the circle to see to the arrangements.

The sound of the drum and flute brought Yamun's attention back to the shamans. The droning melody of their chant was just ending when he came back to them. Taking their horsetail wands, the shamans sprinkled the still body of the priest with milk and then stepped away from the pallet.

"Well?" demanded Yamun, only to be hushed by Crowmask.

"Wait, we will know in a little while." The shaman's voice echoed from inside the mask. The three squatted down on their haunches. Yamun stood behind them, fiddling with his knout. Finally his patience could take no more and he resumed his pacing.

After several minutes Yamun heard a cough. He turned and strode back to the pallet. Koja was struggling to prop himself up on one elbow. The shamans clustered around, their masks pushed up from their faces. They fussed over the priest, pushing him back down each time he weakly tried to sit up. Crow-mask turned to Yamun. "He lives, Illustrious Khahan. The spirits of the Sky God, Teylas, have favored him with their blessing."

"Good," commented Yamun, stepping past the man. He looked down into Koja's wan face. Dried blood still caked the back of his skull, although the wound, magically healed, had already knit. "Well, envoy of the Khazari, want to go riding?" He laughed at his own joke while Koja winced in pain at the thought.

One of the shamans tugged at the khahan's sleeve. "Gently, Great Lord. He is still very weak."

Yamun grunted in acknowledgment and squatted down beside the sickbed. He waved the shamans back so he could be alone. "You live."

Koja nodded weakly, tried to raise his head, and fell back in pain. "What—where . . . ?" His questions drifted off.

"You're outside Quaraband. I had you brought here so the shamans could work their spells on you."

Koja took a deep breath and composed his thoughts. "What happened to me?"

"You were thrown from your horse. My guard brought you in, almost dead. It took a little time, but the shamans healed your wounds." Yamun's legs were getting stiff, so he rocked gently from side to side to stretch. "The men who failed you have been punished," he added, assuming the priest would demand justice without delay.

A cloud of confusion swirled in Koja's eyes, only in part from dizziness. "Why have you done this?" Remembering his manners, he rephrased the question. "Why has the kha-han, Illustrious Emperor of the Tuigan, come here to see to the health of this insignificant one? You have bestowed great favor on me."

Yamun scratched his neck, thinking of how to explain it. The reasons for his actions seemed obvious to Yamun, so he assumed that those same reasons were clear to everyone. "Why? You're a guest in my yurt. It wouldn't be good if you died while you were here. People would say my tents were plagued by evil spirits."

The khahan paused and smiled. "Besides, what would your prince think if I sent him a message saying 'Please send another priest, the first one died? I don't think he would be pleased." Yamun picked up a pebble and rolled it between his fingers.

"And now," Yamun said softly, "I've saved your life." The warlord tossed the rock aside.

Koja was at a loss for words. "I am unable to repay you for this, Great Lord," he whispered at last. A shiver ran through his body. His chest felt tight and restricted.

Yamun smiled broadly, the scar on his lip giving it a leering quality. His eyes remained squinted and hard. "Envoy of the Khazari, I need a new scribe. The last one proved unreliable."

Koja gulped painfully. "Unreliable?"

"He forgot his loyalties."

Koja remembered the bloody head and Yamun's quick justice. "You mean—"

"He told me what others wanted me to hear," Yamun interrupted. "So, who do you serve?"

Koja hesitated in fear, then swallowed and answered. "Prince Ogandi of the Khazari, Great Lord." He closed his eyes, waiting for the blow.

"Hah! Good!" Yamun bellowed. "If you'd betray your proper lord to serve me, what kind of loyalty could I expect?" He slapped his thigh in satisfaction. "But now, you will do your prince service by serving me."

"Great Khan, I—"

Yamun cut off his protests. "Your prince ordered you to learn more about me and my people, didn't he?"

"Yes, but how did you know?" Fearful that his letters had been found, Koja struggled and finally managed to sit up.

"Because that's what I'd have you do. Now, as my scribe, you'll be very close to me and have the chance to learn many things, won't you?" Yamun scratched at his chest.

"Yes," Koja answered hesitantly.

"Good. It's decided." Yamun stood once again, rubbing the soreness out of his back. The khahan turned and looked toward the tents of Quaraband. "You've met the second empress. What do you think of her?"

"She is . . . strong-willed," responded Koja, picking his words carefully.

Yamun snorted. "She tried to get something from you, I see. Remember, she will never give up, and she is powerful. Most of the wizards and shamans heed her words."

"I will remember."

"As my scribe," Yamun continued, still looking away, "she may seek your favor. Look over there." He turned and pointed across the small circle.

Koja looked where Yamun pointed and saw the bound prisoner. Up to now the man had been mostly silent, except for slight whimpers of pain. Koja was barely able to recognize him as the rider from his escort. Yamun raised his hand, signaling to his guard. Two men stepped from the ranks. Each carried a large, flat stone. Seeing them, the prisoner began to scream and beg for mercy. Impassive to his cries, the men set to work.

With a quick cut of the knife, the guards slashed the bindings that held one leg. One man quickly grabbed the victim's leg, twisting the ankle upward, while the other Kashik slid one stone underneath. The prisoner, still screaming, tried to kick free, but he was held fast. The second guard raised his stone high over his head.

"Stop them, Khahan!" Koja cried out as he realized the guard was about to smash the stone down. The effort it took to shout caused him to fall into a wracking fit of coughing.

"Hold!" Yamun commanded. The Kashik lowered the stone he held over his head.

"Why should they stop?" Yamun demanded of Koja once the coughing passed.

"This man has done nothing. You cannot blame him for my accident," Koja protested.

"Why not?" Yamun countered. "He failed to protect you. Therefore, he must be punished. At least he will live. His comrades were drowned."

His mind already weak from shock, Koja was amazed at Yamun's words. "It is not his fault that I was hurt. I will not have him harmed," the priest finally said with conviction. Exhausted, he fell back on the pallet.

Yamun sucked on his cheek as he listened to the priest. "Do you request his life?" the burly warlord asked.

"His life? Yes, I do," Koja answered as he lay on his back.

Yamun looked over to the prisoner. The man was watching them, his eyes filled with fear and expectation. "Very well, priest. According to custom, I give him to you; he's your slave. His name is Hodj. If he commits any crime you'll be punished. That too is our custom."

"I understand this," Koja assured Yamun, closing his eyes.

"Good. Now, as for Bayalun, she'll assume that you're loyal to me. She hates me," he said matter-of-factly, "and so she'll hate you. Always remember that I'm all that stands between her wrath and you." Yamun signaled the guards to release Hodj and then left to find his horse.

Koja watched the khahan ride off as the bearers came and hoisted his pallet onto their shoulders. All the way back to Quaraband the priest silently said his prayers, calling on Furo to protect him until he saw his home again.

- 3 -
Lightning

For four days, Koja lived in a special white yurt raised on the outskirts of Quaraband, just outside the boundary of the magic-dead lands. Here he stayed on his pallet, resting and regaining his strength. Once a day the shamans came and unfurled their white sheet and set out their offerings to Teylas. Beating their drums and howling out chants, they cast spells to heal and fortify him. Every day, after they left, Koja would sink into deep concentration, praying to Furo for strength and forgiveness. Though he told no one, the priest was mortified, fearful that Furo and the Enlightened One would shun him for having accepted the healing of another deity.

By the fourth day, the shamans were marveling at Koja's speedy recovery and priding themselves on the efficacy of their spells. To their minds, Teylas clearly favored them by accomplishing the healing of this foreign priest. The shamans told the khahan of this wondrous progress, explaining that the priest must somehow be special.

Four days also gave Koja time to learn his new servant's qualities. Although Hodj was a slave, Koja refused to treat him like one, and, instead, gave him the liberties and confidence of a trusted servant. Hodj responded to this and seemed to care for his new master. The first morning Hodj made tea in the Tuigan style—thick with milk and salt. Koja almost choked, and a tea-brewing lesson immediately followed. Thereafter, Hodj brewed tea Khazari-style—thick with butter—although he made an awful face as he set it out for his master.

While recovering, Koja had little to do with his days but listen. Hodj rarely spoke, but the shamans were another matter. Their lengthy conversations usually centered on beliefs, but ranged across a variety of subjects.

Soon, Koja had enough new information to add to his letters. He lit the oil lamp that sat on his small desk and unfolded a thin sheet of paper, the page softly crackling as he smoothed it out on the top of the desk. The white paper appeared straw yellow in the dim circle of light from the lamp. Taking up his brush, Koja began to write in tight, controlled strokes.

The khahan claims to command more than one hundred thousand men, in four different armies. I know too little to say if he is a boastful man. Three of his armies are led by his sons. The fourth commander is Chanar Ong Kho. He is a vain and proud man. There are also many lesser khans among the Tuigan. Most of these I have had no chance to meet.

The khahan has a wife, the Second Empress Eke Bayalun, his own stepmother. She surrounds herself with sorcerers and holy men, and seems to have sway over the shamans of the people. That she does not love her husband is clear, and her feelings may be even stronger. There is some chance that overtures to her would drive a wedge between the khahan and his wizards.

Having written everything he could, Koja was left with nothing to do but brood. In particular, he was worried how to get his letters to Prince Ogandi. In Semphar, trusted messengers carried them by the Silk Road to Khazari. Here, his only choice was the khahan's riders, and Koja certainly did not trust them with his messages. He wished he could send the letters safely back, but that was not possible. However, there was little Koja could do, since he had to stay until the khahan at least gave some answer to Ogandi's offer. Am I doing the right thing, he worried, in serving as Yamun's scribe in the meantime?

After four days of rest, Koja was fit enough to get about. He was still weak, but Yamun pressed him to return to the royal compound. The khahan needed his scribe. So, reluctantly, Koja returned to Quaraband and assumed his duties as the khahan's court scribe.

There was not much to these duties, mostly sitting quietly to the side during the khahan's audiences, noting any orders or proclamations Yamun made. It was quiet work, indeed so much so that Koja learned little more about the khahan than he already knew. Two weeks of that drudgery passed before anything of note happened.

It was very late at night, almost midnight, and the three men remaining in the royal yurt were almost exhausted. Yamun sat half-sprawled on his throne, drinking wine and resting. Koja, still only two weeks at his new duties, yawned as he patiently worked with a pile of papers. In the darkness at the side of the yurt was one of Yamun's nightguards. In his black *kalat*, the man almost disappeared into the gloom. He sat still, trying to remain bright and alert, knowing he would be beaten if he fell asleep.

His writing table pulled up in front of him, Koja sat transcribing the day's judgments and pronouncements. As he worked, the priest stopped to listen to the hammering roars of thunder and staccato pounding of rain against felt. The thunderstorm raging outside made him start each time a new crash shook the yurt. Such storms were the distant battles of the god Furo against the evil spirits of the earth—at least that was what he had been taught. Still, this storm, the first since Koja had arrived in Quaraband, was greater than any the priest had ever heard before.

All day the sky had been gray, promising a storm of swelling power. While the khans had watched the sky fearfully, the khahan had been edgy, waiting for the rain to come. In the early evening, the storm broke. Abruptly, Yamun dismissed the khans and the servants, sending them out into the downpour. Since then, Yamun had been sitting, drinking wine and occasionally issuing orders, but his tension had not subsided. By this hour, the khahan moved wearily and his temper was short.

Yamun swallowed a gulp of wine from a chased silver cup. "Write out this order, scribe," he said brusquely.

Koja neatly set aside the notes he had been working on and laid out a fresh sheet of paper. His vision was blurred by the long hours he worked. His tired fingers dropped the writing brush, splattering the drops of black ink over the clean white page.

"You'll have to be stronger than that, scribe," Yamun growled, irritated with the delay. "Make yourself tougher. You'll have days and nights with no sleep when we begin to march."

"March, Great Khan?" In two weeks of taking down proclamations, Koja had yet to hear any mention of the armies of the khahan going on campaign.

"Yes, march. You think I intend to sit here forever, waiting on the pleasure of others—like your Prince Ogandi? In time, I must march," the stocky man snapped back. "Soon the pastures here will be gone, and then we must move."

"Great Khahan," Koja pleaded as he rearranged the papers, "would it not be easier for you to find another scribe? Surely one of your people, somebody stronger, could do the job."

"What's this? You don't like being my scribe?" The khahan glowered over his cup at Koja, his foul mood getting worse.

"No, it's not that," Koja stuttered. "It's . . . I am not brave. I am not a soldier," he blurted out. Terrified, he turned his attention to the sheets in front of him, mumbling, "Besides, I never thought there was so much work. I mean—"

"You thought we were ignorant and didn't know how to keep records," Yamun interrupted in cold tones. Koja despaired. All his attempts to explain his weaknesses were only making things worse.

Yamun slid forward out of his seat, bringing himself close to Koja. "I can't write and I can't read, so you think I'm a fool. I know the value of these." He grabbed up a handful of Koja's papers from the little writing desk. "Great kings and princes all rule by these slips of paper. I've seen the papers sent out by the emperor of Shou Lung. I, too, am an emperor. I'm not some little prince who goes from tent to tent, talking to all his followers. I am the khahan of all the Tuigan and I will be more."

Koja looked in silence at the khahan, startled by the outburst.

Still, the skepticism must have shown on the priest's face. Yamun heaved to his feet, splashing wine over the carpets. "You doubt me? Teylas has promised it to me! Listen to him out there," he shouted, pausing long enough for Koja to hear a particularly loud thunderclap. "That's his voice. Those are his words. Most people live in fear of him. They pray and scream, afraid he'll call them to the test. But I'm not afraid. He's tested me and I still live." Wobbling slightly from the drink, Yamun walked toward the door. "He's calling to me now. Today."

Koja stayed at his seat, trying to make sense of Yamun's ranting. The nightguard, however, dashed over to the doorway and flung himself down on the carpet. "Great Prince," he entreated, "do not go outside! I beg it of you. There has never been a storm like this. It is an evil omen. Teylas has released his spirits upon us. If you go out they will try to snatch you away. Teylas is angry!"

"See," Yamun shouted across the yurt at Koja. "They all fear the storms, the might of Teylas. These are my soldiers—children! Move, guardsman," he ordered, turning his attention back to the cowering man. "I don't fear the wrath of Teylas. After all, I am the khahan. My ancestor was born the child of Teylas and the Blue Wolf."

Arrogantly, Yamun strode past the kneeling man and unfastened the door flap. The heavy cloth immediately flew open with a crack. Cold rain blasted through the open doorway, swept in by the powerful wind. Foul ashes swirled up in choking clouds from the braziers. The warm air suddenly drained away.

"There. That is the might of Teylas," Yamun bellowed, motioning toward the storm. "Come, scribe, since you don't believe he talks to me."

"Please, Great Lord," Koja begged, shouting over the wind, "stay inside.

"No! You'll come and see because I've ordered it." He strode over to Koja, grabbed him by the shoulder, and half-dragged him to the doorway. With an unceremonious push, Yamun shoved the priest into the blasting rain.

Koja stumbled and slipped, sliding down into the cold mud. Rain splashed into the slop and splattered thickly against him. A lance of lightning cut jaggedly through the night sky, illuminating the entire horizon. In the brief stab of light, Koja saw the dark form of Yamun standing over him, face to the sky, mouth wide open. The light lasted only an instant, and then the world was plunged back into darkness. Yamun's strong hand grabbed the priest's robes and hauled him out of the muck.

The two men set out, struggling and sliding their way down the slope. They walked through the icy mud, out the gate, and past yurts until they reached the horse pens outside the capital. Wind and rain lashed against their faces. Rivulets ran from Yamun's hair into his mustache, dribbling into his mouth. Huge drops ran down all sides of Koja's shaved head, washing away the gobs of mud.

"Teylas!" shouted Yamun, spitting water between each word. "Here I am! Listen to me!" A distant bolt of lightning dimly lit the steppe, casting weird shadows over the pair. The wind swept the rain away from their faces for a moment and then whipped it back again. The hollow rumble of the distant bolt barely carried over the wind.

"He listens," Yamun said confidently, letting go of Koja's shoulder. Suddenly unsupported, the priest stumbled backward and fell, floundering along an unexpectedly steep part of the bank. Oblivious to everything, Yamun strode forward until Koja could barely see the older man's bulky silhouette. Splashing through pools of foul, muddy water, Koja did his best to catch up.

Finally, the priest fell back into the mud, exhausted from stumbling and slipping in pursuit of the khahan. Occasional flashes of lightning had guided Koja, but now he had lost sight of Yamun. Horses screamed and whinnied somewhere nearby, their shrill cries rising over the rattling rain. Koja pushed himself out of the mud and splashed off in the direction of the noise.

"Teylas!" Yamun's voice came from somewhere off to the priest's left.

"Khahan!" Koja shouted, hoping Yamun would hear him.

A stroke of lightning, almost overhead, flooded the sky with light and thunder. Though his eyes hurt from the light, Koja could see Yamun off to the left. Around him were the shadowy shapes of horses, rearing and prancing in panic.

"Yamun Khahan!" he shouted. There was no answer.

The lightning illuminated the ground again, as if in response to Koja's shouts. In the moment of light, he saw Yamun, arms stretched to heaven, at the center of one of the horse corrals. The rain formed streaks of silver all around him.

Determined, Koja plunged forward into the darkness. His feet squished into the mud and threatened to slip out from under him at any second. Rainwater dripped down his eyebrows, blurring his sight. His robes, sodden and filthy, sagged and pulled on his frame.

Koja's shin smashed against something hard and solid—a fence. Shocked by the pain, the lama tried to hop back on one foot, then lost his balance. Both feet shot out from under him, kicking into the air. He sat in the muck at the foot of the corral fence, rubbing away the shooting streaks of pain that started at his shin and ran up his leg.

"Teylas, listen . . . powerful . . . rule . . ." Yamun's voice floated in snatches over the howling wind. Koja peered through the fence. He was close enough to see into the corral now, although he still could not make out anything clearly. Shielding his eyes from the rain, Koja peered through the horses' legs, straining to see Yamun.

The dim form of a man standing all alone was barely visible to Koja. The mares and stallions had all moved as far from him as possible, pressing their bodies against the fence. They stamped and kicked, their eyes wild with fear.

"Take my offering of thanks, Teylas. I have united my people, but with or without you, I must conquer," Yamun shouted. Koja heard the words clearly as the wind dropped away to nothing. The rain pelted down in straight sheets, the thick drops deprived of their driving force.

Koja could see Yamun more clearly now. The khahan stood with his feet planted widely apart, arms akimbo, head tilted to the sky. He paid no mind to the rain as it pounded against his face. His clothes were plastered wetly to his body, but the khahan didn't care. He stood still, waiting.

There was a dazzling burst of light as the storm renewed its fury. Before the glare had died away, there was another stroke of lightning, closer and brighter than the first. It was followed by another, then another, and another. The explosions of light became continuous, first from the east, then west, north, and south. The rumble of thunder grew louder and more shattering, until it was a continuous barrage. The whinnies of the horses became screams of terror, piercing over the bass rolls of thunder.

Koja, trembling in fear, clapped his hands over his ears and sank down as close to the ground as he could. The posts of the corral thudded and shook as the panicked horses reared and lashed out with their hooves. Even though the sky was bright, Koja could barely see the khahan through the flailing hooves, but the man was unmoved by the pandemonium around him.

Just as Koja felt the storm was at its height, a luminous ball of sparkling blue swirled around Yamun, illuminating him clearly. It crackled and sizzled, a leaping electrical fire. Miniature bolts arced from the center, scorching and snapping as they hit the ground. At its heart, Yamun stood, unaffected by the charged flame.

Koja sat, dumbfounded. Then it dawned on him that the khahan might be in danger. "Great Lord!" he shouted over the roaring storm.

"Yamun Khahan!" the priest shouted again, cupping his hands to add more volume to his voice.

In response a spark arced from the khahan and hurtled toward Koja. Flinching, Koja threw himself aside as the charge lazily flew past him. It hit the ground behind him and exploded in a shower of muck. The force of the blast knocked him forward into the fence, driving the air from his lungs. Koja sagged against the corral, stunned.

More sparks began flying from Yamun, drifting out over the corral. As each ball of lightning detached itself, the radiance enclosing the khahan diminished slightly. The horses went into a frenzy, galloping and wheeling to avoid the drifting sparks. The fence, too high to jump, penned them in.

There was a sizzling pop and a scream of equine pain. The steeds redoubled their efforts. The fence wobbled and banged. Koja slid back in the mud as hooves flailed just in front of his face, but the fence held firm. There was another frenzied whinny and pop, followed by a third. With each, the cries of the horses grew a little less.

Terror took hold of Koja, driving him with uncontrollable energy. He had to get away, get to safety. Panting, the lama crawled away from the corral, dragging himself across the rain-drenched ground. Behind him, the brilliant glow spread from the corral, then began to fade. The wind and rain drowned out the noises behind him. Finally spent, he collapsed like a rag doll, unable to move any farther.

As Koja lay there, the wind began to drop away and the howling rage subsided. The rain changed from a hammerlike pelting to a slower downpour. The water was still icy, and rivers of muck ran into the folds of his robe. Koja's body was chilled to its core. He clung to the ground, trembling, as the lightning and thunder diminished.

"Scribe? Where'd you go?" Yamun's voice carried easily to Koja.

"Here," Koja called weakly, raising his head from the mud. Panting, he got to his feet. "I am here, Great Khan. Wherever that is," he added quietly. With the storm gone, it was too dark to see far.

"Come here, then," ordered the khahan. He sounded unharmed by the storm.

Koja set off in direction of Yamun's voice. He could only hope he was headed the right way. "Great Lord, where are you?"

"This way," came the answer. Koja stumbled along until he found the corral. The fence was still standing, but the pen was silent. Following the fence around, the priest came to the gate. Waiting on the other side was Yamun Khahan, unhurt, although he wavered unsteadily. Spying Koja he said, "Let us go," offering no explanation.

Koja nodded automatically, concentrating on the pen. It was empty; there were no horses, living or dead. The lama looked at Yamun, startled, and then back into the corral, trying to see any sign of the horses or any marks left by the glittering blue fire. There were no steeds, and the mud was so churned up that it was impossible to tell what had happened. The fence showed no scorching or damage from the sparks. It was as if nothing had occurred.

"What happened?" Koja asked in amazement.

"Come on. We go," Yamun said as he stepped through the gate. He moved slowly, with exaggerated care. His stiffness could have been caused by the late hour or the lightning. It was impossible for Koja to tell.

Koja remained insistent. "What happened?"

Yamun guided the priest by the elbow, firmly squeezing it as they walked along. By now the wind was only a chilly spring breeze and the freezing drops of rain had given way to a fine drizzle.

"I talked with Teylas, my father, the Lord of the Sky."

Koja stared at Yamun, believing him possessed or victim of some demented illusion. Perhaps Yamun meant it only figuratively, he decided. Many people, he knew, "talked" to various gods and never received an answer. Lamas and wandering priests were the only ones he knew of who could contact the fearsome powers of the outer planes and expect some kind of reply.

Yamun noticed Koja's skeptical stare. "I talked with Teylas." The khahan's voice was filled with conviction.

Koja didn't say anything. There wasn't anything he could say that wouldn't sound patronizing or obsequious. He slogged up the muddy slope alongside Yamun in pained silence. "You were glowing," he finally said.

"Was I? I can never see what happens."

"You've done this before?" Koja sputtered.

"Of course. Teylas demands his offerings." The khahan waded through a wide puddle.

"But you're not hurt."

Yamun stepped over a fallen cooking pot. "Why would Teylas hurt me? I'm the Illustrious Emperor of the Tuigan, and a son of the Blue Wolf."

Koja cocked his head at that, trying to decide if Yamun was serious or playing some grotesque joke.

"Teylas will not strike down his own clan." Yamun splashed through the mud, not breaking his stride.

"Then what happened to the horses?" the lama finally asked.

"Teylas took them." As Yamun spoke, his breath fogged the air. The temperature was dropping quickly in the wake of the storm.

"What?"

Yamun stopped walking and turned to face Koja. The khahan's shoulders sagged with exhaustion, but his face, especially his eyes, were still vibrant. "The horses now serve Teylas in his realm. Don't you make sacrifices to your god?"

"You sacrificed them?"

"Teylas took them. I didn't touch them." Yamun pointed out.

"Flaming blue sparks flew from your fingers," Koja said, explaining what he saw.

"That was the power of Teylas," Yamun replied. He turned and resumed walking toward the Great Yurt. They continued on in silence through Quaraband.

At last they returned to the door of the royal yurt. Yamun threw open the flap and was about to step inside when Koja stopped him.

"Please wait, Great Lord," Koja blurted, barely observing proper courtesy. Yamun stopped in the doorway, looking back over his shoulder.

"What did Teylas tell you?" Koja asked, bowing slightly as he spoke.

Yamun looked at the priest. A small, sardonic smile crossed his face. "He—"

"He what, Illustrious Emperor of the Tuigan?" Koja prompted, unable to suppress his curiosity.

Yamun looked slowly at the sky, and saw the starlight visible through the thinning clouds. "He showed me the entire world, priest, from the great water in the east to lands of the west. I saw Shou Lung and this 'Cor-meer' you spoke of." The khahan, eyes blazing, turned back to the priest, yet seemed to focus on something farther away. "Green lands and forests, waiting to be conquered—and all I have to do is reach out and take them."

Koja stepped back as Yamun spoke. The khahan's voice was slowly growing as the warlord saw his vision once again unfold before his eyes. "Teylas promised you these things?" Koja ventured fearfully.

"Teylas promises nothing. He only showed what I could have. It's up to me to take it," Yamun answered coldly. The priest's question dimmed the fire in Yamun's eyes. "I will be emperor of the world."

"The world is large and has many emperors, Yamun Khahan," Koja pointed out. The priest shivered in his wet robes.

"Then I'll conquer them, and they'll be the slaves of my khans." Yamun leaned slightly against the doorframe of the yurt. "And you'll tell the story of my life."

"What?" Koja gasped in astonishment.

"You will write the history of my rule. I will be a great emperor. As my historian, you will be honored by many." Yamun stepped inside the yurt, and Koja followed him, still arguing.

"But—but—I am just an envoy, Great Lord. Surely there must be someone better."

The nightguard, the same man who was in the yurt when they left, ran up to the door and dropped to one knee alongside the khahan. "Great Khan!" he said in surprised relief. "You live! I will tell my brothers that you have safely returned."

"You'll stay until I dismiss you," Yamun countered as he walked past. "Koja of Khazari, you will write the history of my life—starting from right now. No one else will do."

"Great Lord, I serve Prince Ogandi. It would not be right." Koja hurried across the yurt.

"I don't care. You'll write it because I need you—who else would write the truth? Mother Bayalun? Her wizards? I wouldn't trust them. My generals? They're like me—they don't know this magic of writing. You—" He wagged his finger at Koja. "You, I trust. And that is why I choose you."

"Lord Yamun, I am very flattered, but you barely know me. I have a responsibility to my prince. I cannot serve you." Koja realized he was knotting his fingers.

"You're in my tent, in my land. You will do what I say," Yamun commanded. He began unwrapping the wet sash from around his waist.

"And if Prince Ogandi bids me otherwise?" asked Koja as he nervously squeezed the water from his cuffs.

"Then I will deal with your prince." Yamun spoke in slow, measured words.

"I'm loyal to Khazari," Koja pressed, his throat getting dry with tension.

"It doesn't matter. I trust you. There's no more discussion to be had of this." Yamun tossed his wet sash aside and settled himself on his throne.

Koja rubbed his head in frustration. He was stymied. In desperation he tried another ploy. "Isn't there a saying of your people about a man who tells the truth?"

Yamun looked about for his wine cup. " 'A man who tells the truth should have one foot in the stirrup,' " he quoted. "It's good advice. You should remember it."

Koja finally gave up and spoke his mind. "I do not want to be your chronicler, Yamun Khahan."

"I know."

"Then why do you make me do it? Why do you need a biographer?"

"Because Teylas revealed that I should," Yamun said testily as he pulled at one of his sodden boots.

"But why? What good would I do you?"

"This is no longer amusing, scribe. There will be no more argument," Yamun snapped, his voice rising in volume. "You will write the history of my great deeds because I am the khahan of the Tuigan and I say you will. Every king and every emperor has someone to make songs about them. You will write mine. Now leave until you are called for!" With a jerk Yamun pulled the boot off and threw it aside.

Stiffly, Koja walked out of the tent, giving only a slight bow and turning his back to the khahan upon leaving. The tent flap slapped shut with a wet flop.

After the priest left, Yamun sat brooding, staring into his glass. The wind whistled around through the small gaps in the smoke hole. Drips fell in the corners where the rainwater had soaked through the seams of the tent.

After the nightguard had laced up the flap of the tent, Yamun spoke. "What do you think?"

"Me, Great Lord?" the guard asked in surprise.

"What do you think of the Khazari priest?" Yamun said, pointing to the door.

"It's not for me to say, Great Lord," the guard deferred.

"I'm asking, so it is. Come closer and tell me."

Intimidated by the khahan, the man hesitantly came forward. "Noble khahan, I apologize for speaking so boldly, but I speak because you have ordered it. The foreigner is disrespectful."

"Oh," Yamun commented as he began tugging at his other boot.

The guard became more confident. "He argues and does not heed your word. He is only a foreigner, yet he dares challenge you."

"And what should I do?" Yamun asked, jerking on the stubborn shoe.

"He should be flogged. If a man in my *tumen* spoke as he did, our commander would have him beaten!"

"Your commander is a fool," Yamun observed, adding a loud grunt as the boot came off with a thick pop.

The guard looked up, his eyes wide with astonishment.

Yamun continued. "What if everyone obeyed me and never questioned my word? Where would I get my wise advisors? They'd be no better than a worn boot." The khahan held up his own mud-caked boot and then tossed it aside.

Humbled, the guard nodded automatically.

"Why do you think the truthful man has one foot in the stirrup? Truth is not always what people want to hear. Learn and someday I will make you a commander," Yamun finished, suppressing a yawn. He struggled to his foot and began unfastening the toggles of his robes. "Now, I'm tired and will sleep alone tonight. See that my guards are in order and send someone to the women's tent. Tell the ladies they won't be needed. You will sleep at my doorstep."

"By your word, it shall be done," said the guard, touching his head to the floor, acknowledging the duty the khahan had given him. He ran to the doorway and loosened the laces enough to bark out his orders.

Before the guard finished, the khahan had struggled out of his clothes and collapsed, exhausted, onto the hard wooden bed set up behind his throne.

- 4 -

Chanar

It was late the next morning when an escort of black-robed dayguards arrived for Koja to lead him to the royal compound. Reluctantly, the priest gathered his writing materials together. Today he was not eager to enter Yamun's presence, not after what had happened last night. Although the wild night out in the storm was clear in his mind, except for the moments where he had succumbed to blind panic, Koja still had no understanding of what had happened. That, along with the idea of becoming the kha-han's biographer, frightened him.

Taking the horse waiting for him, the priest set out. One man rode alongside him, holding the reins of his horse. Ever since Koja's accident, the guards had taken the utmost precautions with his mount. None of them wanted the for-eigner's horse to go galloping off again.

The rain from the night before had altered the dry steppe. The snow cover had melted to patches and pools of slushy mud. Grasses and flowers, filled with bright vibrant green, had sprung up where none had been before. The ground around the Great Yurt was checked with swatches of fresh green and barren areas of churned mud. Small, black-headed birds hopped around the edges of these mires, pok-ing at the standing water with their beaks. Children charged at them, scaring them off, and then splashed mer-rily through the muck. The legs and the hems of their robes were caked in mud.

Passing through the entrance to the khahan's compound, the guards dismounted and led their horses up the slope. As they marched to the royal yurt, Koja looked out across the the horse pens, trying to decide which corral had been the scene of last night's terrifying visitation. There was nothing to distinguish one from another, so he couldn't be sure which of them was the one.

"Captain," Koja called out as he hurried to ride alongside the officer in charge, "did anything unusual happen last night?"

Slowing his pace, the officer turned to look at Koja. "Unusual? Teylas sent a storm."

"Yes, but more than that. Did the nightguards report anything strange?"

The captain looked at him suspiciously, his eyes narrowed. "Strange? I did not hear of anything strange."

"I heard rumors some horses had escaped."

"A man who listens to his neighbors seldom hears the truth." The captain once again picked up his pace, making it clear he would answer no more questions.

As he neared the top of the hill, Koja saw that the court was to be held outside today. The area was already prepared. Felt rugs in bright red and black patterns were laid out over the sodden ground, layered thickly to keep the topmost ones dry. A small stool for the khahan sat near the doorway to his yurt. Behind the seat towered the khahan's horsetail standard, a sign that he was present in his compound. On the left was the khahan's golden bow case as well as a quiver filled with blue-feathered arrows. On the right side of the standard was a saddle of polished red leather. A white trim of sheepskin decorated the saddle's edges, and its silver fittings gleamed brilliantly in the sun. A tray with cups, a kettle, and a pitcher sat beside Yamun's throne.

"And let his horses graze in our pasture," boomed the khahan from nearby. He was walking up the hill along another trail, evidently returning from some business. He was still dressed in the thick layers of the his sleeping robes, and his hair was loose, undone. Koja could see the tips of his toes under the long hems, unshod and covered in cold mud.

With Yamun walked an old, stoop-backed khan, who was absentmindedly nodding as the khahan gave his orders. The ancient man was a short, thin fellow with patchy spots of hair and a perpetual stoop. Koja recognized the man as Goyuk Khan, one of Yamun's trusted advisors.

Behind those two followed an entourage of guards and attendants. There were several unsmiling dayguards in heavy black *kalats*, hands always at the hilts of their swords. Yamun's quiverbearers, his personal servants, carried his morning clothes and a silver-hilted sword in a bejeweled scabbard. At the end of the group came one servant carrying a hooded falcon, the khahan's prized hunting bird, out for its exercise. All told, Koja counted at least thirty people. Yamun acted as if they were not there.

Koja had been told the khahan had two thousand quiverbearers in his service and another four thousand dayguards. No one had ever estimated the number of nightguards, the finest of the bodyguard, because the khahan had decreed anyone that curious would be beheaded. Koja had no doubt the khahan would carry out the sentence, too.

Yamun casually tracked mud across the carpets and took his seat on the throne. Goyuk bowed and took his leave to carry out the khahan's orders. Koja stood, waiting to be recognized, his shoes slowly filling up with cold mud.

"Bring my bird," Yamun ordered.

As a falconer walked forward, another quiverbearer ran up with Yamun's hawking gauntlet and a small dish of raw meat. Yamun pulled on the thick glove, adorned with mottled red leather cut from the belly of a giant fire lizard, one of the strange creatures that roamed the steppe. The servant stood by with the meat ready.

Yamun held out his arm and coaxed the falcon onto his hand. Even hooded, the bird spread its wings and tried to fly away. The khahan held the bird by its jesses and gripped the leash in his teeth. He whispered soft words through clamped jaws as he took off the bird's hood. The falcon blinked and flapped again, trying to get away. Yamun held out a strip of raw meat. The falcon snapped at the morsel, tossing its head back to get the piece down. When the bird settled down, Yamun spit out the leash.

"Welcome to my tent, Koja of the Khazari. Sit and enjoy the flesh of my lambs, the milk of my horses," the khahan called out, giving the traditional greeting that preceded each day's audience.

"I thank you, Illustrious Emperor of the Tuigan, for your generosity," Koja responded with a slight bow. Like the invitation, his answer was repeated every day, a part of the ancient ritual that ruled the lives of the Tuigan.

"Well, then, come and sit. Quickly—there's a lot to do today. I want to go hunting later," Yamun said, dispensing with etiquette.

"Yes, Great Lord," Koja said as he hurried to his seat.

"You will come, too. You will hunt with me." Yamun handed the fierce bird to the falconer and dismissed the servant with a wave. "But first you must be my scribe for a little bit more—just for today."

Koja nodded and took his seat, laying out his papers, brushes, inking stones, and pressed cakes of powdered ink—both red and black. A servant set out a small dish of water for mixing the powder.

Yamun waved his hand to his waiting attendants. "I'll dress now," he commanded.

The quiverbearers ran forward, unfurling a long strip of white cloth. Four of them took positions in a square around the khahan, their eyes turned, holding the fabric up to form a screen. Other servants set piles of clothes inside the screen, then backed away.

"Bring my women to dress me."

After a short delay, two young girls came from the direction of the women's tents. Koja guessed they were little more than eighteen years old. They were Shou in appearance, with glossy black hair, pale skin, and narrow eyes. The girls hurried forward in quick, mincing steps, the way court ladies were trained to do. Each wore a tight silk dress and the towering headdress of an unmarried woman. Combs carved from the bones of exotic monsters held their hair in place. Giggling shyly when they saw there was an audience, the two girls stepped inside the screen and set to work.

"These are the princesses Water Flower and Spring Peony," Yamun boasted over the screen. "Gifts from the Shou emperor. He sends me more than wine. These two are princesses of the royal blood, and he has given them to me. Has he done this for your prince?" Yamun wriggled as the girls pulled his outer robes off.

Koja didn't answer, trying to discreetly keep his eyes lowered. He looked up briefly. The khahan's bare shoulders were covered with long, narrow scars.

"Dressing is not all they are good at." Yamun broadly leered. "But then, you would not know that. Is it true you priests never touch women?"

Koja flushed at the question. "Purity of mind and body is the path by which we seek Furo," he said defensively.

"So then women are impure?" Yamun asked, an incredulous tone creeping into his voice.

Koja could hear more giggling behind the screen.

"Passions cloud the mind and corrupt the spirit. We live to control our passions and purify our minds, so we can achieve perfection in thought and deed." Unconsciously, Koja settled into the cross-legged pose assumed by the priests of his temple when at their lessons.

"Hah! And what does that get you in the world?" Yamun held up his arms as the princesses undid his trousers.

"Only one with a pure spirit can enter into the presence of the Enlightened One."

"So if you avoid women you might, just might, get a chance to see your god?" Yamun had ducked from sight behind the screen.

"Something like that, yes." There was a lot more to the philosophy of the Red Mountain Temple, but Koja wasn't about to go into it now. Preparing for his work, Koja mixed his inks.

"What does your Enlightened One do? Does he reward you and strike down your enemies with lightning?" Yamun's voice was muffled as fresh clothes were pulled over his head.

"The Enlightened One fills us with perfect understanding and harmony. With that we do not have enemies."

"Phah. What if I were your enemy? Would your perfect understanding protect you?" Yamun stepped out, dressed in long, loose robes of red and yellow silk, embroidered with leaping tigers. The quiverbearers and the women gathered up the dirty clothes and carried them away.

"I have faith in Furo and the Enlightened One."

"I have faith in my bow and my sword," Yamun pronounced as he strapped on his sword. "They are the power. Teylas gave them to me, and he can strike down his enemies from the sky. Teylas is a god you can use."

Koja was astonished by this last statement. "Gods are not used."

"Teylas would take back the power if I did not use it, so he is a god to be used," Yamun snapped with a slight sneer.

Dressed and accoutered, Yamun sat in his chair, ready to hear the morning's business.

"Don't you fear offending Teylas?" Koja asked as he wetted the writing brush.

"Why?"

"Well," Koja offered hesitantly, rubbing at the back of his neck, "others might call your words presumptuous. You might be wrong in interpreting Teylas's will."

"Others have not been given the power by Teylas. That is why I sit in judgment of the khans, and we have kept them waiting long enough," he announced, pointing to the quiverbearer coming up the hill. "It is time for business."

"Yes, Great Lord," Koja said, setting out a clean sheet of paper.

"Enough 'Great Lord.' Today I permit you to call me kha-han, with no other titles." Yamun looked to the quiverbearer as the man reached the courtyard. "Who waits?" the kha-han asked, pointing to the gate at the bottom of the hill.

The servant knelt, bowing his head. "Glorious khahan, the khans of the Jeun and Bahkshir bring petition that you hear their cases, and one of Chanar Ong Kho's men has come say-ing his master has returned. The general awaits your plea-sure to make his report."

"Tell Chanar to come," Yamun said, irritated. "He should have presented himself when he arrived. Jeun Khan and Bahkshir Khan will wait until this afternoon."

Koja sat up straighter and smoothed out his orange robe. "Khahan," he asked hesitantly, uncertain of the liberties of his new status as historian, "just where has General Chanar been?"

"Eh? You don't know?"

"No, Great Lord—"

"Khahan," Yamun corrected.

"No, Khahan," Koja said, biting his lip over the fumble. "I only heard that he was gone, sent away."

"Good. You weren't meant to know."

"I what?"

"You were not meant to know where he went," Yamun said slowly and clearly. "Again you thought I was simple. Koja of the Khazari, in my empire you learn what I want you to learn and nothing else. Learn that," he stated with finality.

A servant in a white *kalat* stepped up to the edge of the carpets and knelt down, pressing his head into the mats.

"Speak," Yamun ordered, reluctantly recognizing the man.

"The honorable second empress, Mother Bayalun, ex-presses relief that the khahan of all the Tuigan is once again unharmed by Teylas's wrath. She gives the greetings of a mother unto her stepson, of a wife unto her husband," the servant announced.

Yamun scowled. "Take my greetings to my stepmother and my wife, Mother Bayalun, at my pleasure."

The man stayed in his place, head to the carpets. "The second empress wishes the indulgence of her husband and wonders if she might attend on the khahan his morning."

"Mother Bayalun knows she is always welcome. Go back and tell her she can attend if she wants," Yamun lazily answered. He waved to dismiss the man.

"I thought you did not care for the second empress," Koja commented as the white-garbed man hurried out of sight.

"I don't, scribe. I married her because tribal tradition demanded it," Yamun explained.

"Then why do you let her attend?"

Yamun stretched his arms forward, working the kinks out of his shoulders. "Why not? She would learn what happens anyway. If I send her away, she becomes suspicious and makes trouble. Here, I can see what she's doing. I pick my battles better than that."

Koja nodded. "I see."

"Good. Now," Yamun said, turning to Koja, "prepare yourself. General Chanar and his aides are coming, and you will have to take down all that is said. Now you will learn where General Chanar has been."

Koja looked toward the gate of the stockade, easily spotting the stiff-backed form of the general, mounted on his horse. Unlike all others who passed through the gate, Chanar refused to dismount, remaining in his saddle as his stocky white mare pranced up the hill. Behind him trailed three aides, on foot, their horses at the gate.

As he rode forward, Chanar kicked and whipped at his pony, getting it to rear and prance. The beast was already spirited, but the general was determined to get it to perform more to make his entrance all the more exciting. The aides following him kept a good distance back, lest his horse lash out at them.

At last, Chanar reached the top of the hill. With a final spur, he reared his horse back, bringing its hooves down just short of the carpeting. A quiverbearer ran forward and took the animal's reins, holding the horse while Chanar dismounted. Swinging one leg over the horse's neck, the general easily slid from the saddle and landed on his feet in the mud with a loud plop.

"Greetings to my khahan," Chanar said loudly. He looked to all those around him. " 'Though I was far, when my khan called, quickly did I come,' " he said, quoting an old poem.

" 'Many are my enemies, but like rotten trees they fall,' " countered the khahan, quoting from the same poem.

"Greetings to my brother Chanar," Yamun continued. "May the Sky God always make your horses fat and your lambs many." A quiverbearer scooped a ladleful of kumiss. He handed it to the khahan. Yamun took a drink from the ladle. The yellow-white liquid clung to his mustache. The ladle next passed to Chanar, who noisily gulped a large swallow and handed it back. The servant walked back to Yamun, but the khahan waved him to Koja.

"Today, he also drinks from my cup."

Chanar looked in surprise from Yamun to Koja as the servant passed the ladle over. He opened his mouth to say something, then closed it just as quickly.

Steeling his stomach, Koja took the ladle with both hands and gulped a swallow of the bitter drink. Suppressing a gag, he gave the silver ladle back to the servant.

The khahan turned to the east and poured a little kumiss on the carpet. Then he turned to the south and the west, doing the same at each spot. Only the north, an evil direction, was avoided. Meanwhile the servant took the horsetail banner from its stand and lowered it in front of Yamun.

"Teylas lead us on the hunt. Teylas lead us in battle. Teylas make our wives fertile," Yamun chanted in a toneless voice as he sprinkled the last of the kumiss over the banner. The servants took the cup and banner and set them back in their places. Yamun, the formalities over, sat back on his throne.

"Sit, Chanar, and report," the khahan said casually.

Slowly and with noticeable reluctance, Chanar sat beside Koja, eyeing the priest venomously.

Just as the general was about to speak, a procession

arrived from Bayalun's tent. The second empress led the
small group, of only a few servants. Stepping onto the carpets, she bowed to the khahan. "I thank my husband for
permitting me to attend." Her silver-brown hair shone
richly in the morning sun.

Yamun nodded respectfully to his stepmother. "Your wisdom is always welcome to us." Mother Bayalun quickly took
a seat opposite the men.

"Now, make your report, General Chanar," bade Yamun.

Chanar took in his breath slowly, composing his thoughts.
After a slight pause he began.

"Following your orders, I went first to Tomke's *ordu*. He
camped all winter on Yellow Grass Steppe, but with the
spring now, his pastures are almost gone—"

"He's not to move until I tell him," Yamun interrupted, addressing his comment to Koja. The priest dutifully noted it
down, writing with quick strokes.

"As I said," Chanar continued, "the grass there is almost
gone. He hopes to move east toward the Tsu-Tsu people, but
he waits for your orders."

"How are his men?"

"Tomke let many of them go home during the winter, to
reduce his grazing. He has three *tumen* left—Sartak's, No-
gai's, and Kadan's—in addition to his own." Koja counted
them off on his fingers. "They are not full. His wizards
count perhaps thirty *minghans*."

"*Minghan*?" Koja softly interrupted. "What is this? Please
excuse me, but I need to know for the letters."

Chanar answered him contemptuously. "A *minghan* is one
hundred *arban*. An *arban* is ten men."

"Ah," Koja said, working out the figures on a small abacus,
"Tomke has thirty thousand men."

Yamun scowled. "He's let too many men go. Order him to
call them back immediately."

Koja quickly wrote the command on a fresh sheet of paper and handed it to a waiting quiverbearer. The man presented the paper on a tray, along with a stone coated with

red ink. The khahan took his seal, a small silver block with a top in the shape of a bird, from under his shirt. The underside was carved in the contorted Tuigan script. Yamun dipped the seal into the ink and pressed it on the sheet. The sealbearer backed away, blowing the ink dry as he went.

"Continue," ordered the khahan.

"He has not sent many scouts," Chanar noted. "The Tsu-Tsu seem peaceful. He thinks they will come over to us without fighting. The lands behind him, to the west, have been conquered. He has recruited some soldiers from them, but they are poor warriors. He says they are too weak to rebel, and I agree with him. They are dogs."

"Dogs bite," observed Yamun. "What do you say, historian?"

Koja was startled by the question, too surprised to be diplomatic. "If they have been treated well, they will not rebel. But if Tomke has ruled them harshly, they will fight more fiercely than ever before. My own people, the Khazari, have fought so in ancient times against wicked emperors of Shou Lung."

"So, the Khazari are not just mice," commented Chanar with a faint sneer.

Koja colored at the slight and bristled to make a reply.

"Enough," Yamun firmly interrupted. "Good advice. Chanar, how was my son treating them?"

"I didn't ask," Chanar replied sullenly. He shot an evil glare at Koja.

"Someone should find out. Send Hulagu Khan. Draw up the orders to see that it's done."

Koja nodded and made a brief note.

"Was there anything else at Tomke's camp?" Yamun asked, returning to Chanar.

"He's met with the chief of the ogres from the northern mountains. They want to fight alongside us. He wants to know if he should send the chief to your *ordu.*"

"What are they like?" Yamun tugged at his mustache, considering the offer.

"They're strong. Their chief stands twice the height of a man and likes to fight. I say we use them."

"What do you know of ogres, historian?" Yamun asked, curious to see if the priest had any insight on these beasts.

Koja thought back to the scrolls in his temple that showed ogres as hideous, blue-faced monsters locked in combat with Furo. "They are treacherous and violent beasts. I would not trust them."

"Hmmm." Yamun sat wrapping the long end of his mustache around his finger, considering the choices. "The Tuigan do not fight alongside beasts. Tell Tomke to have nothing more to do with them."

Koja scribbled out the order and passed it along to the sealbearer.

"Unless you've got more to say about Tomke, tell me how Jad's camp was," Yamun commanded after he'd struck his seal on the last order.

"Jad sets his camp at Orkhon Oasis, five hundred miles southeast of Tomke. His pasture and water are good, and he has held his men in hand."

Koja suddenly paid more careful attention. He didn't know where the Orkhon Oasis was, but southeast was the direction of Khazari.

"How many?" Yamun queried.

"Five *tumen*—Hamabek, Jochi—"

"Enough, I do not need their names. What does he have to report?" Yamun scratched at his brow.

Chanar paused to pick at his teeth and spit into the mud at the edge of the carpet. "His scouts said they traveled south into the mountains. The peaks were so high that snow never melted from the tops. There they found a mountain that breathed fire and spit stones at them. There was a race of little bearded men there who lived underground and prayed to the mountain. These little men were wonderful craftsmen of iron. The scouts claimed when they tried to cross it, the mountain killed many of them with magical burning stones. I think they lied and they were afraid to go on."

"Mother Bayalun, have your wizards ever told you of a mountain like this?" Yamun queried.

The second empress looked as if she were asleep. At Yamun's words, she slowly raised her head. "They have never spoken of such a place, my husband."

Koja didn't remember any fire-breathing mountains to the southeast, but Khazari was on the edge of a great range of peaks. Such a strange thing was certainly possible.

"You should send a truth-seeker to question the scouts," Chanar continued. "Jad is too lenient with them."

"How many scouts went out and how many came back?" Yamun took off his cap and set it on the ground.

"I did not ask," Chanar replied, as if it was beneath him.

"Then how do you know they lied?" countered Yamun.

Chanar sat silent, brooding over the khahan's rebuke.

"Is Jad ready to march?" Yamun finally asked.

"His men are in hand, as I have said," Chanar responded. He looked down, shielding the anger in his eyes from the khahan.

Koja made notes, both for the khahan and himself. He needed to find out more about Jad's—Prince Jadaran's—army: where it was, and what Yamun intended to do with it.

"And what of my youngest son, Hubadai? Has he heard from the caliph of Semphar?"

"No, Yamun," Chanar said, using the khahan's familiar name. "The caliph apparently didn't believe the demands I delivered at the council."

"Scribe, were my demands unclear?" Both Yamun and Chanar turned their attention to Koja.

Koja cleared his throat and took the time to answer carefully. "Khahan," he said, watching Chanar out of the corner of his eye, "General Chanar presented your demands quite clearly."

"What exactly did Chanar Ong Kho demand?" Bayalun asked suddenly.

Koja's mouth went dry as he wondered just why Bayalun was asking. "I apologize to General Chanar," he began, "if my words do not do him justice. It has been some time since I heard him speak. He said that all caravans crossing the great steppe would pay taxes to the khahan of the Tuigan." Koja paused, rubbing the stubble on his head nervously.

"Is that all?" Yamun queried. Chanar sat up straight, ready to protest.

"Oh, no," Koja said hurriedly. "He also said that all kingdoms must offer you tribute or submit themselves to your rule."

"It seemed quite clear to me, Great Lord," Chanar offered.

Yamun nodded in agreement. "So, the caliph has not responded?"

"No, Yamun," Chanar noted. "No word has come from Semphar."

"Perhaps the caliph does not believe you have the power, Khahan," suggested Koja. "After all, Semphar has a large army and many cities. Indeed the caliph is called the 'Chosen Prince of Denier' and the 'Great Conqueror.' "

"The 'Great Conqueror' will learn," Yamun said grimly. "How many men does Hubadai have at present?"

"He has kept all his *tumen*, five of them, ready. I, myself, advised him to await your orders," Chanar boasted.

"Did you?" Yamun commented. He smiled faintly, though any warmth in his expression was twisted by the scar across his lip. The lama could not decide if Yamun was being sarcastic or not. If he was, Chanar apparently did not notice.

"Yes, Yamun," Chanar said proudly. The general sat up straighter and puffed his chest out.

"Scribe, send this to Hubadai," Yamun ordered, settling back on his stool. "He's to divide his command into three parts. He will lead one, and I'll send commanders to lead the others. No man of his army will go hunting except for food, to save the horses. If a man breaks this law, the first time he will get three strokes of the rod. The second time, he will have three times three. The third time he will get three times times three times three. His men are to have two weeks of food ready at all times. The horses must have sufficient fodder on hand. He must be ready to go to war on the day he is ordered." Koja wrote furiously, trying to keep up with the rapid-fire pace of Yamun's order.

"His men must have their weapons ready," the khahan continued. He signaled a servant to bring him a drink. "Each man must have two lances, two bows, and four hundred arrows. Any man who doesn't will be beaten—five lashes of the rod. Any man whose horse is not ready will be beaten for the same. Any man who goes home to his family will be captured and given to his khan for punishment."

Koja finished writing with a flourish. He held his brush poised, ready to resume writing.

"The morning audience is over," Yamun abruptly announced. "Tonight there will be a feast to honor the safe return of Chanar Ong Kho. Let all who welcome his return attend."

Chanar was stunned. Although pleased about the feast, he expected a longer meeting with the khahan. Always in the past he had enjoyed Yamun's favor. Now, it seemed things had changed. Reluctantly, he stood to go, bowing to the khahan as he started to leave. Koja also got to his feet, wincing as his legs refused to unbend.

"Koja," Yamun suddenly said, using the priest's personal name for the first time, "I want you to stay. I'm curious about your prince."

The priest waited as the khahan ordered, obedient if baffled. He also sensed Chanar's dark looks behind him. The general stalked away, keeping his counsel to himself.

"I will go now, too, my husband," Mother Bayalun pronounced. Yamun didn't answer.

After Bayalun and Chanar had departed, the khahan ordered the servants to bring drinks, black kumiss for himself and hot wine for Koja. He once again lounged back on his stool. "Now, Koja of the Khazari, I've let you learn something of our plans. Perhaps now you can tell me what sort of man your Prince Ogandi is." Yamun yawned.

Koja paused, uncertain of what to say. How much could

he reveal without betraying his lord? How much did he owe to the khahan?

Down the slope, Mother Bayalun caught up with Chanar as he was walking toward his white mare. She hobbled alongside him, prodding the ground with the tip of her staff.

"Greetings to our brave general," she hailed. "Will you take a little time to visit with an old woman?"

Chanar looked at her carefully. The sunlight gave her face a warm glow. It was a mature beauty, livened with self-confidence and will. Bayalun gave Chanar a smile, knowing and tempting. "Old woman" was hardly the way Chanar would describe her.

"Greetings returned, Mother Bayalun," Chanar replied. A part of him was intrigued. It was not like Bayalun to be so forward.

"I couldn't help but see you are alone today, instead of with your *anda*, Yamun."

Chanar slowed his pace to match hers. "You are very observant." His voice went cold. He glanced back to the khahan's yurt. Yamun and the foreign priest were sitting in close conversation.

"I have just come to apologize and say that I do not think it is proper." Her tone was soothing to his injured pride. "You have been traveling much of late, General Chanar."

Chanar turned in surprise at her concern. "I have been doing Yamun's wishes."

"The khahan has messengers to carry out duties such as these," Bayalun said as she steadied herself on the staff. "He sent you to Semphar—"

"It was an honor!" Chanar insisted.

"Naturally, though hardly taxing on your abilities," she answered, unperturbed by his outburst. "The priest you brought back is quite a prize of war." Chanar glared at her, needled by her barb.

"Of course it was an honor to go to Tomke's *ordu*, too," Bayalun added as she stopped walking. They were near her tent. The second empress turned and looked back toward the khahan. "Since you have been gone, Yamun has spent much time with the foreigner. He has named the priest his grand historian."

"I know," Chanar muttered sullenly. He followed the empress's gaze to where the two men sat.

"Other things have happened while you carried messages," Bayalun noted ominously. "Yamun consults the priest for advice, listens to his word. It could be the priest has enchanted Yamun."

"Bayalun, you know no spells can work here. He—" Chanar tipped his head toward Yamun's tent. "—chose this place with you in mind."

"There are ways other than spells to enchant, General," Bayalun reminded Chanar as she turned to enter her yurt. "The priest is dangerous—to both of us."

"Not to me. I am Yamun's *anda*," Chanar corrected. He didn't look Bayalun in the eyes.

"Chanar, things have changed. More things could change. Look up there. That should be you talking to Yamun, not the Khazari." Bayalun pulled aside the tent flap. "The khahan forgets you, forgets all the things you have done . . . forgets you for a lama." She paused again for effect.

Chanar let his head sink so that his chin almost rested on his chest. He watched the second empress from the corner of his half-closed eyes. The light of the morning sun highlighted her figure, the slimness showing even through the heavy clothes she wore. "You're right," Chanar conceded, "Yamun should listen to his khans, his *anda*—not strangers."

"Of course," Mother Bayalun agreed in a magnanimous tone. "The khahan needs good advisors, not bad ones. If he is not careful, Yamun may forget the Tuigan way. Then, General Chanar, what will happen to us? Come into my tent," Bayalun cooed as she stepped through the doorway. "I think we should talk more."

With a cold, friendless smile, Chanar stooped and stepped inside. The tent flap silently fell back into place.

- 5 -

The Valiant Men

C ome, Koja," Yamun bellowed, "sit here beside me!"
Under the night sky, Yamun sat in half-darkness,
illuminated by the flickering flames of a large, foul-
smelling fire. Thick smoke from the burning dung
drifted lazily into the chill, star-studded sky. Koja wrapped
the sheepskin coat around himself and walked into the ring
of light that marked Yamun's campfire.

The feast celebrating Chanar's return had already begun
by the time Koja arrived. It was now late in the evening. The
sky was black, and the moon was three quarters full. Tonight it shone with a reddish hue, dimly illuminating the
landscape, casting thick sepia shadows over everything. Behind the moon trailed the string of sparkling lights. Tuigan
tales said these were the nine old suitors scorned by Becal,
the moon. According to the story, she in turn pursued Ten-
gris, the sun.

The celebration was no small affair. In the walk to the top
of the hill where Yamun's yurt stood, Koja passed a dozen or
more fires. Around each was a circle of men, eating and
drinking. At several fires the soldiers sang wailing, obscene
songs. At one, two squat burly men were stripped to the
waist, arms locked around each other as they wrestled in
the dirt. Their companions roared and shouted out bets.
More than a few troopers had already drunk themselves
into a stupor and now lay around the fires, snoring in sotted
bursts. Koja hurried past these fires.

DAVID COOK

During his hike, Koja noticed a change in the quality of the men. Near the base of the hill were men who carried iron *paitzas*, the lowest pass issued by the khahan. Koja knew because he recognized a few of the men as commanders of a *jagun* of one hundred soldiers. Serving as the khahan's scribe, the Khazari had seen these men in audiences before Yamun. Also around these fires were common dayguards, now off duty. The dayguard troopers were the least important of Yamun's elite bodyguard, but they still had greater status than the rest of Yamun's army.

At the next ring were lesser *noyans*, commanders of *minghans* of one thousand soldiers. Koja did not recognize most of these men, but guessed their rank by their talk. The priest acknowledged the greetings of the few he had met.

At the innermost circle, clustered around Yamun's fire, were the greater *noyans*, the commanders of the *tumens* of ten thousand men. All of these men were khans of the various tribes, important in their own right. Occasionally one would leave his fire and slowly approach the center, where the khahan sat. However, even the khans took care not to alarm the nightguards who stood around Yamun's camp.

"Come and sit, Koja," Yamun repeated to the priest, who still stood at the edge of the firelight. "You'll be my guest." He waved to an empty space on his left. A quiverbearer quickly rolled out a rug and set up a stool for Koja.

The priest glanced about furtively, looking for Chanar. This feast was in the general's honor, and Koja didn't want to accidentally insult the man. Chanar was already irritated enough as it was.

Koja couldn't spot the general among the faces around the fire. Several of Yamun's wives, old Goyuk, and another khan Koja couldn't identify sat close to the khahan. An iron pot hung from a tripod over the fire, simmering with the rich smell of cooking meat. Several leather bags, undoubtedly kumiss and wine, sat on the ground next to the revelers.

"Sit!" insisted Yamun, his speech slightly slurred. "Wine! Bring the historian wine." The khahan tore at a clublike shank of boiled meat.

"Where is General Chanar?" Koja asked, pulling his shear-ling coat out of the way as he sat down. He had traded a nightguard an ivory-hilted dagger for the coat and then spent the rest of the afternoon cleaning the lice and vermin out of it. Now, it was tolerably clean and kept him quite warm.

Yamun didn't answer Koja's question, choosing instead to talk to one of his pretty wives. "General Chanar, where is he?" Koja asked again.

Yamun looked up from his dalliance. "Out," he answered, waving a hand toward the fires. "Out to see his men."

"He has left the feast?" the priest asked, confused.

"No, no. He went to the other fires to see his commanders. He'll be back." Yamun swallowed down another ladle of ku-miss. "Historian," he said sternly, turning away from his wife, "you weren't here when the feasting began. Where were you?"

"I had many things to do, Khahan. As historian, I must take time to write. I am sorry I am late," Koja lied. In truth he had spent the time praying to Furo for guidance and power, hoping to find a way to send his letters to Prince Ogandi.

"Then you have not eaten. Bring him a bowl," the khahan commanded to a waiting quiverbearer.

A servant appeared with a wine goblet and a silver bowl for Koja, filling the latter from the steaming kettle over the fire. The pot held chunks of boiled meat, rich with the smell of game, swimming in a greasy broth. A second servant of-fered a platter covered with thick slabs of a sliced sausage. Koja sniffed at it suspiciously. Aware that Yamun was watch-ing him, he chose one of the smallest slices. At least Furo was not particular about what his priests ate, Koja thought.

Closing his eyes, the priest took a bite of the sausage. He had no idea what the meat was, but it tasted good. Fishing into his coat, he pulled out an ivory-handled knife, mate to the one that bought him the coat, and poked the meat around in the bowl, stabbing out a large chunk of gristly flesh. The meat was hot and burned his lip. Koja took a quick swallow of wine to cool his mouth.

"The food is good," Koja complimented his host.

Yamun smiled. "Antelope."

"Lord Yamun kill it on the hunt today," one of the khans said from the other side of the fire. It was Yamun's advisor, Goyuk. The old man smiled toothlessly, his eyes nearly squeezed shut by wrinkles. "He only need one arrow. Teylas make his aim good."

There was an impressed murmur from the others around the fire.

"Goyuk Khan lost most his teeth at the battle of Big Hat Mountain, fighting the Zamogedi," Yamun explained. The old man nodded and smiled a broad, completely toothless smile.

"That is true," Goyuk confirmed, beaming. Toothlessness and strong drink gave his speech the chanting drone of a soothsayer or shaman.

"What is the sausage made of?" Koja asked, holding up a piece.

"Horsemeat," Yamun answered matter-of-factly.

Koja looked at the piece of sausage he held with a whole new perspective.

"My khahan! I have returned!" a voice called out of the darkness. Chanar, still dressed in the clothes he wore that morning, lurched into the camp. He had a skin tucked under one arm, dribbling kumiss across the ground. He held a cup in the other. As Chanar got close to the fire, he stopped and stared at Yamun and Koja.

"You are welcome at my fire," Yamun said in greeting as he sipped on his own cup of kumiss.

Chanar stood where he was. "Where is my seat? He has taken my seat." The general pointed at Koja.

"Sit," Yamun ordered firmly, "and be quiet." A servant unrolled a rug on the opposite side of the fire from the khahan and set out a stool.

Slowly, without taking his eyes off Yamun, Chanar

slopped more kumiss from his skin. He let the bag drop to the ground and slowly drained the cup. Satisfied, he stepped to the seat put out for him and sat down with a grunt. He glowered at Yamun from across the fire.

Koja was uncertain if he should break the silence. As he sat there, he could feel the anger forming and solidifying between the two men. The women disappeared, slipping from their seats and fading into the night.

"Khahan," the priest finally said, "you made me your historian." Koja's mouth went dry and his palms began to sweat. "How can I be your historian if I don't know your history?"

For a moment Yamun didn't answer. Then he spoke slowly. "You're right, historian." He turned his gaze from Chanar. "You've not been with me from the beginning."

"So, how can I write a proper history?" Koja pressed, diverting Yamun's attention from the general.

The question seized hold of Yamun's mind, and he mulled it over. Koja quickly glanced at Chanar. The man was still staring at Yamun. Finally, the honored general's eyes flicked toward Koja and then back to the khahan. The priest could feel the tension begin to ebb as both men's thoughts were diverted.

"What should you know?" Yamun wondered aloud. His fingers began to toy with his mustache as he considered the question.

"I do not know, Yamun. Perhaps how you became khahan," Koja suggested.

"That is no story," Yamun declared. "I became khahan because my family is the Hoekun and we were strong. Only the strong are chosen to be khahan."

"One from your family has always been the khahan?" Koja asked.

"Yes, but I'm the first khahan of the Tuigan in many generations. For a long time the Tuigan weren't a nation, only many tribes who fought each other."

"Then how did this come about?" Koja spread his hands to indicate the city of Quaraband.

"I built this in the last year—after the last of the tribes submitted to my will," Yamun explained offhandedly. "But that's not my story."

The khahan paused and sucked at his teeth. Finally, Yamun began his tale. "When I was in my seventeenth summer, my father, the *yeke-noyan*, died—"

"Great pardons, Yamun, but I do not understand *yeke-noyan*," Koja interrupted.

"It means 'great chieftain,' " Yamun replied. "When a khan dies, it is forbidden to use his name. This is how we show respect to our ancestors. Now, I'll tell my story."

Koja remembered that Bayalun had no such fear for she had named Burekai freely. The Khazari bit his lip to restrain his natural curiosity and just listen.

"When I was younger, my father, the *yeke-noyan*, arranged a marriage for me," continued Yamun. "Abatai, khan of the Commani, was *anda* to my father. Abatai promised his daughter to be my wife when I came of age. But when the *yeke-noyan* died, Abatai refused to honor the oath given to his *anda*." Yamun stabbed out a large chunk of antelope and dropped it into his bowl.

Across the fire, old Goyuk mumbled, "This Abatai was not good."

Yamun slid back from the fire and took up the tale again. "The daughter of Abatai was promised to me, so I decided to take her. I raised my nine-tailed banner and called my seven valiant men to my side." The khahan stopped to catch his breath. "We rode along the banks of the Rusj River and near Mount Bogdo we found the tents of the Commani.

"That night a great storm came. The Naican were afraid. My seven valiant men were afraid. The ground shook with Teylas's voice, and the Lord of the Sky spoke to me." The khans at the fire glanced up at the night sky when Yamun mentioned the god's name, as if expecting some kind of divine response. "The storm kept the Commani men in their tents, and they did not find us hidden behind Mount Bogdo.

"In the morning, To'orl of the right wing attacked. My

seven valiant men attacked, too. We overturned the Commani's tents and carried off their women. I claimed the daughter of Abatai, and she became my first empress." Yamun stabbed the meat in his bowl and took a bite. Steam still rose from the boiled antelope.

Koja looked at the faces around the fire. Chanar sat with his eyes closed. The other two khans listened with rapt attention. Even the boisterous singing that had started at one of the nearby feast-fires didn't distract them. Yamun himself was excited by his own telling, his eyes aglow with the glories of olden days.

"Now that I defeated the Commani people, I scattered them among the Hoekun and the Naican," the khahan added as a postscript, between bites of antelope. "To To'orl of the Naican I gave five hundred to be slaves for him and his grandchildren. To my seven valiant men, I gave one hundred each to be slaves. I also gave To'orl the Great Yurt and golden drinking cups of Abatai.

"That's how I first made the Hoekun strong and how I got my first empress," Yamun said as he finished the story.

Chanar opened his eyes as the recitation ended. The khans smiled in approval at the telling of the tale.

"What happened to the first empress?" Koja asked.

"She died bearing Hubadai, many winters ago."

Koja wondered if there was a trace of sorrow in the words.

"And what happened to Abatai, khan of the Commani?" Koja asked to change the subject.

"I killed him." Yamun paused, then called to a quiver-bearer. "Bring Abatai's cup," he told the man. The servant went to the royal yurt. He came back carrying a package the size of a melon, wrapped in red silk, and handed it to Yamun. The khahan unwrapped it. There, nestled in the cloth, was a human skull. The top had been sliced away, and a silver cup was set in the recess.

"This was Abatai," Yamun said, holding it out for Koja to see.

The hollow eyes of the skull stared at Koja. Suddenly they flashed with a burning white light. Koja jumped back in surprise, almost toppling off his stool. The bowl of meat and broth in his lap splashed to the ground. "The eyes, they—"

The eyes flashed again, the light flickering and leaping. Koja looked at the skull more closely and realized he was seeing the reflection off the silver bowl through the hollow eye sockets.

"What's wrong, little priest, did you read your future in the bones?" Chanar quipped from across the fire. The old khan, Goyuk, guffawed at the joke. Even Yamun found Koja's reaction amusing.

"He's dead and what's dead can't hurt us," Yamun said with conviction. He turned to Chanar. "Koja is filled with the might of his god, but fears bones. True warriors don't fear spirits."

Koja flushed with embarrassment at his own foolishness.

"We must drink to the honor of the khahan," Chanar announced, hauling himself to his feet. He stepped around the fire and stopped in front of Koja. Uncorking his skin of kumiss, he splashed the heady drink into the skull cup. He took the skull from Yamun and handed it to Koja. Unwillingly, the priest took it in his hands.

"Ai!" Chanar cried, the signal to drink. He tipped his head back and drank from the skin.

"Ai," echoed Yamun and the khans. They raised their cups and took long swallows.

Koja looked at the skull cup in his hands. The eyes were still staring at him, and the brain recess was filled with a milky pool of kumiss. He turned the cup so it wasn't facing him.

"Drink, little priest," urged Chanar, wiping his mustache on his sleeve, "or do you think the khahan has no honor?"

Yamun looked at Koja, noting that the lama had not joined in the toast. His brow furrowed in vexation with his newly chosen historian. "You don't drink?"

Koja took a great breath and hoisted the skull up to his

lips. He closed his eyes and gulped a draught of the wretched drink. Quickly, before they could urge him to take another swallow, the priest held the skull out to Chanar.

"Drink to the khahan's might," Koja gasped.

"Ai," called out the khans, refilling their cups.

Chanar grinned at the look of distress that flickered over the priest's face. He took the offered cup and drained it in a single gulp. Taking the skull with one hand, he filled it again with kumiss and handed it back to Koja. "Drink to the khahan's health," he said with a wicked smile.

Koja choked.

"Ai," slurred out the khans. The toasts were starting to take their toll.

"Enough," interrupted Yamun, pushing the drinking skull away from Koja. "My health doesn't need toasting. I've told a story, now it's someone else's turn." He looked pointedly at Koja.

"I've a story to tell," Chanar snapped, before Koja could speak up. "It's a good story, and it's all true." He stepped back to give himself more space, kicking up the ashes at the edge of the fire.

Yamun turned to Chanar. "Well, what is it?" he asked, barely keeping his irritation under control.

"Great khahan, the priest knows how you beat the Commani with the help of the Naican and your seven valiant men. Now I'll tell of what happened to one of those seven valiant men." Chanar dropped the skin of kumiss and stepped away from the fire.

"Yes, tell us," urged the toothless Goyuk Khan.

Koja looked at Yamun before he voiced his own opinion. The khahan was impassive. Koja couldn't tell if he was displeased or bored, so he kept his own mouth shut.

"After the khan—the khahan—," began Chanar in a loud voice, "defeated the Commani, he gave them to his companions, like he told us. He told his seven valiant men to gather the remaining men, young and old, of the Commani. 'Measure all the men by the tongue of a cart, and kill all those who can't walk under it,' the khahan ordered."

"Measure all the men by a cart," Koja asked meekly. "What does that mean?"

"Any male who cannot walk under the hitch of an oxcart is killed. Only the little boys are spared," Chanar answered curtly. "We killed all the men of the Commani, like the khan ordered. He wasn't the khahan yet, you understand." Chanar circled around the fire, pacing as he spoke. "So, we killed the men.

"Then the khan gave out the women and children to us, because he was pleased with his warriors. He went to the seven valiant men and said, 'You and I are brothers of the liver. We've been *anda* since we were young. Continue to serve me faithfully and I'll give you great rewards.' He said this. I heard it said." Chanar kicked an ember at the edge of the fire back into the flames.

"The valiant men were pleased by these words." Chanar paused, looking at Yamun. "There's more to the story, but perhaps the khahan doesn't want to hear it."

"Tell your story," insisted Yamun.

Chanar nodded to the khahan. "There isn't much more to tell. Perhaps you know the tale. One of the valiant men told the khan, 'We are *anda*, brothers of the liver. I will stand at your side.' And I heard the khahan promise, saying, 'You are of my liver and will be my right hand forever.' When the khan went to war, this valiant man was his right hand. With his right hand, the khan conquered the Quirish and gathered the scattered people of the Tuigan—the Basymats and the Jamaqua. His right hand was strong."

Chanar's story became more impassioned. He stomped about the fire, slapping his chest to emphasize his points. "I never failed or retreated. I went with the khan against the Zamogedi when only nine returned. I fought as his rear guard, protecting him from the Zamogedi. I took the khan to the *ordu* of my family and sheltered him. I strengthened the khan when he returned to the Zamogedi to take his revenge. Together we beat them—killing their men and enslaving their women and children.

"All this because I was his *anda*. When the Khassidi surrendered to me, offering gifts of gold and silk, weren't those gifts sent to the khahan? 'These things that are given are the khahan's to give.' Isn't that the law?" Chanar faced the other khans at the fire, directing his questions to them, not Yamun or the priest.

"Is true, Great Prince," mumbled Goyuk to Yamun, his toothless speech made worse by drink. "He sent it all to you."

Satisfied with Goyuk's answer, the general turned to face the lama.

"But now," Chanar growled, narrowing his eyes at Koja, "the valiant man no longer has gifts to send and another sits at his *anda*'s right hand. And that's how the story ends." The general turned from the priest, stalked back to his stool, and sprawled there, satisfied that his point had been made.

With a sharp hiss, Yamun stood and took a step toward Chanar, who watched him like a cat. The khahan's fists were clenched tightly, and his body swayed with tension.

"This is no good," Goyuk said softly, laying his hand on Yamun's arm. "Chanar is your guest."

Yamun stopped, listening to the truth in Goyuk's words. Koja quietly slid his stool away from the khahan, fearful of what might happen next. The singing from the other fires started up again.

"Nightguards!" snarled Yamun. "Come with me. I'm going to visit the other fires." With that he wheeled and strode off into the darkness. The guards streamed past, and the quiverbearers followed after, carrying food and drink for the khahan no matter where he stopped.

Those around the fire watched the entourage wend down the hillside. Koja sat quietly, suddenly feeling himself among enemies.

"This is a dangerous game you play, Prince Chanar," observed Goyuk, leaning over to speak softly in Chanar's ear.

"He can't kill me," Chanar confidently replied as he watched Yamun march down the hill. "The Khassidi and many others would go back to their *ordus* if he did."

"Is true, you are well loved, but Yamun is the khahan," the old man cautioned.

Chanar dismissed Goyuk's comments with a gulp of kumiss. As he drank down the cup, he once again saw Koja on the other side of the fire.

"Priest!" he hissed at the lama. "Yamun trusts you. Well, I am his *anda*! You are a foreigner, an outsider." The general leaned forward until his face was almost in the flames. "And if you betray the Tuigan, I'll have great fun hunting you down. Do you know how a traitor is killed? We crush the breath out of him under a plank piled with heavy stones. It's a slow and painful death."

Koja paled.

"Remember it and remember me," Chanar warned. With those words, he threw the rest of the kumiss on the fire and stood. "I must go to my men," he told Goyuk Khan, ignoring Koja's presence. The old khan nodded, and Chanar walked off into the darkness.

The rest of the evening seemed to pass quickly and slowly all at once. At first Koja was content to sit near the fire, keeping away the increasing chill of the frosty night air. The servants kept refilling his golden goblet, having long since taken the skull away. The old khan, Goyuk, seeing that the priest wasn't going anywhere, began to talk incessantly. Koja only understood about half of what the codger said, but smiled and nodded politely nonetheless. The khan talked about his *ordu*, his horses, the great battles he had fought in, and how a horse had kicked out his teeth. At least, that is what Koja thought he was discussing. As the night went on, Goyuk's speech became increasingly unintelligible.

Several times, Koja tried to get up and leave. Each effort brought a storm of protest from Goyuk. "This story is just getting good," he would insist and then demand more wine for the priest. Eventually, Koja wasn't even sure his legs would work if he did manage to get away.

At last, the kumiss and wine had their effect. The old man

nodded off in midsentence, then snapped back awake and
rambled on for a while longer. Finally, Goyuk bedded down,
moving the stool out of the way and wrapping the rug
around himself. Koja, too tired to walk back to his yurt, followed custom, rolling the thick felt rug tightly around himself. Within a few minutes he was sound asleep.

Down the slope, a hooded servant slipped among the
fires, seeking out one man. At each circle he stopped, standing in the shadows, staring at the faces. Finally, at one fire,
where the drinking was the most riotous, the servant found
the man whom he sought. Moving through the darkness, he
sidled up closer to his goal. The revelers were too involved
with their drink to notice him. Softly, he leaned up and
whispered in the ear of his man.

"The khadun, Lady Bayalun, hears that you have been
wronged this night," he hissed. "'Is Chanar to let himself be
usurped by a stranger?' she asks."

"Eh? What do you say?" the drunken General Chanar
blurted in surprise.

"Shhh. Quietly! She fears you fall from Yamun's favor—"

Chanar moved to speak, but the messenger quickly
pressed his hand on the general's shoulder. "This is not the
place to talk. The khadun opens her tent to you, if you will
come."

"Hmm . . . when?" Chanar asked, trying to look at the man
without turning his head.

"Tonight, while the eyes of others are occupied." The messenger waited, letting Chanar make his decision.

"Tell her I'll come," Chanar finally whispered. Without another word, the messenger faded back into the darkness.

* * * * *

The campfires had burned down to lifeless ashes, and
only thick plumes of smoke rose up into the blackness of
night. Koja found himself sitting up, shivering in the cold,
rugs and robes fallen off his back. It didn't strike him as odd
that he could see the sleeping forms of men, the empty

yurts flapping in the breeze, even in perfect darkness. They were just grayer forms against the black plain.

There was a clink of rock against rock behind him and then a soft wet scrape of mud on stone. Wheeling around, he was confronted by a man in yellow and orange robes, hunched over so his face could not be seen. The man's hands were doing something, something that matched the sounds of stone against stone.

"Who—," Koja started to blurt out.

The man looked up and stopped Koja in midsentence. It was his old master from the temple, his bald head lined with age. The master smiled and nodded to the priest and then went back to his work, building a wall. With a scrape, the master dragged a trowel across the stone's top, spreading a thick layer of mortar.

Koja slowly turned around. The men, fires, and yurts were gone. A low wall encircled him, trapping him beside the campfire. Turning back, Koja watched his master lift a square block and set it in place atop the fresh mortar.

"Master, what are you doing!" Koja could feel a growing panic inside himself.

"All our lives we struggle to be free of walls," intoned the master, never once stopping his work. "All our lives we build stronger walls." With a scrape and heavy thud, another stone was set in place. "Know, young student, of the walls you build—and who they belong to."

Suddenly the wall was finished, towering over Koja. The master was gone. Koja heaved to his feet and whirled about, looking for his mentor. There, in front of him, was a banner set in the ground. From its top hung nine black horsetails—the khahan's banner. He turned the other way. There was another, with nine white yak tails—the khadun's banner. Stumbling backward, he tripped and fell against another—a golden disk hung with silken streamers of yellow and red—Prince Ogandi's banner. Panicked, Koja fell to the ground and closed his eyes.

A sound of heavy breathing, and a blast of steam across

Koja's face forced him to look again. The banners were gone, and the wall that circled him shivered and moved. It became a great beast, black and shimmering. A pair of eyes, inhuman and cold, stared down at him.

"Are you the khahan of the barbarians?" the beast boomed.

"No," answered Koja in a weak whisper.

The eyes blinked. "Ah. Then you are with him," it decided. "That is good. Finally, it is time." The eyes glowed brighter. Fearful, Koja looked away from the baleful gleam. There was a rushing of wind and then the shape was gone.

Looking up, the priest saw his master again. "Be careful, Koja, of the walls you build," the old lama called out. The master faded, growing dimmer to Koja's sight, until there was nothing but the dull gray horizon. Then there was nothing at all.

The priest woke slowly, dimly remembering the voices from his sleep. A sharp tang welled up at the base of his skull, tingling the stubble of his neck hair. Involuntarily, the thin priest inhaled deeply. Suddenly, he was wide awake, sneezing and gagging, his nostrils filled with the smoke of burning manure. He flailed about, then opened his eyes. Thick wads of stinging smoke assailed him. Koja crawled out of his rug and into clear air.

"It is a good day," a wavering voice somewhere to Koja's left said.

Still blinking, the priest looked toward the voice. He could hardly see the speaker because the dawn sun blazed behind the man's shoulder. Koja shielded his eyes from the orange-red glow with one hand and rubbed away the last of his tears with the other. Sitting next to the thickly smoking campfire was the ancient Goyuk Khan, poking at the coals with a stick. He looked back at Koja and smiled one of his broad, toothless grins.

Koja weakly smiled back. His head felt thick from drink and pained from his sudden awakening. His mouth was gummy. The years among the lamas had not prepared him for a night of feasting with the Tuigan.

"Is time to eat," Goyuk said. He didn't look the least bit haggard from the celebration. Poking the fire again, Goyuk fished out an ash-covered lump, bits of burning coals still clinging to it. Picking it up carefully, he brushed the embers away with his dirty fingers and held it out to Koja.

Koja looked at it dubiously, knowing full well that he had to take it or offend the old khan. It looked like a scrap of the horsemeat sausage, roasted in the fire. He gingerly took it, juggling it between his hands to avoid burning his fingers.

"Eat," urged the khan, "is good."

"Thank you," said Koja with a forced smile. He ate it down quickly, doing his best not to taste the meat. Breakfast finished, Koja struggled to his feet to look for water. The sun had barely risen over the horizon, but already men were about. The guards were changing, the dayguards replacing the nightguards. Quiverbearers and household slaves were going from yurt to yurt, preparing for the morning.

Not everyone was awake, however. Koja weaved through the sleepers clustered around the feast-fires. Most of the revelers were still snoring blissfully, unusual for the Tuigan camp, which was normally bustling by this hour. Some were wrapped in their blankets and rugs, curled closely around small mounds of smoldering embers. However, more than a few were sprawled haphazardly over the ground, their *kalats* pulled up tight around them. Koja guessed many of them slept on the same spots where they had passed out the night before.

After much futile searching, Koja finally collared a servant carrying a bucket of water. Scooping it up with his hands, he gulped down a mouthful. Though cold enough to numb his fingers, the priest splashed the water over his face and head, vigorously rubbing his skin to clear his brain.

One of Yamun's quiverbearers presented himself to Koja. "The Illustrious Emperor of the Tuigan, Yamun Khahan, sends me to ask why his historian is not in attendance at the yurt of his lord." The servant remained kneeling before the lama.

Koja looked at the man in surprise. He hadn't expected the khahan to conduct business so early this morning. Furthermore, the priest didn't realize his presence would be needed so constantly. "Take me to his yurt," he ordered.

Obediently, the servant led Koja through the clutter around the feast-fires. Reaching the tent, the man announced Koja's arrival. The priest was quickly ushered inside.

This morning the yurt was arranged differently. Yamun's throne was gone, and the braziers had been moved to the sides of the tent. The flap covering the smoke hole was opened wide, as was the door, allowing rays of sunlight to dazzle the normally gloomy interior. In the center of the yurt, in a shaft of sunlight, sat a circle of men. Yamun was bareheaded, his conical hat set aside. The light gleamed off his tonsure and brought out the red color of his hair. He still wore the heavy sable coat he had worm the night before, though now it was mud-stained and smudged with soot. The other men had likewise removed their hats, making a ring of shining bald domes in the center of the yurt. Koja was reminded of the masters of his temple, although they didn't sport the long side braids favored by these warriors.

"Historian, you'll sit here," called out Yamun as the lama entered. He slapped his hand on the rug just behind himself. Koja walked around the circle and took his seat. Chanar, bleary-eyed from the night's festivities, sat on one side of Yamun. Goyuk sat on the other. There were three others wearing golden cloths and embroidered silks, signs that they were powerful khans, but Koja did not recognize them. Their rich clothes were travel-stained and rumpled. At the farthest end of the circle, sitting slightly away from the rest, was a common trooper. His clothes, a simple blue *kalat* and brown trousers, were filthy with mud and grime. He stank powerfully, Koja noticed as he walked by.

The khans glanced toward Koja as he sat. Goyuk smiled another of his gaping smiles. A look of displeasure sparked in Chanar's eyes. Yamun leaned forward, drawing their attention to the sheet spread out in front of them.

It was a crude map, something which surprised Koja. He hadn't seen any maps since arriving, and he had assumed the Tuigan had no knowledge of cartography. Here was another surprise about his hosts. The lama craned his neck, trying to get a view of the sheet.

"Semphar is here," Yamun said, continuing a conversation begun before the priest entered. He thrust a stubby finger at one corner of the sheet. "Hubadai waits with his army at foot of Fergana Pass." He traced his finger across the map to a point closer to the center. "We're here."

"And where is Jad?" asked one of the khans Koja didn't know.

"At the Orkhon Oasis—there." Yamun pointed to the far side of the map.

The priest strained even harder to see where Yamun was indicating. All he could make out was a blurry area of lines and scribbles.

"And Tomke?" the same khan asked. He was a wolf-faced man with high, sharp cheekbones, a narrow nose, and pointed chin. His graying hair was well greased and bound in three braids, one on each side of his head and a third at the back.

"He stays in the north to gather his men. I'm going to hold him in reserve," Yamun explained. There was a grunt of general understanding from the men listening. They studied the map for a few minutes, learning the dispositions of the armies.

"What will you do?" Goyuk finally asked, his nose practically touching the map as he screwed up his eyes to see the lines. "Semphar? Or Khazari?" At the mention of Khazari, Koja scooted sideways a little, trying to find a better angle to see the map. By leaning to the left, he could see it clearer.

"Semphar must fall. They've refused my demands. Hubadai will march against them." The khahan traced a line on the map. Again there was a murmur of approval. Chanar glanced at the wolf-faced khan, giving him the tiniest of nods.

"Great Yamun," the man said, "I must speak because it is my duty under heaven. Your son Hubadai is a brave and valiant warrior, but he is young and has not gone to war often. The caliph of Semphar is a mighty ruler. Our spies tell us he has many soldiers protected by great stone walls. It would be wisdom to send a wise and experienced warrior to instruct and aid your son."

"My son is my son. He must fight," Yamun snapped.

"Of course, Great Khan," Chanar noted. "He must command. Perhaps Chagadai does not mean you should send a new commander. Send someone you can trust to advise Hubadai. Make this advisor commander of the right wing."

"Hubadai is young and his temper is quick," pressed Chagadai, the wolfish khan. "Send him someone to cool his rashness, someone who knows the traps of war. Send someone your son can learn from."

" 'A wise man has a wise tutor,' " Chanar offered.

"They speak wisely, Yamun," wheezed out Goyuk.

The khahan looked at the khans around the circle, pondering the advice. "Chagadai's advice is good," Yamun finally said. "But who should I send? You, Chagadai?"

"Great Lord, my wisdom is the wisdom of the tent," the khan demurred. "I do not have the cunning for war. Send a warrior who has served you well."

"I am too old," said Goyuk, before Yamun could even ask him. "Send a young man."

"What about you Chanar?" Yamun asked.

"I hoped to visit the yurts of my people," the general began, "but by your word, it shall be done."

"Then it is done," Yamun concluded. "I hoped you would ride by my side, but you must serve my son now. He'll listen to you."

"You have my word, Semphar will fall." Chanar bowed, smiling as he did so.

"But what about Khazari?" inquired Goyuk, pointing at the map. Koja, peering over their shoulders, could see that Chagadai pointed to the same general area of the map as the

Orkhon Oasis. So Prince Jad was camped near Khazari, he thought.

"Before we talk, we must hear the reports of the scouts," Yamun said. "Come forward, trooper."

The soldier at the back slid forward and prostrated himself.

"This man led the scouts I sent to Khazari. We will hear his report. But first," Yamun said, turning to Koja behind him, "you must go. Wait outside. You will be called when you are needed."

"Yes, Khahan," Koja said softly, concealing his bitter disappointment. Yamun's face was impassive, unconcerned, but Chanar looked at the priest with smug satisfaction. As quickly as he could, Koja hurried out of the yurt.

Outside, the revelers were waking up. Koja, with nothing else to do, sat down on his haunches beside the doorway. He strained to hear anything of the conversation inside, but the thick felt of the yurt swallowed up the words.

Koja sat there, disconsolate, watching hung-over khans wander away from the scene of last night's feast. The day-guards walked among the circles, kicking awake their brothers who had passed out the night before. A few half-hearted fights broke out, more loud arguments than real brawls.

One did turn into a serious battle as two men wrestled across the ground. Their fight quickly attracted others, and soon there was a shouting crowd around the battlers. Yamun and the khans came out of the yurt shortly after the fight started, but no one seemed very interested in stopping the conflict. Yamun and the others stood by as the two brawlers rolled around, trying to get each other in a deadly hold. Within minutes, though, one man screamed, and the fight ended as quickly as it had started.

Ignoring Koja, who sat expectantly by the door, the khahan called down to the big wrestler. "You are a good fighter."

The man knelt where he was. "Teylas has given his strength to me," he answered.

Yamun raised an eyebrow at the man's words. "What's your *ordu*?"

"I am Sechen of the Naican," the wrestler answered. "I have killed five men with my bare hands, Khahan." Behind him the dayguards dragged his dead opponent away.

"Sechen, you're proud and shameless. I like you," Yamun said impulsively. "From now on you will serve at my side."

Sechen fell into the dirt, humbling himself before the khahan. Inarticulate cries of thanks poured from the man's lips.

Koja looked in horror at the big wrestler. The khahan had just honored an admitted killer, praising the man for what he had done. Astonished, the priest looked at the emperor of the Tuigan. The man showed no shame or conscience for what he had just done. Koja had almost forgotten just what the Tuigan were. For all their cunning craftsmanship and military skill, the Tuigan were still uncivilized barbarians. Koja wondered if they could ever be anything more.

Yamun finally finished speaking with the wrestler, but the grateful man was still kneeling at his feet. Looking at Koja standing beside him, the khahan gave no notice of the priest's horrified expression.

"We have reached a decision, lama," Yamun said. "I have an answer for your prince."

"What is the message I am to take to Prince Ogandi?" Koja finally, hesitantly asked, his voice trembling with rage and fear.

"You don't. The Tuigan ride to Khazari with their own answer. No one speaks for us," Yamun pronounced. "And your prince will hear from me very soon."

- 6 -
On The March

Elsewhere in the royal compound, another meeting was just beginning. It was a furtive liaison in one of the yurts used as a storehouse. The tent's felt walls were black, darkened by powdered charcoal. The smoke hole was sealed shut, and the door flap was tightly closed. It was an isolated yurt, seldom visited or disturbed.

Outside, a few soldiers, wearing the blue *kalat* of common troopers, leaned on their lances. Their eyes were far from idle, though. Under a guise of nonchalance, the men constantly scanned the area, ready to warn of any intruders.

Inside, the black yurt was barely lit by one small lamp. It burned fitfully, the little circle of light it cast growing and shrinking with each flicker. The dim glow revealed rolls of fabric, sealed baskets, rugs, and stacks of metal pots. Nestled in all this, within the circle of light, were General Chanar and Mother Bayalun. She was dressed in a simple robe, hardly fitting to her station. Around her head she had wrapped several coils of a shawl, until her face was hidden in shadows. Her staff leaned against a bale beside her.

"Did you do as I instructed?" she demanded, leaning forward to look the general in the eye.

"Everything," answered Chanar with cocky self-assurance.

"And Chagadai?"

"He played his part," Chanar said with a smile. "What did you promise him?"

"More than nothing," she answered, avoiding his question. "What is the result?"

"He rides to the Sindhe River to meet with Jad. Then they go to Khazari." The general warmed his hands over the lamp.

"Excellent. Soon, Chanar, you will become the true khahan," Mother Bayalun said coldly. "And where are you to be?"

"I am to ride to Fergana Pass to advise Hubadai." Chanar heard something and stopped speaking. He sat up straight, looking about him to see the source of the noise. The dark walls of the tent quivered in a faint breeze.

"Relax, my general," Bayalun said soothingly. "We are alone. My guards outside will make sure of that. Now, take this—" She handed him a small leather bag. "Mix it with some wine tonight, then drink it. It will make you sick, but don't worry, it won't kill you. Yamun will see that you are too sick to travel."

"Why do this?" he questioned, eyeing the bag dubiously.

Bayalun grabbed his hand and stuffed the bag into his fingers. "Don't be a fool," she said sharply. "We need each other alive. And you need to be here, in Quaraband—not with Hubadai. When the khahan is dealt with, you must be ready to move, so that means you must stay here with me. How are you going to do that? Tell Yamun you don't feel like riding out today? That it's an unlucky day?" She gently squeezed his fingers. "Use the powder or he will become suspicious."

"Oh," Chanar said, slowly coming to understand. "What if he orders a cart to take me to Hubadai?"

"He won't," she contended. The khadun's patience was starting to wear thin. "He has too much to do. Tell him you will take care of your arrangements. He'll believe you."

"And then what?"

"Then you wait. Things will work just as we've planned. And then—" Bayalun reached out and laid her hand gently on his arm. "We will lead the Tuigan to their true glory."

"Yes." Chanar savored the thought. "When I'm khahan, I'll get rid of these foreigners."

"Of course," Mother Bayalun said, stroking his arm. "That is the whole reason we're doing this, isn't it?"

Chanar grinned wolfishly, openly admiring the older woman. She was not passive, a mere ornament like Yamun's Shou princesses. She was bold, a woman for a true warrior.

"But quickly," she urged, breaking the mood, "you must go before anyone becomes suspicious by your absence. Leave now. My men will make sure the way is clear." She pressed on his arm, sending him on his way.

Chanar moved to go with only a little reluctance. Her words reminded him of the plan's dangers. Going to the door, he peered out through a tiny gap. After what seemed an interminable minute of watching, he slipped out through the doorway. There was a brief flash of sunlight, and then the tent fell dark again.

Bayalun sat on the pile of rugs, leaning on her staff, her eyes closed as she thought. Her plans were going well. Nothing had gone wrong, but that worried her. She was certain that by now there would have been some mistake. "Perfect plans are made by fools," or so went the old proverb.

"Does he suspect?" said a soft, yipping voice from the darkness.

Mother Bayalun looked up slowly, not showing any surprise at the new speaker. "No, but that's through no help from you. Your clumsiness almost gave you away," she snapped. "What are you doing here?"

A large fox, honey brown in color, walked into the light. Moving opposite Bayalun, it settled back on its haunches. With its front paws, it produced a long pipe from the leather bag it carried slung around its neck. "I wish you people would move your tents. It would make things a lot easier. I'd change out of this form, but these damned magic-dead lands prevent me."

"Why are you here, you insolent creature?" Bayalun demanded, thumping the rolled-up rug beside the fox-thing.

"My master sent me," it explained as it stuffed tobacco into the pipe and tamped it down with a paw more human than foxlike. "Are we stuck with that dolt?"

"Who?"

"The buffoon who was just here," the fox explained. He dug into his bag and pulled out a smoldering ember, casually holding the burning coal in his paws. "Stole it from a fire outside," the fox offered before she could ask. He set the coal to the pipe.

"Don't light that in here!" Bayalun snapped. The fox looked up at her in surprise. "The smoke will give us away."

"To whom? Your guards? They're the only ones outside." The fox drew a long puff on the pipe, blowing out sweet smoke from the combination of tobacco and strange herbs. "This shape lets me get around easily, but it is so tiring. Especially when everyone wants to chase you." It puffed on the pipe again, watching Bayalun's increasing irritation with an unconcealed glee.

"You take too many risks! Someone saw you?" Bayalun asked with alarm.

"Some saw a fox, nothing more," the creature replied confidently.

"Carrying a bag!"

"I was careful. Stop worrying like an old woman. I've done this all my life, which is longer than yours—even if you are one of those half-spirit Maraloi." The fox-thing blew smoke up toward the ceiling.

Bayalun started at the mention of the Maraloi. "How did you know?" she demanded. "No one knows of that."

"The emperor of Shou Lung knows. Your father was one of the Maraloi, spirits of the great northern wood. Humans think the Maraloi don't exist. You and I know better." The fox tapped its pipe, shaking out the excess ash. "But, the man you were talking to—"

"Will present no problems," Bayalun said, a little subdued. "He thinks we only plan to get Yamun out of Quaraband so he can seize power. He has no idea of my true intentions."

"*Our* true intentions," corrected the fox, rubbing its back against a rough-sided basket. "Ahh," it sighed.

"Our intentions," Bayalun noted. "And just what does your master intend?"

"He is concerned. He wants to be sure that everything is as he agreed." The fox-thing suddenly dropped its casual air. "Yamun Khahan continues to unite the tribes, and his army grows larger. Soon even the unbreachable Dragonwall will be threatened by his might. There is a chance its magic may not be able to hold him back. You assured my master that there would be peace between Shou Lung and the Tuigan."

"There has been no change," she answered defensively. "Once I have control, I will see that the peace between the Tuigan and Shou Lung remains unbroken. But, your master has certain obligations to fulfill, too."

"Of course," assured the fox between draws on its pipe. "That's why he sent me."

"What?"

"You needed an assassin, an expert in disguise. Am I not," the fox said as it stood and took a little bow, "brilliant at disguise?"

"Not if that's the best you can do," Bayalun shot back. She was furious with the *hu hsien*, this inhuman trickster of the spirit realm. She was equally furious with the Shou mandarin who sent it. The mighty of Shou Lung think they can toy with me, she cursed silently, but I'll show them just how dangerous that can be. "Go back to your master and tell him to send me a real assassin, not a clowning animal."

The fox bit down hard on the stem of its pipe. "You will take whomever my master sends," it snarled, baring its fangs as its animal side boiled to the surface. "Now, old woman, I'm tired of this. Tell me what I am to do."

Bayalun relented. "There is a post you can fill—assuming you can look human—among the khahan's dayguards. Then you will be close to him. You must take it and wait." Bayalun twisted the staff between her hands as she explained things.

"That's all? How will I know when to act?" the beast asked.

"I will send you a message," Bayalun answered.

"How?"

"That's all you need know," she snapped, frowning at the beast's curiosity. "Too much knowledge and you become a danger to everything. Tomorrow, present yourself to Dayir Bahadur—in human form. He commands a *jagun* of the day-guard and will see to your position. Then, wait for my word." She narrowed her eyes, waiting for any more questions. None came. "Now, you may leave."

The fox blew a puff of sweet smoke. "I haven't finished my pipe," it declared.

"Leave now," Bayalun hissed, "lest I complain to your master."

The fox pricked up its ears. "Careful, or I will *complain* to your lord." The *hu hsien* watched the empress's reaction. "I find you interesting, half-Maraloi. Your husband might be strong enough to seize the riches of Shou Lung, but you want him dead. Your ambitions are strange."

"Yamun Khahan killed the *yeke-noyan*—my husband, his father—so he could rule the Hoekun. I will never forgive him for that." Besides, Bayalun thought, with the khahan dead, I will control the Tuigan. Chanar will be khahan, but I will have the power. "Now, no more questions."

"Very well, I will take my leave," the fox-thing said pompously. It closed the lid on the pipe and stuffed it back into the pouch. Dropping to all fours, it smiled a foxish smile at Bayalun and lightly leaped away into the darkness.

After the creature had left, Bayalun waited patiently for some time. She was in no hurry. Haste ruined careful plans. She had learned that from experience.

* * * * *

It was impossible to keep secret the fact that the khahan was on the move toward Khazari, and by the afternoon the news had spread through all of Quaraband. Yamun's women had emptied out the Great Yurt and had started to take it down. Within an hour, the yurt was stripped of its felt walls, the frame standing like a skeleton atop the hill.

The dismantling of the royal yurt was a signal to the rest

of the city. Men rode from their tents, extra horses in tow, to assembly areas outside Quaraband. Each *arban* of ten men gathered to form the *jaguns* of one hundred and in turn the *minghans* of one thousand. For every unit there was a specific meeting place, so that the men could be organized quickly. Throughout the day, yurts disappeared from the valley as preparations were made to move out.

Men loaded Yamun's throne onto the back of a huge cart, which was roofed with a smaller version of the royal yurt. The cart, pulled by a team of eight oxen, was Yamun's capital while on campaign. During the work, the khahan set up his headquarters in the sunshine. He sat on his bed, a small wooden-framed thing with stubby legs. Koja sat on a stool nearby, along with several other scribes, mostly Bayalun's wizards and holy men. All of them furiously scribbled down orders, rolling up the sheets as they were done and thrusting them into the hands of waiting messengers.

Koja had just finished writing out a sheet of orders meant for Hubadai at Fergana Pass. "It is to be there in no less than five days," insisted Yamun as the priest handed the scroll to a rider.

"By your word, it shall be done!" the rider shouted, sprinting to his horse before he had even finished speaking.

Koja leaned to the scribe next to him, a young man with a thin, black goatee and shaven head. "How can that be?" Koja asked, pointing his writing brush at the departing rider. "How can he deliver a message so quickly? Do they use magic?"

The young priest shook his head, barely looking up from his work. "He is an imperial messenger, so he can use the posthouses. He will ride all day, changing horses at special stations. Then another man will take the message at night." The priest bent back to his work.

Yamun dictated orders for hours, going into minute details for the impending march. By his orders, the army was divided into three wings, with Yamun in command of the center. Troops were assigned, and *tumens* and *minghans* dispatched to the different wings. Commanders received orders concerning the amount of food to carry, the number and types of weapons they were to employ, and how many horses each man was to have. The khahan appointed *yurtchis*, the army's purveyors, to supervise the camps and find supplies as they marched. Many of the orders concerned the condition of the horses, setting penalties for galloping them unnecessarily or working them too hard.

Koja wrote until his fingers were numb. The nightguard came to relieve the dayguard as the sun set. Lamps were brought, and the scribes continued to work by the dim glow.

Finally, Koja walked back toward his tent, the nightguards in his wake. His legs moved mechanically as his mind slowly dozed off. All he could think of was the pile of cushions that waited for him at the yurt—soft cushions and warm blankets that would cradle him while he slept.

When the priest got to his tent, he stopped. A barren circle of crushed grass filled the space where his yurt had stood. In its place were two horses and a camel, hobbled to keep them from wandering, a small mound of sacks and baggage, and the curled-up shape of his servant, sleeping on the ground.

Koja moaned. It was to be another night sleeping under the stars. Searching through the baggage, he found a set of rugs. Resigned to his situation, Koja lay down, using his leather bag for a pillow, and pulled the rugs tight around him. Within a few minutes, lulled by the snoring of his servant, the priest was sound asleep.

In the morning, Koja awoke to find that Quaraband was gone. All that remained was a field of waste—fire scars, muddy tracks, and garbage. A line of creaking carts drawn by lowing oxen lumbered across the green steppe, carrying the households deeper into the trackless plain. Many miles away, in a more secluded spot, the city would be rebuilt by the women and children. There the families would wait until their men returned from war.

File after file of soldiers moved out, leading their mounts across the river and away to the east. The water, normally clear, was a turgid, brown flow. The banks had been turned into quagmires by the churning tread of man and horse. There were shouted good-byes to wives and children, assuring them of their safe return. Horses whinnied; oxen lowed.

An *arban* of dayguards rode to Koja's camp. "Come with us, grand historian. The khahan commands you to ride with him."

"Wait until I have eaten," Koja requested, refusing to be rushed.

"No," insisted the chief of the *arban*. "The khahan leaves now."

"But my food—"

"Learn to eat in the saddle," the experienced old campaigner said helpfully. He signaled his men that it was time to go.

Back aching from a night on the ground, Koja gingerly climbed into his horse's saddle and rode to join the khahan's train. Behind him, his servant led a small string of pack animals.

The journey quickly fell into a pattern that would become routine over the coming days. The army moved at a brisk pace; even the oxcarts moved faster than Koja expected. For him, the ride was painful and jolting. The horsewarriors traveled for ten hours a day, stopping only occasionally to let the horses graze and water themselves. Fortunately, the animals were tough, wiry little mounts, much different from the well-bred and magnificent steeds that Koja had seen in Khazari and Shou Lung. Surely, the priest thought, these animals must draw some of their nourishment from the air. With the exception of a small bag of millet at night, the men made no effort to feed the horses, letting them survive on the new shoots of grasses and tough scrub they found on the steppe.

By the time Yamun called for camp on the first day, it was

dusk. A few yurts were standing here and there, tents of the khans, but the bulk of the army simply slept under the stars. Each man laid out a small felt rug to use as a mat, taking his saddle for a pillow. The mares were milked and driven into clusters around a single tethered stallion, where they stayed for the night, grazing and sleeping. Each *arban* camped as a group, kindling a fire at their center. The men worked together to prepare their evening meal.

As the red horizon of twilight gave way to darkness, the glow of campfires covered the plain. Koja ate at the camp of the khahan, served by the quiverbearers. Dinner was a simple stew of dried meat and milk curds, bitter yet bland, brown-gray in color. Nonetheless, Koja ate it with enthusiasm. A meal, any meal, was welcome.

After dinner, Yamun found Koja alone in the dark. "Priest," he began without any preamble, "the khans are unhappy with you. They think you will try to curse the army. A few suggest I should get rid of you." He said no more, but gazed at Koja.

The priest swallowed, suddenly feeling Yamun's stare. "Khahan, as I have said, my duty is to Prince Ogandi. Still, your intentions may not be hostile, so I should not bring misfortune to you," he said in a single breath, not giving Yamun the chance to interrupt.

"No wonder you're a diplomat," Yamun said, sorting out the answer. "Remember this—you owe me your life. You were dead and brought back at my command. Betray me and I'll take it back."

Koja nodded.

That night, the lama returned to his own campfire. Hodj was already asleep. The nightguards sat at a small fire a little way off from Koja's. The lama dug into his bags, finally pulling out the small packet of letters he had written. He opened them and surveyed the sheets he had prepared for Prince Ogandi. Each page was covered with fine brush-strokes, column upon column of neatly arranged characters. The sheets represented hours of work in his tent, hours inking out pages of crabbed text. They were supposed to have been the sum and goal of his existence, at least while among the Tuigan.

"The prince might find these useful," he said to himself. He looked over the yellow sheets of rice paper.

"Or he may already know everything I've written," he countered. "In any case, he will know the intentions of the khahan soon enough."

Koja stared at the pages. Yamun had treated him well, showing him kindnesses and trust far beyond what his position warranted. If he sent the letters, which might not even be useful, he would betray that trust. Koja sighed and paged through the letters again. If he didn't send the letters, would it matter to the prince anyway?

"Yamun Khahan, you are wrong," Koja said clearly, as if there was anyone to hear. "I am a very bad diplomat." He touched a corner of the top sheet to the coals of the campfire in front of him. The flame eagerly devoured the flimsy paper. One by one he burned the sheets, watching their ashes rise into the night sky.

In the morning, the letters were only a few crumbled wisps of ash. As Koja rolled awake, Hodj stirred the last of the ashes into the fire. Soon, the servant poured out cups of tea, one thick with milk and salt for himself and the other with butter and sugar for Koja. Apart from the tea, however, this morning's breakfast was different. Instead of boiling a porridge of millet and mare's milk or reheating last night's dinner, the servant spooned globs of a white paste into a leather bag. He filled the sack with water and sealed it tightly, then he hung one bag from the saddle of each horse. Next he took several strips of dried meat and slid them between the saddle and the blanket.

"Later we eat," Hodj answered, patting the saddle. "Dried meat and mare's curd. See, the meat softens under the saddle, and the horse's bouncing will mix the curd for you." The servant proudly showed Koja how it was done. "And I made tea, master." Hodj held up another bag.

After tea, Koja once again took to the saddle. Although the pace this day was no slower than yesterday's, perhaps even faster, it seemed less frenzied and chaotic. The scouts resumed their patrols. Operations began to function without the khahan's hand guiding every detail.

By midafternoon, Koja found himself riding with the khahan, undisturbed by messengers and commanders.

"Khahan, I am wondering," Koja began, his curiosity coming to the fore once again. "We are well beyond the deadlands of Quaraband. Why then do you ride and rely on scouts when simple magics could make everything much easier?"

"Priest," Yamun answered, "count my army. How many could I move by simple magic? An *arban*? A *jagun*? Even a *minghan*? What would they do? Hold off the enemy until more arrived? We ride because there are so many of us."

"But surely the scouting could be done by spells," Koja suggested.

"You've got some sight?" Yamun asked. He reined back his horse to a slower pace, a concession to the saddle-sore priest.

"A little, yes." As they slowed, riders began to pass them, churning up dust. Koja's eyes smarted as the air grew cloudy.

"Then tell me what's ahead, beyond my eyesight."

"Where?" Koja asked, peering through the haze thrown up by the army.

"Ahead, priest—the way we're going." Yamun smirked, pointing with his knout.

"But there's so much ahead of us. If you told me what I should look for—"

Yamun broke into laughter. "If I knew what was there, I wouldn't need your sight!"

Koja clapped his mouth shut. Embarrassed, he rubbed his head, keeping his eyes lowered.

"See, priest," Yamun explained, still laughing at Koja's embarrassment. "That's why I use men and riders. I send them out with orders to look and see. They'll ride back and tell me what they have found. I learn more from soldiers than I ever will from wizards and priests."

Koja nodded, pondering the lesson's wisdom.

"Besides," Yamun concluded more darkly, "I'd have to rely on Mother Bayalun for magic."

There was a silence between the two men, although the world around them was hardly quiet. A constant chorus of shouts, song, snorting whinnies, and the steady, droning thunder of horse hooves filled the air.

"Why?" Koja finally asked, unwilling to phrase his question completely.

"Why what?" Yamun asked without turning.

"Why does Mother Bayalun . . . hate you?"

"Ah, you noticed that," Yamun reflected. He snapped his mare's reins, urging the horse to go a little faster. Koja had little choice but to follow pace. The ride became rougher.

"I killed her husband," Yamun said in even tones when Koja had caught up with him once again.

"You killed your own father!" the lama gasped in astonishment. He fumbled with his reins, trying not to drop his knout.

"Yes." There was no sign of remorse in the khahan's voice.

"Why? There must be a reason."

"I was meant to become the khahan. What other reason is there?"

Koja dared not speculate aloud.

"Bayalun was the first wife of my father, the *yeke-noyan*. Her son was to become the khan. I was older, but my mother was Borte, the second wife. In my sixteenth summer, the prince was twelve and he died. He fell from a horse while we were out hunting."

Yamun stopped as a messenger from the scouts rode toward him. Yamun waved the man on to Goyuk.

"You see, I was destined to be the khahan, even then. Mother Bayalun, though, she accused me of killing the prince." Yamun turned in his saddle to talk to the priest.

"Did y—" Koja stopped himself, realizing the question he was about to ask was hardly diplomatic.

Yamun eyed the lama sharply, his gaze stabbing like ice.

"She used her seers to convince the *yeke-noyan* I did. Even when the Hoekun were a small people, she had great power with the wizards." Yamun paused and scowled.

"Anyway, my father turned against me. I escaped from his *ordu*, taking only my horse and weapons. I went to Chanar's father—Taidju Khan—and he took me in and fed me. He treated me like a son."

"That's when you and Chanar became *anda*?" Koja ventured.

"No, that was later. Chanar didn't like me then. He was afraid his father loved me more. He was right." Yamun stopped talking and spat out a mouthful of dust. Unfastening a golden flask that hung on his saddle, he swallowed a mouthful of mare's milk.

Koja realized that his own mouth was thick and dry. Still, he didn't care to try the milk brew Hodj had prepared, and the tea was all gone. Taking the long cowl of his robe, he wrapped it over his mouth and nose, screening out some of the thick dust.

"Taidju swore to help and gave me warriors from his own people. We went back to the tents of my father. One day he was riding with some of his men and I found him. He wouldn't listen to me, so we fought. I couldn't shed his blood."

"Why not?" Koja's voice was muffled.

"The *yeke-noyan* was royal blood. Shedding his blood would be a bad omen," Yamun explained as if he was talking to a child.

"What happened?" Koja scratched at the top of his head, paying close attention to the words.

"I seized my father as he galloped by, and we fell to the ground and wrestled. I had to break his neck so I wouldn't spill his blood. After he was dead, I went to the Hoekun *ordu* with Taidju's people and declared myself the khan." Yamun unconsciously mimed the actions as he spoke.

"If Mother Bayalun created all the trouble, why did you marry her?" Koja asked. His horse became restless, so he gripped the reins tighter.

"Politics. Custom. She was powerful." Yamun shrugged his shoulders. "Mother Bayalun has the respect of the wizards and shamans. Through her they are protected. I could not have her turning them against me. Besides, she realized that I was meant to be khahan."

"So why does she stay in your *ordu*?"

Exasperated, Yamun snapped, "Why, why, why. You ask too many questions. Which snake is better, the one in your talons or the one in the grass?" With that, the warlord wheeled his horse toward Goyuk and called out, "What've the scouts seen?"

Koja rode the rest of the day without seeing the khahan. He worried that he had offended Yamun, so he tried to occupy his mind by watching the surroundings. The land was slowly changing. The gently broken steppe was giving way to steeper, harsher hills. Small gorges cut through the dry and rocky ground. Outcroppings of sandstone jutted through the surface in heavily eroded heaps. Snow drifted into the hollows. There were fewer patches of grass and more scrubby brush, but it was probably only the result of twenty thousand horses passing through the countryside.

That night, the army divided into a number of smaller camps. Koja left Hodj to set out the rugs for another night under the stars. The priest walked toward Yamun's oxcart, brushing the dust from his clothes.

"Greetings, Khahan," the priest hesitantly called to Yamun. Sweat-caked dust clung to the ruler's silken clothes. Grime coated his face. Yamun unceremoniously scooped a ladle of kumiss from a leather bucket and guzzled it down.

"Food!" he ordered, wiping the kumiss from his mustache with his sleeve. He scooped up another ladle of the drink. "You don't sleep, priest?"

"No, Lord Yamun," Koja said softly. "I waited to speak with you."

"Then get on with it," Yamun said gruffly. "I want to sleep." He filled the ladle once more.

"I ask to be your envoy to the prince of Khazari." He spoke in a quick monotone, trying to keep himself from panicking.

"Eh?" Yamun stopped in midswallow, looking sharply at Koja over the top of the ladle.

The priest straightened his robes and stood up a little straighter. "I want to be your envoy to the Khazari."

"You? You are Khazari," he sputtered in surprise.

"Khahan, I know it is unusual," Koja hurriedly continued, shifting uneasily on his toes. "But I know my people, and I have learned much about the Tuigan. I am sure I can make them—"

"Yes, yes, that's fine," Yamun said. "Still, these are your people. How do I know you won't betray me?"

"I owe you a life," Koja answered simply.

"What is the truth?" The khahan probed. "Not your rationale—the truth."

Koja sucked in his breath. "Because I want to save Khazari," he blurted. "If you conquer, what will you do with the country? You have not made plans. You know how to conquer, but can you rule?" Koja clamped his jaws tight, waiting for Yamun's outburst.

The khahan slowly returned the ladle to its bag. He paused by the kumiss sack, staring past Koja. Finally, he slapped his knout against the leather bag.

"I'll think about it," he announced at last, his voice cold and unfriendly. "Now I am going to sleep. We ride early in the morning."

"By your word, it shall be done," Koja said with a trembling voice as he made a low bow. The khahan had already turned away, his heavy coat flapping around his bowed legs.

* * * * *

The next day's ride was uneventful, even tedious for the priest. It seemed like a constant battle against minor irritations—biting flies, hunger, and thirst. Dust, churned up by thousands of horses, settled into everything. To Koja it seemed that his robes crackled with the stuff. Dust coated his scalp, which now bristled and itched with a stubby growth of hair; it caked on his eyelids and lined his throat. The hot afternoon sun raised tiny drops of sweat that ran like mud down his arms. All afternoon his horse thudded along in a monotonous, pounding rhythm.

With the evening came a welcome relief from the jolting, bone-breaking ride. Koja gladly turned his horse, a gray and yellow pony with an unmanageable urge to bite, over to Hodj for the night. The lama had taken to calling the horse Cham Loc, after an evil spirit who fought the mighty Furo. Relieved of his mount, the priest decided to walk out the cramps in his muscles.

The army had camped in a bowl-shaped depression, where several streams flowed in together. Koja climbed to the top of a small sandstone promontory on the edge of a steep hill. His guards scrambled along behind him.

On the overlook, the lama sat watching the sunset, a brilliant band of red-orange topped by a sapphire-blue sky. Koja was reminded of another time, when, as a child, he sat at the edge of a towering cliff and watched the long shadows of the mountains fill his valley below.

From his vantage, Koja could see the entire campsite spread out before him. The fires clustered into small knots spaced almost evenly across the floor. In between them were occasional clumps of moving darkness, only a small part of the thousands of horses set out to graze for the night.

"Each fire is a *jagun*," explained one of the guards, pointing toward the shimmering lights.

Koja looked out over the plain with a greater appreciation for the size of the army. He guessed there were a thousand, perhaps several thousand fires dotting the entire valley floor. Absentmindedly he began counting the lights of the *jaguns*.

"We must go now," interrupted one of his guards, "before it gets too dark."

The sun had slid almost out of sight. It cast so little light that Koja could barely see his black-robed guards.

The priest climbed down from the rock, heeding the suggestion. Quietly, he made for the fires of Yamun's camp. The guards hurried after him, carefully staying as close as was their duty but no closer. As they approached Yamun's fire, the guards stopped as they always did. Koja went the rest of the way alone.

Tonight, there was a small group around Yamun's fire, just the khahan and a few of the *noyans*. A *kaychi*, a singer of stories, was sitting cross-legged near the fire. He was a young man, smooth-faced with rounded features and a carefully groomed mustache and goatee. Across his lap lay a small two-stringed violin, his *khuur*.

"Are you at peace?" asked Yamun when Koja was within easy speaking distance. It was a standard greeting that needed no answer. "Sit."

Koja took the seat offered him and accepted a cup of wine a quiverbearer poured. The storyteller struck the first note on his instrument and then put his bow to it, beginning his tale. He sawed at his *khuur* madly as he sang. His voice leaped from high, quavering notes to hoarse growlings.

In a moment between the *kaychi*'s songs, Koja turned to Yamun. "Khahan, although I spoke rashly yesterday, I ask you to consider my request." The priest spoke softly, so only the khahan could hear.

Yamun grunted. "In time, priest, in time. I need to think about it. You'll know in time." The khahan pointed to the *kaychi*, commanding the man to wait.

The singer set aside his instrument. Yamun stood and raised his kumiss ladle to the other khans. "Our friendship has been raised."

The khans around the fire raised their ladles and repeated the toast. That finished, they got to their feet, stopping long enough to kneel to the khahan.

Koja rose and, after a moment's hesitation, knelt too. Before the khahan could call him back, he hurried away. Returning to his own camp, Koja crawled into the rugs and furs Hodj had laid out. Within seconds of lying down, the priest was sound asleep.

When he opened his eyes, Koja was once again on the hilltop overlooking the valley, watching the sun set over the army. The colors were splendid, more intense than he had ever seen them before. The troops formed a black, seething mass, arching and humping over the ground. The men fused and joined into a single being, a freakish thousand-legged centipede, then a dragon that coiled around and bit at itself. The fires flared up, becoming the pinpoints of its eyes. Soundlessly, it writhed and shuddered toward him. Arms, hands, and horses' heads heaved out of the mass and fell back. Koja looked down at his hands, held out in front of him. They were covered with huge droplets of sweat. He suddenly felt fear, a fear that locked every joint in his body.

"It is good to see you, clever Koja," said an emotionless voice behind him. The fear was suddenly gone, and the priest automatically turned toward the speaker. His guards stood at the base of the rock, upright and unmoving. Beyond them, standing on the slope, was his old master. Wrinkles lined the high lama's eyes but his face was bright and clear, not ravaged by age. He was dressed in the formal vestments used on the festival days—yellow, flowing robes with a red sash over one shoulder, a white pointed cone with flaring earpieces for a hat.

"It has been some time since I saw you, Koja," the old man said. "Greetings."

"Why, master—"

"Quiet, Koja," the old master said softly, cutting the younger man off. "Soon you must face the walls you have built, walls stronger than stone. There are secrets in walls, buried deep beneath them. Learn the secrets of your walls."

Koja came forward to grasp his teacher's hand, but the distance between them never closed. The young priest opened his mouth to speak, but the older lama droned on in a curious monotone, now suddenly a voice not his own.

"Your lord is called by one more powerful than he. This spirit that calls him seeks aid. Before you can do your part, your lord will fear you are against him. Be ready to prove yourself." The figure turned to go.

"What? Which lord? Who? Which lord? Wait! Do not leave! Tell me what I should do!" Koja shouted toward the fading figure.

The old lama didn't answer. He only disappeared into the distance of the steppe. Just as quickly as Koja's old master came, he was gone. "The one who calls waits behind you." The master's voice came drifting out of the darkness.

Koja sat alone, staring into the ebbing light. Behind him, he could sense the creature, clawing and scrabbling its way up the hill. Its grasping hands were getting nearer, reaching for him. He wanted to turn but knew he couldn't. The fear that locked his joints had returned.

The thing had reached the top of the rock. Koja could not hear it or see it, but it was there, reaching for him. Sweat poured down his face, dripped off his fingers. Something cold and reptilian lightly brushed his shoulder.

Koja jerked awake and sat bolt upright. Hodj leaped back, terrified at the effect his simple touch had had on his master. The priest was wild-eyed and panting, his robes soaked in sweat.

Hodj stared at his master, then turned back to his work with a slight shrug. Without comment the servant brewed tea and set a cup before the priest. He then began to prepare fresh bags of churned curd. By the time Koja finished his tea, Hodj had the horses ready for the day's ride.

That day the army marched hard. The normal pattern of riding, then grazing, was broken. They stopped only once, long enough for the men to milk their mares. Hodj tended to this task while Koja took the chance to stretch his pained legs.

The respite was over all too soon. "We go!" shouted a

yurtchi. Servants hastily finished their work and ran back to their horses. Almost as suddenly as they had stopped, the horsewarriors were on the march again.

By now, it was getting quite dark, but the riders continued into the night. With the sun gone, the warriors took to guiding themselves by the stars. They used the faint moonlight to pick their way along. Throughout the entire mass of men, only a few torches glittered.

Nothing shown as brightly as the khahan's camp. The great tent cart was illuminated for the first time since the journey began. Bright light shone through the doorway, blinking on and off as the door flap swayed. A swarm of quiverbearers rode around the wagon, carrying torches to light the way for messengers. The nightguards hovered in the shadows, ready to spring to their master's defense.

The army traveled long into the night. Moonlit shapes swayed close, then faded away into the darkness. The snorts of the horses and soft conversations drifted through the night. Occasionally there was a thud, followed by a bitter cry or curse and a burst of laughter as a dozing rider fell from his saddle to the amusement of his comrades. Koja lost track of time and place.

"Master, we stop. I've made your bed." Hodj's voice soaked through the fog, slowly bringing Koja back to consciousness. The sun burned brightly overhead, but the air still felt cold and thin. The pain of twenty-four hours in the saddle burned through every one of the priest's muscles, wracked his back, and twisted his hips. Slowly, his feet dragging over the ground, the lama tottered toward his bed.

The images of his latest nightmare came silently to Koja. Who is my lord? he wondered. Ogandi or Yamun?

Does it matter what I do? the priest's exhaustion-numbed mind finally asked. No, came the answer, only sleep matters. The decision made and eyes closed, Koja pitched forward, snoring almost before he hit the coverlets.

* * * * *

Chanar stared at the scene in front of him. A translucent image of the army, strung out over dusty hills, filled the center of the tent. Bayalun stood, half-hidden by the moving images on the opposite side of the yurt. Between them was a small glowing crystal, the source of the magical scene. "So, Bayalun, Yamun's reached Orkhon Oasis. There—you can tell by the cairn next to the spring. Is it time?"

"Not yet. We cannot be too obvious," the second empress cautioned. "If we strike now, the suspicion will fall on me and everything will be undone. Now that we're out of the deadlands, we can watch them closely. When the right time comes—a battle or something else—then my agent will act." She walked through the image to Chanar's side and placed her hand lightly on his chest. "Patience, brave general. Patience will reward us."

Chanar's eyes moved from the mighty army before him to Bayalun and back again. He bit his lip to restrain his impatient desire.

"Soon, very soon," Bayalun assured him. "Until then, have patience."

- 7 -

Manass

Master," Hodj said softly in his nasal voice. "Master, the khahan wishes to see you."

Koja opened his eyes and discovered that he was looking at a broad field of night stars. He blinked and scanned the sky. In one direction the scintillating points swept as far as he could see. Looking the other way, the lights were blocked by a silver-black range of peaks, mountains outlined by the light of the waning moon.

"Lord Yamun summons you, master," Hodj repeated.

"I hear, Hodj," Koja answered. With his arms, he slowly pushed himself up. His shoulders and back were stiff and pained, but not anything like the agony he had felt earlier. Still, he didn't think he'd be leaping and dancing about for a while. In fact, moving with as little bending as possible seemed like a good idea.

"Help me up."

Hodj slid an arm around the priest and pulled the thin lama to his feet. Koja wavered there unsteadily, lightly testing his weight on each leg before releasing the servant. Satisfied that his knees were not going to buckle underneath him, Koja took a few steps to gently stretch his cramped muscles. While he did so, Hodj hurried into the yurt to fetch clean clothes.

It took Koja a little while to realize this camp was different. His yurt was raised. He turned in a circle, looking over the camp. All around were shadowy, moonlit domes, the rounded shapes of the felt tents. Small welcoming fires blazed on the dusty prairie among the tents. Short, squat, Tuigan men wandered among the fires.

Drifting through the night came the wail of a band of musicians, the scraping notes of the *khuur* and the rhythmic rattle of a yak-hide drum. A singer suddenly added to the cacophony, wailing in the two-voice style peculiar to the steppe. Somehow the man produced both a low, nasal drone and a high-pitched chant at the same time. Koja was glad the musicians were some distance away, as he had not yet learned to appreciate the finer points of Tuigan music. It all sounded like the screeching of evil spirits, or at least what Koja thought evil spirits sounded like, since he had never really heard any screech.

Hodj came out of the tent with Koja's bright orange silk robe, which the priest had packed away for the journey. Although he found his master's insistence on clean clothing odd, Hodj tried to do his best to fulfill the priest's wishes. He helped Koja pull the robe on over his travel-stained garments. It was too cold to take them off, even though the clothes were caked in dried sweat, dust, and grease. Finally somewhat presentable, the priest set out for Yamun's tent.

On his way there, Koja noticed that the soldiers seemed in a very different mood this night. On the surface they were happy and cheerful, but the priest sensed a grim and resolute mood underneath. Around many of the fires, men sprawled against their saddles, drinking ladles of kumiss and swapping stories. At one fire, a thick-mustached trooper held his sword between his legs and scraped along its length with his honing stone. A bright glint of metal caught the priest's eye at another fire. There, another soldier sat cross-legged, a suit of armor stretched out in front of him. It was a fine piece of workmanship, with the same cut as the man's *kalat* but made of overlapping scales of polished steel. He was carefully checking it over, testing the strength of the stitching that held each metal scale to the thick leather backing.

Yamun's camp was larger and more elaborate than the previous night's. The tent-wagon was gone and, instead, Yamun's white-chalked yurt had been raised. The khahan's standard stood next to it. Nearby was another tent, almost as large, patterned with black and white stripes. A smaller standard, unfamiliar to Koja—a pole topped with a silver crescent and a human skull—stood outside its door. There were more nightguards present than usual, all in full Tuigan-style armor and tensely alert.

Koja was hastily ushered into the khahan's tent. Yamun and another younger man sat at the yurt's center, leaning over a low table that had been set in front of them. Trays at their side held cups of Tuigan tea and piles of gnawed bones.

The younger man stopped talking when Koja stepped through the threshold. He turned and stared at the priest. His face, although similar to Yamun's, was more pinched and less heavily lined. His right cheek was badly pitted by the pox, and a half-moon-shaped scar made a pale mark on his forehead. Like Yamun, the stranger had a red tint to his hair. The man's locks were tied in two thick braids that dangled below his shoulders. Silver and shell ornaments capped the ends of his braids.

The stranger wore a long, tight-fitting robe of black silk, imported from Shou Lung and cut in the style of a trooper's *kalat*. Raised patterns woven into it gave the robe a shimmering texture. Beaded red cords, fixed in place with hammered silver bosses, hung from his shoulders. Embroidered across the front of the robe, in red and gold, was a serpentine and leaping dragon against a sea of brilliant blue and silver clouds. A saber, the scabbard covered with deep blue lapis lazuli, hung from his broad golden belt. Koja was surprised by this, for few visitors were allowed to bear weapons within the khahan's yurt.

Yamun didn't glance up as the lama entered, instead continuing the discussion with the newcomer. "Your men are too close to the river. Move your forward *tumens* back. Set their camps between the two hills to the south. You'll keep your own tent here. Have your commanders report to me in the morning." The younger man sat quietly, noting all of Yamun's commands.

"You summoned me, Khahan," Koja said, kneeling on one knee with his head bowed.

"Sit," grunted the warlord, pointing to a space alongside the table. The younger man said nothing, but watched Koja carefully as he took the place indicated.

"Join us in tea, historian," Yamun said, setting his own cup on the table. This is Jadaran Khan, commander of the great left wing. He's been here for a day, waiting for us to arrive."

Koja realized the man sitting next to him, the commander of the great left wing, was Yamun's second son, Prince Jad. He turned and, still seated, bowed respectfully to the royal prince. "I am honored by the brilliance of the commander of the great left wing," Koja lauded, being as polite as he possibly could.

"Enough of that," interrupted Yamun. "We've been talking while you slept. Tomorrow my army rides to Manass. You know this place?"

Koja grew pale. He nodded. "Manass is in Khazari."

"Is it strong?" Prince Jad asked. His voice was similar to Yamun's, but with a nasal twang.

Yamun raised his hand in admonition to his son. The prince instantly fell silent. "Is Manass your home?" the khahan asked casually, as if making small talk.

"No, Lord Yamun," Koja answered guardedly.

"Then none of your clan is there," Yamun said with finality. "That's good."

Jad looked to Yamun to be sure he had permission to speak. "Who rules Manass?" he asked timidly.

"Prince Ogandi, of course," answered Koja. "But he does not live there," he quickly corrected.

Jad nodded. "Who, then, is the khan of this *ordu*? How many tents does he have?"

"I do not know," Koja said apologetically. From Jad's words, he grasped that neither the prince nor Yamun really knew what Manass was. They thought of it as a camp, a collection of tents.

Koja's first instinct was to inform them of their error. Just as he was about to speak he stopped, his mouth open, the words tumbling back down his throat. They would learn the truth soon enough, he decided.

"It doesn't matter," Yamun assured the priest, pouring more tea. "We'll see these things with our own eyes, hear them with our own ears. I won't ask my historian to speak against his people." He raised his cup to the priest. "Ai! I drink to my clever and wise friend."

"Ai!" toasted Prince Jad, his own cup raised. They both noisily slurped at their cups of tea.

"Ai," echoed Koja, a little less enthusiastic than the other two. He sipped slightly at his cup, drinking as little salted tea as possible.

Yamun set his cup firmly down on the table and leaned forward toward Koja. His breath reeked with the smell of sour milk. "I ask my historian, though, to go to his people and give them a message. You've seen my people and how I rule them. Tell your people how I'm generous and kind to my friends. Describe to them the wonders and riches you've seen. Count out the size of my army for your leader." A look of puzzlement crossed Koja's face. "Don't worry, you have my blessing. 'A thief can't steal what is already given.' "

Yamun wiped a drop of tea off his chin with the sleeve of his robe, then continued. "And, when you are done, you must also tell this leader something. Say he must recognize me as the Illustrious Emperor of All People and submit his city to me."

Koja swallowed hard when he heard the new title Yamun was claiming for himself. "They'll never do that."

"Tell the leader of Manass that if he doesn't submit, I'll have him and all the members of his family killed. Tell everyone that death is the punishment for those who defy me, but that I'll spare those who do not resist. And then you must return to me with the answer."

"If you kill them, who will rule for you, Khahan? You can conquer Khazari, but what benefit will that be?" Koja steeled himself as he spoke. "Unless you have governors of your own, you will need the rulers of Manass to keep the peace. But—"

"But nothing. The matter is decided," Yamun snapped. He sat upright, his muscles tense. Koja noticed that Jad was also stiff and hard-faced.

"Now," Yamun pronounced as he rose to his feet, "it's time for you to go and rest. This meeting is over. You may return to your tent, Koja of the Khazari."

The audience ended, the priest quietly slipped back outside and returned to his yurt. During the walk, Koja pondered the surprising outcome of the audience. Certainly the Tuigan warlord was wiser than it seemed. Still, now the khahan's mind was set on Khazari. Koja wondered if Yamun had planned beyond the conquest. Perhaps, he finally decided, I can guide Yamun and protect Khazari at the same time.

In his tent, Koja did not sleep well. All night he awoke in fits, wondering in the darkness what he should do. What should he tell his fellow Khazari? Recommend they surrender or urge them to fight? He was a Khazari, or at least he was when he started this trip, but now he was not so sure. If he told his people to surrender, was he betraying them?

It was a puffy- and red-eyed priest who greeted the dawn the next day. Even the brilliant golden sky that lit the jagged mountains of Khazari could not raise his spirits. Seeing the peaks of his homeland only furthered his feeling of despair. Reluctantly, Koja joined the assembled company of Yamun, Prince Jad, guards, quiverbearers, and messengers. The group mounted their horses and rode along a rising, winding trail that led them up out of the valley and onto the high plain of Khazari.

By the light of day, Koja looked down on Yamun's army. With Jad's arrival, it had swelled to almost twice its number, fifty or sixty thousand men. The yurts filled the narrow valley floor, and dotted among the tents were herds of horses.

Rings of pickets surrounded the camp. At the head of the valley, in the direction they were going, a mass of men was forming up. Rank upon rank of mounted warriors, an entire *tumen*, were preparing to march on Manass.

"I brought you up here to see this. These men come as proof of my word," Yamun explained when he noticed Koja's worried look. "I don't think this *ordu* of Manass can withstand an entire *tumen*." The khahan spurred his horse ahead, angling to join the front of the column.

The troops assembled, the *tumen* set out on the route to Manass. They followed a road, little more than a rutted path, that had been used for centuries by the caravans from Shou Lung—caravans that could no longer cross through the great steppe. From what Koja was able to infer, the army was still a half-day's ride from the city. The khahan was advancing on Manass with only a part of his army, while other *tumens* were to cross the border at other mountain passes.

The small command group rode throughout the morning at the front of the *tumen*. Yamun was preoccupied with his messengers, and he gave a constant stream of orders. A scribe rode at his side, scribbling out the commands, his paper balanced precariously on a little board that, in turn, rested across his saddle. Koja wondered where the scribe came from or if the fellow knew the fate of his predecessors.

Jad rode well away from the priest, surrounded by men of his own bodyguard. At times the prince would ride over to have a word with his father, but apparently had no desire to talk to the priest. Koja didn't mind this. He was not in the mood for company. His own thoughts and concerns possessed him so much that he hardly even noticed the passage of time or the terrain they rode over.

The priest was struck with some surprise when the riders around him suddenly reined up short. The party had just cleared the top of a small ridge. The scouts in the lead came circling back toward the khahan's dayguards.

"Priest, come forward!" Yamun shouted to Koja. This was a moment the lama dreaded. He lightly spurred his horse forward, trotting it up to Yamun. The guards moved away, eyeing the surrounding hills suspiciously.

"There," announced the khahan, standing in his stirrups. He pointed down the slope toward the other side of the valley they had just entered. A small river ran through the valley floor, winding in lazy oxbows through tiny, barren fields. On the near bank of the river was the city of Manass, its white limestone walls shining in the noontime sun.

Koja was surprised by what he saw of Manass. It was much larger than he expected. In tales, the town was never as great as Hsiliang, which was close to the border with Shou Lung, or Skardu where Prince Ogandi lived. Still, Manass was described as one of the guardians against the raids of the mounted bandits who sometimes boiled out of the steppe.

Apparently Prince Ogandi considered the threat of barbarian raids a serious matter, for Manass seemed well fortified. The city was enclosed entirely within a wall. Although it was difficult to be certain, Koja guessed the main wall stretched more than a quarter-mile on each side to roughly form a square. The fortifications were in good repair.

The main gate was large and closed by heavy wooden doors. A gatehouse, several stories in height, was built over the entrance. Other towers rose at the corners. The walls of these were heavily plastered with whitewashed mud, and the roofs were fireproofed by yellow-brown clay tiles. A broad walk ran across the top of the wall and connected each tower to its neighbors.

Within the wall, Koja could see a cluster of yellow-brown roofs broken by the gaps for streets. The city was laid out in a regular grid, the streets running in straight lines according to the advice of ancient geomancers, earth wizards who came long ago from the great cities of Shou Lung. Only occasionally was this orderly pattern broken, perhaps on the advice of these soothsayers or maybe just to accommodate the needs of the citizens.

As Yamun and his party studied the city, a faint sound

came to their ears. It was a long, droning blast with overtones of a higher-pitched whistle. Koja recognized the sound from his years at the temple. It was the wailing note of a *gandan*, a huge straight horn. It took a man with strong lungs to blow one of these instruments. Outside the walls, only a few farmers were in the field, it being too early in the spring to start planting. Those few, however, began a hurried rush to the safety of the citadel.

"Well, they've seen us," Yamun declared. "Go, priest, and deliver my message. Take ten men from the dayguard as an escort." Yamun didn't wait to see his orders executed, but wheeled his horse about and set to the business of arraying his ten thousand.

There was only a little delay as the ten guards were assembled for the escort duty. Koja sincerely wished the wait could have been longer, but before long he was riding through the fields, surrounded by the bodyguard. One of them bore the yak-tail standard of Yamun Khahan.

When they reached the gate to Manass, it remained closed. A deep bass voice hailed them from the gatehouse overhead. "State your business for entering the White City of Manass." The sentry spoke in Khazarish. Koja abruptly realized it had been weeks since he'd heard the clipped sounds of his native tongue.

The bodyguard looked at Koja, waiting for him to speak. Unconsciously standing in the saddle in a futile attempt to get closer to the speaker in the gatehouse, Koja called out in his thin voice, "I am an envoy of the Brilliant Shining White Mountain, Prince Ogandi. I am Koja, lama of the Red Mountain Temple, son of Lord Biadul, son of Lord Koten. I bring a message from the one who calls himself the Illustrious Emperor of All People, the ruler of Tuigan, Hoekun Yamun Khahan. I come under a banner of truce. Open your gates so I can speak with the governor of your city."

Koja waited for the gate to swing open. The doors did not move.

"Who are the men with you?" the voice shouted back.

"They are my escort and bodyguard," explained Koja. "Surely the mighty warriors of Manass are not afraid of ten men." Koja didn't know about those in the city, but he was certainly afraid of them. He was more afraid, however, of the reception he might receive inside if the bodyguards were not present.

"Do they come in with you?" A new voice was shouting out questions now. Koja guessed a higher-ranking officer had taken over the negotiations.

"The khahan of the Tuigan would consider it insulting if his men were made to wait outside," Koja pointed out. "In fact, he might suspect us of plotting against him." Koja looked to the guards on either side. They apparently had no understanding of what was being said—he hoped.

"Your guards must not draw their weapons. Is that understood?"

"Yes," Koja yelled back. His throat was getting sore from all the shouting.

"And there are to be no spellcasters—understood?"

"Only myself," Koja responded, sitting back in his saddle, "and I am a simple lama of the Red Mountain."

There was a period of silence. Koja shifted uneasily in the saddle, looking to see how his guards were taking all this. They sat still in their saddles, waiting for something to happen.

"Priest?" the voice called out.

"Yes?"

"Know this. Should you make the slightest sign to cast a spell, you will be killed before you can complete it. Is that understood?" The voice spoke the last with great emphasis.

"It is understood," Koja answered clearly.

There was a drawn-out scraping noise as the gates were unbarred. It ended with a loud clunk, and then the massive wooden halves began to swing open. With grunting strain, a team of soldiers pushed the gate open wide enough for the riders to pass through.

"Do not draw your weapons," Koja charged his men, "or

we will all surely die. Remember, your task is not to get me killed."

Inside the gate was a company of archers, their weapons nocked and ready. The men stood tensely, lined up on one side of the street instead of both, so their arrows wouldn't accidentally kill their own men if there was a fight. The soldiers wore simple cotton robes, dyed in blues and reds. Koja suspected the robes covered armored suits of leather and mail. Each man wore a pointed cap decorated with the brilliant green plume of some strange bird or beast.

At the far end of the line stood their commander. He was easily identified by the gleaming suit of metal scales he wore. Each scale had been polished to a sheen, so that the officer sparkled wherever he went. In the noonday glare, his armor was almost blinding. "Welcome, lama of the Red Mountain," he said, bowing slightly.

"I am honored to be welcome," Koja replied, using his best diplomatic skills.

Koja cautiously urged his horse through the gate, not wanting to venture too far into the city. He was still very uncertain about the reception he might receive.

"You and your men will leave your horses here," instructed the gleaming commander. "Then you will accompany me to the governor."

Koja translated the officer's words. There was some grumbling from the men about leaving their horses. Koja pointed out that if they did not, they could not go any farther. Reluctantly, the troopers dismounted and handed their steeds over to grooms, who appeared seemingly out of nowhere.

"Follow me," ordered the commander with little ceremony. "Watch, fall in." The archers slung their bows, drew heavy curved knives called *krisnas*—a favorite weapon of Khazari warriors—and took positions on either side of Koja and his escort. The swarthy, robed Khazari eyed the shorter Tuigan suspiciously and kept their weapons ready.

As he marched through the streets, Koja studied the city.

Although he'd never been to Manass, its houses were much like the ones of the small village he grew up in. They were larger here. Most had one or two stories and were built from carefully stacked rocks. The narrow side streets were clogged with goods left outside—jars too large to put anywhere else, half-finished baskets, even outdoor looms. Doors and windows lined the street and curious eyes watched him from the shadows.

The streets remained empty as they marched through the town, but the rickety wooden balconies that thrust out from many buildings did not. Curious children and veiled women crowded on these, threatening to bring the precarious structures crashing down with their weight. Koja saw few men until the procession rounded a corner and entered a large plaza.

This was obviously the heart of Manass. At the plaza's far side was a broad, low building, whitewashed and brightly painted with bands of sutras done in vermillion, cobalt, yellow, and green. Koja recognized the writing and the style. The scriptures were from a sect of the Yellow Temple, rivals to the Red Mountain in power. He read them to himself. "Bohda of the brilliant, five-flame heaven, master of the thirteen secret words, brought to the mountain by the King-Who-Destroyed-Bambalan, so bow to the east . . ." The rest of the verse continued around the building, out of sight. Koja guessed that the inscription was a charm used to ward off evil magic and the evil spirits of the mountains.

The front of the building was dominated by a low portico that ran its entire length. Men, dressed in armor—heavily padded coats of yellow and red that reached to the ankle—and carrying wicked looking staff-swords, formed a wall at its base. More men, equally armed and armored, stood in the narrow streets that entered the plaza, blocking the other routes into the city. Sitting on the portico, near the center, was a group of five men.

Koja bowed to the officials. Foremost of the five was a tall, slender man. A banner behind him portrayed a multi-armed, sword-wielding warrior—the King-Who-Destroyed-Bambalan. This ancient hero was the founder of Prince Ogandi's line and was now revered as a a savior by the people. The figure was the official seal of Khazari. Koja assumed the slender man was the town's governor.

Just behind the governor was a man in loose, draping robes of red and blue. Stains and holes marred the brilliant colors of his clothing. His hair was thick, long, black, and unwashed. In his hand he held a thin iron rod, four feet long, hung with chains and metal figurines. Koja guessed he was a *dong chang*, a wizard-hermit from the high mountains. Most of these men led reclusive lives, seeking only to perfect their magical craft, but sometimes they ventured out of their cold caves and returned to the civilized world. Koja shuddered slightly when he looked at the man. There were many stories about the *dong chang*, few of them pleasant. It was rumored they were actually dead creatures, kept alive by their own meditations and practices.

The third man was clearly a scribe, as indicated by the writing materials spread around him. Koja quickly passed over him to study the remaining men on the stand.

The last two on the porch were a surprise to Koja, even more than the *dong chang* had been. It was obvious to Koja that neither man was Khazari. They wore the long, tight-fitting silk robes of Shou Lung mandarins, the bureaucrats of that great empire. One seemed quite aged, while the other was more youthful, just verging on middle age. The elder had a thin mustache and a fine, wispy goatee, both carefully groomed. His hair was balding and faded, and his eyes drooped in heavy wrinkles. Age spots marked his cheeks and hands.

The younger man's features more clearly showed his Shou heritage. His face was not swarthy like those Khazari around him. His hair was black and straight, bound in a long queue. He wore a small round hat with a long yellow tassel. His face was serious and hard.

As Koja studied these men, the guards that accompanied

him from the gate slowly fell back, forming up in two lines to block the street they had all just come up. His own men moved to form a horseshoe around him, open at the front. Their hands went instinctively to their weapons.

"No fighting!" hissed Koja when he noticed their movement. "Keep your weapons sheathed."

"We shouldn't die like the staked goat before the tiger," urged one of the men under his breath. "Better we fight."

"If you do not touch your weapons, the tiger will not strike," Koja whispered back. "You will fail the khahan if we die. Wait." The troopers stood still, but not a man lowered his hand.

"You claim you are Koja of the Khazari," said the governor from his seat. "You must be willing and able to prove this . . ."

"I am," Koja assured the man, standing as straight as he could.

"It will cost you your life if you're deceiving me. Manjusri, make the test," the governor ordered, signaling his wizard to the front.

The *dong chang* stepped forward and raised his hands, presenting the iron rod toward Koja. The priest's guards went for their swords. Koja grabbed the wrist of the nearest man. "Wait," he ordered. The wizard waved the rod in circles and murmured a deep chant. His eyes were closed. There was a sudden puff of wind that fluttered the magician's robes and tossed his hair about. Suddenly, it stopped. The hermit opened his eyes.

"He speaks the truth, Lord," the wild-haired wizard pronounced. The gaunt fellow returned to his place behind the governor.

"Well then, Koja of the Red Mountain, I am Sanjar al-Mulk, commander of this city in the name of Prince Ogandi. State your message to me as if it were to him." There was no tone of warmth or friendliness in the man's voice, only a faint trace of sneering contempt and disgust for the priest in front of him.

Koja swallowed nervously and crossed his hands in front of himself. "I am a Khazari—"

"Come forward. I cannot hear you," ordered Sanjar. Koja walked closer to the porch and began again, shouting a little louder.

"I am a Khazari, like those of you here. I bear you greetings from Hoekun Yamun, khahan of the Tuigan, who styles himself Illustrious Emperor of All Peoples. He has sent me to you, my people and my prince, to deliver a message. The words of the khahan of the Tuigan are this: 'Submit to me and recognize my authority over your people or I shall raze your city and destroy all those who refuse me.'"

As Koja finished those words, there was a murmur of shock and surprise from the men in the plaza. Many eyes turned to Sanjar. The governor's face was purpled with rage and indignation. "Is that all this barbarian has to say?" he shouted in fury at Koja.

The priest wiped his sweaty palms on his robe. "No, Lord Commander. He also bids you to look over your walls from your highest tower."

"I've seen the reports from the sentries. Your khahan has gathered himself a sizable force of bandits. And now he wants to style himself Illustrious Emperor of All Peoples. He's got a lot to do before he can claim that title," Sanjar sneered. "Does he really think he can capture Manass with that puny force?"

"Yes, he does, Lord Commander."

Sanjar snorted in derisive, insulting laughter. The old Shou gentleman at his side joined in, though he veiled his smile behind a fan. Koja bit his lip to refrain from speaking. Sanjar was treating the whole thing like some great joke, as if the khahan were some thieving buffoon or a common raider. Although he knew the commander was making a grave error, Koja found himself unwilling to speak up. He didn't like Sanjar al-Mulk very much and trusted the Shou mandarin even less.

"It is to be assumed that the brave khahan has chosen a

time by which this insignificant city must reply?" asked the old Shou mandarin suddenly. He spoke fluent Khazari, but with a thick Shou accent.

"The khahan of the Tuigan requests his answer by sundown today," explained Koja. The old man nodded.

"Perhaps sometime tomorrow? After all, there is much to consider here," the mandarin offered. He made no effort to conceal his contempt.

"The khahan is adamant. The answer must be given today." Koja waited to see what the governor would say.

The mandarin leaned over and whispered in Sanjar's ear. The governor's smile was replaced by a grim scowl. He stood up from his chair.

"You will not have to wait so long. This is my answer: Kill them all except the lama. Leave him alive to tell his impudent bandit-lord that Prince Ogandi finds the company of civilized men more to his taste. Tell him injury to Khazari is injury to Shou Lung. Let him think on that!"

Koja was thunderstruck by Sanjar's words.

"What did he say, priest?" demanded one of the Tuigan, sensing the threat in the governor's words.

The lama roused to action. "Quickly," Koja shouted in Tuigan to his guards. "Defend yourselves!"

His words were almost unnecessary, for the Tuigan were already in motion. They sprang back, leaping on the guards who blocked the way back to the gate. The sergeant of the *arban* shouted out commands to his men, driving them like a wedge toward the wall of guards in their path. The lead warrior feinted a high cut and then suddenly shifted it, thrusting his sword under the Khazari's guard. The sharp steel slashed through the soft armor and sliced into the man's arm, shearing down to the bone. The Khazari screamed as his sword dropped, his arm now useless. The other Tuigan hurled themselves into the attack, hoping that sheer fury and surprise would carry them through.

Koja stood flat-footed as the warriors swept past him. He had never been in a real fight before. The speed of the battle stunned him.

The Tuigan slashed deeper into the ranks of the guards. Several Kharazi were already down. One lay clutching at his throat, his blood soaking the ground. Another had crawled out of reach, clutching at his belly, trying to keep the gaping gash across his abdomen closed. Two others lay unmoving. Steel rang against steel; harsh gasps and pants punctuated the battle. Already the guards were starting to waver as the small band of Tuigan drove forward.

"Stop them!" shouted Sanjar, his voice screeching with rage. "Don't let them get away!"

Suddenly Koja heard a droning murmur behind him. He wheeled about just in time to see the *dong chang* shake his iron rod in the direction of the battle. As the wizard finished the spell, a paralyzing force settled over the lama. He tried to fight it, calling on the inner strength his master had taught him to use. In his mind he chanted sutras of power, focusing his thoughts to a single point.

Then, just as suddenly, the paralysis was gone—and so was the noise of battle. Looking cautiously behind him, Koja saw his Tuigan escort and some of the Khazari guards frozen like statues. Each man had been caught in the grip of a magical rigor, locking him in place. Some were lunging, others parried. A few had fallen over, their weight off-balance when the spell struck. Not one of them twitched, blinked, or moved in any way. Around their feet was the blood of their opponents, still flowing. Koja felt his knees go weak.

"Excellently done, Manjusri," the governor said, rising from his seat. "Let the lama take the soldiers' heads back as our answer. Then hang the bodies from the gate."

Several men ran forward with their *krisnas* to carry out the grisly task.

- 8 -
Retreat

The screech of wood on wood signaled the closing of the main gate behind Koja. The Khazari had seated the lama backward on the horse and, with a slap on the rump, sent the beast galloping out the gate. The priest's hands were tied behind him, fastened to the pommel, and bags hanging from the saddle squished and thudded softly against his legs. In these sacks were the heads of his Tuigan escort. The blood soaked through the fabric and onto the hem of his robe.

As he watched Manass recede, Koja heard horses coming his way. There was a jerk at the reins, and the horse stopped. A knife cut away Koja's bonds. Freed, he practically leaped from the saddle, animated by fear and anger. While he stood there, the troopers remounted, leading his horse with them. Before Koja could protest, one man leaned down and hauled the priest up behind him. Then, wheeling their horses, the troopers galloped back toward the Tuigan lines.

In the time it took Koja to deliver the khahan's message, Yamun had been busy. The ridge where the horsewarriors had entered was now a solid line of men and horses. The riders were packed three, sometimes four ranks deep. The different standards—poles with banners, tails, golden ornaments, and carved totems—thrust up throughout the lines. Each marked the position of a different commander.

Koja's rescuers quickly rode past the ranks of hard-bitten campaigners. The priest marveled at the nonchalance of the men who were likely to soon be in battle. Some slept at their mounts' feet, while others drank and boasted of the great deeds they would do today. Most of the men simply watched and waited.

Galloping forward, the troopers delivered Koja to the khahan's banner, set in the center of the long line. Yamun sat on a pure white charger, his son on a white mare at his side.

The troopers opened the sacks and laid out the heads of Koja's escort for Yamun to see. Some of the dead faces stared at him, while others had their eyes closed. Yamun stared back at the heads, rage building inside him. "What happened?" the khahan demanded tersely.

Koja told of the meeting while Yamun strode up and down the line, looking carefully at each head. The priest could see the look of hatred twist Yamun's visage. The Tuigan turned to his scribe as the priest described the last moments of the battle.

"See that their widows and children are taken care of for the rest of their lives," the khahan ordered, speaking in a tight, controlled voice. The scribe took down the words and sent a runner to learn the dead men's names. "Cover them up," Yamun ordered, and then he wheeled back on Koja.

"Where are their bodies?" Yamun demanded of the lama.

"The governor ordered them hung from the gate." Koja spoke softly, out of respect for the dead.

"Then, this is his answer?" Yamun mused grimly. The question was rhetorical, and Koja made no effort to answer it. "We attack." He turned and strode back to his couriers. "Sound the horn! Send in Shahin's *minghan*!"

The standard-bearer ran to the front of the line. There he dipped Yamun's war banner, with its horsetails and gold, five times to the east. At the same time another messenger blew three sharp blasts on a ram's horn. On the east flank, one of the banners, a silver disk hung with blue silk streamers, dipped five times. A line of one thousand horsemen broke from the front and trotted down the slope into the valley.

Even with his limited battle experience, Koja knew a thousand men couldn't take the walls of Manass. The thick gate was soundly closed, so the riders would not be able to gallop in, and they carried no ladders to scale the walls. Their lances were useless against the hewed stone. In his mind, Koja could see the attack: the warriors would gallop forward, shooting their bows from horseback, aiming at the top of the wall. Few of their shots would find a target. Most would only shatter against the stone. The archers in the towers and the battlements would wait, allowing the riders to come closer, and finally draw back their bowstrings and let loose a flight of arrows. The sharp points would cut down the riders like barley under the scythe, just as the governor had promised. Koja rode over to where Yamun was hearing the latest reports from Quaraband.

"Lord Yamun, those men are certain to die!" the priest shouted, pointing to the attackers on the valley below. They were now riding at a gallop.

"I know," he answered without looking up. "This report says Chanar hasn't left Quaraband yet. How long ago did you ride?" he queried a pock-faced messenger.

"Two days, Great Lord," answered the messenger breathlessly.

"But your men!" Koja urged in alarm, pointing toward the valley. "They're all going to die!"

"Be ready to return faster than you came. Now go eat," the khahan warned. Yamun didn't react to Koja's words. The messenger bowed in his saddle and trotted his horse away. As he left, Yamun finally turned his attention to the lama.

"Priest, you may be wise but you have much to learn," Yamun said in irritation. "I ordered Shahin to go forward so we can count their arrows. You did very poorly at noting their strengths, so Shahin must go."

"Count their arrows? You mean he's supposed to learn the strength of Manass's garrison? How?"

"Watch," Yamun instructed. He walked his horse forward, urging Koja to come along. The pair rode to where the

standard-bearer stood. From that spot they had a clear view
of the valley floor. "Watch and learn how we fight."

Koja looked down on Manass. Shahin's riders had assembled just out of bowshot of the walls. The distant thumping
of the *minghan*'s war drum echoed up from the fields. The
riders grouped themselves into wedge-shaped *jaguns*. Shahin, marked by his standard, sat toward the center of the
line. The standard waved to the right and then dipped.
There was a ragged shout, and the right wing of riders
broke away, galloping madly toward the walls. Koja
watched in fascinated horror. The Tuigan were riding to
certain doom.

Before the charging men had covered even half the
ground to the walls, victims of the Khazari archers started
to fall. A man swayed and wobbled in his saddle; a horse's
front legs buckled, somersaulting horse and rider under the
hooves of another charging steed. The bass roar of the
hooves was punctuated by the faint screams of beasts and
men.

The khahan watched the battle intently, his face impassive to the death below. "This is suicide!" Koja cried angrily,
his own frustration at the pointlessness of the deaths well-
ing up in his chest.

"Of course," Yamun said, not even trying to defend his
actions. "But now I learn the enemy's strength's and weaknesses. See, look how many have died in the charge."

"You sent them out so you could count the dead?" Koja
gasped in disbelieving horror.

"Yes. From this I'll know the skill of Manass's archers. See
how many times they fire? How they stand on the wall?"
Yamun turned his horse and rode back to the main camp.
Koja stayed forward, unable to tear himself away from the
deadly farce below. He was stunned that Yamun Khahan,
the great leader of the Tuigan, a man who had conquered so
much of the steppe, would use his men so callously.

On the field below, the first wave of soldiers was returning from its charge. Dead men and horses marked the

course of their attack. Wounded horses thrashed on the ground or hobbled back toward the line. Dismounted riders scrambled over the battlefield, such as is was, rounding up mounts and galloping back to their fellows. Even before the right wing had finished forming, the signal was given and the left wing charged.

The hideous cycle repeated itself. The riders galloped forward, falling as before. This time the priest watched them carry their attack to its conclusion. Suddenly, a little over half the distance covered, the horsemen pulled up, wheeling their horses about. As they spurred their mounts back toward their lines, each man fired an arrow over his back. There was a faint, singing hum as the volley flew on its way. A few of the men on the walls tumbled and fell, some flopping over the battlements, but far too few when compared to the losses of the riders. Still, Koja could only marvel at the foolish bravery and skill of the Tuigan.

Yamun returned as the last charge straggled back from Manass. A horn blared, sounding a recall of Shahin's men. Forming into ragged groups, the riders began to gather up the wounded and straggle back to the safety of the Tuigan lines. As they withdrew from the battlefield, the gates of Manass opened and a continuous stream of riders poured out. Amazingly the Khazari raced out from the safety of the walls, chasing small knots of exhausted Tuigan, thinking the riders were broken. Shahin's warriors kept their nerve, retreating just ahead of the fresh enemy. Here and there, Khazari knights overtook their prey and overwhelmed the Tuigan troopers, but the bulk of Yamun's men avoided death. Koja marveled at the discipline and control of the troopers. There were no signs of rout or panic.

"You said the lord of Manass promised to ride us down, didn't he?" Yamun suddenly asked Koja.

"Yes, Khahan," Koja answered, shading his eyes to make out what was happening below.

"Then this lord's a fool." Yamun stroked the neck of his mare. "I need a plan. If only General Chanar were here."

Koja was surprised at the mention of the khan. "How so, Lord?" he questioned.

"Chanar's a fox, historian. He's a clever one on the battle-field. Between us, I know we'd have a plan." The khahan studied the battlefield below, stroking at his mustache as he thought. The Khazari riders had ridden well beyond the range of their bowmen on the walls. They rode helter-skelter, apparently out of the control of their commanders.

Abruptly Yamun sat up straighter in the saddle and a cold smile came to his lips. "Signal the men off the ridge, out of sight!" he shouted to the standard-bearer. "Then signal Sha-hin to get back here." The khahan wheeled his horse about and trotted back to the khans waiting at his camp. Koja fol-lowed, curious as to what the khahan was up to.

"Khans, I've a plan. We'll move the men off the ridge. Then we attack with three *minghans*." There was a gasp among the khans.

"Three thousand men cannot win," Goyuk said with a scowl across his wrinkled face. "It is not good, Yamun."

"Tomorrow is when we'll win. Remember the battle at Bit-ter Well?" Yamun hinted. Goyuk's face brightened. "Into the tent," the khahan ordered, bustling the surprised warriors into his yurt. Koja stepped to follow, but a pair of guards stepped into his path. Before Koja could call for the khahan to intercede, the door flap fell shut.

The meeting went on for almost an hour, during which time messengers came and went. While he waited, Koja saw the troops shift and move their lines, making a show of re-treating from Manass. When the meeting finally ended, the khans hurried to their positions. Yamun and Jad were busy with reports and messages, making it impossible for Koja to question either man. The priest could only guess what would happen next. Finally, Yamun ordered a seat prepared on the ridge. Koja followed behind, waiting for events to unfold.

"Now," ordered Yamun as he looked over the valley. A sig-nal blared behind Koja. The standard-bearers ran forward again and waved their poles. There was a rumble of shouted commands, jingling harnesses, and drumming hooves as more troops began to stream down the slope.

The late afternoon sun was falling low in the sky by the time the three *minghans*, three thousand men, reached the fields outside Manass. Koja was confused and curious. He still didn't see how without siege equipment—ladders, ropes, and the like—Yamun hoped to breach the walls of Manass. Perhaps there was something the lama didn't know about warfare. It looked to him like a foolish waste of lives. This attack would fail, leaving more dead and wounded. What could Yamun intend by these hopeless attacks? the lama wondered.

Koja could not contain his curiosity anymore. Perhaps in his role as historian the priest could learn Yamun's plans. He strode through the throng of messengers, seeking out the khahan for some type of explanation. As he came forward, he was surprised to be greeted by the hulking Sechen and another guard of the Kashik.

"You will come with us, Khazari," said the wrestler. The guard's voice was hard and tinged with an unpleasant threat. Koja decided not to argue. "The khahan has given orders for you to be confined to a yurt. You will come with us." Sechen drew a knife meaningfully.

"But I've done nothing!" protested Koja.

"You are Khazari. Come with us or die." The guards flanked him, each taking one arm. Resigned and more than a little fearful for his safety, Koja allowed himself to be whisked away.

The guards placed him in a small empty yurt. Koja had no idea where his servant or his belongings were. Sechen and the other man took position outside the door. Koja, with little else to do, sat near the door, trying to glimpse the activity outside and listen to whatever he could hear.

For a long time, nothing in particular happened. Then, as the sun was almost set, he heard a familiar thunder. Horses, a large number of them, were on the move. Soon the noise grew louder and louder. Koja could only imagine the scene on the other side of the ridge. The *minghans* were advancing with the setting sun at their backs, to blind the archers on the walls. The lama strained to hear more. Faintly, echoing through the dusk, were the blasts of horns and the deep, staccato roar of war drums. A ringing, higher note rose above the lower rumble. At first, Koja could not place it, then he realized that it was the sustained cries of screaming horses and men.

The battle for Manass had been joined, and all Koja could do was listen.

The noise continued for about an hour after sunset, gradually growing fainter and less insistent. Koja sat still, rapt by every crash, cry, and wail that reached him. The battle was a failure, the lives were wasted; he was convinced of this. He imagined the ground outside Manass was strewn with gutted horses and broken men. Koja choked back an involuntary sob at the thought of the suffering pointlessly inflicted.

This was Yamun's vision of conquest. It was a dream, filled with blood, valor, and death, but nothing more. Koja wondered if this, the futile attack on Manass, was really what Yamun's god had shown the khahan in that thunderstorm. Was this what Yamun wanted?

Before today, the priest thought Yamun would conquer Khazari. He also had been sure that Yamun could somehow be persuaded to leave it unharmed and safe. Koja had tried to hint and suggest the possibilities for peaceful rule. What hope was there of that now? If the khahan was willing to send his own men to certain death, Koja knew Khazari could expect no mercy from the Tuigan warlord.

Images of the dream came back to him as he began pacing around the yurt. His old master had talked of his lord, and the strange creature claimed Koja was with the khahan. Who was his lord? Prince Ogandi had sent him as ambassador to the Tuigan. The khahan had sent him as ambassador to the Khazari. Now he was a prisoner. Koja felt lost, the events of the day casting his own actions into doubt. There was no treaty between the Tuigan and Khazari as a result of his actions. Instead, there was an army on the border of his homeland. He, as envoy, had failed his prince.

Exhausted, the lama sat back down and prayed to Furo for guidance, silently whispering his sutras as he sat huddled near the door. Finally Koja realized what he must do. As a lama of the Enlightened One, Koja must guide the khahan to be a true ruler, more than just a warlord.

His decision made, Koja strained to hear any sounds of the struggle, but the tumult of battle had ceased. Koja sat patiently, until sleep finally settled over him.

The guards came and woke the lama during the night. It was dark and bitterly cold in the thin mountain air, and Koja was shivering from the instant he awoke.

"Quickly," ordered Sechen, "come with us." The lama groggily heard the words without really understanding them. The guard grabbed him by the arm and pulled him to his feet. "It's time for you to go."

"Go where?" Koja managed to ask as the Kashik pushed him through the doorway. His bodyguards were being none too kind.

"Away. We're leaving," Sechen offered as explanation. It didn't tell Koja much. The guard pushed the priest toward a horse. Servants were already setting to the task of taking down the yurt. Indeed, the camp seemed to be astir, but in an oddly silent way. The normal sounds of breaking camp— the grunted shouts, clatter of cups, even the braying of camels—were all missing. The men, even his guards, spoke in hushed tones. The fires, normally blazing, were damped to the lowest coals.

"I would like to see the khahan," Koja declared as he became more aware of where he was.

"You will," answered a guard, much to Koja's surprise. A servant held the horse for Koja to mount.

"What is going on?" Koja demanded one more time. Somehow he suspected the question was futile.

"Be quiet," Sechen hissed. The other guard nodded in agreement, smiling with a mouthful of crumbling, decayed teeth. They roughly hoisted the priest into the saddle and then mounted their own horses. The big wrestler reached over and took Koja's reins, leading his horse along. There was no clopping of horse's hooves; the pace was marked instead by a soft plodding. Koja looked at the lead horse and saw that its hooves were wrapped in bindings of rags. Wherever the army was going, they were taking great efforts to do it quietly.

The group rode in the darkness for some time, going mostly downhill. All around, Koja could hear the quiet movements of other riders. Shapes moved in and out of his vision. The lama wondered if they were moving to Manass. Had it, against all possibilities, fallen to Yamun's attack, or was the khahan secretly reinforcing whatever remained of the three thousand men already encamped outside?

As the hours went by, the priest became confused. They traveled too long to be going to Manass, even though they went slowly.

With the dawn, Sechen and his fellow guard finally came to a halt. They were on the edge of a rocky bluff overlooking a flat valley floor. A line of birches marked the course of a small stream that cut through the valley. Behind Koja were more trees, making the tops of the low mountains dark blue-green in the morning light.

While Sechen watered the horses, another nightguard came with a message for the wrestler. "The khahan orders you to send the priest to him," was all the man had to say. In a very short time, Koja found himself in Yamun's camp.

The Khazari priest expected the camp to be like a furious beehive of activity, with Yamun hearing reports and issuing orders, couriers galloping in and out, and commanders plotting out strategies—just the way he imagined any great leader's camp must be during times of battle. When he got there, however, he was astonished. Yamun Khahan, his son Jad, and the old Goyuk were all sitting on stools, drinking hot cups of Tuigan tea.

Slightly off to the side was a wrinkled, old wizard. In the weak light of the dawn, the sorcerer looked drawn and lean, radiating an otherworldly feeling. Perhaps it was the effect of spending a life steeped in strange magics. Koja knew that the arcane arts took a toll on their masters, sometimes even draining them of vitality.

Like the others, the wizard was sipping a cup of tea, although he did not join in the muted conversation. Instead, the wizard sat close enough to their circle to listen, but looked the other way, watching the sun rising over the ice-frosted peaks of Khazari.

Yamun and his companions did not appear to be hurried or concerned, rather more like a group of men relaxing before a hunt. They looked up, noting Koja's presence. Jad made a show of watching the tree line while old Goyuk smiled his bland smile and noisily sucked up his tea.

Yamun stood as Koja came closer to the circle. "Welcome," he said evenly. Koja could not guess what Yamun's temperament was. "Sit. Have some tea."

Koja dutifully took his place, trying to decide how he was being treated. In just a day, he'd been a diplomat, a prisoner, and now—well, he just didn't know. So many things had been going on, and none of them seemed to make sense. "Khahan," he inquired, "am I your prisoner or your envoy?" Koja chose his words with care, trying not provoke the khahan into some rash action.

"In my land you are my historian," Yamun explained, rubbing at his chin. "In Khazari, you are Khazari. Some of my khans think you are a clever spy for your people. I do not want them worrying about you."

Koja stammered, "But—but, Great Lord, you sent me to Manass to deliver your ultimatum just yesterday."

"Yes, but remember, you asked. I thought you could persuade them to be reasonable." The khahan took Koja by the arm and led him away from the others. "You didn't. And you came back with ten dead men. There have been questions."

"Questions?" Koja's voice hardened in unexpected anger.

"They are groundless and insulting," Yamun assured him.

"But there are questions . . . so you have me confined," Koja said, a trace of bitterness in his tone.

"Yes," Yamun said simply. "It was for your own safety."

"My own safety, Yamun?" Koja asked skeptically, irritated at the suggestion.

"If you wander about before a battle, people think you are a spy. If you don't, no one kill you. Is good plan," chortled Goyuk, interrupting from the other side of the circle. The old man seemed to be in a particularly good mood this morning.

Koja mulled over the old general's words. There was some sense to them, but he still wondered if Yamun had some other reason for his confinement. "What happened last night? I heard sounds of fighting," the priest questioned, trying a different subject.

"Are you the khahan's man or Prince Ogandi's man?" Jad interrupted. He stood, watching Koja carefully. The prince's eyes were dark and hard. Finally, the priest broke the stare, stealing a look toward Yamun.

The group fell silent, waiting for Koja to answer. Yamun settled back on his stool, fingering a small knife while he watched the priest carefully. Goyuk did a poor job of pretending to be interested only in his tea, but he, too, watched the nervous lama from the corner of his eye. Only the wizard looked away, seemingly unconcerned. Still, Koja could see the mage flexing his wrinkled hands, the long fingers practicing the motions needed to cast a spell.

Koja tried to consider his choices carefully, but his mind was filled with memories that tugged and pulled against each other. There were the oaths of loyalty he swore—to Ogandi, to the Red Mountain Temple, to the god Furo. There was his father, sitting next to the fire in wintertime, then Yamun bending over his pallet and Chanar's hate-filled glare. Overriding all these images was the dream of his old master standing in the darkness, building walls.

"I have no lord," he whispered. The memories faded from his mind. Jad relaxed, but showed no pleasure in the priest's words.

Yamun stirred and stepped forward. He laid one hand on his son's shoulder and the other on Koja's. "My historian is an honest man. 'Liars never say no, fools never say yes,'" he quoted, looking at Jad.

"Ai!" agreed Goyuk. He raised his cup high and then took a long noisy slurp.

"Ai! To our success today," pronounced Yamun, letting the two go. Jad found his cup and raised it in a toast. Koja fumblingly found his own cup and raised it up.

The men sat and drank another cup of the hot tea. Even Koja was thankful for the salted brew. It soothed his tired, tense nerves. The priest had no idea what was to happen this day, but for now he was content to wait.

Finally, Yamun spoke. "It's time to get ready." Jad and Goyuk nodded in agreement and stood. "Goyuk, take command of the right. My son, you lead the left. I'll take the center. You, Atraslb," he commanded, pointing at the wizard, "will stay with me. As will you, Koja."

"Where are we going?" the lama asked hesitantly, hoping that he might now get an answer.

"It is time to put my plans in motion," was all that Yamun would say.

- 9 -
The Trap

Yamun Khahan paced along the bottom of the dusty gully, kicking at stones and scraping little patterns in the dirt with his toe. Occasionally he stopped and marched up the slope and stood at the edge of the tree line to gaze across the plain. To his left and right, sheltered in the gully, were two thousand horsemen, huddled below the level of the plain.

In preparation for the coming conflict, Yamun wore his battledress—a glittering steel breastplate engraved and chased with flowers, a leather skirt sewn with metal plates, and a golden pointed warhelm. A coif of chain mail hung from the back of the helmet, covering his neck. The metal draped on Yamun's body clinked as he walked.

For the last three hours or more, the khahan, Afrasib, Koja, and a host of troopers had waited, more or less patiently, in the gully. The dry wash ran a jagged course, coming down out of the hills to the north and then angling to the southwest, where the mouth of the valley opened into the broader fringes of steppe. A thin stand of willows and tamarisk lined the banks, giving shade to the weary men. Koja, tired of watching Yamun pace and tired of waiting, sat against the base of a tree. Sechen stood nearby, never letting the priest get far from him.

Even in the shade, Koja was sweating. The big wrestler had found a suit of armor for the priest, a heavy thing of metal plates stitched to leather, in the style common to the

Tuigan. The armor was ill-fitting, with absurdly big shoulders and long, droopy sleeves, but Sechen had insisted that he wear it. "You might be hit by an arrow," the guard warned. The helmet Sechen had produced fit little better than the armor.

Koja watched as the khahan turned from the plain and came back down the embankment. Yamun fretted back and forth, impatient for something to happen.

"Why do we wait here, Khahan?" Koja asked as Yamun ventured close.

Yamun, stopped short by Koja's question, scowled at the priest and almost snapped a sharp reply. Then he relented. "We wait here to capture Manass, historian. At least that is the plan."

"Manass?" Koja asked, amazed. He struggled to his feet, the armor scraping against the tree trunk. "Here? But how?"

"They're going to enter the trap," Yamun answered, marching back to the gully's edge. Koja noticed that the khahan spoke with less than his usual absolute conviction. The warlord looked to where Koja stood. "Come here, priest."

Koja joined the khahan, walking awkwardly in the heavy armor. Yamun pointed toward the upper end of the valley, where the land rose to a low pass nestled between the mountains to the east. The trail to Manass crawled over the pass.

"Look there," Yamun instructed, pointing to a spur that ran down into the valley floor from the north. "See the dark line? That's Jad and his men." Koja squinted, barely able to see the line Yamun indicated. Years scanning the emptiness of the steppe had sharpened the khahan's eyesight far beyond Koja's.

"Goyuk's men are across the valley, near those trees," Yamun continued as he swept his hand across the plain, stopping on a wooded slope.

"If you say so, Khahan," Koja responded, unable to see any sign of troops there. "But, you are here and Manass is far away. I do not understand how you plan to conquer the city by fleeing from it."

"Manass will come here, if all goes as planned," the khahan murmured, his head sank to his chest. Lifting his chin, he continued in a stronger voice, "We will *bring* Manass here, historian."

"How?"

"You told me how the lord of Manass acted. He calls us bandits," Yamun answered, turning away from the plain. "So I act like a bandit." He looked at Koja. The lama's expression showed he was still confused.

"Yesterday I attacked and lost—on purpose." Yamun held up his hand, stopping the startled outburst Koja was about to make. "Not many men died. Their orders were to make it look good and then flee. This morning I left one troop near Manass, to lure the garrison out, make them pursue. I just hope Shahin Khan can do the task. If Chanar were here, I know they'd follow. There's nobody better for baiting the enemy." He gave the lama a wan smile.

"But why should the garrison leave the city walls?" Koja asked. He shrugged the oversized armor back into place.

"Their commander is foolish. Yesterday, when Shahin retreated, the Khazari left their walls and chased our men. They did not have to, so last night I made a feint. My 'bandits' attacked Manass and failed." Yamun pointed toward the ridge. "This morning the Khazari see a retreating enemy. They will chase Shahin, hoping to destroy him." Yamun stopped and took off his helmet. Sweat ran down the back of his neck. "If that's not enough, Shahin has orders to burn whatever he comes across near the city.

"That will force the lord of Manass to come out. He must protect his herds and his people." Yamun wiped the sweat from his forehead. "He would be disgraced if he hid behind walls of stone. From what I've seen, he'll want to fight. After all, we're only bandits." Yamun set his helmet firmly back in place.

"And then?" probed Koja.

"Then Shahin lures the Khazari here," Yamun stated calmly. "Shahin will ride past us, and we will stay hidden.

On the signal, my men strike the Khazari on the flank while Jad and Goyuk close in from behind."

"And if no one chases Shahin?" Koja asked.

"Then I've guessed wrong about the lord of Manass," Yamun answered. "He would be wise to stay home, but he will come." The khahan scanned the horizon as he spoke.

Koja waited for Yamun to dismiss him. Finally, the khahan turned to other details. Koja went back to his tree and tried to settle in for a nap. Although the lama was tired, sleep wouldn't come.

Flies buzzed lazily overhead. Another hour went by without Shahin's arrival. The morning was slowly becoming a hot spring day. There was nothing for the priest to do but wait and pray.

"They come, Yamun Khahan," panted a messenger who ran up and knelt at the great lord's feet. "The scouts signal that Shahin is coming."

Yamun turned from the man, waving forward another messenger. "Go to Prince Jad. Tell the prince his father reminds him not to move until the signal is given." The messenger hurried to his task.

At the announcement, Koja scrambled to his feet. "Things are almost ready," Yamun eagerly explained. "Shahin's done it. Now all we need to do is close the trap." The khahan strode up the gully's side and watched the pass.

"Khahan, will this be dangerous?" the priest asked, joining Yamun. So far, Koja had only seen battles, never been in one.

"Of course," Yamun replied. "All battles are dangerous." The khahan shaded his eyes and continued to watch, ignoring his historian.

"May I cast some spells—purely for protection? I am not a warrior—"

"No!" Sechen growled, stepping forward to guard Yamun. "No spells." The muscular wrestler glowered down at the priest. Koja lurched back in surprise.

Realizing what he had done, Sechen suddenly stepped back and knelt at Yamun's feet. "Forgive my anger, Great

- 157 -

Lord. I was only trying to guard you."

Yamun studied the man carefully. "You mean well, Sechen," he said, reassuring the fretting giant. Turning to Koja, Yamun said, "You'll take your chances with the rest of us. No spells."

The decision made, Yamun climbed a small rise of crumbling rock, Koja and his guards in tow, to get a better view. Koja reached the top with sweat running down the sides of his glistening, stubbly scalp.

"There's Shahin," Yamun abruptly said. He pointed to the far ridge. Shielding his eyes, Koja could barely make out a thin sliver of moving gray. The khahan scrambled down the slope and headed for his standard, waving his arm to bring the army to attention. Koja, panting and sweating even more, stumbled down behind him.

By the time the khahan reached his standard, messengers were already starting to arrive. Yamun pushed his way through the crowded gully, past the expectant troopers. As he did so, a messenger ran forward and dropped to one knee. "Jad reports that his men are in position," the man called out.

"Good. Standard-bearer, use the white banner for the right," Yamun commanded without breaking his stride. The trooper bowed quickly to show his understanding.

"Scouts say Goyuk is ready," added one of the khahan's aides. He was little more than a boy, perhaps fourteen or fifteen years old. His face was still round with baby fat.

"Why hasn't Goyuk reported this?" Yamun snapped, the aide falling in beside him. They squeezed past a knot of horses eagerly pawing at the ground. The troopers stroked the animal's muzzles, trying to calm them.

"I don't know, Lord," answered the aide apologetically.

"Then find out!" the gruff warlord growled.

"Shahin has reached the valley floor, Great Lord," yelped a messenger who galloped up to the top of the gully. Yamun stopped and scrutinized the man as the courier swung from the saddle.

"Who's your commander?" the khahan queried.

"Buzun. One of Shahin Khan's men, Great Lord," the man hastily answered, falling to one knee. Streaks of sweat colored the dust on his clothes. One braid of the man's hair had come undone, and the other was caked with grease and dirt. His eyes were staring and hollow from lack of rest.

"What of the enemy?" the khahan demanded as he walked up the slope to question the man. "Does Shahin have anything else to report?"

"The garrison is chasing him, half a mile behind, maybe a little more, Great Lord. No more than a mile," the messenger said. Koja climbed up to where the warlord stood.

"How many men chase Shahin?" pressed Yamun.

"Three *minghans* of riders. Two of men on foot—but they are farther behind."

"Damn!" Yamun grumbled. "They can't be allowed to escape." He wheeled to his aides. "Send riders to Jad and Goyuk. Tell them not to attack until after the footmen pass by. They're to give a signal, the war drums, when the infantry is in the trap. We'll hold our attack until they signal. You—" Yamun turned back to the messenger. "Go back to Shahin and tell him to harry the riders, slow them up. I want the enemy pushed tight together. Tell Shahin his losses are not important."

The messenger bowed quickly, fired by the khahan's urgency. "Get this man a fresh horse!" Yamun bellowed down to his aides in the gully. "You—give him your horse!" He jabbed his finger at the nearest trooper. Startled and flustered, the man dropped to his knee.

"By your word it so—um—so shall it be!" he shouted. The man led the horse out of the gully, bowing to the khahan at every step.

Yamun turned back to the messenger. "Go! I want those Khazari chasing Shahin in full pursuit!. Understand?"

"Yes, Khahan," the man shouted, scrambling to his feet.

Yamun didn't even wait for the courier to leave before he turned his attention to the lines of troops filling the gully.

"Give the word," he told the aide still at his side. "It's time to prepare."

Those simple words had an electrifying effect on the army. There was a murmur of voices as the order was passed along, then a chorus of creaking leather and metal. Men hustled up off the ground, where they had been lounging. Saddle cinches got a final tug. Honing stones were dragged in one last scrape along already sharp swords. Heavy, stifling armor was pulled on. Kumiss bags gurgled as veterans poured themselves a drink; there was no telling when they would have another chance. Horses pawed at the ground, shifting unsteadily under the sudden load of metal-clad men. A whisper of chanted prayers drifted on the wind. Like a wave on the ocean, men mounted their horses, the action flowing outward from the khahan's word.

Then they waited, waited for the nine-tailed banner of the khahan to be raised high and the war drum to be sounded. These were their signals, and not a man would move until they were given. Those that rode forward too early would be beaten. Those that fled, beheaded.

Koja climbed into the saddle of his own horse, a cumbersome task in the oversized armor that he wore. The scale mail bagged out around his chest giving him the appearance of a large metal-plated balloon, or, with his pointed helmet, an upside-down top. The helmet promptly slid forward and smacked against the bridge of Koja's nose. The weight of the armor on his shoulders was crushing. Koja uncomfortably shifted in the saddle. He knew a warrior's life was not for him.

Yamun rode to Koja's side, unable to suppress a devilish grin at the priest's comical appearance. "There's going to be a battle—more than I planned. Shahin will need help in holding the cavalry long enough for the infantry to be caught in our trap," the khahan explained. "You're to ride with me, where the guards can protect you. Even so, you may have to fight."

Koja pushed the helmet off his face. "I'm no warrior," he protested. "It is against the teachings my temple to harm another. I cannot risk offending my god. Khahan, I cannot fight."

"Then you can get your head smashed in. The enemy's not going to be so fussy," the warlord pointed out. "Here, take this." He held out a heavy metal-studded club. "It doesn't take much to use. Just don't bash your horse in the head." The scowling warlord grabbed Koja's wrist and slipped the weapon's thong over his hand. "Keep that on, so the mace doesn't go flying the first time you swing it."

The weight of the mace pulled Koja to one side. A hand grabbed his shoulder and pulled him back into the saddle. A sharp snicker came from behind him. Koja turned in time to see a dayguard laughing at him. There was something about the look of the man that disturbed him, something not quite correct. The man's face didn't seem quite human. Koja blinked and wondered if exhaustion and sunlight were playing tricks on his eyes. Noticing the priest's stare, the dayguard quickly slipped behind a horse and disappeared from sight.

Mounted, Yamun's soldiers sat as silently as they could, trying to catch the first sight of Shahin and his men. Warriors stood in their saddles, shading their eyes to break the glare from the sunny plain.

It was a sound that first warned of Shahin's coming: the steady reverberation of galloping horses. Alerted, men strained to see their approaching companions. A plume of dust rose from the valley floor, driving fast in their direction. New sounds reached the army: garbled but piercing screams, resounding metallic rings, even an occasional shouted command.

"Up!" Yamun yelled to the standard-bearer. The nine-tailed banner rose over the gully. A ragged shout spontaneously erupted from the line as men urged their horses forward. The steeds scrambled up the bank, tearing at the soft dirt with their hooves.

"Hold!" shouted Yamun as the double line reached the edge of the trees, still hidden from sight. The standard-bearer waved the banner from side to side. The standards of the three *tumens* did the same. The lines drew up and came to a halt. Koja could hear the commanders of the *jaguns* shouting at their men to dress out their lines, evening out the ranks.

Koja swallowed what tasted like a mouthful of dust. He quickly recited sutras to Furo, trying to remember any that told of success in battle.

With growing speed the dust cloud whirled toward Yamun's position. Shapes formed out of the murk, becoming wild horsemen who whipped furiously at their mounts. The distant drone of hooves grew to a deep, rolling thunder; the cries and shouts became more distinct. As the priest sat watching, Shahin Khan's golden banner flew past. The riders continued down the valley, following the narrow angle of the dry wash. The dust of their passing roiled up and swept over Yamun's men in the tree line, hiding them from sight.

"Excellent," shouted Yamun over the fading din. "Shahin's men kicked up enough dust to cover us. Keep the men back until the signal's given."

The drumming hooves and whoops of the riders gradually died away, though the dust still hung thick in the air. Koja wrapped a scarf over his mouth and squeezed his eyes shut. Around him he could hear men coughing and horses prancing with excitement.

The noise of Shahin's men was replaced by sounds of the Khazari cavalry's galloping pursuit. The dust clouds had barely opened up when another wave of riders burst out of the gloom. The pounding hooves, the jingling of metal, and the shouts were all the same, but the riders charging past were wearing the yellow and blue of Manass.

Koja nervously glanced down the line of warriors to his right, a line that faded into the haze. The mounted men were grim-faced, hands tight on their reins. They, too, watched the passing riders nervously, waiting for the kha-han's signal. The priest looked back to Yamun and saw him sitting, grave and impassive, only the slightest look of concern on his face. Koja pulled the scarf from his mouth and leaned sideways to ask the khahan a question.

Then, a different rumble, fainter and lower in pitch, added to the noise. It was the deep boom of war drums, rolling from the distance. Yamun suddenly sat straight and raised his hand to the signalmen beside him. "Bows and drums," the khahan commanded.

The aide next to the khahan quickly took his own bow and nocked a strange arrow with a carved, bulbous head. Instead of aiming at the enemy, the man pointed the shaft upward, as if he were shooting at the clouds. The rank of signalmen prepared similar arrows.

At a slight nod from the khahan, the archers shot their arrows skyward. A chorus of howling shrieks pierced the din. Koja, startled, yanked on the reins of his horse, almost charging his mount into the chaotic fray. Sechen seized the bridle and held the horse in. "Whistling arrows," the big guard shouted, nodding upward where the shafts still flew, mournfully wailing over the galloping riders.

The whistling signal electrified the waiting troops. Koja watched as each man eagerly pulled a bow from his case and, with precision, nocked one arrow while gripping a bundle of others in his hand.

The khahan dropped his hand. Another flight of whistling arrows flew, followed immediately by a loud twang, like a badly tuned instrument, as the ranks fired their bows. The shafts hissed through the air, stabbing into the gloom. From the plain came a ragged chorus of startled cries. Through small gaps in the swirling dust, Koja saw a field dotted with a few dead and wounded. Other horsemen milled in confusion, panicked, as they tried to find the source of the attack.

Before the enemy could recover, Yamun's warriors shot again and again, sending their arrows into the slowly lifting murk. The cries of the wounded mixed with commands shouted in lilting Khazari that only Koja could understand. Officers were desperately trying to regain control of the confused mass. Men screamed of their injuries or called for their friends and horses. The dust began to settle, revealing a battlefield filled with confusion and fear.

"Now, before they recover, charge!" the khahan ordered. The nine-tailed banner waved forward, and the war drums were sounded. Down the line Koja could see the three banners of the *tumens* take up the signal. Three thousand men leaped from their positions.

Koja pulled back on his reins, holding his horse from the rush. The mare pranced and bucked, champing to join the tide that rushed outward. Even with Sechen holding the bit of Koja's horse, it was hard to restrain the skittish steed.

Only after the ranks had swept past did Yamun move forward. Steadily, the khahan and those with him gained speed to keep up with the galloping warriors strung out in front of them. Soon they were abreast of the stragglers—lamed horses, fallen riders hurriedly remounting, and nags that couldn't keep up. Koja clung to the pommel as he plunged forward, straight for the thin wavering line of enemy riders.

For Koja, the battle dissolved into a chaotic collection of scenes. There was no sense of order or place. It was not like the battles Koja had imagined: organized, proper, almost stately. Instead, the charge was like opening the doorway to the realm of Li Pei, the great judge of the underworld.

The first seconds of the attack were the clearest. As the leading men of the Tuigan tore into the flank of the Khazari cavalry, Koja could see the looks of utter astonishment and fear on the enemy's faces. The Khazari were still confounded by the torrent of Tuigan arrows and didn't seem to expect a charge.

The two armies met. A sound, like a peal of thunder, tore through the milling crowd. Koja had never experienced that instant when two lines met. The shock of first impact— horses, men, lances, and armor driving together—staggered him.

Almost instantly the two forces swirled into a mass. The Tuigan rode straight into the enemy, using their momentum to cut deep into the heart of their foes. The Khazari wheeled in confusion, and they lashed out in all directions. Commanders shouted orders to their men, desperately trying to regroup their units.

Before Koja could fully grasp the situation, Yamun and his command were among the enemy. An unshaven warrior with a gaunt face, dressed in a dirty silk robe with gilt trim, thrust a lance at the priest. Instinctively, Koja swung his mace up, batting at the oncoming shaft. The lance head ricocheted off the mace's shaft and skittered past his arm, bouncing off the metal plates of his armor. As the man swept past, a big fist shot out from the right, cracking the Khazari on the chin. The warrior toppled and thudded off the flank of Koja's mare. Sechen pulled close to the lama and grinned, holding up his fist in pride. The priest twisted back, horrified at what was happening. The fallen Khazari was nowhere in sight; he had vanished beneath the surging horses' hooves.

After that, Koja could no longer tell who was winning or even who was friend or foe. His horse leaped over a mortally wounded stallion that flailed madly on its back. Wild screams rattled around the terrified priest. A warrior stood, tottering. His body was braced against the end of a broken lance, which had been driven completely through his chest. Another soldier swayed weakly in his saddle, clutching the bloody stump of his wrist. His eyes were glazed and almost rolled completely back. He babbled prayers to some god. Two troopers grappled with a third, trying to throw him from his saddle.

Abruptly the fighting seemed to stop. The charge had carried Yamun's men through the enemy. The effect was dramatic. The sudden appearance of the warriors had set the Khazari cavalry into panicked flight. The broken lines streamed back the way they had come, ignoring their officers, leaving their wounded behind.

"Signal the pursuit," Yamun bellowed to the standard-bearer. Already the commanders of the *jaguns* were gathering their men. The standard waved, and the war drums quickly picked up the signal. Not allowing the Khazari troops a moment to regroup, Yamun hurled his riders after them. The lines of Tuigan cavalry quickly fanned out.

A rider wearing the armor of a Tuigan dayguard furiously whipped his horse, overtaking Koja. Some headstrong young warrior out to impress his khahan, the lama thought. He looked to see who it was, on the faint chance he knew the man. To his amazement, it was the dayguard he had seen earlier, the man who had aroused his suspicion. Hard behind the man came Afrasib, the wizard. He held no weapon but a slender bone wand. A flashing spark shot from the end, then a sudden gout of flame exploded far to the right. A wavering line of smoke hung for a second in the air. The wizard laughed aloud, deriving some maniacal pleasure from the destruction.

Suddenly, Yamun's group ran into another cluster Khazari, men who had no intention of turning their horses and running. There must have been twelve or more of them grouped under a commander. Sechen's momentum carried him through the defenders. His charge scattered the group. Some of the Khazari lancers veered off toward Yamun's standard-bearer, forcing the man away from the khahan. Two charged toward Koja, only to be met by the priest's guards. The suspicious-looking dayguard continued to whip his horse mercilessly, driving it toward the khahan. Koja wanted to call the man back, then realized the guard's job was to protect the khahan, not him.

Koja saw the dayguard, his foxlike face gloating, move close behind Yamun. The priest assumed the fellow was only coming to the support of his ruler, but he suddenly lunged forward, thrusting his lance into Yamun's back.

The khahan howled in rage and pain. Twisting in his saddle, he swung his saber in a blurring backhand swing. There was a brief, dull sound as Yamun's blade sheered through the man's collarbone and cut into his chest. The would-be assassin dropped his lance in surprise. Blood flowed freely from the rent in his armor. He fumblingly drew his sword and weakly jabbed at the khahan. The thrust missed, but pierced Yamun's white mare in the rump. At the same time, the Khazari lunged forward, sensing an opportunity to strike.

Yamun's mare squealed in pain from the dayguard's blow and lurched forward, crashing through the two enemy riders. One man's horse staggered, knocked sideways by the charging mare. The rider clutched at the mane to keep his balance, forgetting his attack. He quickly lost his balance and fell to the ground.

Still acting with fearful speed, Yamun recovered from his backswing and thrust his sword forward, sweeping the point up. The tip of his saber slid under the bottom of the other Khazari's breastplate. With a quick twist and pull, Yamun gutted the trooper. The man's eyes widened in surprise and pain, his hand automatically reaching to his belly. The lance dropped from his dead fingers, and his body slowly fell forward. The khahan's sword, still half-entangled in the body, was twisted from his grasp.

The khahan suddenly sagged back in his saddle, too exhausted to recover his weapon. Dark red blood, his blood, soaked the back of his armor and stained the silver fittings of his saddle.

Koja realized there was no one else around to aid Yamun. Instinctively, Koja jammed his heels into the belly of his horse, driving it forward. The dayguard assassin, clinging to his saddle, was about to strike the defenseless Yamun from the rear.

Urgency drove Koja to form a mystic shield of deflection around the khahan. With one hand wrapped in the reins and his legs clamped around the chest of his mount, the priest tried to trace the arcane symbols in the air and chant the necessary sutras. Only the grace of Furo could save Yamun now.

The assassin's sword lunged straight and true for Yamun's neck just as Koja's spell was completed. An unseen force seized the khahan and moved him away from the attack. It was not enough. The tip of the assassin's blade struck Yamun's shoulder, splintering through the armor and drawing new blood.

The swing pulled the assassin forward, toward the khahan. Just as the man reached the limit of his lunge, Yamun reached out and grabbed the assassin's arm. Fiercely the old warrior yanked, dragging the treacherous dayguard off his saddle. A long-bladed dagger appeared in Yamun's other hand. Without letting go, he punched the blade into the killer's side. The man gave out a horrible, inhuman scream, then writhed and twisted in the khahan's grip. Even injured, the warlord refused to let go.

At that instant, the dismounted Khazari ran forward, his blade swung high. Yamun saw it coming out of the corner of his eye. An agonized grunt escaped his lips as he heaved the squirming assassin, still spitted on his dagger, into the air. The body crashed headfirst into the Khazari, and the two of them slammed to the ground.

A thunderous yet screeching roar reeled Koja's senses. Waves of sound hammered at his eardrums. Just in front of him, Yamun clutched at his skull, rocking in agony. The khahan crumpled and fell off his horse, hitting the ground like a slab of meat.

Tears of pain welled up in the holy man's eyes, blocking his vision. The howling scream ended as quickly as it had started. Gasping against the pain, Koja clutched at his horse's mane and wiped the tears from his eyes. Looking back, the priest saw Afrasib, a look of smug victory on his face. As the wizard rode forward, he pointed the bone rod, the wand of fire, at Yamun's motionless body. Koja could see the wizard's thin shoulders heave with laughter, even though all sound was blocked by the roaring pain in the priest's ears.

Koja knew he must do something, for the protection he'd

already cast on Yamun was useless against the wizard's magical attack. Fortunately, Afrasib seemed to pay the lama no mind. Desperately, Koja looked around for someone to come to the khahan's aid. The Tuigan attack had done its job too well; Yamun's troopers were caught up in chasing the fleeing enemy. Ahead, the lama could see the big form of Sechen, but the man was too far away to do any good now.

Koja thought of the spells he knew. He needed one that would stop Afrasib completely, not just hurt him. So long as the wizard was alive and able to move, he was dangerous. The only chance, Koja realized, was to freeze the wizard in place. The lama fumbled through the small bag hanging from the pommel of his saddle, searching for the right ingredient to work the spell. Under his breath he mumbled praises to Furo and the Enlightened One. Now, more than ever, he needed their assistance.

Quickly, Koja's fingers closed on the small iron ball he needed for the spell. Tearing his hand from the sack, the lama flung the pellet at Afrasib, while shouting out the words of the spell. Still unable to hear, Koja could only assume that he said the words correctly.

Instinctively, Afrasib recoiled from Koja's throw. His body rocked back in the saddle and, as the iron ball struck, froze in an oddly tilted pose—one arm upraised to ward off the pellet and his body arched backward. His face was twisted with surprise and anger. The wizard stayed in the saddle for just a moment, and then tipped sideways, body still locked in his comical pose. Afrasib hit the ground, still stiff and unbending.

Koja collapsed against his mare's neck, breathing the sweet saltiness of its sweat in relief. Then he remembered Yamun. Awkwardly, the lama slid off his horse and stumblingly ran to where the khahan lay, faceup in the dust.

Before examining the body, Koja was certain that Yamun was dead. Then, unexpectedly, Yamun's eyes fluttered. Koja stopped, disbelieving. Quickly he rolled Yamun over to examine his wounds. One sword stroke had laid open the back of the khahan's left shoulder. Blood still flowed from it, soaking into the khahan's armor.

Using a dagger, the priest slashed away the leather straps of the armor, peeling away the heavy shirt. The floppy sleeves of his own oversized suit of armor got in the way. Frustrated, he hurriedly struggled out of the heavy scale mail. Tearing away a piece of his own robe, Koja packed the cloth against Yamun's wound and continued his examination. Farther down Yamun's back was a hole where the lance had struck. Again Koja hacked with his knife to see the wound. It was small compared to the cut on the shoulder, but it had driven deeper. Blood and bile seeped out of it. The edges were purple and swollen. Koja pressed at the wound gently. Yellow-green pus oozed out under his fingertips.

"Poison," he said aloud. Koja went back to his examination, then suddenly realized that he could hear. The knowledge reminded him where he was and, fearfully, he looked around in case an enemy was creeping up on him. There were no Khazari nearby, but Koja saw Sechen and the standard-bearer headed his way.

"Over here!" he shouted as he leaped to his feet. "Here! Yamun is here!" His words had an electrifying effect as the two Tuigan whipped their exhausted horses into motion. Sechen didn't even bother to slow down as he approached. The big warrior leaped from his saddle, sword drawn.

"Back, Khazari demon!" Sechen snarled as he sprang forward, pushing the little priest away. "You'll die for this!"

"He is dying! Look at them! Look at the wizard!" Koja shouted in frustrated anger. He pointed at Afrasib's frozen form. "I might keep him alive! Just let me work."

. At that moment the standard-bearer shouted, "Sechen, come here! Look at this!" He was standing where the dayguard assassin and the Khazari had fallen. The trooper was underneath, apparently killed by the fall. The dayguard lay sprawled, facedown on top of him.

"Look," said the man. With the toe of his boot he gingerly

rolled the dayguard over.

Sechen sucked in his breath in surprise. The man that lay there was not a man at all. His face had been replaced by that of a large fox. The soft brown fur of its muzzle was thick with blood. Its hands were long, slender paws, but with human fingers, not like an animal's.

"By mighty Furo," Koja breathed, looking up from Yamun's side. "That's a *hu hsien*."

"What's that?" Sechen demanded.

"An evil spirit," Koja answered hastily. "It attacked the kha-han. Now let me help!"

The Tuigan warriors looked at each other, each hoping the other had an answer.

"Very well," Sechen decided, "but if he dies, you die." He squatted near the lama to watch his every move.

Koja quickly set to work. "Get the bag off my horse," he ordered. The standard-bearer hurriedly fetched the bag, passing it to Sechen.

The first problem was the poison. Taking an herb from his bag, the lama pressed his hands on the lance wound and uttered a prayer. There was a heat beneath his palms as the spell began to take effect. "The khahan's been poisoned. I cannot stop the venom right now, but I have slowed the poison to keep it from killing him out here. This may give me time to pray for a cure." Koja carefully explained everything he did to defuse Sechen's suspicions.

That finished, he examined the wounds again. They were bad, but probably not serious enough to kill the khahan. Still, if Furo allowed, it was best to heal them now. Bowing his head in prayer, the priest counted out a rosary on his beads. When he completed the plea to Furo, Koja's hands itched and trembled with the power coursing in them. Gently he placed a palm on each wound, then pressed them down firmly. Yamun stirred and groaned under the pain. Blood seeped through the lama's fingers. The heat once again grew under Koja's hands, this time stronger and lasting longer.

DAVID COOK

Sechen sucked in his breath through his teeth. "Look. His wounds are closing," he whispered. Pinkish-white skin grew before Sechen's eyes, knitting the wounds shut and leaving only a slight scar. At last, Koja took a deep breath of relief and took his hands away. He tore off another shred of his robe, spit into it, and daubed away the blood and fluid to check his handiwork. Koja watched the khahan's chest rise and fall until he was satisfied the man slept quietly.

"The khahan is better," Koja explained as he sat back in the dirt, shaking from exhaustion. "However, the poison is still in him, and he could still die. Can you take him back to camp?"

Sechen nodded. He looked at the priest in wonder.

"Are you sure? What about the battle?" the lama asked.

"You saw. This battle is over. We won. Prince Jad and Goyuk Khan will finish things here." Gently, Sechen lifted the khahan in his arms.

"Then get him to his tent. He needs rest," Koja urged.

"By your word, it shall be done," answered Sechen. "But you will come with me." Sechen nodded to the standard-bearer. "He will tell the prince what has happened." Koja struggled to his feet and helped Sechen hoist the khahan into his saddle. Yamun barely opened his eyes.

"Oh, yes," Koja said, "the wizard, Afrasib, lies over there. He helped the *hu hsien* and would have killed Yamun. Right now, he cannot move, but he will recover soon. You might want to do something about him." The standard-bearer looked at the oddly frozen figure on the battlefield and grinned unpleasantly. Before Koja could stop the man, the trooper ran over and neatly slit the spellcaster's throat.

"I've always wanted to do that to one of Bayalun's lackeys," he coldly proclaimed. As Koja sat, stunned with horror, the standard-bearer mounted his horse and galloped away to inform Prince Jad of the khahan's condition.

"He should have kept the wizard alive to question him!" Koja shouted.

"Priest, the wizard got what all Bayalun's kind deserve.

Just consider yourself lucky not to be among them," Sechen grimly explained as he led their horses back to camp.

* * * * *

That night there was a council in Yamun's tent. Outside, the finest and most trusted of the nightguards ringed the yurt. Each was dressed in full armor and heavily armed. They were nervous and jumpy. Already several rabbits had died from rapidly fired arrows when they made a little noise in the bushes. The guards eyed each other as well. The rumors were already circulating through the camp— stories of treachery among Yamun's bodyguards, whole cadres of wizards, and evil monsters rising out of the ground.

Those inside the yurt were no less tense. The spacious tent was almost completely dark. A small iron pot of glowing red coals provided the only illumination, barely lighting the grim faces of the men present. Yamun lay on his bed, conscious but very weak. There was very little color in his face. Under Koja's supervision, he was covered with several layers of heavy felt blankets. Perspiration beaded on Yamun's brow as the priest tried to sweat the poison out of the khahan's system. Sitting on the rugs at the side of Yamun's bed were Jad and Goyuk, little more than dark shapes in the darker yurt.

Koja had spent the last hour carefully telling his version of the day's events. Jad sat with his head bowed to the floor. Goyuk nodded as he considered the priest's words. Koja, now finished describing how he had treated the khahan's wounds, sat silently with his hands on his knees, waiting for the others to speak.

"It is good to have gods on your side, even if they are the gods of strangers," Goyuk said in a rambling tone. It was very late and the day had been long. Fatigue was showing on the old khan's face; his eyes drooped and he slumped as if he were some exhausted vulture.

From his bed, Yamun sighed and focused on the big guard

at the back of the yurt. "Sechen, did it happen as the lama said?"

The guard shambled forward, nodding. "What I saw is as the priest said, Khahan," the wrestler answered, stiffly bowing.

"I remember the guard attacking and the wound," Yamun added. He pushed himself up onto one elbow. "Historian, you saved my life. Therefore, Koja of the Khazari, I ask you to be my *anda*." Yamun weakly extended a hand to the priest. There was a gasp from the group.

"Great Lord! I—I am not worthy of this," Koja stammered, his face reddening with embarrassment.

"That's not for you to say. I choose who will be my *anda*." Yamun pushed his shaking hand out toward Koja.

"Father!" protested Jad. "You are weak and need rest. Think on this later."

Yamun growled, "Be silent, my son. Koja saved my life and that has earned him the right."

"Yes, Khahan," Jad replied, cowed.

Yamun looked toward Goyuk to see if he had any objections. The old khan only sucked on his gums, keeping his counsel to himself. The khahan shifted his gaze back to the lama.

"Well, priest?"

Koja took a breath to steady himself. "I cannot argue with your wishes. I am greatly honored. I accept." He took the khahan's hand.

"Then we are *anda*. From this day, you are Koja, little brother of Yamun." He gave the priest's hand a weak squeeze and then dropped his arm. "From now on you must call me Yamun."

Koja looked at the others. Goyuk was unreadable, his old, lined face barely betraying any emotions. Sechen looked stern as always, but there was a glimmer of respect in his eyes. The prince's brow was furrowed with concern, and he avoided the gaze of the priest. Koja was not sure if he was upset or merely confused.

"The men have fought well today," Yamun continued weakly. "Jad, report on the battle." He closed his eyes and let a ragged breath escape his lungs.

The prince roused himself, putting whatever thoughts he had to the back of his mind. "Father, your plan succeeded. The foot soldiers followed the riders into the trap, and Goyuk and I were able to surround them. The khans have taken many prisoners." Jad bowed slightly toward his father, who was not watching.

"What of losses? Shahin's men?" whispered the stricken khahan.

"Goyuk and I lost few men. The foot soldiers couldn't catch us, and we simply shot arrows at them until they surrendered. Your men did not fare badly, though they lost more because they were involved in the heaviest fighting. Shahin's *tumen* has lost many brave warriors, Great Lord. More than half of his men are killed or wounded." The youth waited for some word from his father.

"Not too bad," Yamun commented with a sigh. "Give the prisoners the choice of service or death. Those that join us are assigned to Shahin's command." He coughed a little and then wheezed out the rest. "What about Manass? The governor?"

"He was cowardly and did not come out, Father. Our messengers have already delivered the heads of his generals. I thought you would want this done," Jad answered, sliding closer to the bed. "He sends back messages of peace and friendship. Manass will be ours."

"And soon all of Khazari," added Goyuk, glancing at Koja to see how the priest reacted.

"Indeed, all of Khazari," agreed Yamun.

"Were the assassins from Manass?" Jad asked.

"It makes sense," Goyuk concurred.

"No, it doesn't," Yamun disagreed with a weak sigh. The two khans looked at him in surprise. "Why would the governor send his army if he had assassins? Besides, Afrasib is one of Bayalun's people." The khahan let the point sink in for a moment while he recovered his strength. "What was this creature called, the one that attacked me?"

"A *hu hsien*, Khahan," Koja explained as he fixed Yamun's covers. "They are evil spirits who often do men harm. I heard tales of them at my temple. They appear as foxes normally, but can disguise themselves as people. It is said the emperor of Shou Lung uses them as spies because they can change their shape."

"It could have been this emperor," Jad offered.

"The emperor of Shou," Yamun mused. "Perhaps."

"You have many enemies, Yamun," Goyuk pointed out. "Why would this emperor attack you now?"

"Why, indeed?" Yamun slowly pulled one arm out from under the sheets and began to stroke his chin. "Perhaps he fears me. Perhaps he knows that I can conquer his land." Yamun's eyes glazed slightly. Koja quickly wiped the khahan's sweaty brow with a warm cloth. Yamun closed his eyes and then spoke again. "So, one of Bayalun's wizards was involved."

Koja nodded. "Yes, Khahan—er—Yamun."

"You shouldn't have let them die," Jad pointed out. "We could have made him talk."

"Your father's guards were most incensed and did not heed my suggestions," Koja answered defensively.

"Still, they should not have died," Jad snapped, his jaw stubbornly set. "Perhaps we'd now know who was responsible for the attack on the khahan."

"Do you have their bodies?" the priest suddenly asked, turning to Jad and Goyuk.

The prince was taken aback by the lama's question. "Yes. Yes, we do," he answered, flustered.

"Perhaps you can have your answer," Koja offered mysteriously. "See that their bodies are not burned. If mighty Furo is willing, I will speak to them." Confused, the prince looked into the gloom at the priest.

"Afrasib is Bayalun's man. Then she's suspect, unless the wizard acted on his own. Bayalun. The emperor of Shou.

Perhaps one, perhaps none," the khahan murmured feebly from his bed. "I do have many enemies." Yamun paused, his strength temporarily exhausted. The others sat silently, considering his words.

"How long can I be dead?" the khahan asked suddenly.

"What?" Jad blurted out.

"I want everyone to think I'm dead. How long can you keep the army together?" Yamun turned toward Jad.

The prince thought for a little bit. "Without you, two, maybe three days. There are already rumors."

"I say four or five days. The men are good men. They listen to your son," contradicted Goyuk, punctuating his comment by sucking on his lip.

"Jad, you'll keep them together as long as you must. No one must know what's happened me," Yamun said in the best commanding tone his weak voice could manage.

"But, why?" Koja asked. "Don't you want to reassure your men?"

"Someone—Bayalun, the Shou emperor, or someone else—wants me dead. They're sure to have more plans in mind. If I'm dead they'll reveal themselves by their actions," Yamun explained as if he were talking to a child. His speech was stopped by a fit of coughing. Jad and Goyuk looked away, politely ignoring the khahan's weakness.

The priest helped Yamun sit up to clear his throat. "You need rest." Yamun, still wheezing, tried to wave Koja off, but the priest refused to take his seat. He pulled the blankets up to wrap them over the khahan's shoulders. "You need rest now, unless you want to die."

Yamun was wracked by another fit of coughing. "All right," he gasped out. "Go to your tents, all of you. Jad, I'm depending on you. Listen to Goyuk and the priest. Now, leave me." He sank back onto the cushions, breathing noisily between the intermittent coughing fits.

Jad and Goyuk exchanged worried glances and then bowed to the floor. Silently the two took their leave. As they went out the door, Koja took a blanket from a pile at the foot of Yamun's bed and wrapped himself up in it. He curled up on the floor beside the Illustrious Emperor of All People and tried to make himself as comfortable as possible. Tonight he would stay in Yamun's yurt, to watch over his patient—his *anda*.

– 10 –
Dead Voices

The only glow that lit the darkness came from a rough crystal, the size of a large egg, nested on a tripod of wrought iron. The stand's small legs ended in finely chiselled rams' heads covered in gilt. Small, facetted garnets decorated the curling horns of the beasts, tapering back into the black iron of the supports.

The crystal shown dimly with the warm colors of sunlight. Chanar marveled at it. Staring into the stone was like looking out on a sunny morning through a small hole in the tent wall. Warmth and light danced in front of his eyes, just beyond his reach. When he stared into the stone closely, he thought he saw shapes flicker and fade deep in its heart. He wondered what Bayalun, sitting across from him, saw as she hunched over the orb.

The khadun chanted. Her nose was practically pressed against the crystal, and her hands were carefully cupped around the base of the tripod.

Chanar squirmed. His legs were going to sleep, but he didn't want to move for fear of disturbing Bayalun. She had been sitting in the same position for the last half-hour, repeating the same chant over and over again. Chanar wondered how she managed it. The chant was mind-numbing. At first he thought it was Tuigan, badly distorted, but that quickly proved to be wrong. Whatever she was saying, it was in no language Chanar had ever heard. The general was sure of that. He'd had thirty minutes to listen and be certain.

Abruptly Mother Bayalun ended the chant with a huffing sigh of exhaustion. She sat up straight, arching her back, and rubbed her temples hard with her fingertips. The crystal still glowed between them.

"Look," she commanded as she lightly touched the stone. The stone's glow shimmered and then expanded, filling the air between them. Bayalun spread her hands open and the light spread, too.

A scene formed and grew within the light. It was a yurt in the bright morning sun. Guards stood rigidly outside, ringing it. A tall standard set near the doorway flapped in the breeze.

"That's Yamun's yurt!" Chanar exclaimed.

Mother Bayalun laughed. "General Chanar, you are so charming," she said. "Yes, that is the khahan's tent." She stood up, leaning heavily on her staff, and stiffly walked to his side. "Look," she commanded again.

Chanar peered closely at the scene. "There's old Goyuk . . . and Jad," he whispered, pointing at the image.

"There is no need to be quiet," Bayalun croaked out. She stopped to clear her throat. "They cannot hear us."

Chanar nodded, still watching the scene. He stepped back to give the image space. The general wasn't about to let it touch him.

"Look!" Bayalun suddenly hissed. "Look at the banner! It's just as they said." She pointed at the pole standing in front of the yurt. From it, gently swinging in the breeze they couldn't feel, were nine black yak tails.

"The sign of death," Chanar said softly. He stared for a time at the slowly waving tails. "Yamun's dead?" He turned to Mother Bayalun, not really accepting what he saw.

"Of course," she assured him confidently. "Why else would they fly the banner?"

Chanar bit back the desire to scold Bayalun for her callous words. The dead deserved respect. "I want to see Yamun's body," he suddenly demanded. His green silk robe glittered and shone in the light from the crystal.

The sorceress shook her head. The hood fell from her face, allowing her rich gray and black hair to hang free. "It cannot be done. There are protections on the royal yurt, placed there by Burekai—my husband. The crystal cannot see inside it."

"Then how do you know he's dead?" Chanar countered. He eyed the image suspiciously.

"Because he must be. They would not fly the banner if he was not dead." Bayalun's face showed her absolute conviction.

The general considered her reasoning, pulling at his knuckles while he stood there. Chanar agreed after a moment. "But why don't they keep his death a secret? Without the khahan, the army will fall apart."

"The men must already know," Bayalun offered as she circled the glowing image. "Otherwise, you are right, Goyuk and Jad would keep the death a secret."

Chanar nodded, agreeing with her conclusions. "That would be Goyuk's way—until he could get Jad safely in control of the khans."

Bayalun looked at Chanar through the image. "Of course, we will dash any plans Goyuk has formulated."

Chanar smiled cruelly and then watched the scene, absorbed in his own thoughts. Figures came and went—Jad, Goyuk, Sechen, and Koja. As the bald-headed lama stepped out of the royal yurt, Chanar spit on the floor in disgust. "That one dies," he snarled, jabbing a finger at the priest.

Bayalun snorted to herself. "As you wish." She had no intention of giving the priest to Chanar just to satisfy his pride. The lama might be useful. After all, he was an emissary of the Khazari and an avenue to the Red Mountain Temple. If nothing else, she would keep the lama just to remind Chanar of her power. However, for now she was not going to tell him of her plans.

"Before you can execute anyone, Chanar, you must be khahan. We still have that to do," she reminded him in regal tones.

Chanar grunted in irritation. "Well, what now?"

"First, we wait while the army bickers and grows restless. Those two cannot hold the army together for long," Bayalun pointed toward the khahan's tent. Goyuk and Jad stood outside it. "Then, you will arrive and give them order."

"What if Jad keeps the army together? He's Yamun's blood, after all," Chanar pointed out as he stepped closer to Bayalun.

"Then we will deal with him, too. The army has khans who will listen to you. It will just take a word here and there to keep them unhappy." She smiled reassuringly. "With my magic, you can appear to them in a dream."

Chanar frowned at her suggestion. This, he thought, was not the proper way to become the khahan—using dark arts to sway the minds of warriors. "Why don't I just go there and speak for myself?"

"Don't be in such a hurry. Let the young prince stumble and fall." Bayalun stepped into the image; Koja and the others swirled like ghosts around her. She bent over slowly, supporting herself with her gold-topped staff. With one long, sharp finger she tapped the crystal and muttered a word under her breath. The image suddenly withered away.

"Strike a light," she ordered. While Chanar blew on the small pile of coals that smoldered in a metal bowl, she carefully lifted the crystal off the tripod and wrapped it in a leather bag. "General, you must be ready to leave at any time. Timing is everything in this. Too early and the khans will suspect you. Too late, and Jad will have rallied the *ordus* to his banner. Either way you will lose your chance." She looked up from her work and stared sharply at him. "The men will serve under you, will they not?"

"They love me," he answered. "They trust me."

"You had better be right." The khadun crossed the tent and undid the door flap, a clear signal for Chanar to leave. He bowed slightly to her and stepped out through the door.

After Chanar left, Bayalun sealed the tent flap and knelt

down near the brazier. After taking one last look around, she was satisfied that she was alone. Quickly the sorceress whispered a few mystic words and sprinkled a handful of incense into the coals. The powder burned quickly, billowing into a heady puff of white smoke. The smoke rose, twisting and massing. Gradually, it formed into a face, a man of Shou features, handsome, with steady, dark eyes.

"Greetings to the khadun of the Tuigan people," said the face in a whispery, hollow voice. The words were spoken in perfect Tuigan, though colored with a distinct Shou accent.

"Greetings to the Minister of State," Bayalun replied. "May he live forever."

The face smiled, the smoke drifting away at the corners of the mouth. "All is well?" it asked, puffs of smoke swirling from its mouth with each word.

"The khahan has been struck down," Bayalun answered gloatingly. "It happened in battle. Soon there will be a new khahan." She tapped the floor decisively with her staff.

"None suspect our involvement?" the form asked in soft words.

"Do not worry, mandarin. No one knows your empire sent an assassin." Bayalun mocked the mandarin's fearful caution.

The smoky face ignored her tone. "It is sad for your people. Surely none chosen as the new khahan can hope to match the illustrious glory of Yamun Khahan. The new khahan will need many advisors and learned men to help him through these difficult times." The face was growing indistinct, as smoke trailed from its nostrils and ears.

"And, of course, Shou Lung will offer them," Bayalun noted. "Remember too, the new khahan will also need friendly, helpful neighbors—and assurances of their goodwill."

"We have already decided the gifts that will be sent, Khadun," the minister said sternly. "Are you trying to renegotiate? Many of your people would be angry if they learned what you have done."

Bayalun's face purpled slightly. "They might blame Shou Lung instead," she snapped back. "A khahan, any khahan, is dangerous to you if all the tribes follow him alone."

"This is true. Then we understand each other perfectly," the face said faintly. "Now it is time for me . . ." The last words trailed off into silence, and the smoky face became nothing but a shapeless mass.

Standing, Bayalun waved her staff through the vapors to break up the cloud. There was no particular reason for it, but she felt powerful doing it. Moving stiffly, her arthritis flaring up again, she crossed the tent and undid the door flap to let in the cool morning air. A beam of sunlight illuminated the room. With little else to do but wait, she sat in its pleasant warmth and rested.

Today has been a good day, she reflected. Everything seemed to be working as she had planned. There was only one minor concern. Neither the *hu hsien* nor her wizard had reported. Afrasib had strict orders to keep her informed. It wasn't like him to forget her commands. He was normally so diligent and attentive.

Still, Afrasib's failure was only a minor problem. Most likely, the wizard had not had a chance to contact her with his spells. Besides, all that really mattered was that Yamun, her stepson, was dead. Now, the khadun had to place Chanar on the throne before any rivals could challenge him. Once Chanar was khahan, she would rule the Tuigan through him.

* * * * *

In Yamun's tent, the three conspirators, Koja, Jad, and Goyuk, hovered around the khahan's sickbed. The warlord was barely awake. His face was pale gray, tinged with a hint of blue. His breath came in labored sighs, wheezing in and out. A damp film of perspiration trickled across his shaven tonsure. His braids, which normally hung from his temples, were undone, spilling the graying red hair over his embroidered pillow. His eyelids wavered between almost closed and not quite open.

Jad pulled the priest aside, away from Yamun's hearing. "You said he would get better," the prince whispered. There was a touch of danger in Jad's words, perhaps fueled by desperation.

Koja swallowed nervously. "He has lived through the night, Lord Jadaran. That was the first struggle."

"Then why hasn't he gotten better?" Jad demanded, pressing the priest back toward the wall.

"I—I don't know," Koja feebly protested. He suppressed a tremor that started to come over him, brought on by fear and exhaustion. For two days the priest had slept no more than an hour. Judging from Jad's appearance—hollow-eyed and haggard—the prince had rested no better.

"You don't know!" Jad snapped in frustration, slamming his fist into the carpeted wall beside Koja. "What do you know?"

"Lord Jadaran," Koja said firmly, his patience gone, "I am no expert in poisons. I have closed the khahan's wounds and lessened the poison's fire. I did what I could, thank the almighty Furo. There is nothing more I can do. His life rests on the scales of Li Pei."

"Li Pei?" Goyuk asked, just catching the end of the conversation.

"The Strict Judge, the master of the dead who weighs the karma of men."

"This no sound good" Goyuk commented, shaking his head.

"So you say there's nothing you can do, priest?" Jad asked, slowly realizing that events were out of their control.

"There is nothing I can do for the khahan," Koja said carefully, "but there is still something I can do."

"What's that?" old Goyuk asked.

"Speak with the dead. It is difficult and maybe a little dangerous," Koja explained, "but Furo has blessed me with this ability."

"Wonderful. You propose to wait for my father to die and

then talk to him!" Jad growled. He spun away from the priest and strode to the khahan's sickbed.

"Not the khahan." Koja followed after Jad, trying to explain. "I meant—"

A sigh suddenly escaped from Yamun's lips, and his eyes fluttered. "A plan?" the khahan breathed out softly. Weakly looking toward the others, he tried to speak again, only to falter and fall back upon his pillow.

Koja wasted no time with more speech. Quickly he pulled back the covers and listened to the khahan's chest. His heart was still beating, and his breathing was slightly stronger. Still, his color was pale blue-gray, and his sweat was cold. The priest squeezed at the khahan's tough and weather-beaten hands, checking the firmness of the muscles.

The lama waved to a servant to bring a pot of simmering herbs. It was placed carefully at his side, along with a colorful strip of woven cloth. The lama dipped the cloth in the pot and gingerly lifted the steaming fabric out, holding it up to cool. Finally, Koja laid the herb-infused cloth across Yamun's chest, folding it back and forth several times. With shaking fingers, the priest pressed it into position and then carefully covered the khahan once again with the blankets.

The lama finally got up from his examination. "He heard us. It is a sign he is getting better." Jad's face broke into a shaky smile of relief. "But only a little better," cautioned Koja.

"But what is this plan, lama?" Goyuk asked, breaking the tension.

Thankful for the excuse to change the subject, Koja hurriedly launched into an explanation. "Khans, Furo has seen fit to answer my prayers and grant me the power to speak with the dead. Not with the illustrious khahan," he hastily added, "but to talk to one of his assassins."

"What good is this?" Jad asked, looking away from his father.

Koja shook his head. "I may learn something about the poison used on the khahan. You may learn who is to blame for the attack."

"I know who is to blame—didn't you yourself say the creature was an agent of the Shou? And didn't you say the governor of Manass had a Shou advisor at his side? What more is
there to know?" Jad said, dismissing Koja's last suggestion
with a wave.

"There was Afrasib, too," Goyuk pointed out. "How does
he fit in?"

"He was a wizard," Jad snapped, as if that explained it all.

"The khahan, he would find out. Try what the lama say,"
Goyuk urged.

Jad took a deep breath. He was young and unused to making such important decisions. "Goyuk," he said slowly, "because you advise this, I'll try the priest's ideas." He pivoted to
face Koja. "What do we do?"

"Have the bodies brought to the tent, and we will perform
the rite to summon their spirits. Then you can ask your
questions through me."

"You mean to bring the bodies here, to the royal yurt? I
won't allow it," Jad said defiantly, his young eyes flashing.
"Since my father is stricken, I'm in command. The dead
bodies will pollute the yurt. That cannot be allowed."

"But I must have the bodies. I must touch them," protested
Koja.

Jad mulled over the lama's words. "Very well, but it must
be done in secret, and it cannot be done here." The prince
got to his feet and paced back and forth as he gave his commands. "Goyuk, have one of the nightguards—not the
dayguards—go to Sechen the Wrestler's yurt and order him
to come with us. Issue a proclamation: all khans are to as-
semble their men this evening for a review by their prince.
That will keep the curious occupied and out of our way."

"By your will, it shall be done," Goyuk declared as he left.

"Thank you, wise counsellor," Jad replied as the tent flap
fell closed. Exhausted, the son turned back to his father.
Spotting Koja, Jad stopped. "And you, priest, go and get
yourself ready."

Koja bowed and then left. There was little he needed to prepare, but he obeyed all the same. Yamun would manage without his care for a little while. As he walked back to his yurt, Koja could feel the gloom that had settled on the camp. The warriors were tense, uncertain of the future.

Back in his tent, Koja quickly gathered the few things he would need. Hodj prepared him a hot meal, the priest's first in days. The food revived Koja, bringing him back from the edge of exhaustion. The meal finished, the priest opened his scrolls and once more reviewed the sutras he needed to know for the upcoming rite.

He was still reading when Sechen brought horses. Packing up a small pouch, Koja joined the others. They rode silently across yesterday's battlefield. Most of the dead men were gone, taken by relatives or friends to be properly buried. A few still lay where they had fallen, their bodies looted. Still, the battlefield was far from clean. Littering the field were the bodies of horses. Nearly all the dead animals had been left to rot. The victors had taken what saddles, bridles, and tack they could carry, but the carcasses were left undisturbed. Only a few horses had been butchered for their meat. Most were puffy and bloated after many hours in the sun. Vermin were feasting on the carcasses. Vultures squawked at the riders as they went by. Jackals yipped when the men ventured too close.

Jad worried that they were being watched as the group rode along. The prince had forgone his fine white stallion with the black and red saddle for a plain black mare and a saddle borrowed from one of the dayguards. He did not want to attract undue attention. Several of the dayguards had asked to ride along, since the prince was almost certain to be their new khahan, but he had firmly refused them.

Ahead of the prince, Koja, too, rode quietly, thinking of what was to come. He was worried. When he'd made the offer to summon up the spirits of the assassins, he hadn't considered the possible results. What if he were wrong and the assassins were paid by Prince Ogandi? The farther they rode, the less confident Koja became.

"Down there," said Sechen, interrupting the thoughts of both men. "We hid the bodies down there." He pointed to a small overhang that projected from the other side of the gully. "That way there would be no questions."

"Good," Jad said. "You have served my father well. He will see that you are rewarded."

"To serve him is my only reward," answered the wrestler. Koja had no doubts the man meant every word.

Stopping at the edge of the gully, the group dismounted in the shade of the trees. Sechen hobbled the prince's stallion so it could not wander. The rest slipped off the bits and bridles so the mares could graze comfortably. The mares would naturally stay near Jad's stallion, so there was no need to hobble them. Leaving their mounts, the men slid and stumbled down the bank to where the bodies were hidden.

If the battlefield hadn't already stank of death, they would have smelled the bodies some distance away. With so much death around, the smell of the corpses was only a minor thing. The heat of the day had not been kind to the dead. Drawn by the decay, flies buzzed thickly around the small shelf where the bodies were tucked. Sechen reached in, brushing the cloud of insects away, and pulled the corpses out.

The bodies had already started to rot, and something had been gnawing at them. A noxious, poisonous wind exhaled from their inner cavities as the two corpses came tumbling out of the crack. They flopped and rolled down the slope until they jammed up on a small pile of rocks. Koja felt a quick squeeze of queasiness and resolutely choked it back. This was all his idea; he couldn't be sick now. Goyuk and Jad stepped back, well away from the bloated remains. Sechen quickly hurried away as soon as his job was done.

Koja was not as fortunate as the others, for the spell he meant to cast required him to touch the bodies. However, he was slightly prepared. He pulled a spice-infused cloth and pressed it over his face. The heady smell made him dizzy, but at least now his nostrils weren't filled with the odor of rotten flesh.

"Get started," Jad said impatiently.

The priest thrust a small stick of incense into the ground, then waved to Sechen. Reluctantly, the tall fellow shambled over with a small metal cage hung from a chain. In it glowed a hot ember. Taking the chain, Koja picked out the ember with silver tongs and touched it to the incense. Within seconds, a thin stream of sweetly scented smoke rose up from the little stick. As the incense filled the air around him, Koja settled back and began chanting sutras. He had never used these prayers before, but knew they were the words needed to summon back spirits.

The others watched him silently. Still suspicious of the priest, Jad signaled to Sechen, making like he was drawing a bow. The wrestler nodded in understanding. Quietly he took up his bow and held it ready, just in case the priest attempted to cast a spell on the prince.

Everyone waited nervously for Koja to finish his chant. It seemed that the priest droned on forever. The words were hypnotic, seductive.

Koja was oblivious to the strange sound of his chant. All his concentration was spent in uttering the words Furo poured into his mind. Simply saying the chant required an effort that cramped the muscles of his face. His upper lip trembled, and the back of his neck tingled. He could sense forces swirling about him, called by the musical quality of the words. His vision narrowed to a single point.

Then, abruptly, the words stopped. Koja leaned forward and touched the cold, blue forehead of the dead wizard. A pale red light swelled out of the late Afrasib's slack mouth, winding slowly around the dead wizard's face. Gradually, the orb rose, trailing tendrils of light that continued to play over the cold face. As the orb moved, it elongated and increased in size.

Koja sat back in surprise. Summoning up dead spirits was new to him; he had no idea what to expect. No one at the

Red Mountain Temple ever mentioned a glowing light like this. As he watched, the light shimmered and expanded, slowly forming into something—a wispy, transparent form of Afrasib. The spirit opened its eyes, black voids, and stared directly at Koja. The lama shuddered as he looked into the dark pits.

The priest spoke over his shoulder to the others, behind him. "The spirit is bound here for a short time," Koja whispered, afraid he might disturb the thing that hovered over Afrasib's body. "Quickly, what are your questions? I can only ask a few, so choose them carefully."

"Ask who it worked for," Jad hissed, sitting stiffly upright, concealing his fear.

Koja turned back to the spirit. "Who ordered you to kill Yamun?"

"The one who wanted it done," the spirit answered. Its voice came from midair, somewhere in the vicinity of its former mouth. It was Afrasib's voice, but cold and monotone.

"Ask the name," urged the prince.

"What is the name of the person who ordered this killing?"

"Ju-Hai Chou." The words drifted softly throughout the gully.

"Who is Ju-Hai Chou?" Jad wondered aloud. "No, don't ask that. Ask about Bayalun."

"Did Eke Bayalun know of the attack?"

The spirit languorously replied. "Mother Bayalun knows many things. Would she not know this?"

"Now the spirit questions us," the prince muttered in disgust.

"I cannot hold him much longer, Prince Jadaran," cautioned the lama. Sweat had broken out on his brow, and the strain of keeping the spirit bound was telling on him.

"Who is Ju-Hai Chou?" Goyuk broke in, taking up Jad's previous question. "This may tell us more."

"Who is Ju-Hai Chou, the one who ordered you to kill

Yamun?" Koja strained to keep the spirit from slipping away. The light wavered and dimmed, then returned.

"The *hu hsien*," the voice echoed faintly. The image started to dwindle.

"What was his plan? Quickly, priest, ask!" Jad shouted, sensing that the contact was fading.

"Afrasib, what was Ju-Hai Chou's reason?" Koja blurted out.

"He was sent to help," the spirit intoned.

"Who sent him?" Koja quickly asked, before the spirit could fade.

"The Minister of State," was Afrasib's cryptic reply.

"Who was Ju-Hai Chou help—" Koja didn't finish the question. The light had shrunk in on itself, leaving only a small point that hung in the air for a few more seconds and then disappeared completely. The priest slid back from the dead bodies, thankful to Furo that it was over. "I am sorry. The spirit escaped me. It was very strong." He pulled off the scented cloth and bowed to the prince in apology.

Jad grunted, sounding a little like his father. "What about the other? We can learn more from him."

Koja rubbed his shaven head, and looked at the body of the fox-man. The gaping gash that shattered the creature's chest was black and thick with flies. "I do not think it will work. He is not a man. His spirit is not the same."

"Then we've learned nothing," Yamun's son said in disgust, brushing the dust from his *kalat* as he stood.

"We have a name—Ju-Hai Chou," the priest pointed out. He was relieved that no names from Khazari had come up.

"And we have a mandarin's title," Goyuk added. "Big herds grow from small sheep."

"Perhaps," Jad conceded as he climbed back up the bank. "Still, I don't see anything useful in it." The rest of the group got up and followed.

They rode back to the khahan's camp with little conversation. The midday sun beat heavily on the corpses covering the battlefield. The stench grew stronger. Koja never before realized that war left behind such death and decay. He knew that some men died in the battle and others often suffered hideous wounds, but the aftermath was always something forgotten, ignored. Nobody ever told of the horses' screams or the bloated bodies of the unburied that covered the ground.

The group reached the camp without any interruption, detouring only a few times to avoid some packs of jackals that refused to flee from their approach. As they wound their way back through the warriors' tents, the men came out to greet them. The troopers stood quietly with their heads downcast as the prince passed. At first, the men seemed mournful for the loss of Jad's father, their khahan. Watching them line the way, the priest could sense an uneasiness among the men. The mourners fixed their gaze on Jad, as if waiting for him to do something.

From the back of the crowd, a man suddenly broke into an anguished chant, improvising a lament to the fallen khahan.

> "The winds of heaven are not balanced.
> The body of birth is not eternal.

> "Who drinks the sacred water of life?
> In our short lives, let us enjoy.

> "The winds of heaven are beyond touch.
> The lives of men are not eternal.

> "Who drinks the sacred water of life?
> In our short lives, let us enjoy."

The singer's voice cracked as his lyric soared and trembled. Quickly the other men took up the chant, repeating the singsong verses, embellishing on them. Voices broke above the mass to carry the words higher.

The song spread ahead of the prince, greeting him at every turn on the way to the khahan's tent. It seemed that every trooper turned out along their march. Khans knelt in respect as the prince rode by. Men, even the horribly wounded, struggled to get to the front of the press, where they could make themselves seen. Koja watched as a crippled trooper, his foot lost in yesterday's battle, was carried forward by his companions, his pallet hoisted over their heads. It seemed to take all his effort to sing the simple lyric, but sing he did, hoarsely bawling out the words.

A surging mass of men followed them up the hill to the khahan's tent. As their numbers grew, the tension increased. "Let us see the khahan!" someone screamed. "Let us see his body!" There was a grumbling swell underneath the song as more and more men called out to see the khahan's bier.

"Guards, keep them out!" Jad shouted over the noise as he entered Yamun's compound. The dayguards dashed forward, forming a triple line around the gate. Their weapons glinted in the sun, a bristling line of sword points. Officers on horseback shouted commands, their steeds prancing behind the line. The menacing black forms of the dayguards pushed forward, forcing the crowd back. Jad and the rest of his party disappeared into Yamun's tent, Sechen at the rear.

Koja hurried to check the khahan. Yamun was still alive and breathing, a victory for the day. The blankets were soaked in sweat and his color was still like that of the ice high in the mountains of Khazari. Hastily, Koja stripped off the coverlets and demanded new ones. A quiverbearer hastened to fulfill the request.

Jad came to the sickbed and watched for a moment, saying nothing. The khahan was asleep, and there was little the prince could do. Satisfied that Koja was attending to Yamun, he turned back to Goyuk. The old khan had just finished offering a prayer to the small felt idols that hung over the door. Reaching into a bucket of kumiss by the sill, Goyuk dipped his fingers in the brew and sprinkled it on each idol. He kowtowed to the little red cloth figures and then turned to join the others.

"You should remember the old ways, Jadaran Khan," chided Goyuk. "Teylas be angry with you." He pointed to the doorway, leaving no doubt what he wanted the prince to do.

Jad held his tongue. Although Goyuk was presumptuous to speak that way to him, the prince knew that the old man was right. Obediently, he knelt down at the door and offered up his prayer, going through all the motions to make the ablution. Outside the doorway, he could hear the muffled chanting of the men. Jad wondered how long they would be satisfied to wait.

Goyuk beamed a toothless smile as Jad finished the ritual. "You are a good son. Maybe you make a good khahan, too."

The suggestion caught the prince by surprise. "My father isn't dead yet," he snapped. The weight and pressure of the day were catching up with him, and Goyuk's intimation only added to his rage and frustration.

"No, no, of course not," Goyuk quickly agreed. "But the time may come."

The prince let himself relax slightly, accepting Goyuk's explanation. "If it comes to that, I hope I'll have your support. There are many things I don't know, much I need to learn. You've always served father well, and I'd like you to do the same for me."

"Of course," said the old man, following Jad back to the sickbed.

"Lama, how is the khahan?"

Koja frowned. "The sweating may have driven the poison out of his blood."

Jad nodded impassively. "Are you certain?" he pressed.

Koja bit at his lip, then replied honestly. "No, Prince Jadaran. I *think* that he will live. I cannot *promise* that he will live."

Jad walked to the yurt's door and beckoned Koja to his side. The prince pulled open a corner of the door flap as Koja joined him. "Hear the men, lama?" he asked, putting his hand on Koja's shoulder. "They fought for him. If his assassins were alive, that crowd would rip them apart with their hands and then feed the guts to the jackals. If he dies in your care, I could not stop them."

"I still cannot promise you anything," Koja insisted. He stepped away from the door and looked Jad firmly in the eye. "I do not want to fail."

"Nor do I," echoed Jad. He looked back out the doorway and coldly murmured, "I wish I could give them the ones behind all this. Especially Bayalun."

"This you cannot do," consoled Goyuk, his sharp ears picking up Jad's softly spoken words from across the tent.

Jad let the tent flap drop. "Why not? Her wizard struck down my father," he argued. "The men would believe me."

"You have no proof she do this," Goyuk said, tapping the carpet where he sat to emphasize his point. "Think like your father. She has many relatives, many friends. You must have proof, not suspicions. Besides, the wizards and shamans protect her."

"Then what do I do?" Jad cried in frustration. "I need proof before I can act, but this viper works freely against us. I need to find Yamun's killer!"

"Wait, Jad. Be like the tiger hunting for the deer. Whoever it is will make a mistake. It will happen soon," Goyuk advised. "Ambition will cause them to blunder. We must wait until that happens."

"How long can we keep the army together, just waiting? We need to do something." Jad squatted beside Goyuk, looking to the old khan for guidance.

It was Koja, however, who spoke, from the side of Yamun's sickbed. "A funeral. If the khahan is supposed to be dead, there must be a funeral."

Jad glared over at the lama. "What good will that do, priest? It will only remind them the khahan is dead."

Koja stood and moved to where the two men sat. "It will keep the khans busy—and keep them following your orders. And it may give your father time to get well."

Jad stopped and considered Koja's words. He glanced to

Goyuk, and the old khan nodded in agreement.

"If you give orders for the funeral," Koja continued, "the khans still listen to your words. They will grow used to following your commands. It will keep them from grumbling and give the men an outlet for their pain."

Jad, chin sunk to his chest, watched Koja while the priest explained his plan. As he finished, the prince raised his head and spoke. "You are much more than a simple lama. I see why father has seen fit to name you his *anda*."

– 11 –
Reunion

Bayalun stood in front of her yurt with Chanar at her side. Surrounding both of them were Bayalun's guards. The troopers stood tensely alert as the khadun read from an ancient scrap of yellow paper. Chanar peeked at it over her shoulder. He could read—a little anyway—and wasn't about to miss a chance to show off his meager skill to Bayalun. To his dismay, what he saw was unintelligible, a strange and twisted script. Worse still for his pride, Bayalun read from the unrolled sheet with ease, her tongue tripping over the tortured phrases.

As she spoke, a gloom settled over them and the colors leached away from everything. Chanar tensed with fear as the world went gray—the white robes of the guards, Bayalun's black hair, the red silks of his own shirt, even the orange glow of the fire. Then, there was nothing.

Abruptly, there was something. Solid ground slammed up under his feet, wiping away the brief feeling of floating. Chanar staggered, but several of the guards stumbled and fell. Bayalun managed to remain on her feet with ease. At any rate, they had arrived in Yamun's camp.

And apparently they were not welcome.

The men of Yamun's Kashik who surrounded them held drawn swords ready. The guards were a grizzled group, seasoned campaigners wearing dirty black *kalats* stained with blood. They watched the newcomers with hard stares. Black beards and braids were thick and foul with grease.

Only their scarred cheeks were free of the filth. Chanar recognized many and knew their names from previous battles. Watching them, the general moved slowly and carefully. These guards were poised to strike. It was clear in the way they stood, the way they held their swords, and the friendless look in their eyes.

Bayalun's guards stood no less at the ready, their sword tips wavering in anticipation. Chanar slowly drew himself up. He was a khan, a prince of the Tuigan, not some thief. Looking his imposing best in a red robe and gold vest embroidered with blue dragons, Chanar glowered at the Kashik around him.

"Let me pass! I bring the khadun of the Tuigan to see the body of her husband," Chanar shouted. His face was clouded and dark, and his eyes narrowed to hard, unfriendly slits. The battle-hardened, bloodthirsty old brawler in him rose to the fore. "Clear the way or die!" he bellowed, drawing his sword with a menacing flourish. The general's shoulders heaved as he pumped himself up with fury and courage.

The Kashik shifted on the balls of their feet, preparing to meet his charge. They had their orders, and Chanar's threats were not about to make them falter.

"General Chanar, you cannot teach asses courtesy," Bayalun said softly. The general glared at her for having the audacity to interfere at such a critical point. "Put away your sword. These ugly mules haven't the wit to be frightened. You—" She pointed at the largest guard with a flick of her finger. "Go and ask Yamun's son if the khadun must change his guards into the asses they truly are. Then he can bray out his orders to them." She smiled wickedly, an easy feat for her.

The fellow, whom Chanar recognized as an old, tough sergeant named Jali-bukha, went dead white at Bayalun's words. Eyes wide open with fear, the sergeant nodded and quickly ran toward the khahan's yurt. Bayalun looked at Chanar with a triumphant smile. "It will not be long," she confidently predicted.

With difficulty, Chanar swallowed his pride. He was one of Yamun's seven valiant men. He didn't need a woman to tell common warriors to get out of his way. Someday, he knew, there would come a time when her words and threats would no longer suffice. Then she would have to come to him for support.

Behind his back, Mother Bayalun hid her contemptuous smile. The general believes he can do this alone, she thought. But, she reminded herself, the dear general is necessary. The wizards and some of the people might follow her, but the rest of the army would never accept Bayalun's commands. She needed General Chanar to keep Yamun's—her—empire intact.

The sergeant reached the door of the khahan's yurt, less than one hundred yards away. Barely waiting to be announced, he threw open the tent flap and breathlessly stood in the doorway. Seeing the prince glaring at him for the intrusion, the sergeant flung himself to the ground. "Prince Jadaran, I bring a message," he declared while gasping for breath. "Eke Bayalun and General Chanar, they have just arrived!"

"What?" the prince exclaimed. "Here?" He clenched his fists in frustration. With a curt wave, he dismissed the sergeant and then spun back to the others. "What are we going to do?" He whirled on Goyuk, expecting the advisor to instantly provide an answer.

"Show them . . . in," came a weak voice from the other side of the tent. Astonished, Jad turned slowly toward the source. There, on his sickbed, was Yamun. Somehow, he had struggled up onto one elbow, raising his head enough to look at them. His face was hollow and pale. A tic quivered his cheek, a small sign of the massive effort he was expending. "Get me up," he whispered hoarsely. "I will meet with my . . . wife." Koja hurried to his side, quickly mounding pillows for Yamun to lean on.

"Father, you're not strong enough!" Jad protested. "There

must be something else we can do."

"No. Bayalun must know I live. Otherwise, she will make trouble. And Chanar deserves to know the truth." His voice trailed off weakly. The khahan rested for a little before speaking again. "Go. Greet them. Give me some time, but don't tell them I live. . . . I will be ready."

Jad stood still, uncertain if he should obey these orders. Koja looked up, firmly meeting Jad's gaze. "We will make sure Yamun is ready."

"Let all who disobey you know this is by the word of the khahan," Yamun mumbled, reciting the formula. Even in his weak voice, there was no uncertainty.

Resigned, Jad bowed to his father and turned to go.

"And order the Kashik to double their guard," Yamun added as his son departed.

Accompanied by the sergeant, Jad marched the short distance to where Bayalun and Chanar waited. The Kashik stepped aside to let the prince pass.

"Greetings, Mother," Jad said with forced civility. There was little warmth in his voice, although nothing in his expression noted anything less than filial love. "You should have warned of your coming. A proper reception could've—well—been prepared." His smile was broad and utterly heartless.

"I am sure your preparations would have been most complete," Bayalun parried. She did not even bother to pretend friendship to her stepson. "We did not want to put you to such trouble."

Using her staff, Bayalun pushed her way past Jad and began marching toward the khahan's tent, ignoring everyone around her. She continued to talk, unconcerned whether Jad was following her or not. "In Quaraband, there are rumors that Yamun is slain. I came to investigate these. Now I see the mourning banner in front of my husband's tent. Why was I not informed?"

The prince quick-stepped to fall in beside Bayalun, avoiding the backswing of her staff as he did so. "We had no one who could reach you quickly. We've sent a messenger." It was a part lie; he and Goyuk had carefully avoided letting the news travel beyond the camp.

"What about Afrasib, my wizard? He could have reached me," the khadun asked warily.

"I think not. He died in yesterday's battle, slain by the Khazari," Jad lied.

The old sorceress stopped suddenly, taken aback by her stepson's announcement. "Afrasib is dead?" she asked in sad disbelief. "It is not possible."

"Most certainly, he's dead. His body was brought back from the field of battle." Jad couched his words carefully this time.

"I shall see his body later," Bayalun decided, brushing an errant gray hair from her face.

As Bayalun came to the doorway, two more Kashik stepped in front of her, blocking the way with crossed swords. Irritated, the khadun poked at them with the gold head of her staff. Although they flinched as she thrust it forward, neither man moved.

"Unless you want me to hurt these men," she snapped at the prince, "you should order them to move." She squinted at the guards with mock ferocity and wagged her staff under their noses.

"They only want to protect you from evil spirits. There is death here," the prince explained, reminding her of the old taboos. "The yurt is ill-omened. Yamun's body lies inside." Jad carefully avoided making eye contact with his stepmother.

"I have seen enough death that this will do me no harm," Bayalun informed her stepson. Taking up her staff, the khadun thrust it forward. The sleeve on her arm fell back, revealing the smooth, golden skin that belied her age. Bayalun pushed the guards aside and stooped through the doorframe.

Jad waited for Chanar to enter, then brought up the rear, trying to suppress his panic. Had he stalled long enough?

Was the khahan ready to receive them? He edged his hand to his sword, in case things went badly.

Bayalun took only a single step through the door and stopped. Chanar, his head bowed to get through the door, bumped into the khadun and stepped back in surprise. Looking over Bayalun's shoulder, he lurched back farther in greater astonishment. Jad easily slid to the side, out of the way, his eyes goggling at Yamun's throne.

Bayalun let out a sharp gasp of incredulity, and her staff almost slipped from her grasp. General Chanar simply gaped in shock. There, opposite them, was Yamun, alive and sitting on his throne. His legs were spread, his hands resting on his knees, his head held upright, chin jutting forward. He was dressed in his finest armor, a bribe the emperor of Shou Lung had sent a year ago. The metal gleamed in the dim light—a golden breastplate sculpted with muscles, a pair of flaring silver shoulder-guards, a skirt of the finest metal chain, and a helm of gem-encrusted brass and gold, tapered and fluted to a point. A pure white horsetail, braided with ribbons of red silk, hung down from the helmet's tip.

Under all the trappings it was difficult, almost impossible, to see Yamun's face. The lamps were hung far and high from the khahan's seat, casting his features into darkness. His hands were covered with thick gauntlets.

At the head of the men's seats, close to the khahan, sat Koja, cross-legged. The hollow-eyed priest studied the pair who had just entered with anxious curiosity. Beside him was Goyuk, still dressed in the filthy robes from yesterday's battle. The old khan had dug out his pipe and was carefully tamping it full of tobacco. He glanced toward Bayalun and Chanar, and then returned his attention to his pipe, scarcely giving them any notice. Behind the khahan were the nightguards. At their head stood Sechen, his arms hidden in the folds of his *kalat*. The guards stood stiffly erect, their eyes boring in on the visitors. They made no attempt to hide their hatred.

"Come forward," the khahan said softly. His resonant

voice carried clearly across the room. Cautiously, eyeing all those around her, Bayalun walked forward. Chanar strode beside her, though his gait was less swaggering than normal.

Bayalun was the first to gather her wits. She cleverly composed in a simple refrain, chanting it in a droning melody.

"Greetings, honorable son who rises again.
Your grieving mother is pleased to see you.
Your grieving wife is pleased to see you.
Double blessings flow like water upon me."

Yamun bowed his head slightly toward his stepmother. "Sit," he whispered, pointing to a seat about halfway up the women's row. Bayalun obediently took the seat, accepting the slight insult the position implied without comment.

"Sit," the khahan said in a stronger voice, indicating a seat for Chanar beside Goyuk. Chanar hesitated, for the seat put him at a lower rank than the priest. He started to protest, then thought better of it.

There was a strained silence and, for a moment, Yamun's head sagged. The illustrious second wife watched the khahan with keen interest. Prince Jad, near the door of the yurt, silently drew his sword and caught the eyes of Sechen. The giant nodded slightly, indicating his readiness.

"Have this pipe, Great Lord," old Goyuk said brazenly, sliding forward to hand Yamun the bowl he had prepared. Abruptly the khahan's head snapped up.

"I'll smoke," Yamun answered, his voice sounding a little hollow. Taking the pipe, he lit it and took several long puffs, enjoying the sharp flavor of the exotic tobacco. Koja offered a silent prayer to the Ten-Thousand Protective Images of Furo. At the back of the yurt, the prince once again relaxed his stance.

"You've heard evil rumors, no doubt," Yamun finally said. "Rumors that assassins were sent to kill me. So, no doubt, you hurried here to prove to your own minds how wrong these rumors were."

Bayalun studied the khahan closely, trying to see if his image was some illusion created by the priest. At the same time, she quickly reviewed the spells she had ready, just in case there were more surprises.

"Sadly, there was truth in the rumors. Have the guards bring the body," Yamun commanded Sechen. The towering fellow left his position and exited the tent. Yamun continued, "Yesterday, during battle, a creature tried to kill me. It failed because my *anda*—" At this the khahan tipped his head toward the priest. "He fought to protect me. Let us drink to his fortune." With a feeble wave, he had the servants bring ladles of black kumiss. Hands shaking, he raised his ladle to his lips and tipped his head back for a drink.

As he drank his face came out of shadow. Bayalun clearly saw the deathly color of his cheeks, which were gleaming with cold sweat from the mere effort of sitting up.

Chanar sat ramrod-straight, his hard, narrow eyes on the lama. The others raised their ladles and slurped the drink. The general, though, sat still, refusing to salute the priest.

As the group finished the toast, Sechen coughed discreetly from the door. Yamun acknowledged his presence and everyone turned to watch as the huge Kashik pulled open the door flap. There, wrapped in a freshly butchered horsehide, was the body of the *hu hsien*. The guards kept it just outside the door, so that it wouldn't pollute the khahan's yurt. Even knowing who, or what, the body was, Koja found the creature hard to identify. It's fur had already lost the luster it possessed in life. The gash in its chest was crudely closed, but the decay and corruption had not stopped.

Bayalun looked at the body briefly, only long enough to satisfy herself that it was the Shou assassin the mandarin had provided. It only confirmed what she now expected, so she easily concealed the few emotions seeing the body evoked. Mother Bayalun was disappointed. She had expected much more from the great empire of Shou Lung. Their token of support, a lone assassin, had failed. Now, she would have to press them for greater commitment.

Chanar, on the other hand, looked at the thing with disgust and fascination. He'd never seen such a creature. It didn't surprise him that Bayalun would use beasts and not men. He could see now why her plans had failed, relying as they did on such creatures.

"There are also rumors," Yamun said thinly, interrupting the contemplation of the body, "that you, Mother, were somehow responsible for this." He paused. Unconsciously, the khahan tugged gently at his mustache, his body sagging forward as he did so. "Of course, this isn't true. Still, it would end these rumors if you swore an oath of loyalty to your khahan."

Bayalun glared coldly at her stepson. In icy, measured tones, she said, "You would make your mother and your wife swear to you? Men will say you are without morals for this perversion."

"Men will say worse of you if you refuse!" Yamun snapped, suddenly revealing surprising strength. "Will the khans hear how you are afraid of Teylas's wrath?" Yamun braced himself once more against his knees.

Bayalun realized that she stood alone. Chanar could not, would not, come to her aid without arousing suspicion. Bitterly the woman agreed. "Never before in our history has the khahan dared to demand this of his khadun. May Teylas find this offensive to his sight!" She turned and spat on the rugs.

"Teylas can make of it what he wants. Now, say the oath," Yamun commanded. By his tone it was clear he would brook no more argument.

Bayalun stared at her husband, weighing her choices. She could hear his armor creak to his labored breathing. At last, she kowtowed before the khahan. With her face pressed into the rugs, she recited the ancient words.

"Although your descendants have only a scrap of meat thrown on the grass, which not even the crows will eat; although your descendants have only a scrap of fat, which

not even the dogs will eat; even then my family will serve
you. Never will we raise the banner of another to sit upon
the throne."

"As this is heard by the khahan, Illustrious Emperor of the
Tuigan, so it is heard by Teylas," Yamun murmured in re-
sponse. His body sank slightly as he recited the words.
"Now, dear Bayalun, you're tired. This audience is over."

Burning with humiliation, the khadun struggled from the
floor, pushing herself up with her staff. Eschewing the traditional formalities of departing, she barged from the yurt,
driving aside the guards with a few solid whacks of her
stout wooden shaft.

"Chanar, you will stay. I have questions for you," the khahan ordered when the general stood to go. Chanar froze,
briefly panicked, and then slowly sat back down. He looked
around, wondering if the audience was about to turn into
some sort of trap.

Yamun deliberately let Chanar sit and wait. Just as Koja
decided that the khahan had passed out inside his armor,
Yamun spoke. "General Chanar, my anda, why aren't you in
Semphar advising Hubadai?" He let his voice trail away at
the end.

"I was ill and could not travel," Chanar answered stiffly.
He placed his hands very carefully in front of him. "I sent
messengers telling you of my sickness."

"You could've ridden in a cart, or were you too sick to
travel at all?" Yamun asked.

"I am not an old man—" Chanar stopped suddenly and
gave a quick glance to Goyuk. The khan's normally pleasant
smile was clouded and grim. "I am not a woman," Chanar began again, "who cannot ride. Valiant men do not follow oxen
to the battle. I could not fight from a wagon."

"It is true a warrior should ride into battle," Yamun
agreed. "I'm pleased to see that you're feeling much better.
Now that you are well, why have you come here?"

Wary of the khahan's maneuvering, the general picked his
words carefully. He looked at the floor in mock humility.

DAVID COOK

"The khadun suspected an evil fate had struck you and came to learn the truth. I could not allow the khadun to travel without a proper guard."

Metal scraped wood as the khahan shifted in his seat. "So, you came for the sake of my mother. Learn this, khans," Yamun said louder, addressing Goyuk and Jad. "General Chanar has shown us the proper thing to do. It is true I have chosen two worthy *andas*, the warrior and the lama. Let us drink to their health."

The kumiss was drunk and the toasts were made. Throughout the salutes, Koja tried to stay quiet and avoid Chanar's attention. There could be no misreading the angry looks the general gave him over each ladleful of fermented milk. Koja could also see that Yamun was weakening, the ladle shaking a little more each time the khahan raised it to his lips.

"Yamun," the priest finally called out, "Chanar is surely tired from today's traveling. However, he is too noble to complain, so let me speak for him and ask that this audience end."

The khahan turned toward Koja, about to lash out at the priest for such impudence, when he suddenly saw the wisdom of the lama's words. Turning back to Chanar, he held one hand up to send the servants back to their places. "My *anda*, Koja, is wise. I've kept you too long, Chanar Ong Kho. This audience is over now, and you may leave."

The warlord sat gaping, then, with a crash, hurled the ladle across the yurt, spraying kumiss over the rugs. "He does not speak for me! I need no one to speak for me. I am your *anda*!" he shouted. Not waiting for a reply, Chanar stormed out of the yurt, savagely shoving the guards at the door out of his way.

The door flap had barely been tied shut when Yamun toppled off the throne. Arms weakly flailing, he grabbed at the screen only to succeed in pulling it over with him. The khahan tumbled from the dais in a crash of metal and cracking wood. The gleaming brass helmet popped off his head and bounced across the floor. Koja sprang to his feet, hastening to the side of the stricken khahan. Quickly, he examined the fallen leader.

"He lives, thankfulness be to Furo, but he needs rest," the priest announced as he tugged off Yamun's armor. "Help me get him to bed."

"You shouldn't have put him in that heavy armor," the prince snapped as he hoisted the khahan to his feet, half-dragging him to his bed.

"The khahan insisted on it. I did not want it," Koja shot back, trying to keep his temper under control.

Jad, too, bit back his words. "That would be like father," he conceded.

"He is strong-willed," Koja noted as they laid Yamun's unconscious body on the bed. Goyuk stood near the door, making sure they were not interrupted.

"More than you know, lama," Jad agreed. He looked Koja in the eye. "I was wrong to accuse you." Together, the pair finished making the khahan comfortable. When they were done, Jad called Goyuk from the door.

"Wise advisors," he began, nodding to both Goyuk and Koja, "Bayalun knows our tricks. What do we do now?"

* * * * *

"He knows about you!" Chanar snapped hysterically, his composure completely shattered. He looked at Mother Bayalun, sitting opposite him, his eyes flashing with panic and rage.

"He *suspects*, dear Chanar. If he could prove anything, we would be dead by now," the matronly Bayalun corrected. Her voice was low and ripplingly musical. She took the general's hand in hers and gave it a reassuring squeeze.

They sat alone in a small yurt she had appropriated from one of the commanders of Yamun's bodyguard. Influential and important though the Kashik khans might be, not even they dared refuse the illustrious second empress. It was a simple matter for her to find a tent to her liking and then persuade its owner to vacate. Indeed, the khan had been most willing; he believed the khahan dead, making this a good time to be friendly and helpful to the khadun.

Still, the usurped accommodations were far from lavish. The tent was small and cramped, divided into two sections. Bayalun and Chanar sat in a small reception area. A pair of small wooden chests covered with rugs served as chairs. The khadun had disdained these, choosing instead to sit on the floor next to the oil lamp, which provided a feeble glow. A fine bow of antler horn and lacquered wood, and a quiver of red leather hung on the wall behind one seat, marking it as the master's spot. A suit of iridescent armor, carefully tended and decorated—perhaps the khan's finest possession—hung on a stand nearby. Weapons, helmets, shields, buckets, and utensils decorated the rest of the wall space.

A folding wooden screen separated the other half of the yurt from the reception area. On the other side of the screen was the private area—a small collapsible bed with a carved and inlaid headboard, and chests of clothing and war booty.

"How long before his suspicion gives way to certainty?" the general countered, slowly pulling his hand free from Bayalun's. He closed his eyes and rubbed hard at his temples, struggling to regain control of his emotions. Blood throbbed through the veins of his forehead and the shaven top of his head. His shoulders ached from the tension. "Why can't we just raise our standard and attack him now—just get it over with? We should defeat him in battle, not with a game of words."

"Patience, my bold warrior," Bayalun gently urged. She smiled warmly. His sudden display of temper threatened all her plans and yet fascinated her. "Forgive me. You are a man of deeds, and I have forgotten this. Blood and the sword are meat for you, not politics and words. Patience. There will be battles, I'm sure, but not yet." Chanar could not help but notice the change in her tone.

The khadun moved closer to Chanar. It was important now, more than ever, that the general do nothing rash, that he be placated. She needed to control him, but let him think he was in command.

"Let Yamun suspect," Bayalun continued, her voice dropping to soft murmur. "We will find a way to distract the khahan." She took Chanar's hands again and gently pulled the general to her. He gave a slight resistance at first, then took her in his arms. She stroked his tanned scalp and the thick brown braids that gathered over his ears. Caressingly, she tugged at his tunic, slowly undoing its clasps.

* * * * *

The sun only weakly warmed the layer of frosty dew that covered the ground the next morning. On the plain where the dead lay, the day's chorus of jackals and vultures was beginning. Listening to their cries, an almost comforting sound, Chanar stretched grandly in the doorway of Bayalun's yurt. There was a rustling noise behind him as the khadun stepped into the small reception area, adjusting her headdress.

"Yamun's death standard still stands, Bayalun," Chanar commented. He did not turn from the doorway. Coming up behind the general, she peered over his shoulder.

"Good. It gives us more time. There are many things we must plan. Now, come and eat." A small tray set with cups of salted tea, soured mare's milk curds, and chunks of sugar had been prepared by her guards. The second empress motioned Chanar to sit as she sipped at her tea.

Chanar could tell by the set of Bayalun's jawline that she had already been thinking of the distraction they needed. Taking up a cup, he settled back to listen, leaning comfortably against one of the chests.

"Did you see the khahan's face yesterday?" The khadun didn't wait for an answer. "It was pale, and his voice was weaker than I have ever heard. He did not escape my assassin. He's been hurt." She stared into her salted tea. "He wants to be dead so he can heal. We must force him into the open before he is ready."

Chanar nodded. "Easily said, but everyone believes him dead."

"I have a plan. Which khans are friendly to you?"

Chanar began to rebraid his hair. He thought for a few seconds while he worked. "Several—Tanjin, Secen, Geser, Chagadai—"

"Enough. Talk to them. If the khahan is dead, then there must be a *couralitai* to select a new khahan," the sharp-witted Bayalun explained.

"A *couralitai?*" Chanar exclaimed with a contemptuous laugh. "It'll take months to gather all the khans for a council. By then Yamun will be healed and there won't be a need to pick a new khahan. Bayalun, you've lost your cunning."

The khadun ignored his slight. "No, your khans must insist on it now." She touched his chest with her staff. "Think about it. The Tuigan are fighting two wars—one with Semphar and one here. Things could go badly without a khahan. Yamun's sons might fight each other for the throne. A decision must be made immediately." She lowered her staff. "These are the things you must tell your khans to make them worry. Then they will insist on the *couralitai*. They will even believe it is the right thing to do. Now, do you see?"

Chanar stopped braiding and pondered her words. "That's true. I could speak to the khans. But Yamun might let the *couralitai* happen. Jad might take command," the general said, trying to see all the strategies, all the complications.

"The khahan will not let it happen. He will appear," the second empress replied confidently.

"True. After all, Prince Jad might lose," Chanar mused, thinking of his own supporters.

"That's not why Yamun will appear. It's his pride that will force him into the open. He won't let another be khahan, not even his own son." Bayalun returned to her breakfast. "That is why I know he will appear."

"So, you force him to come out," Chanar conceded. "What good is that?"

Bayalun smiled, not the tender smile of the night before, but the scheming look Chanar had come to know. It drove a shiver of fear through him, the feeling he sometimes got on the verge of battle.

"When Yamun is weak and in the open, we will find a way to strike at him," she promised.

Their plans decided, the two plotters set to work. All morning Chanar made calls on his fellow khans, dropping suggestions, hints, and ominous predictions. At first skeptical of Bayalun's scheme, Chanar was surprised at how receptive the khans were to his words. The *couralitai* gave them a course of action, more so even than Jad's funeral plan. The khans began to clamor for the *couralitai*, threatening to leave if their demands were not met.

It was late in the afternoon of the same day when Jad insisted upon a council of war. Koja tried to prevent it, arguing that the khahan was still too weak, but the prince would hear none of it.

"I want a meeting with my father," he demanded. "The army's breaking up and there's a new problem. Envoys from Manass have arrived to negotiate a peace. I don't know what to do. Goyuk should be there, too; he knows what's going on. And you, too, priest."

No amount of debate was going to sway Jad, so Koja resigned himself to the meeting. Perhaps the prince was right, he thought. Things were getting out of control. He had heard the rumors among the guards. There was already talk of choosing a new khahan. They needed a plan.

In a short time, Jad, Goyuk, and Koja presented themselves to the khahan. Yamun looked stronger and there was more color in his cheek, but his voice was still shaky and weak. He was sitting up in his bed when they entered, wearing an ermine-trimmed robe lined with yellow silk. Koja had insisted that he put on clean clothes as part of the healing process. In truth, the priest only wanted to get rid of the smell.

Jad wasted little time with ceremony. "Father, your death's gone on long enough," he began, almost as soon as everyone was seated. "The khans are talking, demanding a *couralitai*. They're stirring up the men. I cannot hold the army together any longer."

Yamun looked surprised by the news. "A *couralitai* takes many months to prepare. My time of mourning isn't even over."

"They want one now," Goyuk explained, his wrinkled face lined even more deeply with concern. "They say the army needs a leader." His gums smacked together as if to accentuate the point.

"It's worse, Father," added Jad, bowing his head. "The envoys from Manass have come and are impatient to begin negotiations. That's given the khans more to complain about. Already Chagadai and Tanjin have threatened to return to their pastures. That's four *minghans*, four thousand men, Father."

Yamun considered the situation, absentmindedly twisting the sheets. "*Anda*, is my mother still in camp?"

"Yes, Yamun," answered Koja.

"Could this be Bayalun's doing?" the khahan feebly growled as he slapped the bed with a resounding thud. "Or is it spies from Shou Lung?"

There was silence from the group as they mulled over the possibilities. No one offered any answers.

"Yamun, you cannot sit here waiting for something to happen. You should make a plan," Koja suggested, speaking hesitantly.

"My *anda* is right. Tell them to call a *couralitai*," the khahan announced. He choked back a small cough.

"What?" sputtered Jad. "Why not just appear? Show you're alive?"

"Someone is manipulating all this," Yamun declared with certainty. "I'll show myself, but only after they make their move. Let's give our mysterious enemy what he wants, then see what happens. Call it for tomorrow."

"Lord Yamun, if there is a *couralitai*, you must appear—to prove you are not dead. Otherwise they will pick a new khahan," Koja pointed out.

"I know this. Don't worry, *anda*. I'll rest. Now go." With a tired wave, Koja and the others were dismissed from the khahan's presence.

As he stepped into the afternoon sunlight, Koja realized that it had been days since he'd last made any notes for Yamun's chronicle. He wondered how much he could remember. As a historian, he was doing a poor job. Wearily, the lama wandered to his tent to fulfill his duty as grand historian.

– 12 –

The Couralitai

By the earliest light of the next dawn, word of the *couralitai* had spread throughout the camp. Already the khans were gathering for the meeting, moving from yurt to yurt to share the rumors and gossip that would affect the day's business.

Standing near the Great Yurt, Koja could almost hear the chorus of speculation and rumors. With keen, patient interest, the priest watched the ebb and flow of the khans. General Chanar emerged from the yurt of Tanjin Khan and exchanged friendly banter with the *minghan* commander. Koja watched him next cross the camp to another tent, that of Unyaid, a minor commander in the Kashik. Even earlier, Bayalun had been moving about, her staff echoing with its distinctive thunk on the hard ground. The priest had not seen her for some time.

As Koja watched, Jad and Goyuk came his way. They had been out that morning, probing the khans and listening to the rumors. The three shared their information. Koja described Bayalun's movements and noted Chanar's with curiosity. Goyuk and Jad outlined the mood of the khans, who would side with them and who would not. After making new plans, Jad and Goyuk returned to their rounds, sounding out the khans. Koja maintained his watch of Bayalun's movements.

As the lama waited, the quiverbearers began preparing for the grand meeting. The gathering was to take place inside Yamun's compound, about one hundred feet from the khahan's yurt, in a large open area surrounded by the tents of the Kashik khans. A bonfire, mounded with valuable pieces of wood, was built at the far side of the clearing. The khahan's death banner was moved from Yamun's yurt and staked on the side of the circle opposite the bonfire. Young boys carefully swept the ground with broad brushes, and others rolled out rugs in two arcs to provide seating. Beyond the circle of the *couralitai*, servants were brewing tea at small fires, preparing for the arrival of the khans. Leather bags, fashioned from the skins of horses' heads, were filled with kumiss and set out along with ladles. Special seats for Bayalun and Jad were put up beneath the black yak-tail standard. Between these was a special, vacant seat for the departed khahan.

A horn blew a wheezing, off-key note. It sounded easily over the subdued clatter of the quiverbearers. They quickly finished their tasks and faded to the edges of the circle. The khans began to arrive and take seats. Those khans friendly to Bayalun sat on the left of the banner, near her seat, while Jad's supporters filled the places to the right. Most of the khans took places far from both the prince and the khadun, declaring their current neutrality.

The spaces on the rugs began to get crowded. Deciding there was no more he could do where he was, Koja hurried to find a spot with a good view of the action, before it was too late. The priest squeezed in, finding a space among the densely packed Tuigan. As a foreigner, he had no vote in the the proceedings, but even being allowed to watch was a great privilege.

The horn blew again. From the far side of the assembly entered Mother Bayalun, Chanar following a few paces behind. The khadun was dressed in white robes, her long, loose hair half-hidden by a white shawl. A broad sash, woven with stripes of blue and red, hung around her neck. She walked slowly but firmly across the circle to take her seat at the head of the assembly. Chanar took a position among the khans sitting on the left.

The horn blew for a third time. Koja, sitting between a stiff-backed, black-robed commander of the Kashik and a belching, greasy-haired khan whose name he did not know, tensed in anticipation. Instead of the surprise he expected, however, Koja was disappointed to see only Jad and Goyuk venture out to join the *couralitai*. The prince took his seat, barely acknowledging his stepmother. Goyuk stood quietly behind him, ready to advise the khahan's son.

The khans fell silent, expecting the first words of the session. By tradition, these were spoken by the son of the departed. Jad raised his hand and waited for the last murmuring khans to fall quiet. Satisfied that he had their attention, the prince stood up before the assembled nobles.

"Jadaran of the Hoekun welcomes you. As khan of the Tuigan, he welcomes you. Let this council begin."

With these words, the council was open. Custom gave the honor of the next speech to the commander of the Kashik.

A strong, clear voice suddenly rang out. "Illustrious youth, son of our beloved khahan, commander of forty thousand, this one requests that he may be heard." There was a buzz of excitement at these words. The speaker had made the request in most respectful language, using all the proper forms and inflections—but it was not the commander of the Kashik. At the far side of the council, the wolf-faced Chagadai, dressed in a ragged and filthy *kalat*, stood to address the prince. He wore a dirty white turban in the style of the western clans. Without waiting to be recognized, he pushed his way to the center of the circle.

The Kashik commander, sitting near Jad, glared at the speaker. The upstart had deliberately insulted him. The commander looked to Jad for guidance, but the prince was in as much consternation as he. Goyuk leaned forward and whispered in the prince's ear. Jad spoke a few words in response, obviously debating with the old man about what could be done. Next to him, Bayalun sat, unmoved by the startling turn. A faint smile played across her lips. Finally,

Jadaran looked toward the upstart khan. Throwing a resigned look the commander's way, the prince conceded, reciting the formula required of him. "As lord of this *couralitai*, I will hear Chagadai speak."

"May the thanks of Teylas be upon the noble prince," answered the renegade khan. Now that he was recognized, he turned to his fellow nobles in the audience. "Hear me, khans. Know that I am Chagadai of the Uesgir.

"I will not waste time retelling the deeds of my family or all the greatness of the khahan. These things we know. Instead, I ask a question we have all been wondering—where is the khahan? Where is the one who has led our people to greatness? They," he shouted, turning toward Jad, "say he has fallen. Yet they do nothing!" Jad tensed and prepared to interrupt, when Goyuk once again whispered in his ear. The prince bit his lip and nodded curtly, waiting for Chagadai to continue.

"What is the duty of a son?" Chagadai quietly asked, stepping closer to the prince. "When the father is killed, the son should not hide in his tent. He should find the murderers."

There was a grumble among the nobles. Prince Jadaran squirmed, angered by the accusation. Chanar watched coolly from his seat, his tented fingers touched against his lips. Bayalun's smile had vanished, leaving her face a blank.

Chagadai turned back to the assembled nobles. "There are ambassadors from Khazari in our camp. They arrived only yesterday. Now, why do ambassadors from our enemy come just when we are in our mourning? Do they come to share our sorrow?" The khan stopped to mop the nervous sweat from his neck. "They come to negotiate, to negotiate with Jadaran Khan in our hour of victory! He is taking our victory from us. *Your* warriors died in this battle." Chagadai stopped, pacing down the length of the *couralitai*. There was a growing undertone of discontent among Bayalun's allies.

Theatrically turning to them, Chagadai asked, "Is this who should be khahan? Let us choose another."

Jad moved to stand, only to be stopped by Goyuk's hand on his shoulder. "Let him speak," the old advisor whispered. "This is what we want." The prince sank back down, his eyes smoldering with hatred.

"Let Chanar Ong Kho be khahan," shouted a voice from the ranks of the seated khans.

Several of the younger nobles on Bayalun's side clapped their hands, showing their support. The priest glanced around. Jad's supporters, at least those willing to show their loyalty, were few in number. It seemed that the prince faced a serious challenge to his authority.

"Chanar Ong Kho must be khahan!" cried the voice again.

To everyone's surprise, Chanar shook his head, refusing to accept the offer. The general rose to address the assembly. "I thank the wise khans, but these words are disrespectful to the memory of the khahan. I am not worthy of this honor. Let the nomination go to another." There was a sigh of disappointment from Bayalun's side of the group.

Chagadai, still standing in the center of the council, refused to relent. He pressed the offer again. "Let Chanar be khahan!" The man stopped his pace near Jad. Again, the prince made to stand, only to be restrained by the gentle touch from Goyuk. The clapping for Chanar was louder this time.

Chagadai glanced toward Bayalun. She gave a quick smile of approval. The khan was doing well, acting just as she had instructed him this morning.

Slowly, Chagadai faced all the assembly once more. "Chanar will not be khahan," he said with disappointment in his voice. "Still, Jad must show his worth. Perhaps the khahan's killers have been found and perhaps his body is in his yurt. But we have not seen the body. Jad tells us what happened, but shows us no proof. Are we sure the khahan was slain in battle? Perhaps someone else killed him. Someone who does not want us to know the truth. Let us see Yamun's body and learn the truth for ourselves." With those words, Chagadai strode out of the clearing toward the door of Yamun's yurt.

Just as he reached it, Sechen stepped forward and blocked the entrance with his sword.

"Why is Jad afraid?" shouted Chagadai, turning his back to the door so he could address the *couralitai*. Caught up in the excitement and straining to see, the nobles were on their feet. "Let us see the khahan's body!" shouted many from the crowd.

"Then see it you will," said a voice behind Chagadai, echoing from the doorway of the tent.

The khans in the crowd stopped their cries and froze in disbelief. Standing in the doorway was Yamun Khahan. He was dressed in coarse robes of blue serge cinched with a belt of leather and gold. His hair was undone, shaped in a halo around his shaven pate. He leaned against the doorjamb to steady himself.

"The khahan!" whispered the big, crude khan next to Koja. The assembly echoed the man's words like the breath of a wind spirit. Several of the men abruptly knelt, bowing their heads toward their risen leader. Chagadai turned slowly toward his lord, his eyes wide with shock and fear.

Yamun ignored the wolfish khan. Pushing past Chagadai, he slowly but steadily walked into the center of the *couralitai*. Yamun's color was still pale, and it was clear that every step drained away a little of his strength. His brow glistened with sweat from the effort of each footstep. Nevertheless, the khahan never flinched. At last, Yamun reached the center of the circle, swaying slightly on his feet. He turned and scanned the faces of the khans in attendance. "Now, who will be khahan?" he demanded, as if he were some vengeful apparition.

No one answered. No one, it seemed, could tear his eyes from the khahan.

Koja looked toward Bayalun. She was once again smiling the same faintly triumphant smile that had crossed her face earlier. Next to her, Jad was watching the khans, his smile equally triumphant as he searched out the slightest sign of opposition.

"None shall be khahan but you, dear husband," Bayalun said diplomatically. "But some, believing you dead, were eager for a new khahan." All eyes turned toward Chagadai. His thin face grew pale. "They forgot what is proper and called for Chanar to be khahan, ignoring your own sons. They did not even wait the thirty days of mourning that tradition demands." Bayalun tapped the ground with her staff for emphasis.

Chagadai nervously walked down the path, trying to discreetly return to his place. Those khans who had applauded his words sat very quietly in their seats, doing nothing to attract attention to themselves. Yamun turned toward the trembling Chagadai, fixing the man to the spot with his fierce stare. Those between the two men slid out of the way. "These words are true," the khahan growled.

"Great Lord," Chagadai sputtered, falling to one knee and bowing his head. "I did these things for the good of your people. Hubadai attacks Semphar, while we fight the Khazari. We need guidance."

"And my son isn't fit to rule. This is treason."

The nobles whispered in fearful concern. None, however, dared raise his voice in protest.

"Husband and son," Bayalun interjected, "he acted for the good of the Tuigan. If Chagadai knew you lived, he would not have spoken so."

" 'Only a foolish man holds the pecking hawk close to his eyes,' " Yamun angrily retorted, using an old proverb to make his point. "Like the hawk, Chagadai attacks me. He has betrayed me." Yamun strode to where the khan cowered.

Before anyone could object, Yamun drew his sword and thrust it forward. The sword pierced the khan's chest. There was a choked gasp of surprise from Chagadai, then he flopped to the ground, blood spurting from his wound. The dying man twitched and jerked, but finally lay still. Yamun, exhausted by the effort, leaned on the sword, its tip in the dirt, blood running down the blade.

For a moment, no one spoke. The khans, so vocal before,

were unwilling to draw Yamun's ire. The khahan, as he regained his breath, grimly scanned the assembly, looking for anyone who might challenge his actions. Servants hurried forward and dragged the body away, sweeping dirt over the dark stain of blood on the ground.

"You have been told I died in battle," Yamun finally said to his apprehensive audience. "This was a lie, you say: the khahan did not die." Yamun wiped the bloody sword on his robe. "I remained hidden by my own command. I wanted you, my faithful khans, to think me dead."

"Why, Great Khan, why?" one of khans sitting on Jad's side asked hesitantly.

"I was attacked by assassins. I was wounded, but I live. Teylas protected me from this evil attack." He stopped to recover his strength. Suddenly everyone could see his weakness.

"Who did this to our khahan?" Bayalun called out. She looked around, waiting for an answer.

"The Khazari!" answered one from Jad's side of the *couralitai*. Koja suddenly felt uncomfortable, exposed. The commander next to the priest swiveled slightly, one hand on his sword. On the other side, the belching khan slid back, not wanting to sit too close to the lama.

"No, not the Khazari," Yamun snapped. "It was a Khazari who saved me from the assassins. The lama, Koja, fought to protect me from my attackers. For this I've made him my *anda*." The khans on either side of Koja eyed him with surprised respect.

"Who then?" asked a khan.

"Do you want to see my assassins?" Yamun asked, feigning reluctance. Weakened by the effort of speaking, the khahan closed his eyes. The wave of shouted approval from the khans rocked him slightly. Slowly, he took the empty seat between Jad and Bayalun.

"The bodies! Yes, we will see the bodies," the commander next to Koja shouted, urging the khans around him to add their voices to the cry. It quickly swelled and grew as khans from both sides expressed their outrage. Yamun settled back, confident that the khans still followed him.

"The bodies, bring the bodies!" went up the chant.

Yamun raised his hand, commanding silence. "Loyal khans," he shouted over the dying rumble, drawing deeper on his reserves of strength. "You shall see them. Sechen, bring the assassins here."

In the brief moments it took to fetch the grim bundle, Yamun sagged back in his seat. The khahan, Jad, and Goyuk conferred quickly amongst themselves.

Sechen returned, carrying the bloodstained rug, and dropped it with a thud at Yamun's feet. A wave of anticipation rippled through the nobles.

"Now, see who attacked your khahan," Yamun solemnly announced. "An unclean creature and a man!" With the tip of his boot, the khahan carefully pushed a fold of the rug aside. A visible wave of pollution and decay, marked by a cloud of flies, rose up from the rotting bodies. A gasp of astonishment came spontaneously from the assembled group.

"A beast!" hissed a voice filled with disgust. "They send beasts to kill our khahan!"

There were two bodies in the rug: the *hu hsien* and the wizard. The once-bright fur of the fox creature was stiff and dull-colored. Its wounds, more fearsome in death, were sunken, the edges soft and black. Dark patches of decay spread from these, mottling the skin beneath the bristling fur. The eyes were gone, pecked out by birds. A purplish tongue, dry and cracked, lolled out of its mouth. The human next to it was equally decayed, the slashed throat gray and crusted.

Bayalun choked, "Afrasib!" She quickly clamped her mouth shut and avoided Yamun's gaze. Her face was pale. Leaning over, she whispered a word to one of the khans beside her. He nodded and slid back out of sight.

"Who are they?" cried out a thin, pock-marked khan, pushing his way through his fellows to get a closer look at the corpses. The other khans surged forward behind him.

- 224 -

"The beast is a *hu hsien*, a creature of Shou Lung," Jad explained. "The other is the wizard, Afrasib." The prince stopped, letting the khans form their own conclusions.

Eyes, suspicious and hard, started to turn toward Bayalun. She met their gaze firmly, not showing any fear. Slowly and regally, the khadun stood and walked to the dead bodies. She studied the corpses, poking at them with her staff. The khans stepped back, creating a circle around her. She rolled Afrasib's head to the side. "Traitor!" she hissed. Leaning over, she spat onto the dead wizard's face.

"He has betrayed the khahan. The Shou emperor must have bought his loyalty," Bayalun announced, turning back to her seat.

"But who sent these killers?" the pock-faced khan asked, his questions still not satisfied.

"Who, indeed?" Jad asked, looking toward Bayalun.

"The emperor of Shou uses things like the *hu hsien* as spies," Bayalun countered as she stiffly sat down. "Ask Yamun's priest if this is not so."

"It is true," Yamun said. In the crowd, Koja started at the statement. He didn't see why the khahan was siding with the khadun. He must be must be planning something, the lama decided.

"This is what Shou Lung thinks of us," sneered Yamun, still talking. "Their emperor fears us, so he sends evil spirits to kill me. Do we fear the dogs of Shou?"

"No!" came the cry. Even Chanar seemed roused by the khahan's passionate boast.

"Shall we sit here while they send killers—like this—" Yamun jabbed a finger toward the dead *hu hsien*. "He sends beasts to stalk us. Are we deer before the hunter?"

"No!" came the shout again. The khans were gripped by rage. Koja was amazed; Yamun showed no sign of the wounds that weakened him only a few minutes before. The khahan stood tall, his legs spread and set solidly.

"Do we wait for them to destroy us all or do we act?" Yamun demanded, raising his arms to the sky. His eyes were fiery, energetic, and powerful, filled with a blaze of blood-lust. Koja gaped. He'd seen the khahan like this only once before, during the great storm at Quaraband.

The khans responded with an inarticulate roar, too many voices trying to shout out their answer all at once. There were those who dissented, but their words were drowned out by the furious outrage of their fellows.

The flood of rage and anger seemed to invigorate Yamun even further. He surveyed the khans with pride, reveling in their fire and adulation. He let the warriors have their way for a while, then raised his hands for silence. Reluctantly, they hushed to hear his words.

Yamun pushed the khans back from the bodies, clearing himself some space. "This Shou emperor has declared war on us. What shall we do?"

"We must teach them a lesson!" roared out one of the khans, Mongke by name—a thin, bony man with a powerful voice that belied his meager frame.

"How?" demanded Koja, boldly stepping into the circle. "What about the Dragonwall, the great fortification that protects their border? It has never been broken. How will you get through that?" Irritated at the priest's outburst, some of the khans began to shout down his concerns.

"We will conquer Shou because the emperor fears us," Yamun stated with utter conviction. "If this Dragonwall was invincible, the emperor would not fear me. Teylas must have spared me to become a scourge on the emperor, to break his unbreakable wall!"

"A raid!" suggested one of the Kashik khans.

"No, not a raid," Yamun answered coolly. "More than a raid. We'll teach this emperor to fear. We will conquer Shou Lung! I, Yamun Khahan, will be the Illustrious Emperor of All People!" The khahan roared out the last words to the sky, threatening as much as promising. "It is our destiny."

Yamun's eyes blazed. He panted, lustful for the challenge. His heart longed for the fury of battle and the greatness conquest would bring to him.

The excitement of the khans formed into a chant. It was as if Yamun's vision of conquest spread from him to them. It leaped to the khans, took possession of their spirit. Even Koja felt the wild passion, the lust to act that flowed from Yamun.

The khahan stepped back to his seat and surveyed the khans. They looked to him in anticipation: some eager, a few fearful. "Who will go to war with me? Who will share in the riches of Shou Lung?" he shouted to the masses.

The response came in a tumult of yells and clapping from the khans. Koja, in their midst, was almost deafened by the warriors' frantic shouts. Yamun stood before his seat, clearly enjoying the frenzy. His eyes were wild, and his face was flushed and pulsing with energy. It seemed to the priest that the khahan had found his own cure. Here again was the man who could withstand the might of a god's thunderbolts.

"By the will of Teylas, my khans, we will ride to victory!" proclaimed the khahan. "The Dragonwall must fall!"

– 13 –
Plots

Yamun growled at his bodyguards, ten Kashik warriors who circled him at a respectful distance. One of them had clumsily bumped into an armor stand, sending Yamun's gilt mail sprawling. Fumbling to correct his error, man made still more noise. Yamun snarled impatiently for the mortified soldier to stop fussing.

It was one thing to have a bodyguard of ten thousand men who would make camp, patrol at night, and charge boldly into battle; it was quite another thing to have an *arban* of soldiers hovering around you wherever you went. The Kashik, however, upon learning that morning that their khahan still lived, were determined to protect him at all times. It was a great honor for the men chosen to guard the khahan, but it was going to take time for Yamun to get adjusted. Still, the khahan knew better than to argue with the devotion and loyalty of his own men.

The guard finally finished straightening the gear and quietly took his place along the wall of the Great Yurt. The other guards stood silently in their positions. Satisfied that there would be no more disturbances, Yamun resumed his conversation.

Sitting at the foot of Yamun's throne was his *anda*, the grand historian, Koja. "Well, *anda*," Yamun said to him, "soon there'll be more to write in your histories, if you have the time. There's much to be done before we march on Shou Lung."

The priest looked at Yamun sharply, still puzzled by the events of the *couralitai*. "Why have you done this?" he finally asked. "You attack Shou Lung and ignore Bayalun. Is this wise?"

Yamun scowled. "*Anda*, I did what I must." He held out his fists. "Someone seeks to kill me: Bayalun—" He closed one fist. "And Shou Lung." He closed the other. "I will not ignore this insult."

"But Shou Lung is the mightiest of nations!" protested Koja. "Why them and not Bayalun?"

"Bayalun is one of my people. If I strike at her, there will be dissension among the khans. They will demand proof and the wizards will turn against me," the khahan predicted. "Then my empire would be nothing." He lowered his fists. "But, if I attack Shou Lung, my people will stand united in battle, and I will be rid of one enemy. Better one foe than two. That is ruling, is it not?"

Koja swallowed, hearing the determination in Yamun's voice. "But Shou Lung is huge!"

"And their emperor is afraid of me. Scared men can be beaten," Yamun confidently predicted.

Koja resigned himself to Yamun's decision. "What of Bayalun?" he asked as an afterthought.

Yamun dismissed her name with casual wave. "Now that I know her tricks, she will be watched. We will keep her here with us so she can't cause problems. We will keep the snake under our heel."

"I have decided," Yamun noted idly, abruptly changing the subject, "you'll meet with these envoys from Khazari and handle the details of their surrender. I've got to make plans for our conquest of Shou Lung."

"Me, Yamun? Have you forgotten that I am a Khazari? I can't negotiate the surrender," Koja protested.

"Who said negotiate?" the khahan replied sharply. "Just accept their surrender."

"But, there must be terms. I can't just tell them to give up."

"Why not?" Yamun asked, stroking the fine point of his

mustache. "They've got no army to protect Manass. I can destroy anything they send. You tell them that. There are too many things for me to do here. There are orders to give, and reports have just arrived from Hubadai in Semphar." He pointed to the royal scribe, next to whom sat a bundle of papers tied with yellow silk ribbons.

"But, they want my head!" the little lama sputtered, nervously rubbing his scalp.

An ironic smile twisted the khahan's scarred lips. "You will do this because I have ordered it. They want your head, so they no longer consider you a countryman. You see, you are no longer a Khazari."

Koja swallowed at Yamun's words. "What can I do?" Although he did not want this task at all, it was clear that he had to accept the khahan's will.

"I want them to surrender," Yamun repeated, knowing that Koja expected more. "Very well, I want goods equal to ten thousand bars of silver to be paid on the first moon of every new year. Then, they must turn over this governor, his wizard, and the Shou officials you described. They escaped the battlefield and I want them—or their heads and hands."

Koja waited for Yamun to outline more, but the khahan had finished his demands. "That is not all," the priest enjoined.

Yamun counted out his terms on his fingers. "Surrender, goods, and prisoners. What else is there?"

Exasperated, Koja took paper and pen from the scribe, spreading the sheet between himself and Yamun. Koja quickly drew Khazari's borders.

"Yamun, these are not wandering tribesmen you have conquered. The Khazari will not surrender and obey you just because you are khahan—"

"Then I'll destroy their homes and scatter the people among my khans. Tell them that," Yamun threatened.

"No, Yamun, that will not do. The Khazari are not like the tribes." Koja dotted the map with the towns and cities of

Khazari. "They have stone towns and fields. They do not travel from camp to camp. You must set someone to rule them, pass laws, and make judgments."

Yamun leaned forward to study Koja's map. "This is not our way," he grumbled. "But because you say it must be done, I will consider it. For now, tell the envoys they must give me Manass as my own. Then, they must tear down the walls around all their other *ordus*." The khahan pushed the crude map away with his toe. "Make me a good map of Khazari, *anda*."

Koja sighed and thought through the list of demands that Yamun had made. "And what can you negotiate on?"

"My *anda*, there will be no negotiation." Yamun loomed over the priest to add emphasis to his words.

"And if they refuse?" Koja asked softly.

Yamun casually sipped from a cup of kumiss. "As I said: I will destroy every *ordu* in Khazari. Every male taller than the yoke of an oxcart will be put to the sword, and all their wives and little children will be scattered as slaves among my people. Their nation will be no more. That I can do, *anda*." The khahan settled back into his seat. "Scribe, write out my demands. I'll put my seal to it. *Anda*, you can take that with you as proof."

The demands written, Yamun turned to his scribe and ordered him to begin reading the stack of reports that sat beside him. Koja rose to one knee and made a brief bow to the khahan before slowly backing out of his presence. Rapt in Hubadai's account of the fall of Semphar, Yamun didn't even notice his departure.

* * * * *

In her commandeered yurt, Mother Bayalun worked alone, preparing to cast her magical spells. The door to the yurt was carefully fastened, sealing out all light, and her guard had instructions not to let anyone disturb her, not even Chanar, her current paramour. Her hands moving quickly, the khadun set out the materials she needed: a brazier containing a small glowing coal and a small pouch of powdered incense. Softly, in case anyone might be listening, she muttered the incantation, passing her hands over the brazier.

The words finished, Bayalun flung a pinch of incense into the coals. There was a brilliant puff, and smoke coiled thickly into the air, writhing and turning, forming into the face of a Shou mandarin. The smoke made the man's forehead appear soft and puffy, like bread dough, but his dark eyes shone clearly. The smoky face blinked a few times in surprise, as if the mandarin had been awoken by the spell.

"Khadun of the Tuigan," it rumbled in surprise with a hollow-sounding voice, "you called me?"

"Indeed. We must speak." Her breath caused the outlines of the wraith to waver and shift.

"Now is not the best time, Eke Bayalun Khadun," the face said, the puffy features forming into something that looked like a scowl. "The emperor is giving a poetry reading. It is difficult for me to concentrate on both." As if to illustrate the point, the cloud-face's eyes rolled back into its head. The outlines started to spread and rise, breaking up as the contact was momentarily lost. Then the head began to reform as the speaker refocused his thoughts toward Bayalun and the barren steppes. "Speak quickly, Khadun. My time is short."

"Do not order me, Ju-Hai Chou. I am not one of your dog-people," the second empress snapped. She reached for a small fan, a gift from the Shou emperor, to dispel the smoky form.

"Most humble apologies, wise one," said the face with an expression of diplomatic regret. The head tilted a little to bow toward her. "Please inform this simple servant why you have summoned him. You *did* summon me."

Bayalun was accustomed to the mandarin's impatience and paid it no attention. Slowly, the khadun smoothed her robes, adjusting the *jupon*, the overrobe, so that it hung straight from her shoulders. "The Tuigan army is in

Khazari."

"This we know through our spies. Is that all?" There was a trace of annoyance in the mandarin's voice at being disturbed over such petty news.

"The khahan lives. The creature you sent failed." Although the assassination attempt had been a near disaster, she relished telling the Shou minister of state the news. The image's eyes widened in surprise, then quickly became blank.

"Is it alive or dead?" His words were quick and clipped.

"Dead."

"Do they suspect?"

"Me?" Eke Bayalun asked, knowing full well that was not what the mandarin meant. He couldn't care less about her troubles. "Of course they suspect."

The vaporous brows furrowed. "By that you mean your khahan suspects Shou Lung."

"He does not just suspect," Bayalun gloated. "He blames the emperor of the Jade Throne himself. Your little assassin was too obvious and easy to identify—once he was dead. A priest of the Khazari knew quite a bit about your *hu hsien.*"

"A Khazari priest?" the image ruminated, the words echoing around the small yurt. "Who—"

"An envoy of Prince Ogandi. But that does not matter." Bayalun knew perfectly well the mandarin was eager to know more. She relished goading the Shou bureaucrat with these petty secrets. It kept him off-balance.

"Know this," she continued before the mandarin could protest or probe further. "The khahan blames your Son of Heaven and is marching with his army to conquer all of Shou."

The face smiled, parts of its cheeks drifting away. The smoky shape was slowly becoming smaller, leaner. "He is more foolish than we thought. We will easily brush him away like a small insect. He cannot break the Dragonwall." The trace of panic and puzzlement that had been in the voice was gone, replaced by confidence.

"Perhaps," countered Bayalun. "By the time he reaches the Dragonwall, he will have two hundred thousand warriors."

The cloud snorted a puff of smoke in contempt.

"He might also have magical aid," Mother Bayalun stated slowly. She deliberately picked up the fan and gently waved it to cool her face. The image wavered and spread, pushed back by the gentle breeze.

A smoky eyebrow raised. "Unless?" it hissed, picking up the beat of her words.

"I have kept you too long from your duties," the crafty woman said. "Perhaps you should return to your emperor."

The face barely repressed a grimace of frustration. "Perhaps I should have the Gorath come speak with you!" Bayalun blanched slightly at the mention of the Gorath, a creature of great power rumored to be the emperor's personal assassin. The smoke of the mandarin's face swirled and distorted, breaking up in several different directions.

"Threaten me, Ju-Hai Chou, and I will end this alliance in blood!" Bayalun spat.

"Threaten us," the mandarin answered in a cooler, but no more friendly tone, "and we will expose you. There will always be another willing to aid us." The image restored itself to form and glared down from the top of the tent. Bayalun matched stare for stare, stiffly getting to her feet so she didn't have to look so far upward. One hand still clutched the fan.

"Then we must work together," she finally said. Although a powerful sorceress, Bayalun knew that the mandarin's threat was real, just as he knew her threat was no idle boast.

"Indeed," agreed the voice. "What is it you now seek?"

"Your feeble assassin is what brought us to this disaster. Now, you must be ready to give more. Yamun's throne you have already promised—but now he goes to war with you. You'll have to buy your peace. First, you'll have to pay a tribute to get the khans to go home."

"A bribe, you mean."

"Call it what you will."

"And how do we get rid of your troublesome son?" the face asked. Bayalun's magic was fading; the back of the smoke-formed head was trailing off into a cloud of winding tendrils. Suddenly form's eyes rolled back again as the mandarin's concentration weakened.

Bayalun spoke quickly, before she lost contact entirely. "The khahan marches toward the Dragonwall. There you will have to destroy him and his bodyguards. I cannot do this now. They are too suspicious of me. It must be done by the armies of Shou Lung. You can trap and destroy him with my aid. There are those in his army who will help us."

"A trap . . . ," the mandarin's voice echoed, the face completely gone from sight. ". . . meet again . . . Xanghi River." The spell was broken. The vapor swirled out through the yurt's smoke hole.

Vexed by her conversation, Bayalun waited until all the trailing wisps faded away. The heavy scent of incense still hung in the air. Satisfied that all traces of her work had dissipated, Bayalun gathered up her pouch of incense and set the brazier back in its proper spot. Shuffling slowly to the door, for these days she moved stiffer when no one was around, she undid the ties and pulled the flap back. Thrusting her head out into the afternoon sun, she startled the guards, who were standing at ease on either side of the door.

"Send a runner for General Chanar. Tell him the khadun would be most honored if he would attend her." She coughed a bit and realized how raspy her voice was from the smoke-filled tent.

While one guard went off to see that her orders were carried out, Bayalun had the other bring out one of the small chests so she could sit in the sun. Settling in comfortably, she planted her staff between her feet and wrapped her hands around its gnarled wooden shaft. The sunshine cut through the cool spring air and heated her tired, aching body. In a short time, she closed her eyes and relaxed.

To passersby who might not know better, Bayalun was just another matron, dozing in the warm afternoon sun. But she was not asleep. A corner of her mind was still alert and attentive, listening to the outside world. But the rest of her mind wandered, thinking back to other times, more youthful days among her mother's people, the Maraloi.

A series of footfalls brought Bayalun out of her dark reverie. She stretched her neck, struggling to clear her head. Opening her eyes, she saw Chanar waiting impatiently for her word.

"I have come to do you honor," he said pompously. He did not kneel to the khadun, but stood waiting for her to acknowledge his presence.

Bayalun looked up at him over the golden finial of her staff. The general's arrogance was almost palpable, but he still cut a handsome figure. His braids were long and full, and his mustache carefully trimmed. Dressed in armor, he looked the powerful warrior that he truly was, one of the seven valiant men. "Help me up," she said, although it sounded more like a command. Chanar easily hoisted Bayalun to her feet.

The general followed her into the yurt and reached for her waist as soon as the flap closed. Gently she slid out of his grasp and blocked him with her staff. "Do you still have the desire—" Chanar's eyes gleamed lustfully. "To take the power that should be yours?" the khadun concluded.

He stopped where he was, somewhat taken aback by her question. "To become khahan, you mean?"

"Of course." Her light smile mocked him. "What else?"

Chanar turned away, hands clasped behind his back, arrogance and desire rising up to face what remained of his loyalty. "Before—when we spoke—it was 'Who could save the empire if the khahan died?' You spoke of things that could happen, might happen, even hinted that you saw something with your arts. I believed you." Chanar turned back toward her, his face graven with a look of betrayal.

"But then, the khahan shows this . . . thing that attacked

him. I knew you weren't speculating then. You did that. You sent a beast, not even man! Not even Yamun should die like that. You wanted to kill Yamun, but you failed. And now you want to try again—and drag me into it."

Bayalun cocked her head as Chanar spoke, watching him through gradually narrowing slits. "So, that's it," she said in a soft monotone, "your courage leaves you when your hand must hold the reins. You are willing to let me do your work. No wonder you're such a fine general—ordering others to their deaths."

Chanar reddened in anger and embarrassment, and his voice rose to a snarling hiss. "That's not true! I'm braver than any man. You're changing my words. It's just that now I see you want me to be your assassin."

"Foolish man. If I wanted a killer, I could find one who would not have doubts," Bayalun said as she lightly dismissed his rage. She put her hand on his chest. "I do not want a killer; I come to you because I see that you are a leader. And I thought I saw a man, but you are afraid to even hear what I have to say."

Chanar gritted his teeth, biting back the rage. "Yamun is my *anda*," he spat.

Bayalun sprang upon his words like a hawk striking the trainer's lure. Her jaw trembled as she circled round him. "Has he treated you like his *anda*?" she goaded. "Do you drink his kumiss? No, a little, bald foreigner does that for you. The priest sits at his councils, not you. His wet-nosed sons lead his Kashik in battle. Others mock you behind your back."

Eyes flashing as the huntress in her closed for the kill, the widow pressed close to Chanar's side and continued, whispering in his ear. "I've heard them, when the khahan sits with the other khans. I've heard them talk of you. Fool, evil dog, lazy mule—those are things they say. Then they laugh around the fire and drink more kumiss. Perhaps they are right. I offer you the throne of the Tuigan and you will not take it."

"Bayalun, you have your reasons to see him gone! If not me, you'd turn to another for help," Chanar accused.

"Of course I have my reasons, and I will turn to anyone who can help me," came the unhesitating reply. There was no shame in the widow's voice, only a bitter undertone of hatred. "I think of my son. I think of my husband—my true husband, not this murderer I was forced to marry. I have not forgotten them. I have the right," she snapped. "And don't you have your reasons? Yamun will lead us all to destruction, battering our armies against the Dragonwall of Shou Lung. Perhaps the priest suggested this as a way to destroy us all. So, what will you do?"

The second empress took a step backward as she waited for Chanar's answer. He stood there quietly, his chest heaving, fingers slowly unknotting behind his back. The color that had drained from his face was gradually returning. The wind blew against the yurt, creaking the wickerwork sides. The door flap snapped against its wooden frame.

Chanar tilted his head back, looking toward the smoke hole. His lips moved, saying a silent prayer. Finally, he lowered his head and looked the confident Bayalun straight in the eyes, almost as if he were trying to fathom the depths of her dark nature.

She didn't flinch from his gaze, but met it straight on. Defiant, self-assured, savage—these qualities Chanar saw within the glistening blackness of her eyes.

The general blinked, breaking away from her hypnotic gaze. He had made his decision. Carefully Chanar pulled his long, curved saber from its scabbard, letting the weak sunlight that came through the smoke hole play over the blade. With a defiant thrust he jammed it into the carpeting between them. Bayalun gently touched the blade with her staff.

"Tell me what I have to do," he demanded grimly.

"For now, come with me," Bayalun answered gently, the coldness melting away from her now that she had triumphed. Bayalun took Chanar's hand and gently pulled him toward the back half of the tent. "There will be time for talk later."

* * * * *

Koja stumbled through the gloom, exhausted. He had been sitting all day in negotiations with the diplomats of his old lord, Prince Ogandi. He could only see it that way now— Prince Ogandi was the man he once served, what seemed to be centuries ago. This meeting had confirmed Koja's separation from his own people. He could vividly see the look of outrage and fury on the faces of the Khazari diplomats when he was presented as the khahan's representative. His title certainly hadn't helped the negotiations any.

The priest desperately wanted to go to bed and forget this awful day. Emotionally, it had been hideous, perhaps worse in its own way than the terror he had experienced on the battlefield. During the mad charge across the plain, excitement and fear had kept him detached and allowed him to witness the blood and suffering without any emotional response. He wasn't even aware during the battle of how scared he was. That realization only came later. In the tent with the Khazari, however, Koja felt every excruciating second. Their hatred for him seemed much stronger expressed in Khazari. He understood every nuance and connotation of their words. There was little he could do at the time but suffer through it, while demanding their acceptance of the khahan's terms.

Now, he had to tell Yamun the day's results. Reaching Yamun's yurt, the lama leaned against the doorframe while a servant announced him. It was not proper or decorous, but Koja didn't care. He was tired.

The servant came back and ushered the lama in. The khahan was alone, enjoying a late dinner of boiled horsemeat and curd porridge, chomping noisily on the simple food. He looked up from his meal and nodded for Koja to take a seat. Finishing the mouthful, Yamun wiped his face on the silken sleeve of his robe, leaving a greasy swipe on the fine blue fabric. "Welcome, priest. Will you eat?"

Koja nodded, although he wasn't hungry, especially not for the unappetizing dishes set out in front of him. One small advantage of being in Khazari was that he had found some proper food: roasted barley and vegetables. Still, not wanting to insult the khahan, he gingerly took a scrap of meat and a small bowl of the porridge. Chewing broadly, he made a great show of eating. Neither man spoke during the meal.

Finally, Yamun slurped down the last drops of the porridge and then wiped the bowl clean with his fingers. He set it aside and waited for the priest to finish. Koja wasted no time in pushing away his own meal, barely touched.

"They've accepted my terms for peace," Yamun predicted, scratching at the stubble of his thin beard.

"Mostly," corrected Koja. "They still have some reservations."

Yamun looked carefully at the priest. "Such as?" he asked, a steely edge in his voice.

"Of course, they agree to surrender," Koja hurriedly explained, to avoid provoking the khahan. "They are only ambassadors and will have to go back and present your terms to Prince Ogandi. However, they find them generally acceptable."

"What are their problems?" Yamun demanded, cutting through Koja's stalling. He gulped a ladleful of kumiss and waited for Koja to get to the point.

"They want to negotiate the amount of tribute—"

"Haggling?" Yamun shouted in astonishment. "I offer them peace or destruction, and they want to haggle about the price?"

"I'm sure it's only a formality, Yamun," Koja interrupted, speaking as quickly as he could.

The Illustrious Emperor of All People snorted in disgust. "You said there were problems, not just one."

"The governor and his men are a problem, too. The ambassadors want to know if you intend to keep these men as hostages. The demand for the Shou envoys has them concerned." Koja rubbed his temples, trying to make his rising headache go away.

"My intentions are clear. I'm going to kill them. It is this or total destruction. Didn't you make this clear?" Yamun looked away in vexation.

"Naturally. I stressed it to them," Koja assured the squat warlord. "They are confused."

"Why's that?" Yamun scratched his head, picking for a louse that had crawled out of his hat.

Koja discreetly chose not to notice the khahan's preening. "Taking Khazari hostages they understand, but they don't see why you want the men from Shou Lung. They are afraid this will make the Shou emperor angry with them."

Yamun ignored the comment. He set aside his kumiss and asked, "Does this governor have any use as a hostage?"

The priest thought for a minute. "I think he is a cousin of the prince."

"Good. What about the other man, the wizard who killed my men?"

Koja hesitated. He knew the man was no relation to Prince Ogandi, but if he revealed that, Yamun would certainly condemn the *dong chang* to death. That would make him, a priest of Furo, responsible for the murder. Still, if he lied, the khahan would learn the truth sooner or later and would kill the man anyway—and Koja would be in trouble.

"He is not related to anyone I know of, Yamun," Koja finally replied.

"Then he must die. The *jagun* of the men executed in Manass will want vengeance," explained the khahan. "It is known the wizard still lives. This is a great shame for their *jagun*, and it will be worse if he is allowed to escape. Therefore, the wizard will be turned over to them for punishment."

Koja cringed. He knew that the men of the *jagun* would not just kill the *dong chang*; they would make the wizard's death prolonged and agonizing. The only argument to save the wizard's life Koja could think of was that it was wrong, but it wasn't wrong to Yamun. For him, it was the correct thing to do.

"What of the governor?" the lama asked weakly. "Can I promise the Khazari that he will live?"

"Only if they also turn over the wizard and the men of Shou," Yamun stressed. "I'll keep the prince's cousin as hostage, but the others will die."

Koja pondered the offer, judging whether the Khazari would be likely to accept it. It was clear from the meetings today that the Khazari were frightened by the power and savagery of the khahan's men.

"I think they will accept that," the priest decided sadly. He felt unclean. He had managed to save the life of one man, but only at the cost of the other three.

Yamun suddenly yawned. "I am tired now, Koja, and so are you. It is time to rest. Go now." With a nod, he dismissed the priest.

The audience over, Koja returned to his yurt and quickly went to bed. Already tired, Yamun's yawn had seemed to drain him of his last energy reserves. Ignoring the cold meal Hodj had laid out, Koja went straight to bed.

At first, exhausted though he was, the priest could not sleep. He kept thinking of the day's events, particularly the wizard's fate. Koja felt responsible for Yamun's decision. Fretting and guilt-ridden, he fell into an uneasy slumber.

A noise penetrated the gray fog enclosing the priest. It was the grinding clink of stone against stone. He was outside, still dressed in his sleeping robes. The wind was blowing, but he did not feel the cold.

Looking around, Koja could see that it was still night, somewhere on a grassy plain—or what remained of it. The ground was a jumble of cracks and upheaved earth. Bodies of warriors and horses lay half-buried, half-crushed under the churned ground. Some were Tuigan bodies, clearly identified by the war banners flapping spectrally in the wind. Mingled among the troopers were the bodies of other warriors, dressed in antique armors. Koja could recognize only a few. A man here wore the garb of a Kalmyr chieftain, like one the priest had seen on an ancient scroll. Another wore the outlandish armor of a Susen warrior, easily identified by the flaring earpieces on the battered helm. The bodies encased by the armors were dried husks, their mummified skin stretched tight over the bone.

The odd noise came from up ahead. Koja clambered over the mounds of dirt, past the skeletal warriors and broken lances. Reaching the top of the largest mound, he could see a dark shape, a wall of immense size. To the left and right, it stretched beyond his vision. It stood higher than the five-storied palace of Prince Ogandi in Skardu. At the top was a line of battlements, jutting upward like broken teeth. The hammering sound came from its base.

As he drew closer, Koja saw a line of men, futilely battering the wall's foundation with mauls. Like the dead of the broken land behind Koja, these men were dressed in a weird assortment of ancient clothes. There were soldiers from Kalmyr, Susen, Pazruki, and men from lands he could not identify from their garb.

Each man swung his maul at a single spot, a single stone, oblivious to those around him. The ground reverberated with their blows, but no swing left any mark on the fortification.

Fascinated, Koja walked down the line, invisible to the toilers. He passed by a Kalmyri, then stopped to study the man. It was Hun-kho, the great war chief of Kalmyr. Centuries ago, Hun-kho had driven the Shou out of the wasteland, back behind the Dragonwall, only to be stopped by the Shou construction. Koja recognized him from the history texts in the temple.

The dead warlord continued his monotonous task. Koja resumed his walk. Farther on was the infamous T'oyghla of the Susen, a conqueror in his own right. He, too, never faltered from his work on the wall.

Finally, Koja saw an end to the line and a lone, robed figure, apart from the others. This man held a hammer, but did not swing it at the Dragonwall. Compelled by curiosity, the lama ran forward. When he reached the man, Koja put a hand on the mason's shoulder. The figure turned, revealing the face of his old master, horribly shriveled and gaunt. Smiling, the master handed Koja the hammer.

"This is the wall you have chosen. Break it and be free," the old man intoned. Seizing the sledge, Koja watched as the old master faded before his eyes. Suddenly he was alone with a line of warlords.

Automatically, Koja swung the maul. The stone splintered, splitting the smooth surface of the wall. Koja looked at the crack. Something glittered and slid inside it. He swung again and the crack widened. A shape softly ground against the ragged edges of the stone. The line of warlords stopped, turning in dumb astonishment. The lama peered into the crack. Something moved inside the Dragonwall, something huge and scaled.

"Free me," it whispered, the tones musically floating out through the hole. "Free me, Koja of Khazari."

Koja swung the maul. A painful shock ran through his hands as the sledge hit stone. Chips flew, but the crack was no larger. He swung again and again, jolting with each blow. The priest's breath came in ragged pants. His sweaty hands grasped the maul's handle, trying to keep it from slipping away. He pounded frantically, desperate to widen the crack.

Finally, Koja stopped, exhausted. Looking up, he saw the crack was unchanged, unbroken. It was no wider than it was when he started. There were no chips or scratches in its surface. Frustrated, he slumped down at the foot of the wall, the spirit drained out of him.

"You alone cannot free me, Koja of Khazari, any more than these others who have tried and failed." Lit by a faint glow, the warlords returned to their task.

"Who are you?" Koja gasped to the mysterious voice.

"I am Lord Chien, master of the ocean," the voice said haughtily. "I am the Dragonwall."

"Why can't I free you?" Koja asked as he clambered to his feet.

"I await your lord. Together you will have the might to humble my captors." Dark scales slid past the crack in the wall, then a baleful eye, yellow and catlike, came into view.

"Guide him," the strange voice continued. "Bring your lord to me and together you will free me."

"Why do you call me?" Koja demanded as he stared at the huge eye.

"You are his man. He listens to you. The others, here, know the price of failure. They are doomed to stay, tormenting me, until the wall is no more." Koja looked at the toiling lords and shuddered.

"And if I do these things?" the lama asked, backing away from the crack.

"Then I will have my revenge!" roared the voice. The ground shook with the spirit's words, then the eye disappeared from view.

Shaking, Koja turned. There was his master again, strong and healthy once more. The old man gently took the maul from Koja's grasp. The lama knew it was time for him to leave. Instinctively, he headed back the way he had come, past the conquerors and over the lands of the dead. Just as he reached the hill's top, his master called out faintly. "Everything is in balance, apprentice. Change one thing and you will destroy something else. There are walls all around you. Choose carefully the ones you will destroy." The words echoing around him, Koja walked back into his yurt, into his bed.

Blinking, Koja sat up in the near-darkness of his yurt. The events of his dream remained clear in his mind. Without knowing quite why, the lama hastily dug out his writing supplies. Huddled close to the light of a glowing brazier, Koja began to set down every detail.

- 14 -

Dreams and Destinies

In the next few days, the army's energies were consumed in its preparations to once again go on the march. When the khahan had attacked Khazari, Koja had marveled at the flow of orders given; now he was absolutely stunned. Forty thousand, perhaps even fifty thousand men had taken part in the trek to Manass, and even then only ten thousand had actually attacked the city. The rest were stationed at points along the border, partly to provide a threat to the Khazari, but more to ease the problems of finding food and water for tens of thousands of men and horses.

Now arrangements were being made for an even grander campaign. As historian, Koja discharged his duty conscientiously; he listened all he could and noted everything carefully in a growing pile of papers.

Yamun, for his part, organized his troops while waiting for the arrival of more men. Messengers were coming with greater frequency from Hubadai in Semphar. These reports were taken directly to the khahan. Other riders, wearing the stained yellow robes of Tomke's men, also arrived with their letter pouches bulging.

From different sources, Koja knew that there were one hundred and fifty thousand troopers converging on Yamun's camp. The priest guessed that there would be about two hundred thousand men in the army by the time it reached Shou Lung.

Fifty thousand men were already a burden on the land; two hundred thousand men would break it. Already the stocks of grain and grass in this region were low, because the army had not moved for so many days. In his tent, the khahan drew up plans to move the horsemen to new pastures and lay in supplies for the coming campaign.

To do this, Yamun appointed more *yurtchis* and charged them with the responsibility of gathering supplies. These officials set about their task with swift efficiency. Each day the priest watched another group of blue-robed horsemen, their faces caked in brown dust, return with a herd of lowing cattle, adding the beasts to the growing pastures of cattle and sheep. Other *jaguns* triumphantly galloped past the tents, leading in fine stallions and mares. These prizes would become the extra steeds that would be needed for the upcoming battles. Trains of oxcarts lumbered in with more goods—bags of millet and barley, sacks of flour, bales of rice, barrels of wine, urns of soy, and bricks of tea, salt, and sugar. The *yurtchis*, sitting at a makeshift table, diligently counted in all these provisions, making tally marks on long strips of paper.

All these things Koja noted in his papers as he sat in the doorway to his tent, sipping a cup of tea Hodj had prepared. There were so many details that he could only note them briefly. Finally he had to stop, before he ran out of paper. Carefully Koja packed away his writing materials and stood to leave. He still had to inform Yamun of that day's negotiations with the Khazari.

The lama carefully dusted off and adjusted the skirts of his black *kalat*, the uniform of a nightguard. It was a gift the Kashik insisted he wear; though he was uncomfortable in the dress of a warrior, the priest was not about to insult the generosity and honor of a few thousand tough soldiers. The story of how the priest had saved Yamun's life came out after the *couralitai* and spread to the guards. In recognition of his deed, they more or less adopted him into their ranks. He was now an honorary Kashik and so had to dress the part.

As the lama left the tent, the *arban* assigned to be his bodyguard hurried to catch up. What had normally been a lonely hike to the khahan's tent was now quickly becoming a minor procession.

Today the khahan was holding his court outside. He wore a light shirt of overlapping metal scales that covered his chest, and a pair of heavy, blue woolen trousers that disappeared into the loose tops of his boots. Seeing Koja coming, Yamun dismissed his aides and messengers. Rising, the warlord strode forward and grabbed the little man in a mighty hug.

"*Anda*," he said warmly, stepping back to view Koja's new garb. "I'm glad to see you. The clothes fit you well. Come and sit."

Koja could see that the khahan was in a particularly fine mood. The priest waited for tea and kumiss to be served before speaking, as was proper.

Finally, the drinks were passed. Setting his cup down, Koja began. "Your tea is excellent, Yamun."

The khahan did not acknowledge the compliment. "Have the Khazari surrendered, *anda*?" he asked casually.

"They have agreed to all your terms, including the *dong chang* and the Shou ambassadors. There is only one question they ask," Koja guardedly said. "The envoys wish to know who will rule Manass once they surrender. Will Prince Ogandi still have command?"

Yamun clapped his hands in satisfaction. "I've considered your words about ruling the country, priest. I've decided to put Jad in charge of Khazari. He'll make sure they keep the peace. Besides, he is my son. He should rule."

"This is a wise choice, Yamun." Koja was pleased. Apparently he was having some effect on Yamun's policies.

The two drank their kumiss and tea for a little while longer. Finally, Koja spoke again. "Yamun, what do you know of Shou Lung?"

"Many things, *anda*. You don't think I'm ignorant, do you?" Yamun reached out and refilled his ladle while watching the priest's reaction. "Shou Lung has an emperor, and it is a large country with much wealth, so much that this emperor sends me gifts of great value and princesses of his own blood."

"But what of their army, their defenses, their land?" Koja pressed. "Do you really know how big Shou Lung is?"

"Their army is mostly foot soldiers. They carry machines that shoot arrows—"

"Crossbows," Koja explained.

"Their soldiers are slow and can't keep up with riders. They have some horsemen, but Shou cavalry has never been very good. Even in my father's time, they rode beyond their borders to punish us for raiding. They never had much luck on these trips. So, to protect themselves they keep a wall around their land. These things every khan knows." Yamun presented it all rather matter-of-factly, as if none of it affected him at all.

"Yamun, the Shou are a numerous people, with warriors many times what the Tuigan have. They have many cities much larger than Manass."

"Cities are traps for soldiers, easy to capture." Yamun stretched lazily.

"But there is the Dragonwall," countered Koja.

"Ah, yes, this is the wall they built around their lands," Yamun commented.

"Not all their lands, Great Lord," Koja corrected. "Only along the border with what they call the Plain of Horses— your lands, the steppe."

"Then they are afraid of us." The thought made Yamun even more confident.

"Do you know how long the Dragonwall is?" the priest asked in exasperation. "It runs for hundreds of miles— *thousands* of miles." The khahan was unimpressed.

"There is a story that tells how it was built," Koja went on. Perhaps if the khahan knew how the wall was made, he would understand the power of Shou Lung.

"So now you are a storyteller, too," the khahan said indulgently. He poured out another ladleful of kumiss. "Very well, tell your tale."

Koja sighed, sensing that Yamun was not going to be swayed. Nonetheless, the priest untucked his legs and began.

"The Dragonwall is very old, but it has not been there forever. They say that long ago warriors used to ride out of the Plain of Horses and raid the lands of Shou Lung. In those days, the Shou army could not stop these riders. Each year the raiders took many horses and cattle." Koja paused to sip at his tea.

"At that time a wise emperor ruled Shou Lung. When he saw what the riders did and that his army could not stop them, he went to his advisor, a powerful wizard, and asked him, 'How can I stop these riders?'"

Yamun yawned and waved for the lama to hurry along. The priest spoke more quickly.

"The wizard told the emperor of a dragon khan who lived beneath the ocean—a lake so wide you could not see across it. The wizard said, 'Trick the dragon out of the ocean and tell him to go to the west. There I will meet him, and we will stop the invaders.'"

"Wizards," Yamun snorted. "What am I supposed to learn from this, *anda*?"

"Please, Lord Yamun, let me finish." Koja sighed and then took up the story again. "So the emperor went out in a boat and rowed to the center of the ocean. He stirred up the water with a big stick, churning the mud up from the bottom. Then the dragon khan came out of the water.

"'Who has disturbed me?' cried the dragon." Koja resisted giving the dragon a deep, booming voice, though that is how he imagined the creature would sound.

"The emperor pointed to the west. 'The one who disturbed you ran far away, to a land where there is no ocean. If you hurry, you can catch him.' So the dragon flew into the sky to chase the offender." Koja paused to catch his breath.

"A pretty story, *anda*, but what's the point?" Yamun asked impatiently.

"Well, the dragon flew to the edge of the Plain of Horses. There it saw the wizard, standing on the top of a mountain. 'Are you the man-thing who disturbed my peace?' it shouted out.

"The wizard did not answer. Instead, he uttered a word. The dragon fell from the sky. It's huge coils crashed for hundreds of miles across the ridges of the land. The ground shook, and the body of the dragon turned into the brick and stone of the Dragonwall. All from the power of a single word of a wizard and, ever since, no one has broken through the Dragonwall." Koja waited for Yamun's reaction.

The khahan rose from his seat and stretched. He looked to the sky. In the distance, the mountains were dull blue-gray, fading up to shimmering white peaks. A few storm clouds hung low on the far horizon. Turning back to Koja, Yamun said evenly but forcefully, "You claim that the Dragonwall is more powerful than me. You forget I am the khahan. I can stand in the heart of Teylas's lightning and not get hurt. I'll break the Dragonwall. It is the will of Teylas."

Yamun's words reminded Koja of the most fanatical priests of the Red Mountain Temple, men who could not be reasoned with at all. The lama sat silent while Yamun paced back and forth. The sunlight glinted off the khahan's metal shirt, sending sparkling rays in myriad directions. Finally Koja asked, "What will you do when you get to the Dragonwall?"

"I will smash it like a giant hammer," Yamun boasted, without a trace of doubt in his voice.

* * * * *

A day later, the Khazari accepted the khahan's terms of surrender. Yamun met with the ambassadors for the first time and swore an oath to Teylas with them and formally set forth the terms of their capitulation. All through the brief ceremony, the representatives of Prince Ogandi shot hateful glares at the Khazari priest who sat among their enemies.

The wizard Yamun had demanded be handed over presented a problem; someone had warned him of his fate and he managed to escape. Although he was displeased, the khahan modified the terms so that the sorcerer was named as an outlaw, and the oath-taking continued. At the end of the ceremony, after the ex-governor of Manass was surrendered to the Kashik, Yamun summoned his son, Jad, and gave him command over the Khazari. The prince was presented as the new governor of Manass. From that point on, all judgments concerning Khazari were to pass through his hands. A single *tumen*, more than enough warriors to keep the peace, the khahan pointed out, was detached and placed under Jad's command.

The next morning, Yamun's army broke camp and began the march to Shou Lung. For six days, the troopers rode northeast, heading for the First Pass Under Heaven, the gateway to the broad lands of Shou Lung. Even in early spring, the ground here was dry; the land they traveled marked the very fringe of a cold desert. Compared to their previous trek, Koja found the pace of this journey almost casual, leisurely. As the army moved, it collected more *tumens*: first the forces strung along the Khazari frontier and then a huge contingent that rode in from the west. The slow march was intentional, giving the army time to swell in size. At the start of the march there were about fifty thousand warriors. By the dawn of the sixth day, Koja estimated there were two hundred thousand men, snaking along the trail toward the Dragonwall.

It was late in the afternoon of that sixth day when Koja saw the khahan's banner finally reach the top of the First Pass Under Heaven. The *yurtchis* responsible for the day's march met the khahan there and, after presenting themselves, explained what their scouts found. Koja was too far away to hear them, but his eyes followed their sweeping gestures as they pointed down toward the plain that spread out from the base of the mountains.

From the top of the still snow-covered pass, the plain appeared to be nothing but a smooth expanse of green and brown, broken only occasionally by the darker cuts of gullies and streams. From so far away, in this realm of rock and ice, it looked like a promised land, though it was nothing but grassland, sparsely dotted with stands of trees. In the distance, the smooth ground gave way to rugged terrain. The horizon rose and fell several times, hinting at the chance of more mountains somewhere beyond.

The dark line of what seemed to be a ravine crookedly traversed the scene far out on the plain; the *yurtchis* were pointing at it with some excitement. Studying it closely, Koja realized that it was the shadow of the Dragonwall. Fascinated, Koja traced it with his finger. The wall rose, fell, twisted, curved, and disappeared from sight, only to reappear farther away.

This is what Yamun proposes to attack with men alone, the priest thought sadly. He was suddenly certain that the task was hopeless, whether Yamun had fifty thousand or five hundred thousand warriors. The khahan had no heavy equipment—towers, catapults, and rams—needed for a siege. He had no way to break the masonry wall. Whatever protective magic the wall might possess only made matters worse.

The shouted commands of the Kashik officers roused Koja out of his reverie as the horde started moving again. Carefully, the priest picked his way down the darkening eastern slope toward the campsites chosen by the *yurtchis*, leaving behind the First Pass Under Heaven.

* * * * *

Chanar was not sleeping well. For the past several nights there had been dreams, dreams he couldn't remember but knew were somehow disturbing. Another had just passed, so forceful that he tossed and turned, nearly awake.

Just then, the door flap to his yurt, which wasn't really his, opened by itself. The slight motion was enough to bring him to consciousness. The general's hand darted to his sword, carefully laid beside his bed. Glaring through the open door, he could not see any sign of an intruder. Just as he was about to rise and investigate, the flap closed, again by itself. There was a quick shimmer and suddenly Bayalun, dressed in a dark fur cloak, was kneeling by the doorway, fastening down the ties. She quickly looked up and pressed her fingers to her lips, silencing Chanar before he could even react to her sudden appearance.

"Quiet," Bayalun quickly whispered, crossing to his side. "Prepare to leave."

Chanar looked at her and blinked as his sleep-choked mind tried to sort out what was happening. Clumsily he groped for her, thinking she came to join him at his bed. Fiercely Bayalun pushed aside his advances and jabbed him in the side with her staff. "Get up!" she hissed sharply, clearly not in the mood for romance.

Startled as much by the pain as the widow's ferocity, Chanar sat straight up, ruefully rubbing his side. Awake, the general looked at the khadun, his eyes clearer and his mind starting to function. "What's going on?"

"We must go somewhere, tonight—*now*," she said with passionate urgency. "Get your robes on."

"Are we under attack? What's going on?" Chanar demanded, making no effort to keep quiet as he scrambled out from under the blankets.

"Quiet!" she ordered. "We must go to a meeting, you and I. A meeting with the Shou." Bayalun walked to the tent door, preparing to leave.

Chanar pulled on his trousers and boots, feeling an unaccountable sense of dread. "Where?" he asked.

"Just come with me." The woman didn't wait to explain more, but stooped to undo the door fastenings. Chanar hastily pulled on his mail shirt and grabbed the sword and belt nearby, buckling them on as Bayalun peeked out through the opening. "Keep quiet," she instructed. "We don't want the guards to see us leave."

Chanar shrugged, trying to get his armor to settle into

place. "Why don't you cast a spell like you did when you came?"

"Too risky. *You* do not know how to move invisibly. You'll trip over your own feet. That will certainly attract attention."

Chanar started to rebuke Bayalun, but she slipped out through the door before he could get a word out. Angrily clapping his mouth shut, Chanar followed her into the camp.

The moon was waning, casting a faint light over the camp. With the brilliance of Anjar dimmed, the sparkling points of the Nine Old Men, the stars that trailed behind the moon, showed brightly. Chanar and Bayalun carefully picked their way through the small cluster of tents in the royal compound. They stopped short once, narrowly avoiding the notice of a Kashik guard who was relieving himself just beyond the confines of the khahan's ground.

Once outside Yamun's camp, the two moved much more quickly. Hosts of men lay stretched out on the ground, wrapped in thick blankets, sound asleep. Horses on long tethers wandered among the dozing soldiers. A few men hastened to and fro, since the business of the camp never really stopped. Picking their way past the clumps of sleeping men, the conspirators took an hour to reach the edge of the camp, but no sentry challenged them along the way.

Bayalun softly released a sigh of tension, thankful for avoiding discovery. "Quickly. This way," she whispered, pulling Chanar toward a ravine that cut across a nearby slope. Bayalun set off at a brisk pace, adroitly avoiding stones and clumps Chanar could barely see. Behind her, Chanar cursed under his breath as he stumbled to keep up.

Bayalun was even more surprised than Chanar when a shadowy shape rose in front of them. At first she thought it was a Shou soldier sent to escort them. Then the figure spoke. "Stop!" the shape commanded, speaking perfect Tuigan.

Bayalun jolted to a halt, Chanar almost crashing into her.

"A sentry!" she hissed under her breath. "Quickly, speak to him." She pulled Chanar ahead of her.

"I'm Chanar Khan. Do you challenge me?" the general demanded. "Advance and name yourself." Behind the general, Bayalun slipped off to the left, disappearing into the darkness.

The sentry came forward cautiously, his sword drawn, until he was close enough to recognize Chanar's clothes. The man was only a common trooper. Flustered and nervous in the presence of a khan, the sentry finally remembered his place and dropped to one knee, bowing his head. "Do not be angry, Chanar Khan," he stammered. "I was only following the instructions of my commander."

"Good work, soldier . . . What lies beyond?" Chanar was at a loss for what he was supposed to do now. Bayalun left him stranded there, and he was beginning to think that she'd used him for a fool.

"General, this leads—" Suddenly a black shape sprang out of the darkness onto the sentry's back. The attacker struck with a knife. The guard gave a muffled, bubbling gasp. The two bodies crashed to the ground. Chanar sprang back, drawing his saber, ready to strike. The bodies thrashed about, and then the guard stopped moving.

"Help me up," commanded Bayalun from on top of the sentry. Chanar started, then recognized the black shape as the second empress. He was amazed she could move so quickly and with such strength.

Chanar pulled her up. Her hands were warm and slippery. Panting from the exertion, the khadun leaned against the general to catch her breath. The sentry's blood dripped from her fingers onto Chanar's gleaming mail.

"Help me find my staff," she said weakly.

"You killed him," Chanar said, still disbelieving the speed with which she had struck. He found Bayalun's staff and handed it to her.

"He saw us. Now drag his body into that ravine, out of sight," Bayalun commanded, pointing ahead into the darkness.

Startled into motion, the general grabbed the dead man's heels and pulled the body, facedown, through the dirt, leaving a trail of blood behind. There was a thud and then a clatter of rocks as the body slid down the slope into the gully. Rubbing the blood off his hands with a fistful of dust, Chanar stood at the top of the gully. He was looking into the thick shadows when Bayalun joined him.

"This is a bad omen," Chanar cursed as they wound their way along the bottom of the gully. He fumed quietly. "The guard's death'll be noticed. It's certain to betray us."

"Listen," Bayalun said, her fiery spirit rising, "they'll think the Shou did it. No one knows we are here."

Chanar's tension eased, seeing the wisdom of her words. "It's too bad that man had to die," he finally allowed, "but it was his fate."

Bayalun said nothing, carefully picking her way through the stones. The tumbled slopes of the ravine widened, creating a small, level circle of ground, free of broken rocks. The weak moonlight cast a dim radiance at the center of the clearing, leaving heavy, dark shadows along the edges. Bayalun stopped in one of these shadows, holding Chanar close alongside her. He could tell the second empress was excited; she trembled slightly and her breath came in rapid gasps.

They stood still, waiting. The air was chill, threatening to leave a heavy frost. Chanar thrust his hands into the wide sleeves of his robes to keep them warm and shifted uneasily, trying to maintain his patience.

A whispery voice sounded from the deep shadow on the other side of the clearing. "Welcome, Second Empress Eke Bayalun of the—"

"Enough greetings," the widow interrupted with a sharp thump of her staff. "I've come. Is Ju-Hai Chou here?"

"I speak for the Minister of State," answered the shadow, speaking with the shaky voice of an old man.

"Then know that if Ju-Hai Chou seeks our help to destroy the khahan of the Tuigan he must come himself. We do not deal with *kharachu*," Bayalun noted angrily. Chanar doubted the speaker on the other side knew he'd just been called a slave by the khadun.

"The second empress and her general seek our help to gain the throne of the Tuigan. She will talk to whomever Ju-Hai Chou sends," the voice whispered back in icy tones. Although softly spoken, the words were clear. Bayalun's first demand had failed, and she now considered her next course of action.

"Ju-Hai Chou's representative is acceptable," she conceded, abruptly changing to a gentler tone. "We will stay."

"Ju-Hai Chou will be greatly honored," the voice said politely.

"Listen then," Bayalun began once more, seizing the initiative. "Soon the khahan will ride against the Dragonwall. Perhaps your wall is strong, but he might break through."

"Unthinkable," the old man's voice replied in utter confidence.

"Perhaps, but he is wily and has many men. The unthinkable might happen—especially if the wizards were to help him."

"Their help will make no difference. No one can break the might of the Dragonwall; it is made of more than simple brick and mortar," the voice boasted. "Do you think your khahan is the first to crash himself against it? Other armies have tried and failed."

Bayalun raised her eyebrow in interest as she listened. The Shou hinted at secrets concerning the wall she did not know. Choosing her words carefully, she tried to goad him into revealing more. "Secrets can always be discovered," the khadun suggested ominously, thumping her staff again for emphasis.

There was a sharp hiss from the other side of the ravine. The meaning of her words was not lost on the speaker. "You know?" the Shou snarled.

"I have many sources, *kharachu*," Bayalun lied. She knew nothing of the wall, except what the Shou had let slip. Still, she paused to let the man worry. "Even if the khahan cannot break through, he will forever raid your caravans and strangle your trade with the western lands. All you can do is hide behind your wall until he goes away. You must get rid of him."

"The second empress has some plan?" whispered the voice, somewhat rankled by her observations.

"Indeed. The armies of Shou Lung will destroy the khahan and his bodyguards."

"What will you do while we risk all?" the speaker snapped.

"We will aid you, but we cannot act so directly. We cannot be suspected, or the throne will fall to one of the khahan's sons. If that happens, nothing will be gained," Bayalun explained patiently. "You must attack the khahan."

"Very well. I will," the hidden speaker across the clearing agreed. "What is your plan?"

"You will bring your army out of the Dragonwall and defeat the khahan. In the battle, he will be killed."

"That is all?" the voice asked sarcastically. "And how are we to defeat him?"

"Chanar, explain the khahan's plans," Bayalun commanded, seating herself on a rock.

Chanar stepped forward, standing on the edge of the light. "Yamun Khahan will bring part of his army in front of the Dragonwall. He will attack with this group and then seem to retreat in great confusion. We've done this many times," explained the general. "You must not pursue him. It's a trap. When you don't follow he'll return to attack again. That's when you must be ready to charge."

"He outnumbers the troops we'll have available. To attack then will be suicide," whispered the Shou speaker.

"Only if you attack alone," countered Chanar, "and you won't. Send your army out onto the plain in front of the wall. The khahan won't be able to resist. He will charge. When he does, break to your flanks and let him pass through toward the wall. My men will fall upon him from the rear, and you can strike from the sides. Trapped between the wall and our men, he'll be destroyed."

"And you will become khahan," the voice concluded with a trace of sarcasm.

"And, if the tribute is paid to the khans, there will be peace between the Tuigan and Shou Lung," Bayalun pointed out.

"The bribe will be paid. I will tell Ju-Hai Chou of your plan. You will not hear from us again until after the battle," the voice said flatly. There was a scraping noise from the shadows as the stranger prepared to leave.

Bayalun called out, "Hold one moment, speaker for Ju-Hai Chou. A request."

"What?"

"Send us one of your men to be a runner in case we need to communicate."

"Can't you use spells?" inquired the Shou.

"The runner will be an extra precaution, should I be unable to use my spells. Give us a man. We have clothes ready for him at the edge of our camp." Chanar looked at Bayalun, knowing full well they'd made no such preparations. She met his gaze sharply, warning him to keep quiet.

"It is agreed." There was a pause, then a small man stepped out of the shadows. He wore the dress of a common soldier of Shou—a long padded coat stitched with quilted squares, slipperlike shoes, and a simple metal cap. The runner carried a spear, and a sword hung in a scabbard at his side. In the darkness the colors of his clothes were impossible to see. Nervously, the man, barely more than a youth, moved across the clearing.

"Success to the second empress and the illustrious general," said the shadowed figure across the ravine.

"Indeed. Chanar," Bayalun whispered very softly, "be watchful and ready to use your sword on my signal." She tilted her head slightly toward the Shou soldier. "Quickly now, we must be back before it grows too light," she said in broken Shou, her voice loud enough that the warrior could hear her.

The three set out, following the trail back to the camp.

Bayalun took the lead, then came the Shou warrior, while Chanar brought up the rear. They wound their way along the ravine until they reached the spot where Chanar had hidden the sentry's body.

"Now," said Mother Bayalun without turning around. Chanar instantly took the cue and, before the unfortunate soldier could react, the general's sword bit into the man's neck just below the ear. There was a soft snap as the blade sheared bone. The guard's severed head went tumbling down the slope. There was a quick jet of blood, then, legs and arms still flailing, the body toppled to the ground.

Chanar wiped his blade on the dead man's sleeve, then tore off a piece of the cloth to wipe his mail shirt clean. He retrieved the head and set it closer to the sentry Bayalun had killed earlier.

"Good. Leave the body where it is," the khadun said from the top of the ravine. "When the guards find the bodies in the morning, they'll decide the sentry was attacked by Shou enemies. No one will suspect us. Now, we must get back into camp."

– 15 –

The Dragonwall

The excited jabber of men's voices echoed throughout the royal compound just before sunrise, even before dawn marked the horizon. The noise interrupted Koja's bath. What was normally a luxury, though unappreciated by Hodj, was today an icy ordeal. The air was cold and the water was melted from the snows outside. The commotion in the camp was a welcome excuse to get dressed.

Shivering, Koja quickly pulled on his new black robes, foregoing his normal careful inspection for vermin. He couldn't see how the Tuigan could stand it, lice-ridden as their clothes so often were. Putting the thought aside, he hastily pulled on the soft boots Hodj had found to replace his worn-out slippers. The priest made an incongruous figure—a bald, gaunt man, hardly a warrior, dressed in the rich black *kalat* of Yamun's elite bodyguard.

While Koja dressed, the clamor outside continued. Still fastening the toggles on his *kalat*, the lama scrambled through the door into the predawn darkness. A fire blazed nearby, casting shadows of the men standing around it. Two bodies lay on the ground next to the flames. Koja hurried over to the group—several common troopers, a few more of the Kashik, and stooped, old Goyuk. "What is it, Goyuk Khan?" the priest asked.

"Come and look," the ancient warrior answered, his wrinkled face marked by a grim frown. Scowling, Goyuk pointed at the bodies on the ground. Pushing past the troopers, Koja stopped in horror.

Spread on the ground were the corpses of two men. One was a Tuigan trooper with the front of his *kalat* soaked in blood from a gaping slit in his throat. The other was a strange warrior wearing a heavy quilted robe emblazoned with a single Shou character, the word for virtue. He wore the armor of a simple foot soldier. The warrior's head was carefully set next to the body.

Koja turned away. "Who is it?" he gasped to Goyuk.

The old man deferred to the Kashik commander standing beside him.

"Master lama," the Kashik explained politely, although his voice was cold with anger. "This man was a soldier of the Naican *ordu* stationed on guard duty last night. They found him this morning, along with this other one. He must have met a Shou patrol, and they killed him. At least he killed one of the enemy before he died. It happened over there." The commander pointed toward the northeast, where the ground fell away toward the plain below.

"Does Yamun know?" Koja asked of Goyuk.

The old man nodded, sucking on his lower lip. "He sent me."

Koja looked at the bodies again. There was something here that didn't seem right. "Why?" he finally asked, almost to himself.

"Why did Yamun send me? Beca—"

"No, no," Koja quickly corrected. "Why were the Shou so close to the camp? Did anything else happen?" Koja asked the officer.

"Nothing was reported, master lama," the commander replied.

"They were scouting us, and this man found them," Goyuk said with finality. "It is clear. Hang the body of the Shou up. Now there is work to be done." Having voiced his opinion on the subject, the old khan stomped away, his armor jingling as he went. The Kashik followed after him.

Still unsatisfied with this simple answer, Koja knelt beside the dead trooper and gingerly examined the wound. "How often does a warrior in battle have his throat cut so neatly?" Koja asked, turning to one of the guards who remained nearby.

The guard looked at him, puzzled. "It is rare," he admitted, "but one of the Shou might have attacked him from behind."

"And he still chopped the head off another?" Koja asked skeptically.

"It could happen," insisted the man.

"Perhaps," Koja said, though he was far from convinced. The priest stood, and the guards took the body of the dead enemy to hang out for display as Goyuk had instructed. As they were dragging the corpse off, Koja suddenly had an idea. "Leave the head and this man," he ordered, pointing to the trooper. "Wrap the bodies and keep them safe." There were some questions Koja wanted to ask the dead men, but first he had to rest and pray to Furo for guidance.

The men looked at him with horrified eyes, shocked by his grotesque request. Fearful of what they imagined were the priest's awesome powers, the guards gulped and carried out his orders.

His mind racing with speculation, Koja went back to his tent to have his morning tea and say his daily prayers to Furo. Hodj had already cleared away the bath and set out a pot of hot tea. The drink warmed the priest, driving away the predawn chill.

His tent provided only a brief haven from the commotion of the camp. Outside, the army was already beginning to array itself. Eventually coming out of his yurt, Koja took the horse his bodyguards held for him and rode to where Yamun's standard waved. The dark line of the Dragonwall was clearly visible on the plain below.

Yamun, his aides, and the army's commanders were clustered around the banner, debating strategies for the impending attack. In addition to the khahan there were a few others Koja recognized: Goyuk, Chanar, and the big brute,

Sechen. The priest looked about for Bayalun, but she was nowhere in sight. There were others he only knew by passing acquaintance: minor commanders of the Kashik, Yamun's standard-bearer, and even his old, withered scribe. They formed an impressive group, dressed in their battle armor.

Yamun wore his finest armor in anticipation of his victory. The suit was made up of small metal plates, each fashioned like the scale of a dragon, gleaming gold. Silks of bright yellow, blue, and red hung from the armor, and a gorget of hammered steel circled Yamun's neck and upper shoulders. The khahan's red braids dangled from beneath the conical helm hung with silver chain mail and trimmed with the white fur of a winter wolf. Long metal bracers of polished steel, tooled with tigers and dragons locked in combat, were strapped over the chain mail that covered his forearms. In one hand, the khahan held a silver-handled knout of three thongs. A bowcase of green-dyed wyvern leather hung at his side, along with a gem-encrusted scabbard. The hilt that thrust out from the scabbard was plain and businesslike. A round shield of hammered gold and silver hung on his back.

Yamun's horse, a fine pure-white mare, was as lavishly decorated, fitted with half-barding that matched the khahan's armor. The saddle had high arches at the front and back, covered with plates of tooled silver, patterned with coiling and twisting vines. The saddle frame was covered with a cushion of thick red felt, trimmed with bits of silver mirrors and golden tassels. The bridle, rein, and straps across the horse's croup and withers were completely covered by bosses of gold set with turquoise. In the eastern sunlight, both Yamun and his horse were dazzling.

Those around the khahan, though not as lavishly dressed, were no less splendid. Each commander wore his best armor. Horses were carefully groomed and prepared. Koja was amazed; he'd never realized the khans brought such finery with them. It was likely, too, that this was the first time he had seen them in clothing so clean.

"Welcome, Koja," Yamun said to the priest. "Today we'll test the strength of this Dragonwall." The khahan let his horsewhip dangle from his wrist as he pointed toward the squadrons of mounted men forming up on the slope below them.

The riders were advancing in separate columns lined out abreast of each other instead of the continuous stream they used when on the march. The war standards of the *minghans* and *tumens* were unfurled to flutter in the breeze—streamers of silk, horsetails, tinkling bells, and flashing mirrors hung from cords.

The troopers carried their full war gear with them: a long, springy lance; curved sword; two powerful, compact bows; and a pair of quivers packed with arrows. There were whole blocks of armored men, but the majority wore the same clothes they had every day, a heavily-padded *kalat* being their sole protection. A few carried shields, but most of the riders disdained these, for the shields interfered with their ability to shoot a bow.

Finally, the khahan joined the line of advance, the khans following him. Today was the final march on Shou Lung, several hours out from the Dragonwall. All through the ride, the khans were strangely quiet. Most rode in silence, gathering their thoughts, or held huddled conferences on horseback with their lieutenants. Gradually, as the group drew closer to the Dragonwall, the khahan gave the commanders their final orders and dispatched them to their units.

By the time the Tuigan reached the last ridge before entering onto the plain, there were only three warriors remaining among the messengers who surrounded Yamun: Chanar in his brilliant silver armor, who was to command the left; toothless old Goyuk, commander of the right; and Sechen, who was in charge of Yamun's personal bodyguards. The khahan himself decided to command the center this day. Koja sat on his horse slightly behind this group, not wishing to interfere.

A messenger, barely more than a boy, wearing the white robes of the empress's guard, rode up on a panting mare and made his obeisance to Yamun. The khahan waved him to speak.

"The shining daughter of heaven, the second empress, has sent me to tell you that she has summoned her sorcerers from across the land and they have taken their positions throughout the army." The youth sniffed and wiped his runny nose on a dirty sleeve.

"This is good. Tell her to put the wizards under the command of the khans," Yamun ordered.

The messenger nervously sat straight in his saddle. "The second empress has ordered me to say that she will keep them under her command. The khans do not know the powers of the mages and will use them badly." The boy sat terrified in his saddle, ready to flinch at the slightest move from anyone.

Yamun, who had already gone on to other business, suddenly turned his attention back to the messenger. "She will do what I command!" he snapped. The boy swallowed in terror, even though his mouth was dry.

Chanar rode forward, apparently trying to soothe the situation. "Lord Yamun," he began formally, "perhaps Eke Bayalun is right. Many of the khans do not like the wizards. They would not use them well. Perhaps we should let her command."

Yamun refused to consider the suggestion. "I don't trust her. She's filled with treachery."

"We may need her wizards today," Chanar warned, nodding toward the Dragonwall. "You can always assign someone to see she carries out your orders correctly."

"Is very late to argue," Goyuk added, trying to defuse this crisis before the real battle started.

Reluctantly, Yamun let himself be persuaded. There was no time left for debate, and he believed that the wizards would not be important in the battle anyway. "Assign one *arban* of the Kashik to each wizard," the khahan decided.

"Send a *jagun* of the Kashik to Bayalun. Go, boy, and tell her the men are for her protection."

After the courier had ridden off, Yamun continued his instructions. "Tell the Kashik to kill any wizard, even Bayalun, if any treachery is attempted." Turning to the priest, Yamun then surprised Koja by asking, "*Anda*, can your god let you see the future?"

Initially flustered, Koja quickly replied. "Sometimes Furo can grant such insight."

"Then can he tell us the outcome of today's battle?" Yamun inquired, tugging at his mustache. "Bayalun has not seen fit to bring any of her shamans along to provide the service."

Koja thought for a moment, reviewing the spells Furo had granted him this day. "Perhaps not a perfect answer," he finally ventured, "but Furo might grant some hint of the fortunes of this place. I cannot promise any more."

"Whatever, just do it." The khahan was not particularly interested in the technical aspects of Koja's spells. He was only interested in the results.

"I will need to be closer to the Dragonwall."

"Just ahead, over that ridge," Yamun said with a nod. "Sechen, escort him there and see that he is unharmed."

"By your word, it shall be done," said the big man. Sechen guided Koja and a band of his guards up the last yards of the broken slope until they reached an outcropping of brush. There they found a shaded spot where Koja had a clear view of the wall.

They were less than a mile away from the great Shou fortification. The Dragonwall stretched in a long unbroken line, greater and more massive than it had appeared from the top of the pass. The brick used to build it gave the wall a dull yellow-brown color. Koja guessed it stood thirty feet high. The top was toothed with crenellations. A roadway ran the length of the top, broad enough for a chariot to ride down. At regular intervals, about one mile apart, stood square towers, taller than the surrounding wall. These were obviously watchtowers.

The trail from First Pass Under Heaven wound down from the heights to a massive gate set in the wall. The doors themselves were fully as high as the wall, while the towers were even higher. These gatehouses, smooth-surfaced and rectangular, tapered toward the top. Arrow loops, barely visible on the lower levels, were replaced by balconies as archers' positions higher up. An arching bridge stretched between the towers, over the heavy wooden gate.

Briefly, Koja considered telling Yamun that his spell revealed their situation was hopeless. If the trick worked, he could save untold lives. Morally though, he knew he must work the spell. He could not presume to speak for Furo; such an act would be blasphemy. Besides, he doubted his prediction could sway Yamun's resolve.

Bright flashes of light sparkled on the plain. "They've deployed outside the gate," observed Sechen, whose eyesight was much better than Koja's. Now that it was pointed out, the priest could see the men arranged in a long line. The flashes must have been from their armor and weapons. "They know we're here. Work quickly, historian."

Koja began a breathing exercise to calm his mind. It took a long time, but Sechen was too busy counting the standards of the enemy to notice. Finally, the priest produced a scroll he had made that morning. It was covered with special prayers. Holding it up to the east, he read it aloud, then carefully repeated this process to the other points of the compass. Finished, he closed his eyes and stood quite still, his body unconsciously going completely rigid. Sechen and the guards waited, all afraid to say anything lest they disturb the spell.

At last his overtensed muscles sagged and relaxed, and the priest staggered backward. Blinking, he opened his eyes and stared at the Dragonwall. Furo's power was filling his sight, letting him see the great balance of all nature. All things, living and dead, animal and mineral, were filled with the force of the Enlightened One. Some, such as an ordinary rock, contained only a little, while others—men of powerful will, in particular—glowed brightly with inner power. By seeing these auras through the divine inspiration of Furo, Koja hoped to "read" the harmony of the land, and, perhaps, predict the battle's outcome.

At that moment, Koja saw that a prediction would not be difficult to make.

Before the priest's eyes blazed the aura of the Dragonwall itself, as blinding as the sun. Its brilliance blotted out all other auras, even that of the Shou army deployed on the plain. The intensity was beyond anything Koja had experienced. The priest was dumbstruck. The aura shone from all the way underneath the foundations of the fortification to the topmost towers. The burning fire stretched all along the length of the wall, and in it Koja could barely make out a form, a shape struggling, as if against invisible bonds.

Painfully, Koja forced himself to stare into the heart of this magical fire, to discern what lay hidden in the wall. A claw dug deep into the earth. A ridge of spines reached to the topmost battlements. A pattern of scales blended with the brick and stone. Through it all, Koja felt a power watching him, wrathful and tortured at the same time.

"Furo protect me!" he blurted in astonishment, shattering the enchantment. Suddenly, the scene was gone. Blinded, Koja stumbled back, groping his way down the slope. Sechen leaped after him, convinced the lama had gone mad. The priest eluded his grasp. Undaunted or unaware of the danger, Koja increased his speed and excitement at the same time. By the time he reached the bottom of the ridge, his breath came in ragged gasps. Eyesight returning, the priest hobbled and bounded back to the khahan's party.

"Well, what is it?" Yamun shouted. The lama's obvious excitement was contagious, infecting the khahan with a feeling of hope. "What've you learned?"

Koja finally caught his breath. How could he describe what he saw? A power, a spirit greater than anything he had ever imagined, lay beneath—no, was part of—the Dragonwall.

"Great khahan," Koja began, his chest heaving, "the omens are not favorable. A powerful spirit protects the wall. I am certain it will not let you break through."

Yamun was taken back by the priest's words. Not having a reply, he turned to Sechen, who came running up behind. "What did you see?"

"Lord Yamun," the wrestler said as he stumbled forward, "I saw the Shou army. They know we are coming and have lined up to meet us."

"How many?" Yamun probed, leaning forward in his saddle.

"Twenty, maybe twenty-five standards. I'd guess one thousand men to a banner, like our *minghans*."

Yamun settled back into his saddle. "I've got sixty standards. We'll leave—"

"But Yamun! You cannot break through!" Koja stepped up to the khahan's horse. Soaked in sweat, the priest was frantic, trying to get Yamun to understand. "You will—"

"Quiet!" Yamun roared. "We won't have to." He pointed to a spur of the ridge that Koja had just crossed. "Chanar, take your men to that ridge and hold them there. Goyuk, take one *tumen* and advance; set the rest of your men to protect the northern flank. I'll hold the center." The two khans nodded in understanding.

"Goyuk, you must draw them out. Charge them once, then break and run. Chanar, your men must be ready to close the rear behind them . . . separate them from their wall. I'll be the anvil and you two will be the hammers. Together we will break them." Neither khan had any questions. Their aides would settle on signals to be given with banner and drum, signals that would allow them to attack in unison.

Goyuk and Chanar left to deploy their men. It would be several hours before the troops were in position. That was good, Yamun thought, since it would keep the Shou soldiers standing motionless in the sun for most of the day. Heat and thirst would weaken them. His own men would hardly notice such conditions.

Yamun turned to Koja, who stood nearby, dispirited and dejected. "Priest, I want you to learn more about what you saw." With that the khahan turned away to find some shade. For him, there was nothing more to do now but take a nap.

Leaving the khahan, Chanar galloped down the valley to rejoin his command. Purposefully, he took a long route, one that carried him past Bayalun's camp. Arriving there, he was greeted by a motley collection of wizards—tall and lean, fat and sweaty, some clothed in finery, others scabrous and filthy. The khahan's guards had yet to arrive. Contemptuously, Chanar made his way past Bayalun's lackeys to seek out the khadun herself.

He found her sitting in the warm sun, disdaining the cooling shade. She looked asleep, but without opening her eyes, she dismissed her servants. "Welcome, Chanar. Why do you visit me?"

The general swung down from his saddle and squatted beside the khadun. Quickly, he explained Yamun's plans.

"He's giving us the chance!" Chanar urged, knotting his hands into fists. "Tell the Shou we've changed the plan. They must ride forward and then we will all attack Yamun. We can pin him between us and destroy him today!"

"No. We will do nothing of the kind," Mother Bayalun answered coolly. She pulled the red and blue shawl off her head, letting her graying hair fall naturally to her shoulders. "Think, Chanar, think! If you were the Shou general would you trust us?" She rose from her seat and walked to the door of her yurt. "Don't forget, Yamun will have his guards all around me. We will keep to the plan. For now, let us prove to Yamun we are loyal."

Chanar knew perfectly well that the khahan would never fully trust Bayalun. She was right, however; Yamun could not maintain his vigilance forever. Still, it rankled him to see such an opportunity slip by.

Bayalun sensed his dissatisfaction. "These Shou warriors are no match for the Tuigan," she suggested, appealing to

Chanar's pride. "We would be foolish to trust them to defeat the khahan. Today, Chanar, do what the khahan expects. Tomorrow we will crush him, and you will be khahan."

* * * * *

Four hours passed while the khahan's forces moved into position. During that time Yamun slept under a thorny tamarisk tree. Koja sat in the shade of a rock, meditating and seeking guidance from his god. He hoped that Furo would grant him more knowledge of the spirit he had seen today. As the last of the troops moved into position on the plain below, a servant roused the khahan from his nap. Yamun insisted Koja accompany him, so the priest stopped his exercises and followed him back to the top of the ridge. There they found a comfortable position where they could watch Goyuk's attack. Sechen stood nearby, ready with their horses.

Below, on the plain, was the one *tumen* Goyuk had chosen to make the initial charge. The old khan had divided the ten thousand men into three large blocks. Each block was ten riders deep and about three hundred men wide. The right wing was deployed along the base of the ridge where Koja and Yamun sat. The rest of Goyuk's force stretched off to the left. The priest spotted the old khan's banner, a pole with streamers of blue silk topped by a silver crescent, in the gap between the nearest wing and the center. Across the plain stood the soldiers of Shou Lung, waiting in the broiling afternoon sun.

A rapid roll of drums signaled that all was ready on the plain. Lance tips wavered, creating a sparkling sea of lights. Yamun waved his hand, and his standard-bearer dipped the yak-tail banner to the ground. The signal had been given. The war began.

Koja watched, fearful and expectant, waiting for Goyuk to act. The crescent moon banner trembled, then dipped. In a wave spreading out from that one point, the banners of the *minghans* dropped, transmitting the signal down the length of the front. The ranks of horsemen trembled, but did not move.

A sound rose up from the plain, at first like the breeze through aspens. The sound grew stronger until it echoed like the roar of a thunderstorm. Ten thousand voices were raised in a harsh, piercing war cry. It reverberated until it seemed that the hills themselves were screaming for the blood of Shou Lung.

Goyuk's banner was suddenly raised. The effect was electrifying. The standards of the *minghans* sprang back up. The blocks of men seemed to expand, stretch, and then the entire *tumen* was in motion. The hoarse, echoing shouts of the war cry were replaced by a new sound: the deep rumble of forty thousand hooves hammering the ground. Even at the top of the ridge the ground seemed to tremble.

"Hai!" Yamun cried, leaping to his feet. He chafed with the desire to be at the front, leading the advance. Unable to be there, he paced impatiently back and forth, issuing orders.

Goyuk's men crossed the plain in a well-ordered charge. It was not a wild, pell-mell rush. Instead, the *minghans* advanced at a trot, keeping in a line abreast. Gradually, as they closed the distance to the enemy line, the horses picked up speed, first to a canter, then a full gallop. Across the plain, the spears of the Shou rippled in anticipation.

Yamun waited for the moment when the lead horsemen would suddenly slow their charge just short of the enemy, loose a flight of arrows from their bows, and gallop away, stinging the enemy into pursuit.

That moment never arrived.

From the ridge, Yamun could see the front of the rushing wave of horsemen reach the point where they were in range to fire, just inside the long shadow of the Dragonwall. Down the length of the Tuigan line, the ground rippled, then surged upward, exploding in a fountain of dust and rock. There was a shrieking grind of stone grating on stone and a rolling thunder as the earth's crust tore asunder. Another voice, higher than the roar of upthrusting earth, pierced through the din: the screaming wail of men and horses, their voices fused into a single cry.

Yamun shouted in astonishment and outrage. The front-most ranks of the Goyuk's *tumen* had suddenly disappeared, crushed by dirt and stone. The next ranks, unable to swerve their charging mounts, were swallowed by the curtain of dust that roiled outward. Here and there, the swirling tornado parted to reveal geysers of earth erupting amidst the panicked riders. Boulders tumbled and bounced, crashing through the remaining ranks of horsemen, leaving bloody and crushed bodies in their wake.

Under the onslaught, the *tumen* wavered and began to fall back. The riders farthest from the churning earth wheeled their mounts and began to flee. Their panic was infectious. Standards started to drop as more men turned to run.

Impossibly, one section of the Tuigan line held firm and pressed forward, lunging into the chaotic landscape. At the center of the mass was Goyuk's blue-streamered banner. The dust clouds reached forward, beckoning the entire block of riders into their gloomy arms.

"No! Break off, Goyuk!" Yamun shouted futilely, as if he could recall the riders from where he stood. The khahan whirled to his standard-bearer. "Signal them to withdraw!"

Suddenly, Goyuk's charge was engulfed in dust. Fountains of dirt and rock erupted in the midst of the riders, flinging men and horses like childrens' toys. A pall of clay descended on Goyuk's banner, and it disappeared from sight.

"Eke Bayalun!" Yamun howled. "Get Mother Bayalun! Where are her wizards? They must stop this!" The khahan tore through his small group, screaming out orders, demanding reports, but most of all bellowing for the presence of the second empress to explain the horror he was witnessing. Never had the priest seen the khahan in such a rage.

A rider charged through the ranks of the Kashik behind the khahan, whipping his horse furiously. Leaping off his mount, the man sprawled completely on the ground in front of the khahan, pressing his face into the dirt. "A message from the second empress, Lord Yamun!"

The khahan whirled on the man, poised to strike. "Speak!" he shouted over the rumble from the plain.

Without looking up, the messenger yelled his mistress's words. "The second empress says the magic of the Shou has taken her wizards by surprise. They are unable to do anything. She asks if the foreign priest might know what causes the earth to heave. She humbly begs forgiveness for her failure to—"

"I'll hear her excuses later," the khahan snarled, turning away from the man. The messenger sprang to his feet and backed away, groping for his horse. One of the Kashik, sympathetic to the man's fears, quickly hustled the courier out of Yamun's sight. The khahan looked toward the plain, seeing only men and horses rushing through the clouds of dust.

"My horse!" Yamun demanded. A quiverbearer ran to fetch Yamun's white mare. "Standard-bearer, we're going down there. Prepare to ride!" The guards looked to each other, then hurriedly began to find their mounts and take their positions around the khahan.

Without waiting for his guards to finish assembling, Yamun urged his horse down the steep slope toward the plain. The guards plunged after him, their mounts half-sliding toward the bottom.

Sechen, his tall, muscular body towering out of the saddle, drove his horse savagely to keep up with the khahan. His master was riding blindly into a trap, and the giant was determined to protect him. The pair reached the bottom of the slope well ahead of the rest of the bodyguards.

Small knots of riders rode out of the swirling dust and galloped for the safety of the ridge. Lone men and riderless horses fled in panic. Weapons, shields, and armor were cast aside.

Yamun charged forward and then suddenly reined in his horse before the first knot of routed men. "Form up! Make your stand here! I command you!" The routed men skidded to a halt, brought short by the wild apparition of the khahan that faced them. "Watch them," Yamun ordered Sechen as he galloped off toward another fleeing group.

From atop the ridge, Koja watched the khahan rush from point to point, working to halt the rout and organize a proper defense. The warlord was easy to spot by his banner, white horse, and the swarm of black-robed guards who followed him everywhere. His affect on the men was unmistakable as the broken ranks slowly halted their flight and began to reform into ragged lines. Finally, Yamun turned the task over to Sechen and climbed back up to his command post. As he arrived, a group of guards still clustered in his wake, Koja moved quietly to his side.

Looking very tired, Yamun sat on his stool. For a long time he said nothing, only watched the battlefield. The dust was slowly settling, leaving a clearer picture of the destruction. Across the front was a line of churned earth and shattered rock. Most of the dead or dying lay there, crushed or trapped beneath the fallen stone. On both sides of the wreckage there were still pockets of fighting. A handful of Tuigan riders, the leaders of the foremost rank, were trapped on the far side of the magical earthwork. There they fought, though hopelessly outnumbered and surrounded.

In a few other places, the Shou soldiers had foolishly scrambled forward over the broken ground, believing all the Tuigan were crushed. In pursuing the fleeing horsemen, these small units were also trapped. Battles involving these doomed Shou were brief.

Just when Koja became convinced the defeat had crushed the spirit out of Yamun, the old warlord sat up, shaking off the air of gloom and desperation that had settled upon him. "Find Goyuk, if he lives. I want to know what happened," he commanded, his old energy gradually returning to him. As one messenger left, he turned to another. "Tell Sechen to separate those who fled from the rest of the men. He is to

DAVID COOK

execute those who have no weapons. Of the rest, every man must be beaten for seven blows and every tenth man for twice times seven."

"There are thousands of men down there!" Koja said in astonishment.

"They shouldn't have run," Yamun answered grimly. He continued the orders. "The wizards are to be whipped seven blows for their failure. And if Bayalun argues, tell her she can either have them whipped or give me seven to execute. It's her choice." The man nodded and left to deliver the khahan's orders.

"Tell the *yurtchis* to bring the camp forward. We will be staying here." With a wave, the khahan dismissed the remaining couriers. When they had withdrawn an appropriate distance, Yamun turned to the priest.

"Now, *anda*, why did this happen?" The khahan's voice was hard and measured.

"I do not know. What you saw, if I'm right, was the work of a powerful spirit creature." The priest spoke softly, not wanting to commit himself without knowing more.

"You're saying this . . . creature protects the Shou and won't let us attack the Dragonwall?" Yamun asked incredulously, trying to understand the power he had just seen. His rage and frustration were growing.

"Perhaps. I do not know." Koja looked toward the carnage on the plain.

"Can I defeat it, *anda*?"

"I do not know," Koja sighed. "I have never seen anything like this. I do not know what to do."

"Then think of something!" Yamun shouted, slashing his knout against the ground.

Koja swallowed nervously. "I have had dreams. I think the spirit spoke to me. It called on you, and me, to free it from the wall. It seemed to think that we had some power."

"That's all you know?" Yamun asked, disappointed when the lama stopped talking. "Your plan is to wait for it to visit you in your sleep?"

"If I must, Yamun. Spirits are not easy things to command."
Koja was tired and almost lost his temper with the khahan.
He took a long, slow breath, then added, "I must seek guidance from Furo."

"Talk to your god then. And when you are done, tell me
how to defeat that thing." Yamun thrust his finger toward
the furrowed plain. "The servants will bring you anything
you need. I must attend to other things." Yamun stood to go.
"Teylas's blessing on you, *anda*," he said just before he left.

"And Furo's on you, Yamun," the lama offered. Koja
watched the khahan descend once more onto the plain.

"Paper and brush," the priest ordered of a quiverbearer.
The man hurriedly brought the material and set it before
Koja. Taking up the brush, the priest carefully wrote an elegy for the dead on the field below. The poem was not composed out of artistic desire, however; the priest needed the
verse for the spell he wished to cast. Finished with the
poem, he read it through, then set it aside.

"See that no one disturbs me," Koja ordered the servant.
The man nodded in understanding. The lama closed his
eyes and began to recite prayers. For ten minutes he droned
on, never raising his voice. Then he stopped, opened his
eyes, and touched the paper to flame. The thin sheet quickly
burned, the ashes drifting into the air. The lama closed his
eyes again and waited.

Abruptly he opened his eyes and stood up. The spell was
over; he had communed with his god. With one foot, he
scattered the remaining ashes. A small group of quiverbearers had gathered to watch his strange behavior. Now,
they hurriedly went back to their tasks, afraid Koja would
put a curse on them.

"Where is Yamun?" the lama demanded. One of the servants nervously pointed toward the west. "At his yurt, great
historian." Not wasting any time, Koja found his horse and
rode to Yamun's tent.

When the lama was announced, Yamun quickly cleared
the yurt and had his *anda* ushered in. "Sit and tell me what

you've learned," the khahan said as soon as Koja stepped through the door.

"Mighty Furo saw fit to hear my prayers," Koja said as he took his seat. Yamun got off his throne and sat on the floor closer to his *anda*.

"And?"

"It was a spirit that attacked today, a spirit that is trapped in the Dragonwall," Koja eagerly explained. "The same spirit spoke to me in dreams, although Furo did not say why it chose to."

"But can it be destroyed?" Yamun demanded, holding up a fist.

Koja shook his head. "No, not destroyed. Furo said it craves release. There is some way to free it."

"How, *anda*, how?" Yamun stared at Koja, awaiting his answer.

The lama took a deep breath. "For that, I must consult the spirit of the Dragonwall."

"Then do it," Yamun said as he headed for the door.

"I cannot," said Koja, bringing the khahan to a stop. "I cannot until I rest. These spells are very tiring. I will be ready tonight, before the dawn. And I will need an offering, one suitable to something as powerful as this spirit must be. Is this possible, Yamun?"

"It will be arranged," Yamun assured the lama as he slowly walked back to his throne. "What happens after you talk to this spirit?"

"I do not know," Koja admitted. "I have never done this type of thing before."

A Kashik slowly appeared at the door, making sure that the khahan knew of his presence. Behind him came one of Yamun's couriers. "A message from Sechen the Wrestler, Great Lord," explained the Kashik, stepping aside to let the messenger speak.

"Speak your message," Yamun ordered.

"Sechen sends me to report that Goyuk Khan is dead." The messenger bowed his head and stood quietly.

Yamun walked to the door and looked out over the plain, the pain clear in his face. Slowly and deliberately he spoke, "Shou Lung will pay." His voice implied no threat, no promise, only a certainty that he would break the Dragonwall and gain his vengeance on the emperor who cowered behind it.

- 16 -

Traitors

That night was a somber one in the Tuigan camp. The *yurtchis*, following Yamun's instructions, had moved the tents forward so that by late evening the yurts were in position. Campfires covered the ridge and the near side of the plain before the Dragonwall. Yamun ordered the men to build extra fires to make the army seem even larger. Still, no fire was closer than what Koja, Bayalun, and her wizards determined was safe. The distant tumble of rocks served as a reminder of what could happen to any who ventured too close to the Shou fortification.

The fires of the Tuigan were matched by sparks of flame along the length of the Dragonwall. The Shou troops had withdrawn behind the wall and now lined its ramparts. In the darkness between the two forces, jackals growled and fought over the carrion.

In the royal yurt, Yamun sat, searching for a way to break the stalemate. The khahan had to be prepared, in case Koja failed. Sechen, his duties among the troops finished, stood at his usual place by the door. Bayalun and Chanar sat at the khahan's feet. Though her mood was dark, Bayalun sat calmly. Chanar was openly agitated, distressed by the actions of the Shou. It was not according to the plan. Yamun assumed the general's nervousness was caused by frustration at the day's failure.

From the corner, the scribe read aloud the reports from the scouts. The news was not encouraging. There was no hope of flanking the wall, nor had the riders been able to find any weak spots along its length. Some reported troop movements atop the wall, but the numbers given were not large enough to alarm the khahan. Other scouts screened the army's flanks, watching for enemy repositioning. So far these riders had seen nothing.

Other couriers carried dispatches from Prince Tomke. The khahan's third son was marching with his army to join Yamun. Unlike his brothers, Jad and Hubadai, however, Tomke was cautious and advanced with care. The message claimed it would be several days before his men would arrive. This last piece of news prompted Yamun to send his son an angry rebuke about his troops' slowness.

Finally, the scribe reached a sheet that arrived only a few hours before, a scroll delivered from the Shou. Carefully and slowly, the ancient scholar read the crabbed characters, holding the sheet close to his eyes to see it clearly in the dim light.

Khahan, the note began. *The emperor of the Jade Throne is pleased to call you an equal to his sons.*

You have seen the futility of attacking the unbreakable Dragonwall. It is a truth that if you continue, your greatness will only be dimmed by failure. Let there be no quarrel between the Tuigan and the emperor of all Shou Lung. Depart and go in peace.

As the scribe finished reading the note aloud, Yamun looked at both Chanar and Bayalun. "They want us to surrender."

"So it would seem, Khahan," Bayalun said. Chanar only grunted in agreement.

Yamun picked at his teeth. "Mother Bayalun, why did your wizards fail me today?" The accusation in the khahan's voice was clear.

Unfazed by her stepson's obvious distrust, Bayalun sat proud and stiff-backed as she gave her explanation. "The wizards failed you no more than your own men. They were unprepared for what happened."

"And why did it happen?" Yamun pressed.

"It is a mystery," Bayalun admitted. She lowered her eyes to the floor, abashed at being forced to admit her ignorance.

"When will your wizards know? Tomorrow? That is when they must be ready," Yamun insisted, nodding to the scribe to write the order.

"If my son, my husband, were to rescind his orders to have the wizards beaten, I am certain they will be able to help tomorrow." Bayalun kept looking to the floor, seeking Yamun's favor with mock humility.

"They deserve to be beaten," Yamun snapped.

"Perhaps," the second empress allowed. "But if they are beaten, they will be too weak to fight tomorrow."

"Then give me seven of them, to make an example to the others."

Bayalun stiffened. "No. Their numbers are few and you will need them all tomorrow." She realized her defiance had backed Yamun into a corner with no way to save face. "Tomorrow, if they fail, you may do as you wish with all of them," the khadun offered.

Yamun bristled at her disobedience, knowing he could not force her to comply with the conflict looming before his army. "Very well," he said, his voice tinged by his ill-temper. "Make certain they're ready. There will be no more failures." He pointed at her to accent his words. Her face a mask, Bayalun nodded in understanding.

Finished with the question of wizards, Yamun turned his attention to Chanar. "My general, with Goyuk slain, I'm giving you command of the Ciejan, Ormusk, and Ulu *tumens*. I'll take the rest." Chanar bowed his head in gratitude. "Will your men be ready for battle tomorrow?" the khahan asked.

"Of course, Yamun. But how will we cross the plain?" Chanar gestured in the general direction of the wall. "Their magic will destroy us."

Yamun smiled enigmatically. "Perhaps not. Now, Chanar, my valiant man, we must make a plan. Since we cannot get the Shou to chase us, how do we attack their wall?"

Stepping down from his throne, Yamun sat on the rugs across from his general. The scribe quickly unrolled a long, narrow scroll between the two men. Along one edge was a diagram of the Dragonwall, showing the gates and the towers. Opposite the wall were little circles, denoting the camps of the Tuigan.

Chanar risked a glance toward Bayalun, to see if she knew what the khahan intended. Noting the general's perplexed look, she gave a small, quick shrug to show that she knew no more than he. Chanar looked back to the map, studying it briefly. "First, Yamun, we must find a way to reach the wall. The broken dirt blocks our horses."

"I agree. Mother Bayalun," the khahan called out without looking up from the map, "your wizards must clear a path through the broken earth."

"Yes, my husband," the khadun answered quietly as she looked over their shoulders. "But the men will fear being crushed if the earth moves again."

"Just do what you are ordered. I will worry about the men. How long will it take?" Yamun demanded impatiently.

Bayalun looked to the ceiling, calculating the spells needed to do the task. "By morning, I think."

"Go then and see that it is done," Yamun ordered. "Sechen, lead a guard to protect the khadun. Send me reports on her progress."

"By your word, it shall be done," the soldier and the khadun both said at once. As the pair left, Bayalun eyed the big wrestler venomously. She knew that the man was being sent to spy on her.

Yamun turned his attention back to the map. "If the paths were clear, Chanar, where would you make the attack?"

Chanar studied the map, stalling to conceal his discomfort. The khahan did not suspect that tomorrow the general planned to overthrow him. The khahan was, in fact, giving the traitor an opportunity to personally plan his downfall. His intentions set, Chanar studied the map in earnest.

"I would strike here and here," the general answered, his hand sweeping over the map. He tackled the problem with enthusiasm. Things were almost like earlier times, in the days when he and Yamun made plans to conquer the Dalats and Quirish. Only now, the stakes were much higher and the game subtler.

Quickly Chanar sketched out his ideas to Yamun. The khahan listened, then added these to his own plans, never realizing that Chanar was planning treachery. Together they argued and discussed, working well into the night. It was a slow process, but gradually the two warriors created a plan of battle for the morning.

"I'll have *arbans* sent into the mountains to cut trees for rams and ladders immediately," Chanar promised. "The men will be ready to attack at dawn."

"Excellent, my *anda*," Yamun said. "Tomorrow we will avenge Goyuk. Go and rest. There will be much to do when the sun rises." With a wave he dismissed the general.

As the warrior left the tent, Yamun settled back with satisfaction. Chanar at times might be ambitious, but Yamun thought that he could depend on the general. The plan they had worked out was dangerous, but sound.

Outside the tent, Chanar sought out Bayalun at her yurt. Telling the guards Yamun had posted there that he carried orders from the khahan, the general was admitted with only the briefest announcement. Chanar was not surprised to find Bayalun still awake, meditating over her brazier. Once safely out of earshot of the guard, Chanar told her what had happened. "Why is he planning this? Does he expect your wizards to keep the ground from tearing open again?" Chanar asked in bewilderment.

"I do not know," Bayalun confessed. "I have sat here and pondered on it. The Shou have built some secret into their wall. Of that I am certain. But why Yamun is confident he can overcome their magic is another mystery." She shrugged off these concerns. "Whatever he does, it will not matter. If the Shou kill him with their magic or we catch him in the trap, our plans will succeed."

"Then he will fall," Chanar observed.

"Of course—just as long as he makes the attack." Bayalun glanced toward the vain general with a knowing smile. "Tomorrow, my stepson will be dead. Then we can see about making you the khahan of the Tuigan—as you should be."

Chanar returned the smile, though his heart was pained. Tonight, for a short time, he and Yamun were *anda* once more. Tomorrow that bond would be severed forever.

* * * * *

While Chanar and Bayalun plotted in her yurt, Koja and a small group of guardsmen picked their way between the Tuigan camp and the Dragonwall. Quietly, the company moved through the ruins of the battlefield toward the line of tumbled dirt and stone that marked the limit of that day's charge. Several times the men came across bands of jackals or viler creatures—gigantic centipedes and carrion worms—feasting on the bodies of the dead. The sight sickened the priest, but there was little he could do for the dead now. He said a few quick prayers for the fallen warriors.

The corpses reminded Koja that he should attempt to speak to the dead guard discovered that morning, providing he ever got the chance. There was something about the way the bodies were found that nagged at his brain. It's probably nothing, the lama assured himself so he could keep his mind on the business at hand. However, this was a war, and you can't be too careful.

The band finally reached the churned, rocky ground that marked the beginning of the destruction. "Here, priest?" asked the guide, a grizzled Kashik with long, gray braids.

Koja shook his head and whispered with exaggerated caution. "On the other side, as close to the Dragonwall as possible."

The Kashik looked ahead apprehensively, then began carefully picking a path through the rubble. Strict orders were given down the line not to talk or make any unnecessary noise.

Slowly, the men walked over the top of the mound and started down the loose slope on the other side. Each time a stone skittered down the slope, the men froze, waiting for a challenge. It was a painful hour before they reached the bottom.

The dark shadow of the Dragonwall stood out distinctly ahead of them. Koja and the men were close enough to make out individual soldiers at the top of the wall, outlined against the fires they had built to keep them warm. "Now?" hissed the Kashik at Koja. The lama only shook his head.

Stealthily the group moved forward from shadow to shadow, toward a nearly deserted section of the wall. At last, they were at the base of the fortification. Now, no one spoke. The guards watched warily as Koja sat, preparing his spell.

Alone, the priest carefully unwrapped the offering he brought—the khahan's sword and jewel-encrusted scabbard. He hoped this would be sufficient to contact the spirit. Very softly, he began to murmur sutras similar to those he had used earlier in the day. The lama spoke with exaggerated clarity and care.

At the closing words of the prayer, the priest fell into a trance. Quickly, something writhed out of the wall near Koja. At first it only seemed to be a small tendril of smoke, then it grew, expanding and swelling. Finally it coalesced into the transparent outline of a huge dragon. The long serpentine coils of its body lazily circled the priest. The flowing, fanged face stopped directly in front of him.

The dragon's body seemed to glimmer from reflected light, even though there was no light to reflect: The creature's scales shone with iridescent colors. The spirit was massive and yet moved with an ethereal grace. It looked solid, yet floated lightly. It was a spirit, unreal, yet appeared real before Koja's eyes.

Why have you summoned me? the spirit bellowed inside the priest's mind. Its voice was the voice of Koja's old master, and it triggered the priest's memories of lectures given in the great hall of the temple. The words made the stubble on the back of the lama's shaven head prickle.

"I call you in the name of the Illustrious Emperor of the Tuigan, Yamun Khahan," answered Koja as bravely as he could. His voice was barely a whisper, though this did not matter to the spirit.

Then he has come, came the voice, suddenly keen with interest. A claw, transparent to everyone but Koja, carved furrows in the earth in front of the priest.

"Are you the spirit that lives beneath the Dragonwall?"

I am the spirit of the Dragonwall! roared the dragon, now using the voice of the khahan in Koja's mind.

"Do you serve Shou Lung?" Koja asked, trembling before the might of the spirit.

I do not serve the Shou oxen! crashed the khahan's voice. The dragon twitched and thrashed, as if lashing out at some invisible foe. There was no mistaking the bitterness and hatred in its voice. Koja wished he could flee.

"Are you bound to serve them?" the priest timorously asked.

They are my captors! The priest cringed before the fury-laden voice that assaulted his mind. *I must do as they bid.*

"Did you speak to me—ask me to free you?"

I called to you in hope that you would bring your lord. Together you must free me. This time the dragon adopted the soft voice of Koja's mother.

"Why me?" Koja asked softly. "Why not another in the Tuigan camp?"

There was one other amongst the barbarians I considered, little priest. While she had the magical ability necessary, she cannot be trusted. The dragon growled ominously. *No. Not trusted at all.*

"Who do you mean, great spirit?" Koja said, a little desperation creeping into his voice. "Do you speak of the second empress, Mother Bayalun?"

I will not say whom, but I know that you should look to the bodies of the dead for answers.

"But—"

That is all I will say on that matter, the spirit roared.

"Why have you not sought freedom before?" Koja asked after a short pause. "There must have been others."

Of course there were, little priest. I showed them to you. Or have you forgotten your dream? The spirit had resumed using the voice of Koja's old master. *Many have tried to break through my bonds, but all have failed. You saw them there. That was the price of their failure.*

The dragon paused, fading slightly before Koja's eyes. *And their failures have added to my pain. The Shou devil who tricked me and cast me into the wall placed a condition on my curse. I can contact anyone I think might help me to escape. However, everyone that fails to release me and exact suitable revenge for me against the Shou is allowed to punish me throughout eternity. In the spirit world they stand at my side and hammer away.*

The dragon quivered with anger. *So you see, little priest, I only contact those who have a good chance to succeed in crushing Shou Lung. Otherwise, they add to my torment.*

"How can you be freed?" Koja asked.

I need a sacrifice. This time the spirit chose to answer with Goyuk's voice.

"A sacrifice?"

What does your lord offer his god? That is what I must have, the spirit demanded in Yamun's voice. Its tail lashed at the wall, its prison. *No less, little priest.*

Suddenly, the dragon flowed back into the wall, molding its body to the shape of the stone. But the spirit didn't fade. Instead it expanded, stretching along the length of the wall, past the watchtowers and through the gates. The twinkling of the watch fires played off its scales as its body rippled and grew, until the head and tail disappeared from sight. Slowly, the scales blended into the stone. The iridescent colors faded, the patterns of scale and stone blending together. *I am the Dragonwall,* the spirit whispered as it faded from sight.

Slowly the world returned to normal for Koja. The darkness of the night closed over the priest, driving away the unearthly glow that had surrounded the spirit. From above, Koja could hear the faint voices of the Shou sentries and the flapping of their robes as a cold wind blew across the battlements.

"Lama!" whispered the Kashik guide, seeing Koja stir for the first time in a half-hour. Nervously the man stepped up to Koja's side. "Are you well?"

Numbly, Koja nodded his head. He made ready to go, automatically reaching for the sword Yamun had given as an offering. It was gone. Several long scars marked the ground where it had been.

As slowly as before, the group moved away from the Dragonwall. To Koja their pace seemed agonizingly slow. He was in a hurry to tell Yamun what he had learned. If the khahan intended to free the spirit tomorrow, there was much to prepare.

It took almost two hours for Koja and his men to return to Yamun's camp. By now, it was early in the morning. Dawn would come in a few more hours. Still, the camp was not quiet. Riders were leaving for the mountains to cut timber for tomorrow's assault. The burial details were organizing for the task of burning yesterday's dead.

Koja arrived at Yamun's yurt dog-tired. The khahan was still awake. As soon as the lama arrived, Yamun had the weary priest ushered in.

"Sechen, see that we are not disturbed by anyone." The big man bowed and herded the guards out the door. With everyone out, Yamun sat beside the priest.

"Now, *anda*," the khahan asked earnestly, "what did you learn?" His voice automatically dropped to a conspiratorial whisper. His weatherbeaten face was flushed with excitement, making his scars stand out clearly.

"More than I expected, I think," Koja managed to answer. "There was a spirit there, and I talked to it. At least I think I talked to it." He rubbed his head to massage away a building

DAVID COOK

headache. Fatigue was making it hard for him to think.

"Anyway," Koja continued, "we communicated. I was right, we can free it—or maybe just a little part of it. I don't know for sure. It was very big." The more Koja spoke, the more enthused he became.

"What? Explain yourself, priest. I've no time for puzzles. The army must attack soon." The khahan got up and paced, occasionally slapping his hand against his side.

"I am not sure I can, Yamun," Koja apologized before he began. "Do you remember the story I told you about the making of the Dragonwall?"

Yamun grunted.

"I'm not sure it was just a story. The dragon spirit I spoke to *is* the Dragonwall. The Shou did not build the wall from ordinary earth and stone. The Dragonwall was built with the body of an earth spirit." Koja swiveled as he spoke, trying to face the khahan as the warlord stalked about the yurt.

"But what's the point?" Yamun snapped.

"The power of the wall comes from the dragon spirit. Somehow the builders bound the spirit to the wall so it cannot leave, even though it wants to. It is trapped inside the wall."

"So?"

"So, it seems to think that you—and I—are special. In particular, it expects you to obtain its vengeance by crushing Shou Lung."

"This spirit is wise. After all, I *will* conquer Shou Lung." Yamun rubbed at his chin, considering the spirit's words.

Yamun's boastfulness didn't phase the lama. He knew the khahan was unshakable in his conviction. "Yamun," he continued, "we might be able to free it, at least in this area. Once the spirit leaves, the Dragonwall becomes nothing but an ordinary wall, perhaps even less. Remember, the spirit's power is part of what the builders used to hold the wall together—like mortar for stone."

"You're saying that if the spirit goes the Dragonwall could

be torn down?" Yamun considered the information, trying to make sure he understood everything.

"There will need to be a sacrifice," Koja added.

"Of what?"

Koja thought back to the night in the thunderstorm. "Horses, I think. Fine ones. Isn't that the offering you make to Teylas?" Koja shivered at the thought, uncomfortable at being part of such a rite. Such sacrifices were not the way of the Enlightened One.

"Horses will be no problem," Yamun stated flatly.

"There was something else," Koja added, his voice calmer. "The spirit hinted something about a woman of great magical power. Perhaps he meant the second empress. The spirit said that she was . . . not to be trusted." He looked at the floor, partially out of respect to the khahan and partially out of fear.

"She's never to be trusted," Yamun said, dismissing the lama's concerns.

Koja would not be put off. "No, it was more than that. It was how the spirit said it. I'm worried that someone— probably Bayalun—is planning something."

Yamun continued his pacing, showing no sign of surprise. "If I ask her, she'll only deny this."

Koja looked at the khahan. "I may have a way to check," he offered hesitantly. "You remember the guard and the Shou who were found dead before the battle?"

"What of them?" the khahan asked from across the yurt.

Koja stood up. "The spirit said something about looking to the dead for answers." The priest paused, then added, "Something didn't seem right about those bodies. The guard had his throat cut as if someone had surprised him. If that happened, who killed the Shou?" Koja found himself pacing in time with the khahan.

"Odder things have happened, priest," the khahan cautioned, stopping his stride. He set a hand against the tent post, examining the wood.

"Perhaps, Lord Yamun, but I had the bodies hidden away.

I think it would be wise to speak with them."

"Do you really think these two have anything to do with Bayalun?" Yamun asked skeptically.

Koja scratched his head. "I don't know. Spirits often mislead people," he admitted, "but it is all I can think to do. I am ready. We could find out right now."

The khahan looked at the priest without really seeing him, his eyes focused on something intangible. One hand unconsciously played with the tips of his mustache. "Very well. Try. But you must be quick."

"Certainly, Yamun," Koja answered with a bow. Going to the tent door, the lama gave instructions to Sechen. The wrestler again stood watch, having arranged for Bayalun's guard.

It didn't take long for Koja and Sechen to set everything up in a secluded yurt where their activities would not be noticed. The bodies had been stored carefully, packed in snow to slow their decay. Working quickly, Koja stayed alone in the tent. While Sechen stood guard outside, the lama cast his spells. When he emerged, Koja looked drained. The night's activities were taking their toll on him.

"Remove the Tuigan warrior, but bring the Shou's head to Yamun's yurt," the priest ordered as he hurried past Sechen. "I must see the khahan."

Arriving back at Yamun's yurt, Koja wasted no time in describing what he had learned.

Grimly, the khahan looked toward the priest. "Chanar, too?" he asked, his amazement coloring his words.

"I am sorry, Yamun," the priest automatically mumbled.

"Sorrow is for the weak," Yamun suddenly growled.

Koja only nodded. "What will you do now?"

"Confront them," the khahan said. His face was set in a grim scowl. He called for a quiverbearer to summon Chanar and Bayalun. The servant hurried away with the message.

Neither Koja nor Yamun spoke while they waited. The khahan sat brooding, chin on hand. Koja tried to imagine the dark thoughts passing through Yamun's mind. He couldn't. Yamun's grim mood was beyond him. With a tired yawn, the lama resigned himself to waiting

The servant returned and pulled back the door flap. "Khahan, they are here."

Yamun lifted his head. "Enter." Bayalun and Chanar came into the yurt. "Sit."

Leading the way, the second empress, leaning heavily on her staff, took her place. Chanar followed behind, then Sechen. The two plotters seated themselves on the respective sides of the tent, Bayalun alone at the head of the women's row, Chanar opposite her. Koja moved from his seat, out of Chanar's way. The general eyed the lama warily, then sat down at Yamun's feet. Quietly, Koja slid to the back of the yurt to stand alongside the impassive Sechen. The wrestler quietly opened the door, motioning an *arban* of soldiers to enter.

When all had taken their place, Yamun ordered a basin of black kumiss brought forward. Taking the ladle from the bowl, he held it high, presenting it to the four points of the compass. "Teylas grant us victory today."

The offering finished, Yamun took his seat. "Today we go to conquer a great enemy. Let the men be ready."

"May Teylas grant us victory!" Chanar said in response.

"He will, General," Yamun promised, glaring down at Chanar.

Slowly, Yamun extended the ladle to the last of the seven valiant men. Just as the general reached for it, Yamun tipped it, pouring the black kumiss onto the rugs.

"You were my *anda*," the khahan snarled, flinging the ladle out of reach.

Chanar was white-faced, and his mouth hung open in shock. "But, Yamun. I—"

"Quiet! I know of your treachery. You meet with the Shou. You plot with them."

"This is a lie, Khahan!" Chanar shouted, trembling where he stood. Yamun stepped forward on his dais, his broad frame towering over the ashen general. The khahan's eyes smoldered with fury.

Koja realized that Yamun, enraged with Chanar's deception, had momentarily forgotten Bayalun's presence. The priest looked her way. She had stepped back from the confrontation. The khadun's face was pale, but no fear showed in her eyes, only hatred and fury.

Bayalun took another step back, as if trying to distance herself from Chanar. Her hands reached into the sleeves of her robe. She withdrew a small stone and began to trace small figures into the air.

Koja realized that Bayalun was casting a spell. There was no one close enough to stop her in time.

The lama felt his pockets for some kind of weapon, something he could throw. He hit something hard at his chest, the *paitza*, his symbol of authority. Frantically, he yanked at the cord, pulling the heavy metal plate free.

"Bayalun!" the priest shouted, trying to warn the khahan. Yamun stopped his tirade, astonished by the lama's cry, just as Koja hurled the *paitza* across the yurt. The silver plaque thudded against the khadun's arm, jarring the stone from her grasp. Bayalun screeched with rage and pain, clutching at her side.

"Guards, seize the khadun! Bind her hands. Kill her if she attempts to speak!" Yamun pointed at the second empress. Bayalun's eyes narrowed to slits even as she froze where she stood. The guards were already around her, their sabers drawn. They grabbed the khadun's arms and pinned them to her side. She struggled weakly, but knowing Yamun was serious, said nothing. The guards quickly began lashing her wrists together.

Chanar, seizing the distraction, reached for his sword, determined to fight his way free. Before his sword cleared its scabbard, Yamun drew his own blade and laid the edge against the general's breast. Chanar turned slowly to face the khahan.

"Do not draw it, General, or I'll kill you." Yamun spoke coldly, his eyes steely. "Take the khadun out."

Chanar swallowed. "Why, Yamun?" he asked weakly. The remaining guards closed slowly around him. The general unbuckled his swordbelt and laid it on the ground.

Yamun stepped back and spat at Chanar's feet. "Tomorrow, you and my stepmother—" He turned his glare on the departing Bayalun. "You planned to destroy me."

"This is a lie! Who says this?" Chanar blustered, glaring at everyone around him.

Yamun sheathed his own sword and reached into a leather bag that sat beside his throne. From it he lifted the head of the Shou warrior Chanar had killed.

"This is your accuser," Yamun replied, tossing the head at Chanar. It fell with a thump at the general's feet. Chanar wavered then kicked the head aside with a snarl.

"A dead thing—nothing more. You are a fool, Yamun!" Chanar sneered, no longer trying to hide his contempt.

"Though spirits may trick us, the dead cannot lie," Koja said softly from the back of the yurt.

Chanar wheeled on the lama. "You—this is your doing!"

"No, Chanar. You did this to yourself," Yamun said behind him. "You were my *anda*—the last of my valiant men. I gave you honors and trust, and this is how you have repaid me." Yamun sank back onto his throne, chin sunk to his chest.

"You gave me nothing!" Chanar snarled. "I saved you from your enemies. I fought your battles. My father took you in when your own people drove you out. My warriors made you khan of the Hoekun. I have stood by you, and now you spend your time with a foreign priest while I ride as your errand boy! You will betray us all, send us to death against this Shou wall to satisfy your own ambitions." Chanar's chest heaved with emotion.

Yamun shifted onto the balls of his toes, his hand clenched around the hilt of his sword. "I should kill you—" The general braced himself for the blow. "But I won't."

Chanar stepped back, intimidated and confused.

"Hear this," Yamun announced loudly, although only Koja, Sechen, and the guards were there to hear. "For his courage and bravery, I have chosen General Chanar to stand at my side in battle today. Chanar will be the bravest khan in the center. Make sure that's known throughout the army."

Chanar started in surprise, caught off-guard by the khahan's sudden declaration.

Yamun continued. "Tell them also, that today I've made Sechen one of the khans. Sechen, you will command Chanar's men."

"They are not yours to give," Chanar protested, an edge of panic creeping into his voice.

Yamun whirled on the general. "You are nothing anymore! Have you forgotten? You will stand where I tell you, you will fight where I tell you." The khahan kicked Chanar's sword and scabbard off to the side and stormed closer to his old companion. "You live *only* because you were once my *anda*, and that cannot be undone. Tomorrow, you will ride as a hero in battle. If you die there, your name will be forever remembered as one of my valiant men," Yamun said slowly.

Chanar sagged. His plans had collapsed, and the fight went out of him.

"Take him away and keep a guard on him," Yamun shouted irritably to the Kashik. Turning to Chanar as he prepared to leave, Yamun said, "You will ride with me one last time. If you live, you will be banished from my sight. Go and prepare for battle. Teylas will take us to victory!"

"Ai!" The guards hailed the benediction to the khahan's words. Yamun turned his back as the guards led Chanar out.

"My *anda*, my true *anda*," the khahan called to Koja. "You will stay." Arms nervously crossed, the priest stood quietly by the door.

Yamun turned to face the lama. The khahan looked very tired. "Koja, once again you have acted wisely and well. It pains me that I cannot honor you for what you have done, but it is not a custom for outsiders to become khans."

"I do not seek honors, Yamun," Koja said sincerely. "But what are you going to do with Bayalun? You need her wizards to clear the battlefield."

The khahan joined Koja at the doorway, pulling aside the tent flap to look out on the camp. "For now, we keep her arrest a secret. Guards will visit her wizards. We'll tell the wizards she's ill. Perhaps you can to tend her," Yamun suggested with a mirthless smile. "After we break the Dragonwall, there will be time to decide."

If we all survive, Koja thought to himself.

- 17 -

The Final Assault

It was the largest array of warriors Koja had seen yet. The sun was just rising over the eastern horizon. From the top of the ridge, the priest watched as the creeping rays of morning struck the outermost edge of the right flank. The golden light touched the mass of lance tips, breastplates, shields, bridles, swords, every bit of metal the warriors had. It looked as if some god were pouring gems from the heavens over the Tuigan horde.

Koja guessed that there were two hundred thousand men, perhaps more, gathered on the edge of the plain. They were lined up as far from the Dragonwall as their commanders could manage. After yesterday's disaster, no one wanted his men too far out in the open. The valleys leading onto the plain were choked with columns of horsemen, backed up behind the leading *tumens*. The men were organized into dense blocks, each unit separated from its neighbors. Yamun supervised the disposition of the units from his vantage point on the ridge. Chanar was nearby, ostensibly part of the khahan's honored command. A group of well-armed Kashik accompanied the general wherever he went. Bayalun was being held secretly in a yurt, far from her own guards.

Their mistress's fate kept from them, Bayalun's wizards had done their job well. While the army moved into position, the spellcasters had used their powers to disintegrate boulders and move mounds of earth out of the way. By daybreak, they had cleared several wide, level breaks through the rubble. Surveying the openings from the hill, Yamun decided these were more than adequate for the attack.

In the distance, the Dragonwall, too, underwent a change. In the shadowy, predawn light, the wall was a brooding monolith. As the sun rose, the gloomy walls became red-gold. The towers and cornices were etched in sharp relief against the green and brown land beyond. Along the battlements, a glinting line of light from the defenders' spearpoints shone like small fangs. From where the khahan stood, the Dragonwall's majesty was inspiring.

"Come, *anda*, it's time for battle," Yamun grunted. He looked out over his army. "Today is a great day. I will either conquer Shou Lung or I will lose every man I have."

Koja looked toward the khahan. "I thought you were certain of victory."

"I am—but it may not be today. If I am beaten here, I'll go back and build a new army. I've been beaten before." Yamun shaded his eyes to look toward the Dragonwall. "But, I wouldn't like to lose," Yamun concluded with a wry smile. "Now, *anda*, it's time."

The khahan was dressed as he had been the day before; indeed, the man hadn't changed out of his war clothes at all. Koja himself wore the same suit of armor he had worn at the Battle of Manass, as he had come to call it, although Hodj had at least found the time to size it better. The armor was still heavy and hot, but at least it didn't chafe as badly.

"I am coming, Yamun," Koja answered. He didn't want to be in the middle of the battle, but he had no choice. It was his duty to supervise the sacrifice, which had to take place closer to the wall. Trotting to catch up with Yamun, he reined in his mount alongside the warlord.

"As is the custom of our people," Yamun said, "I have ordered one hundred of my finest white mares to be given to this spirit. Is this enough?"

"I do not know. Would it be sufficient to please your god, Teylas?"

"More than enough I should think." Yamun leaned over in his saddle to issue the final orders to a waiting messenger. Satisfied that the man understood the commands, the khahan sent the messenger on his way. Another messenger came forward to take the man's place.

As he neared the main body of the army, Yamun halted, motioning for the guards to bring Chanar forward. The general sat rigidly on his horse, refusing to look at the khahan. Chanar's pride seemed to be all that was sustaining him.

"Chanar Ong Kho," Yamun said solemnly. "In a few moments we will ride among the army. I will give you the place of honor for our coming battle—leading the first charge against the Shou. I give you this because you are my *anda*, and only because of that. Do not dishonor yourself before the entire army." Chanar made no attempt to answer. "Give him his weapons," Yamun said, then spurred his horse forward.

The khahan's route took him and his entourage through the heart of the two hundred thousand. Koja marveled at the men's discipline. It reminded him just how well trained Yamun's soldiers were. Their insouciance on the march belied their rigid discipline on the field of battle. Two hundred thousand men waited on their horses in strict lines: ten men to an *arban*; one hundred to a *jagun*, which in turn formed *minghans* of one thousand; and the *minghans* were grouped into massive *tumens*. Each *tumen* formed a block of riders ten riders deep and one thousand men across. At their center was the *tumen's* standard, while the banners of the *minghans* formed a line of signal flags each man could see.

Two hundred thousand men and animals made enough noise for their presence to be known. As the khahan passed, the men hailed him with a mighty cheer. Even the ranks far from the khahan were not silent. There was a constant rumble as nervous men and horses waited for the signal to attack.

At last, Yamun, Koja, and Chanar reached the head of the army. Yamun's Kashik were set in the center of the line, at the forefront of the army. The khahan rode out to address them. "Men of the Kashik, finest of my warriors! Today, we will crush the armies of the Jade Throne. Ride under the banner of Chanar Ong Kho, the finest of my valiant men. Go forward and fight bravely, for here we will succeed or die!"

The Kashik raised a mighty shout, beating their lances against their swords. Hearing the clamor, the rest of the army took up the cry. The roar echoed in the valleys and across the plain. Koja could not imagine what it must have sounded like to the Shou defenders on the walls.

At a signal from Yamun, Chanar rode to the head of the Kashik. Two standard-bearers galloped behind, one carrying Chanar's banner and the other the standard of the Kashik. The riders took their positions behind the general. The command assigned, Yamun galloped back to where Koja waited.

Taking a position next to his white-tailed battle standard, Yamun surveyed the length of the line. On one side were Chanar and the main body of the Kashik, eight thousand strong. To the other side of the khahan was a line of one hundred white horses, each led by a Shou prisoner, some of the few taken in yesterday's debacle. Next to each horse was a quiverbearer. The Tuigan's black robes stood out starkly against the white mares.

"Everything is ready, Lord Yamun," a khan said.

"Good. Koja, begin."

The priest swallowed nervously and nodded. Giving his horse a gentle whip forward, he rode out ahead of the army. The prisoners, followed by the guards, led the hundred horses after him. Slowly, the lama rode across the plain, closer to the towering front of the Dragonwall. He continued to ride forward, entering the area that was shattered yesterday in Goyuk's attack. Bayalun's wizards had done a superb job of removing the rubble, their magic cutting avenues through the broken ground. There were still, however, grisly reminders of the men and horses that fell there only a day before.

The priest stopped when he got as close as he dared to the wall. He could see Shou archers training their arrows on the Tuigan procession. Only the presence of the Shou prisoners prevented them from firing. Koja lowered his head, took a deep breath, and then looked up. He felt calm, too preoccupied to be afraid. "Spirit of the Dragonwall," he called out, "hear me! Yamun Khahan, Illustrious Emperor of All People, gives to you a sacrifice of blood. Accept it and go in freedom and peace." Koja whispered a prayer beseeching Furo's forgiveness for what he was about to do. The priest gave the signal as soon as the prayer was done.

Knives in hand, one hundred guards reached out and slashed the throats of one hundred horses. The death screams of the beasts rang in Koja's ears. His own horse pranced and reared, forcing the priest to open his eyes. He could barely keep the mount under control. All around him the mares stumbled forward or lashed at their grooms, blood streaming down their white breasts, soaking the ground. Quickly they fell, one by one, into the dirt.

Koja was dazed. He heard a roar. At first the lama thought it was the war cry of the two hundred thousand men lined up behind him. Then, suddenly, the ground trembled. The shock waves built in strength, and Koja's horse reared and bolted, throwing the priest to the ground. All around Koja the guards struggled to keep their mounts under control.

Scrambling to his feet, the priest looked toward the Dragonwall and stopped in amazement. It was buckling, heaving upward, the foundations tearing from the earth. The brick masonry fell away in sheets, sweeping guardsmen off the battlements. The nearest watchtower heaved outward, rising up before settling into a crumbled heap. Koja looked to the gates. The huge wooden doors groaned against each other. The tall gatehouses swayed. There was a piercing crack as the span between the two towers shattered, raining stone onto the Shou garrison below.

Koja, surprised and terrified, sprinted for the safety of the khahan's banner. The guardsmen around him were also galloping for the safety of the Tuigan line. The ground heaved again, hurling the panting lama into the dirt. Sweat and dust running into his eyes, Koja stumbled to his feet and reeled forward. Unexpectedly, a hand thrust under his arm, squeezing his chest. With a jerk the priest was pulled from his feet and hauled on the back of a galloping mare.

"Hold tight, little lama," Koja's rescuer announced. The Kashik looked back at the priest with a snaggle-toothed grin.

Gasping, Koja clung to the man's waist. Behind him he could still hear the rumbling crash of masonry. "What's happening, priest? What did you do?" shouted the rider over his shoulder.

"More than I thought," Koja shouted back. The guard reined the hurtling steed to a stop just in front of the khahan's banner. Koja tumbled to the ground, and the horseman easily swung his mount around and galloped to his position in the battle line.

"We cannot fight in this madness!" Yamun shouted over the building noise. "Hold the signal for the attack until the wall stops moving!" The khahan sprang from his horse and stormed over to where the lama was sprawled.

"Look!" Koja cried as he glanced back toward the Dragonwall. He pointed to the great fortification.

A great, taloned claw burst through the soil, then another, gouging into the dirt along the structure's foundations. The wall split and cracked, revealing a spiny, scaled back arching and pushing upward. The scales glistened blue and brown along the length of the reptilian hide. Far to the right, away from the gate, the fortification exploded, scattering shards of brick and granite across the plain. Broken men hurtled off the battlements and fell, crushed, to the ground. A coiling tail, forked and pointed, thrashed free of the shattered battlements. Clouds of dust began to roil away from the stone wall, driven forward by the collapsing stone.

The grinding roar of cracking stone and the faint screams of men and horses were overwhelmed by a new sound, a howling cry of tremendous volume. It was part animalistic roar, part shouted cry. Koja wondered if this was the true voice of the dragon spirit.

Suddenly, the great gate shivered. Wood shrieked as the massive doors warped and bent. There was a popping crack as the hardwood valves split, the force of the sudden release blowing the wooden gates outward. The stone gatehouses to either side twisted and heaved. The immense gate of the Dragonwall was shattered.

"Standard-bearer! Get ready," Yamun shouted, barely heard over the destruction. "We ride forward now!" The khahan ran back and mounted his unruly horse.

Koja also ran to a horse. Over his shoulder, he looked back at the wall. There, in the yawning gate, the lama saw a pair of eyes, glistening with a lambent blue fire, fringed by the ornate carapace of a great dragon. It was the same set of eyes he had seen last night.

The vision lasted only a second. Driven by the sudden rush of wind, a column of dust spiraled into the air, explosively pushing the gatetowers to the side. The blockhouses splintered and fell, crashing onto the remains of the wall to either side of the gate. The banners of Shou that once adorned the tower peaks were snatched away by the wind and carried into the sky. Koja watched, too numb to be amazed, as the writhing column solidified to become the twisting serpentine shape of a majestic dragon. Before the priest could see any more, a choking cloud of dust and sand swept over the Tuigan line.

The whirling sandstorm passed in no more than a few minutes. Even before the dust cleared, the thunderous crashes of rock died away. After the chaos that came before, everything now seemed still. Coughing and gagging, Koja struggled with his horse.

"It worked, priest! Better than you promised!" Yamun shouted. Koja turned and looked where the khahan pointed.

Ahead, where the Dragonwall had been, with its imposing gate and towering walls, was a gaping breach. The gate-houses were shattered, the heavy wooden doors in splin-ters. The towers had fallen away from the road, leaving the opening clear. At other points to the left and right, the wall was also breached, tumbled into rough piles.

Yamun barked out commands as he gestured toward points along the wall. "Standard-bearer, signal Chanar. He is to take the Kashik through the center. He will lead the at-tack! Hurry! Hurry, before they can recover!" Yamun yelled at the dazed khans around him, shouting them into motion.

It dawned on Koja that he stood in the path of two hun-dred thousand warriors. Quickly he tried to move his horse to the side, but there was no safe escape. He could either charge forward into battle or risk being trampled where he stood.

"Signal the khans to be ready!" Yamun ordered. The white yak tails dipped, giving the signal the warriors waited for. As the command was relayed through the army, the men of each *tumen* raised their war cry. Once again the air thun-dered with the voice of destruction.

"Attack!" shouted the khahan, nodding to the drummers. The war drums sounded, signaling the Kashik to move. Chanar, for a second, reined in his horse, almost refusing to charge. The Kashik began to advance behind him anyway. Finally the general stood in his saddle and whipped his horse forward. The mount leaped into motion and behind it swept the black-robed mass of the Kashik, eight thousand strong. Before the first men had even reached the crumbled wall, Yamun was shouting orders for the other *tumens* to charge and whipped his own horse forward.

Yamun charged at full gallop, surrounded by his khans. Koja rode in their midst, dragged along by the wave of men around him.

In a moment the Tuigan reached the shattered gate; in an-other they poured through the breach. The Shou garrison that once manned the walls and filled the towers was shattered. Generals and troopers alike had been lost. Those who survived were already streaming back from the broken fortification, some forming ragged units of several thousand, many more fleeing the mounted doom that poured through the gaps. With a howl of triumph, the Tuigan horsemen swept down upon the routed enemy. The great battle of the Dragonwall was won before it had even begun.

Epilogue

Koja sipped on a cup of tea brewed in the Shou style. On his throne, Yamun drank the vile salted brew favored by the Tuigan. In front of the warlord was spread a map of the Mai Yuan province of Shou Lung, which had been found in the rubble of the gatetower. On it Koja had carefully marked the movements of Yamun's scouts in broad, red arrows. They fanned out from a single point on the Shou frontier, reaching like fingers into the interior. The scouts had been riding for many days, some harrying the fleeing enemy and others shadowing the small garrisons that were now on the move. The scope of the Tuigan success had come as a surprise to the khahan, and, Koja suspected, to the Shou emperor, too.

"Yamun," Koja asked, as he blew the steam off his cup, "what will you do now? Continue the invasion?"

Yamun looked up from slurping his tea. "First we'll wait for Hubadai and his men. Then we must fatten the horses. When this is done, I'll conquer Shou Lung," Yamun answered confidently.

The priest didn't doubt the khahan's resolve. Already Yamun had done more than Koja thought was possible. "Shou Lung is huge, Khahan. You do not have the men to rule all of this land."

"Before I worry about ruling it, I must conquer it," Yamun pointed out. "Besides, I have men like you to manage my empire." The khahan rolled up the map. "Now, there is business to attend to." The khahan set his tea aside and called to the quiverbearer near the door. "Bring the prisoners in."

The man quickly stepped outside. There were a few muffled commands and then the door flap was pulled open. Sechen, now a khan, and several Kashik entered the yurt and took positions by the walls. Immediately after came Chanar and Bayalun. The general was still dressed in the clothes he had worn into battle several days ago. They were dirty, bloodstained, and torn. Bayalun wore a simple brown and yellow robe. The sleeves were long, hiding the bonds on her wrists. On Koja's advice, the khadun's hands were bound to keep her from casting spells. The priest did not see any need to gag her. Both conspirators moved slowly, reluctantly. They obviously dreaded this audience.

The guards led the pair to the center of the yurt and roughly pushed them down to their knees. Chanar kept his eyes to the floor, but Bayalun glared venomously at her stepson.

Yamun rose from his throne and slowly circled the two. Finally, he spoke in solemn tones. "You've been proven guilty of treachery against your khahan. Now, I must give my final judgment." At this Chanar raised his head, stubbornly ready to meet whatever doom Yamun might name.

"By law," Yamun continued, "you should be taken into the wilderness and strangled. This would satisfy the ancient codes of our people." He paused and let the prisoners think about their fate.

With a heavy sigh, the khahan continued. "I'll not do this." Yamun stopped at his scribe's table and motioned for the man to write down his words. "General Chanar, I've not forgotten the battles where you stood at my side when all were ready to run. My *anda*, once I swore that I would forgive your crimes though they were nine times nine. This I have done. General Chanar, I let you live. But you will no longer command the *tumens* of the Tuigan. I banish you from my sight, to the command of a *minghan* of scouts." The pained look on the general's face told everyone that he considered that fate worse than death.

Yamun looked down at the scribe, who was furiously writing. "A *jagun* of troops are to be Chanar's guard. If any evidence of further treachery comes to my attention, Chanar will be put to death." The khahan turned to his once-loyal friend. "Perhaps you may work your way back to a command, but do not think to cross me again."

The khahan scowled as he turned to his stepmother. "Bayalun Khadun, you've done much and deserve a painful, long death." The woman stiffened. "However, I have no guarantee that death will end your plotting. Your sorcerous powers could strike from beyond the grave. At the suggestion of my *anda*, you are to retire from worldly life and renounce your claim to the title khadun. Your guards are disbanded. You will spend the rest of your days in the magic-deadlands of Quaraband. Sechen Khan is your jailor. Do you object to this, Mother?"

Bayalun paled. Yamun's sentence was as good as death. However, Bayalun knew that any protests would be futile. "No," she whispered. "I welcome a fate that removes you from my sight."

"Then let all those who oppose these orders know that they are by the khahan's will." Yamun said. "Get them out of my sight. Sechen, see that the orders are carried out." As the two were led out, Yamun scooped himself a ladleful of kumiss. He stood breathing deeply, letting the anger flow out of him. "What do you want to ask, Koja?" he suddenly inquired, seeing the priest still quietly sitting in the corner.

Koja looked at Yamun in embarrassed surprise. Bowing his head to hide his reddened face, the priest finally spoke. "Yamun, I do not understand why you let Chanar and Bayalun live. It is commendable in the eyes of the Enlightened One, but it is very dangerous, isn't it?"

Yamun set down his cup and rested his chin on his hand. "I've given it much thought. For Bayalun, loss of her magic is a horrible fate."

"What about Chanar?" Koja asked, setting his own cup of tea aside.

"Chanar is my *anda*," Yamun answered sadly. "I cannot change that, so I cannot kill him. Once, he loved me." He looked away from the priest. Koja sat quietly, waiting for Yamun to continue.

"He'll have a small command, somewhere my Kashik can easily watch him. Chanar is ambitious, but not that clever. Bayalun was the one behind these plots." The khahan picked up his tea once more and sank back onto his throne.

"What will you do now, Khazari?" Yamun finally asked. "Will you stay with me or go back and be a priest?"

Koja rubbed his itching scalp. The stubble on his pate was getting long enough to irritate. Ruefully, he sighed. "Do not call me Khazari. I know I am no longer that. I might not be priest much longer either. I have not served Furo well. I fear the temple will not have me anymore." He forced a wistful smile, thinking of what he had lost.

"If neither your country nor your god want you, *anda*, who will you serve?" Yamun asked, although he already knew the answer.

Koja took a large swallow of tea. "You, my *anda*. If you will let me stay."

"You can become Tuigan," the khahan offered. He set his cup aside and waited expectantly for the priest's answer. "Watch me conquer Shou Lung. Write your history so that all the world will know of my greatness."

Koja looked at the khahan. It was impossible to ignore the hard, sure confidence in his eyes. Shou Lung was huge, its armies were numerous, but this time the priest did not doubt Yamun's words.

"Yes," Koja said after a while. "The world will certainly come to know your greatness."

FANTASY ADVENTURE

EMPIRES TRILOGY

BOOK TWO

Dragonwall

TROY DENNING

The barbarian horsemen have
breached the Dragonwall and
now threaten the oriental
lands of Kara-Tur. Shou
Lung's only hope lies with a
general descended from the
barbarians, and whose wife must fight the imperial court
if her husband is to retain his command. Available in
August.

BOOK THREE

Crusade

JAMES LOWDER

The barbarian army has turned its sights on the western
Realms. Only King Azoun has the strength to forge an
army to challenge the horsemen. But Azoun had not
reckoned that the price of saving the west might be the
life of his beloved daughter. Available in January 1991.

FANTASY ADVENTURE

THE MAZTICA TRILOGY

Douglas Niles

IRONHELM

A slave girl learns of a great destiny laid upon her by the gods themselves. And across the sea, a legion of skilled mercenaries sails west to discover a land of primitive savagery mixed with high culture. Under the banner of their vigilant god the legion claims these lands for itself. And only as Erix sees her land invaded is her destiny revealed. Available in April.

VIPERHAND

The God of War feasts upon chaos while the desperate lovers, Erix and Halloran, strive to escape the waves of catastrophe sweeping Maztica. Each is forced into a choice of historical proportion and deeply personal emotion. The destruction of the fabulously wealthy continent of Maztica looms on the horizon. Available in October.

COMING IN EARLY 1991!

FEATHERED DRAGON

The conclusion!